AF487420

MEET ME AT THE GATES

Kelly Wyre

www.demented-tours.com

Meet Me at the Gates
Copyright © 2020 by Kelly Wyre
All rights reserved. This work is intended for the original purchaser ONLY. No part of this creative work may be reproduced, scanned, or distributed in any printed or electronic form without prior written permission from Demented Tours LLC. Please do not participate in or encourage piracy of copyrighted materials in violation of the author's rights. Purchase only authorized editions.

Image/art disclaimer: Licensed material is being used for illustrative purposes only. Any person depicted in the licensed material is a model.
Cover Photography: Luiz Clas via Pexels. Visit him at www.luizclas.com
Cover Artist: Demented Tours LLC
Published in the United States of America Demented Tours, LLC
1657 E. Stone Drive
Ste B #139
Kingsport, TN 37660

This is a work of fiction. While reference might be made to actual historical events or existing locations, the names, characters, places, and incidents are either the product of the author's imagination or are used fictitiously, and any resemblance to actual persons, living or dead, business establishments, events, or locales is entirely coincidental.

Warning
This work contains sexually explicit scenes and adult language and may be considered offensive to some readers. This work is for sale to adults ONLY, as defined by the laws of the country in which you made your purchase. Please store your files wisely, where they cannot be accessed by underage readers.

Dedication

For those who know that this life is not all there is.

And even more for those who hope that is true.

Love is infinite.

Chapter One

The walls of hospital emergency room 11A were mint green with gray trim. While they reminded Theo of being seasick on a cloudy day, green was still vastly better than the coral in rooms 1A and 7A. Being in there was like drowning in a bottle of Pepto-Bismol.

There was grit along the plastic baseboards, and a vial of medicine had escaped a cabinet and rolled toward the bed. Theo couldn't read the label. He hoped it was something good. Morphine or Magical Coping Serum or a nice, healthy dose of Fuckitol.

Lower back complaining, Theo hit the button to adjust the bed. He tucked the edges of the pitiful excuse for a blanket under his knees, and he loosened the hospital gown at his throat so it wasn't about to choke him. Tired, Theo went back to staring at the paint. Any color would be better than the rooms in that one hospital in LA. The walls there were putrid yellow. They had reminded Theo of a short story his tutor had made him read when he was about fifteen. "The Yellow Room"? "Yellow Walls"? Something like that. It had been about a woman who had been locked in a room with yellow printed wallpaper, and she went out of her mind.

Theo could relate to both hating yellow and being out of his mind. His had been lost for so long, all hope of recovery was gone. He could only pray that his sanity was nestled in a quiet cabin somewhere enjoying fires, cocktails, and lakeside views. He wished it well.

The curtain across the open doorway standing between Theo's temporary quarters and the bustling hallways of the ER racked to the left. "Mr. Monk."

"Doctor Merrykind," Theo replied to the older gentleman in a polo and jeans. Fresh off the back nine, most likely. Merrykind was slim and had to be seventy if he was a day, but he made the fringe of gray hair look distinguished.

"How's the family?" Merrykind asked, ambling closer and thumbing through Theo's chart. It was two inches thick.

Theo's palms began to sweat. "Fine. They're fine."

"Susan?"

"Mother's great. She's always great." Merrykind had been the Monk family's primary doctor since Theo could remember.

"She's a lovely woman," Merrykind said. He was originally from somewhere in the Southeast, and it seemed that the inhabitants of the backwoods all had the aggravating habit of asking and commenting about family.

"Most people tend to think so," Theo agreed.

Merrykind chuckled. "But you don't?"

"I didn't say that." Mostly because Theo didn't have to. A memory of tall, stately, raven-haired, lavender-blue-eyed Susan Monk floated into Theo's mind. It'd been springtime, and there had been purple blossom petals sprinkled over the ground. Child Theo had first noticed that his beautiful mother had reappeared from the magical place called NewYorkandLondon when he'd looked up from his hands and knees. He'd been crying bloody murder because he'd fallen out of one of the jacaranda trees in front of their estate in La Jolla, California. His palms and legs had been a shredded mess of torn skin and embedded rocks. Theo still had the scars.

Mother had been a giant creature that day, hunched at the waist with her arms at her sides and hands formed into fists. She'd been wearing a billowing white dress, and she'd been smiling the forced, horrified smile of someone who thought of comforting another human being much like everyone else regarded eating maggots. To Child Theo, she'd merely seemed disappointed in him yet again. Essa, Theo's nanny at the time, had come running out of the kitchen and onto the scene.

She'd swept Theo up and carried him off to a

bathroom to kiss his wounds and promise him that yes, Mommy really did love him. No, she wasn't angry. She didn't mean those things about how the cuts weren't bad and he was a big boy now and shouldn't cry. Mommy was just tired from getting back from NewYorkandLondon where her play had been on a really big stage, and she would see him at dinner along with Papa, and wouldn't that be nice?

But dinner hadn't been nice. It had never been anything but awkward and confusing.

Merrykind hugged Theo's chart to his chest behind crossed arms. A crystal-blue stare that didn't miss a trick caught Theo in its crosshairs. "Your mother and father still see me for their annual physicals, you realize."

"They are creatures of habit."

Merrykind ignored Theo's tone. "And they are the picture of health."

Theo swallowed around the lump in his throat. With one thumb, he rubbed the shaft of the fountain pen he'd been using to fill out an impossible-level crossword. He'd been stuck on "A Levantine Coffee Cup," four letters, begins with "Z."

"Your brother Frank, last I heard, is also in fantastic health," Merrykind continued. "Your grandparents lived to be in their nineties."

Eight down had been "Flint and Butane Users," and Theo had written ZIPPO in black block letters. His handwriting was solid and sure. He wished the rest of him could follow suit.

"There is no family history of heart disease. A blessing in this day and age. And you, Mr. Monk—"

"Theo."

"Theodore." Merrykind cocked an eyebrow. Theo allowed Merrykind to use his full name. After all, it'd been Hollywood, not Theo, that had taken the last four letters and tossed them into a recycle bin. Merrykind had been there when Theo was a baby fresh to the world and struggling under the weight of all eight letters and a surname attached to a long history of playwrights, producers, and performers. The man had watched Theo grow up and be molded by people who played pretend for a living. The doctor might be one of the few people in the world who understood what Theo had lost in the transformation.

"You are thirty-nine years old with a personal trainer and chef. You are"—Merrykind consulted his notes—"gluten free, dairy free, and sugar free. Your blood pressure is textbook perfection. Your pulse is sixty, steady as they come. Your cholesterol is incredible, your blood sugar worthy of awards, and all your organs are functioning at optimal levels. Your X-rays are normal, your CT scan clean, and your bloodwork is without a single marker to indicate I should do the other tests that you have requested. A request you've made for the"—a pause for another note check—"second time this year and sixth time in the last eighteen months. Stress test, ultrasound, antibody, deficiency panels…" Merrykind sighed. "If you don't do something quick, Theodore, you're going to outlive us all."

Theo doodled on the corner of his crossword page. He thought the squiggles might be turning into a fox. "I believe I'll need a second opinion."

Merrykind pushed aside the cables attached to Theo's oxygen monitor and blood pressure cuff and sat on Theo's bed. "There've been second opinions. Third, fourth, and fifth opinions. You've been to specialists, the best in this city, LA, and most of the West Coast. I've seen you so often over the past few years that I feel like I should be asking what I should make you for dinner. You've been here six hours and terrorized the staff into a frenzy. They called me in out of desperation. I'm amazed they're not dosing your ice chips with lithium."

"Didn't realize that was an option." Seventy-two down was seven letters for asylum inhabitant. If Theo filled in the answer, he could hold it up like a mirror and see himself.

Merrykind studied him. "How's work? It's that cop show, isn't it?"

Theo capped his pen and twisted it in his hands. It was slippery with moisture from his grip. "*In Force.* Yeah."

"Four seasons?"

"Five."

"Renewed?"

"No."

"But you were in that movie last summer. The funny one with the blonde."

"You saw it?"

"No. I don't do romantic comedies as a rule."

Theo managed a weak chuckle. "Well, don't worry. The critics ruled out my comedic timing too."

"Forget them," Merrykind said with a succinct shrug. "There have to be more offers on your table."

Offers. Piles and piles of paperwork. Scripts. E-mails. Phone calls. Meetings. Theo's chest began to ache like it had six hours ago, when he'd been going for a walk to clear his head. He'd walked at least seven miles over sidewalks and the paved streets beneath Southern California sunshine and clear, bright skies, and he would have needed another three thousand miles to get himself together. Hell, even that might not have been enough. He didn't know what had set the inner beast off this time, but he'd started to get weak in the knees and shaky. The world had started to rotate around him like he was the center of the merry-go-round and the trees and houses had transformed into gigantic demonic horses and grinning painted fish going up and down…up and down. Sweating through his shirt, Theo had Google searched the nearest hospital, seen it was a block away, and he'd staggered across the threshold of the Cardiac Emergency doorways. He'd gasped the words "chest pain," and he'd been whisked away in a flourish of medical staff who had shouted questions at him like auctioneers calling for bids. The moment he was in the professionals' care, he'd started to feel calmer, but the brief respites of smooth sailing never lasted for long.

His chest was so tight, he felt like he'd had pneumonia

for at least a decade. His next breath burned. He got dizzy when he turned his head to look at the monitor, expecting alarms to sound at any moment, but his pressure was normal. His pulse was ticking along around seventy. On paper and on monitors, he was absolutely fine.

"You're all right." Merrykind stood up. He put a hand on Theo's forehead and gently forced Theo against the pillow. Theo closed his eyes and breathed deeply for a count of eight, held it for a count of seven, and let the breath go for a count of six. He wasn't sure the increments were right, but he could never quite remember everything his yoga instructor had taught him.

"There's no infection," Merrykind said evenly, and Theo tried to relax as Merrykind repeated his findings of Theo's ultimate health. Theo was safe, here. There were doctors and surgeons and nurses here. The men and women in this building were paid to keep him alive. For the hours he managed to take up a bed in one of their rooms, Theo didn't have to think about his breathing, his food, his exercise regimen, or if he had remembered the bottle of Xanax that went with him everywhere.

Well, granted, he didn't really have to concern himself with those details, anyway. He had his assistants for that. Brooke used to accuse him of making a habit out of firing an assistant once every six months, no matter what the poor guy or girl had done. They'd fought about it. They were champion fighters. Eleven years of not-quite relationship that was in and out of the paparazzi spotlight could hone anyone's skills at yelling and backstabbing. But when Brooke had suggested, at volume, that he try matched sets of helpers to divide and conquer his life, he'd actually listened. Two could tag team and worked much better than one. Kinsey and Carla were the latest pair of whip crackers who ran his life to the last intimate detail. One or both of them were usually with him every minute of every day. They'd probably come in the bathroom while he was trying to take a shit if he didn't firmly close doors and engage locks. Brooke probably encouraged them to learn how to lockpick. She liked to know everything there was to know about her not-really-but-sort-of-kind-of boyfriend. Theo had no doubt that the Detail Twins were happy to give Brooke daily if not hourly reports. KC and the Nosy Brooke Band.

"You're grimacing," Merrykind said. "Are you in pain?"

Theo unclenched his teeth. "Yes."

"Chest?"

"Yes."

"One to ten?"

"I don't know. Six?"

Merrykind clucked his tongue and unhooked his stethoscope from around his neck. Theo barely felt Merrykind start listening to heart and arteries. He shut his eyes again and tried to think of his inner fortress of solitude or whatever the hell that therapist had called his imaginary safe haven. The image of an empty beach and stormy skies kept wavering, however, and Theo choked on frustration.

For six pleasant hours, Theo had managed to rest and not think about turning forty, getting cast in insipid family dramas where he played a cheating father figure, or about how Brooke was, at that very moment, attempting to spend millions of his money on a small palace that he didn't want. And now here was Merrykind: there to shatter what passed for peace of mind in Theo's overly scheduled, articulated, and exceptionally sad celebrity life.

"I'll get you another dose of anti-inflammatories," Merrykind said, draping his scope around his neck. He shook his head at the monitors and sighed down at Theo. He brushed Theo's hair off Theo's forehead in a fatherly gesture. Theo studied his lap and his crossword, the pen shaking in his fist.

"When was the last one?" Merrykind asked. Theo knew he didn't mean the hospital meds.

"Three hours ago."

Merrykind clucked his tongue and scribbled something

on Theo's chart. "Are those Xanax helping at all?"

"At the moment, I couldn't tell you," Theo said.

"How about the other medication?"

Theo couldn't help it. He laughed with his head back and eyes closed. "Which medication, Doc? Paxil? Zoloft? Lexapro? Ambien? Lunesta? Valium?"

"Any or all of the above," Merrykind said grimly. Apparently he didn't see anything funny about a man determined to come apart at the seams despite greater pharmaceutical efforts.

"I don't know." There was an eye chart in Theo's line of sight from where he rested in the hospital bed. He could read the fine print without any problem. He resisted the temptation to hurl his six-thousand dollar pen at the sign. "I take Ambien at night. Xanax every six hours. I believe I answered most of these questions a dozen times already."

Merrykind grunted dismissively. "Anything for pain?"

"No."

"Are you in pain?"

Theo felt his lips twist. "All the time."

"So—"

"Wrong kind of pain, Doc."

Merrykind paused. He patted Theo's shoulder. "I see."

"Besides," Theo said. "The side effects of those pain bills are a bitch. Being backed up on set is a pain in the ass."

"They make a pill for that too."

"Too bad they don't make one to fix me, huh?"

"We just haven't found it yet, Theodore. Don't lose faith." Merrykind headed for the door but stopped. "Still seeing Doctor Cameron?"

"I am. Twice a week."

"He's good. He tries to help plenty of individuals in the industry."

"I know. Brooke sent me his way."

"Do you need another referral?"

"No. Not yet. This shrink seems to have more patience with me than the rest of them, so far."

Merrykind nodded. "I'll get you the Toradol, and I'm prescribing a steroid pack. Remember to take it as directed."

Theo's insides burned and churned. "And then you're kicking me out?"

"We'll release you, yes," Merrykind corrected. "I'll make you an appointment to follow up with me in a week, see how you're doing." He slapped the cover of Theo's chart closed. "There's a program for cognitive therapy up in San Francisco that has had some amazing results with stress disorders."

Theo rested with his eyes closed again. With every heartbeat, red pulsated across the darkness. "Great. Maybe the third camp for the twitchy will actually work."

"When patients are capable of sarcasm, they are capable of going home."

"You were done with me anyway."

Merrykind's voice was tinged with anger. "I'm not done with you, Theodore. No one is done with you. Your family, your doctors, the entire team that looks after you want nothing more than for you to get better." He took a breath. "Though I probably don't need to tell you that reducing your stress would likely help."

The red behind Theo's eyelids was beginning to crackle with brilliant white. "I'll get right on that."

"Give yourself time to breathe. Take care of yourself and let the people in your life help you."

Theo wanted this conversation to be over even more than he wanted to be able to get through an unmedicated night without having a panic attack. "Thank you for coming in."

"Of course, Theodore. Any time."

It wasn't until after Merrykind had left and the blood pressure cuff had registered a perfectly normal reading for the fourth time in an hour that Theo remembered the name of the short story: "The Yellow Wallpaper." And in it, the woman had been locked up by her husband because she suffered from depression and hysteria. She went insane and started to feel safe only in her land of horrifying and concealing yellow.

Suddenly, the mint green and the capable staff were the opposite of comforting. The walls were too close, and the monitors' hum became the buzz of a killer bee colony.

Theo didn't wait for the anti-inflammatories, the prescription, or the nurse. He unhooked himself from the monitors, found a wad of cotton in the supply cabinet, and eased the needle out of his arm. He held his elbow bent and grabbed his clothes off a chair. He was zipping his fly when an administrative staff member knocked on the glass door and stepped inside. "Oh," she said, and a rosy blush bloomed across her cheeks.

"Yes?" Theo asked, putting his belt through the loops around his hips.

"Ah, you… I am… This is your, ah, statement of what you…owe." The woman cleared her throat.

Theo yanked on his T-shirt and flashed her two rows of capped teeth. The woman quickly became incredibly interested in her clipboard. Theo would say this much for his mother: inheriting her looks definitely had its perks, though he was grateful he'd gotten his father's dark brown eyes instead of his mother's chilly blue. No way would he have been able to face those eyes in the mirror all his life. He'd rather go blind.

"Of course," Theo said to the scarlet woman with the practiced grace he used at functions and meetings. "Here." He took a card out of his wallet. "Run it on this, would you? And I'm in a bit of a hurry, if you don't mind."

"Right away, Mr. Monk." The woman fled, and as soon as Theo had on his shoes and had tucked his sunglasses into the neck of his shirt, he followed her. She had her clipboard ready by the time he arrived at the check-in station. He signed both forms and a piece of paper for the woman's daughter, and he had to stop himself from running out the automatic doors.

Outside it was a perfect spring day. The breeze carried

the scent of the ocean and the perfume of blooming flowers. The hospital was situated beside of a sea of apartment buildings, and it was flanked on the other side by a four-lane highway heading north and south. A twelve-foot concrete wall marched along the highway's edge, keeping down the noise. Theo headed away from the ambulances and across the parking lot toward the black fence surrounding a six-story building in the Green Terrace Apartment Complex. It was Tuesday afternoon at three o'clock, and a school bus slowed on the side street, making a stop. A handful of kids spilled out of the bus with accompanying shrieks of excitement. Their backpacks bobbed in bright green and blue as they ran across a cobblestone drive toward home. He turned north, heels striking the same sidewalk that he had walked that morning.

Merrykind was a good man, an astute man, but the doctor was wrong about one thing: the people in Theo's life had no interest in him getting better. If he got his anxiety—Theo needed a better word for the crippling fear that was the constant undercurrent of his existence—under control, he wouldn't be so easy to manipulate. Theo might be a basket case of the first degree, but he wasn't blind. Nor deaf, nor stupid or unobservant. Lack of control didn't sit well with Brooke. Or with any of the major players in Theo's world: agent, publicist, assistants, assorted staff and managers…

Good God, but Theo's life was a circus, and he wasn't the ringmaster; he was the damned clown.

Theo hiked a gentle hill and checked his phone. He had twenty-four missed calls and twice that many text messages. It was an even distribution among Brooke, Kinsey, and Carla. The messages ranged from Kinsey's sweet and concerned to Brooke's pissed and demanding.

A full flask of guilt dumped into Theo's guts followed by a shot of anger topped with the fire of indigestion. He didn't want to worry people, but when their worry felt more like leashes trying to cut off his air supply, what was he supposed to do? He was a grown-ass man continually treated like a misbehaving toddler, and what was worse was that he was enabling at least half of that behavior with his inability to get his shit together. Was it ever going to get any—

Tires screeched. A car honked its horn, and Theo froze in his tracks. The bumper of the white SUV had stopped a few inches from Theo's left knee. The woman behind the wheel put her hand over her heart and then gave Theo a shaky wave. There was a kid in the passenger seat, who didn't even look up. Near-death experiences were apparently the norm when Mommy was driving.

"Sorry," Theo called, voice hoarse. He staggered back onto the sidewalk he'd not even realized he'd left, and the woman drove on. At least she didn't flip him off, though he probably deserved it. Theo looked this time before he crossed the street, and he trotted to the safety of the other side. He sat on the edge of a stone wall holding up a mound of mulch and manicured trees and realized he was shaking. His diaphragm contracted painfully in a spasm that wasn't quite hiccough and barely shy of dry heave. He held his head in one hand and started his breathing again. It took four rounds of in-hold-exhale before the light-headedness passed. He traced the edge of his cell phone with its screen full of angry texts and emphatic punctuation with his thumb, thinking of cardboard boxes, movers, and how he hated everything he owned.

He'd said he was going to get tea.

He'd been back in California for just over a month. He'd flown in from Canada where he'd finished filming *In Force*. The show supposedly took place in Montana, and shooting in Canada with both film sets at the ready and the great wild north at their disposal was cheaper than LA. Kinsey, the less invasive and more human of the Detail Twins, had been with him, but she'd been bunking with the other crew in a hotel nearby. Theo had a trailer all to himself on-site, and he'd fallen in love with it. There was no marble trim, no spiral staircase, no Renaissance this or handcrafted that. It had a ridiculously comfortable wraparound sectional, a soft double bed, and shades on the windows that would block the light from a nuclear blast.

The moment he'd walked into his home in Carlsbad, he'd missed that trailer and its ability to shield him from the world. Not that he didn't like his house—he did. It was modest by Southern California standards and a closet by Hollywood's. Just shy of two thousand square feet, it faced a quiet road and sat between two other homes with perfectly normal people living in them. On his left were a doctor and the doctor's wife. On his right was some sort of finance guy who worked in LA. They did things like have cookouts and play ping-pong. Nobody cared that Theo Monk lived between them. He was just another man with a demanding job. Theo still wasn't sure if the finance man knew who he was. It was only fair. Theo couldn't even remember the guy's name.

Brooke, however, was not happy with the Carlsbad house. She lived in a loft in downtown San Diego, and she'd been hounding Theo for years to get a home in a more "respectable" area. So it hadn't been too much of a shock when Theo had gotten home from Canada and found Brooke waiting for him. Lying on his dining room table. Wearing nothing but the pearls he'd given her nine years ago, which, as it turned out, was probably the last time he'd actually *liked* Brooke Hutton, small-time actress and social media gossip whore.

"Hi, honey," Brooke had said.

Theo had dropped his bag, willing either Brooke to disappear or his cock to overcome exhaustion and magically become interested in the skinny blonde woman with fake boobs like two oranges dangling in tanned, fleshy sacks. "What are you doing here?" Theo had blurted.

"I have a surprise for you."

"If it's how your tanning stuff spit shines wood, I already knew."

Brooke had rolled her eyes. She dragged a folder from behind her and smiled the grin that spoke of the crocodiles in her ancestry. "I found you a house."

What she'd meant, of course, was that she'd found herself a house that she wanted Theo to buy and let her monopolize. There might have been some vague sense of improving Theo's celebrity image in her motives, but Theo thought those threads were thin at best.

Hoping she'd lose interest in the project with suitable distraction, Theo had spent the next week fucking Brooke into a purring stupor. Since pretty things pacified Brooke even more than sex, Theo had bought a ring at a local boutique, and he'd presented it to Brooke, saying he'd gotten it for her in Canada. They'd invited a friend or two over and relived their young and stupid early twenties with a weekend of sex, drugs, and liquor. Theo had needed a week to recover, and thankfully, Brooke had been elsewhere making kittens cry or whatever it was she did when she wasn't terrorizing Theo.

When the moving company had shown up on Theo's doorstep at seven a.m. that morning, though, it had become clear that Brooke wasn't going to be dissuaded of her goals this time. Carla and Kinsey had been right behind the packing crew, waltzing in and corralling Theo into the kitchen to explain his complicated schedule of signing, paying, decorating, shopping, and transferring himself from one location to another. Everyone thought it'd be so comforting how Theo only needed to show up with his John Hancock at the ready and throw money at the right people to make the process flow smoothly.

For a few minutes, Theo had just stood in his kitchen in his stolen hotel bathrobe and green boxers, chewing on his dry toothbrush. Kinsey and Carla had coffee in reusable, environmentally friendly cups in their left hands, and they each had their tablets in their right hands. They were poised to approve appointments, each woman regarding Theo with hazel and blue gazes, respectively. Kinsey at least looked sympathetic.

Theo had watched a man tape together a box and

begin to stuff the knickknacks on Theo's entry table into bubble wrap. No one asked him a damned thing. No one checked to make sure this was okay. Maybe he'd been telling everyone for the last two weeks he didn't care. Maybe he'd not actually said no. Maybe he had said no, but nobody cared.

Watching those oh-so-not-terribly precious items that some decorator had bought and placed for him made Theo want to laugh and scream. His life was so absurd, but it was also inevitable. That had been the worst sensation of all: the lack of choice or control. Everything was sliding down a slippery, muddy bank toward its final conclusion of muck and mire.

Theo had opened his mouth to agree to the meeting. He'd thought he could get there, refuse to sign, and talk sense into his not-girlfriend who slept with half the West Coast and reported about it anonymously online while giggling to Theo about the stupidity of the industry. He'd thought to say he needed a shower, had wanted that man to be careful with those sculpture things because Theo had yet to figure out what the hell they were, and if they broke now, Theo would never know. He'd had a vague inkling that he should remind the world that in a parallel universe he was a rich, powerful, successful, fully grown man who could ruin them all in a blink of an eye.

What he'd said, however, was "Tea."

"Excuse me?" Carla had replied.

"Tea. I need to get…tea." Theo had stalked out of the kitchen, up the stairs, thrown on yesterday's clothes, and remembered to grab his Xanax, sunglasses, and wallet. On his way out, he'd caught a man going into a guest bedroom that Theo hadn't been in since he'd first toured the house some five years ago. "Be careful with that furniture," Theo'd said. "It belonged to my great grandmother Wilma, and I just couldn't bear it if it got scratched."

"Yes, sir," the moving man had said somberly. When Theo had started to laugh, the man clearly didn't get the joke, and Theo had left slightly ashamed of himself.

Kinsey had chased him outside, saying she would be happy to procure him tea and trying to get answers before he climbed into his Porsche. He didn't like the car. He was too tall for it, and he always felt wadded up behind its wheel. He missed the truck he'd had when he was a teenager. But the Boxter was fast, and it had allowed him to flee from his assistants without a single word about his plans or future whereabouts except that they might involve tea. He'd wondered if anybody remembered he didn't drink tea, hated the stuff, and the hilarity of the entire situation had kept him afloat for the hour and a half he'd fought traffic and had driven south.

When he'd gotten sick of staring at the taillights of the Mercedes in front of him, Theo had pulled off the interstate and driven into an unfamiliar neighborhood. He'd parked in front of a house with a chain-link fence. He'd almost left the keys to his car in the stranger's mailbox.

The delight of misbehaving and being where he shouldn't be had buoyed him for the better part of his walk. He did yoga four times a week, worked with a trainer, and his body fat was lower now than when he'd been a scrawny stick figure in high school. Walking five miles in temperate weather was easy. At least it'd been easy until the panic had suddenly sprung out of the twisted inner workings of his mind and tried to kill him.

Theo reached up and wrapped his hand around the slender branch of a tree. Its bark was smooth and pale, comforting beneath his touch. A line of ants marched up a concrete stone that was three over from the one on which Theo sat. He studied their orderly procession and realized he'd left the crossword book in the hospital. He kept the paperback books in his car and his bags and scattered all over his house. It'd been on reflex that he'd taken one, rolled it up, and shoved it in his back pocket when he'd started his walk this morning. He patted his jeans and retrieved his pen. He'd gotten that, at least. He let go of the branch and began to systematically unscrew and recap the pen. The cell phone buzzed from where it rested on the rock between Theo and the ants. It was Carla. Theo had missed all his appointments for the day, and they were going to start calling hospitals if he didn't answer their messages in the next half hour.

A half hour. Thirty minutes. How far away could Theo be in thirty minutes?

Without bothering to analyze why he wanted to run—his shrink had covered that in their many discussions on avoidance of adult responsibility and fear of confrontation—Theo picked up his phone, thumbed screens, and Google conjured a map of the United States. He flicked to the East Coast and zoomed in. Maine was the farthest point, obviously. There was that lighthouse up there marking the easternmost point of the country. But it was only March, which meant it was still snowing up there. Theo didn't care for frigid. The one and only time he'd gone skiing, he'd broken his ankle. He wasn't going to give the snow another chance to bite him.

He nudged the map down and scanned the Southeast. He didn't love the idea of Florida, and commercial beaches like Myrtle gave him the creeps. Obviously, he could call one of the Detail Twins and have an entire acre of land sectioned off for his use, but the whole idea of this hypothetical experiment would be to choose someplace naturally remote. He wanted something more private, more intimate and…endearing, maybe, for lack of a better word. If he was going to disappear, he wanted to go someplace peaceful and quaint. He studied the landscape and had to zoom in farther to see the fine print labeling the slivers of islands off the coast. He saw Duck, Corolla, and Kitty Hawk. Wasn't that where the Wright Brothers had done their thing? Theo thought so.

Theo stared at Kitty Hawk and then kept scanning the area. He saw Nags Head and laughed. Oh, the irony of ironies: disappearing into Nags Head to escape the nags. He tapped on the city, and the map scooted to the right. On the

left side of the screen was a list of sponsored ads, most of
which were for vacation rentals. Theo chewed on the inside
of his cheek and rubbed the shaft of his fountain pen. The
breeze rustled the trees and the ant train was all but gone,
the last stragglers bringing up the rear.

The car was north of where Theo sat, probably about
a forty-five minute walk. He knew he should get up and go
to it, but his legs had turned to lead. His ass had melted to
the concrete barrier. If he wasn't careful, he was going to
turn into an odd decorative shrubbery, but the more he told
himself to get up and get moving, to answer the messages
and stop fucking around, the less able he was to do anything
at all. He stared at the map. He flipped back to the messages.
He watched the phone's clock tick forward a full minute.

And then Theo went back to the map, stabbed at the
first real estate listing, and dialed the number.

Chapter Two

It was the dream about the stone steps. Muggy, oppressive air pressed on her shoulders like hands kneading her into damp, malleable dough. Her skin was dark, far darker than it was this time around, and her black hair fell to her waist.

He was sitting next to her.

Both of them were small and slim, and though they'd be ridiculed and even publically shunned if they were caught, they clasped hands, their intertwined fingers hidden by the fabric of her long skirt. It was rough against her skin, and her upper torso was wrapped in more beige fabric. He wore a similar skirt, though his was snugger around his legs, and a colorful vest outlined the shape of his shoulders and chest. He was just as dark as she was, and his teeth flashed when he smiled at her. His mouth moved in words of a language that she didn't know, but in the dream, she understood. She was happy. So very happy. Because of what he'd said and because of the feeling of his hand around hers, rough and strong.

"Excuse me, madam, but it appears to be morning."

Hydee ignored the British gentleman who had suddenly appeared in her dream wearing a tux with a towel draped over his arm. She focused on the wide, hot steps, the connection of laced fingers, and the heat of a body so near to her own.

"I believe the rotation of the earth is to blame, madam. Most inconvenient."

The dream faded, and Hydee groaned. She opened her eyes to find the world tinted red by the blanket she'd pulled over her head. She peeked out from the edge of the covers. Her bedroom windows were open, and the light rain tapped the raised hurricane shutters and blew against the screens. Faintly she heard music. She gave serious thought to shutting her eyes and ignoring the world, but the cultured voice was insistent.

"Madam, if you'd be so kind as to rise, I'm certain the day will become all the better with your attendance."

Hydee smacked her alarm clock so the British gentleman who lived inside it would take a nap. She hated loud, blaring noises. They reminded her too much of the hurricane warning sirens. So she had her British butler wake her every morning. Hydee rolled onto her back, stretching as she went. It was barely light outside, and she was warm and comfortable. Her bed was a nest of purple and blue pillows, red and green blankets, and at least one orange cat who not only clashed, he looked positively irritated with her for rousing him before he was ready to move.

"It's not like it was my idea," Hydee said to Oscar the Grouchy. His tail and ears twitched.

"You've got it easy. I have to work. See and talk to people. Smile. Some of us can't survive on canned food and prowling alone, you know." Hydee patted the comforter, and Oscar rose and languidly sashayed over to be scratched. His short hair was soft and warm, and Hydee tried to conjure the peace of the dream steps and the warmth of a foreign sun, but the music reached a crescendo and vibrated her bedroom wall.

Frowning, Hydee tilted her head backward to stare at the oil painting above her oak headboard. An abstract man and woman held hands and walked a rainbow path toward a bright light carved out of the black, blue, and yellow universe. The couple shook again with the thumping of bass through speakers, and Hydee suddenly recognized the tune.

'Do what the music say, you wanna kiss the girl!'

There was a crab and a host of freshwater critters serenading a prince of land and a princess of the sea next door, which could mean only one thing:

It was Changing Day.

Make that two things: it was Changing Day, and she was late.

"Oh God." Hydee tossed covers and cat aside and scrambled toward the bathroom. She sang along to the rest of the song from Disney's *The Little Mermaid*, and she sniffed her underarms. Not too bad if nobody got downwind. Hydee grabbed her toothbrush and shoved it and paste into her mouth. She grabbed a gold-and-blue gypsy skirt with bells sewn into the lining off the floor and stepped into it, hopping on one foot when she lost her balance. She heard a crash next door, panicked, and flung laundry until she found a bra and a tunic blouse that vaguely matched the skirt. Oscar, sensing that his human was having another seizure, zipped out of the room. Hydee started to follow, realized she hadn't actually put *on* the bra or shirt and that she still had her toothbrush, and ran back to the bathroom adjoining her bedroom. That was when she noticed that her waist-length lavender hair was somehow managing to defy gravity and stick out in all directions like a purple halo.

Hydee cussed with her mouth full, spat in the sink, rinsed with one hand, and fumbled in a drawer for a hairbrush and elastic ties. It took her ten minutes to tame her pastel hair into three fishtails that she loosely braided into one long ponytail. By the time she was fully dressed and charging down the dark wooden steps, the playlist had moved on to *Beauty and the Beast*. Hydee found an ice coffee in her fridge and uncapped it. There wasn't time to make the fresh stuff, and Lynne would have brought disgustingly healthy tea, and Adir didn't do caffeine. The weirdo.

Hydee chugged the coffee and dashed from the sunshine-gold kitchen into the sea-blue living and dining room. She found her thong sandals, thought about it, and sat down to pull on her heavy combat boots. It was Changing Day. Things fell and broke and rolled on Changing Day. She'd need to protect her toes.

Oscar scurried over to her, mrowing a reminder that feeding the cat should be at the top of her priority list. Hydee put out kitty chow and flew around the house to find her cell phone. She discovered it buried under a pile of books and magazines on her table. It was dead. So that meant another five minutes finding the charging cord, which was upstairs in her home office, where she journaled and kept her scrapbooks. She got the charger and started to place a habitual kiss to the portrait pinned to a corkboard on the wall, but paused. Even with pale skin, different bone structure, and professionally enhanced teeth, the man from her dreams was still entirely beautiful and completely recognizable. He always was.

Every time she left the room, she kissed him good-bye. The picture was beginning to fade from the daily treatment. That morning, though, Hydee raised her fingertips to her lips and blew him a kiss instead of making it personal. She told herself it was because she liked the older photograph and wanted to preserve it. She didn't let herself think about how it was strange that such thoughts hadn't stopped her until now.

Racing down the stairs for the second time that day, Hydee went to the door leading onto her covered side porch. The front door tended to stick, and the dead bolt was impossible, so Hydee exited toward her backyard with a bang of screen door. She thumped across the porch boards and reminded herself again that the columns really did need another coat of green paint. She could probably get Adir to do it if she bribed him with enough pastries and a historical text or two. The man was a sucker for the past. He and Hydee had that in common.

Hydee took a deep breath of North Carolina beach country air as she walked past her raised herb gardens, around the side of her house, and by the front porch. Her store, The Silver Fox, was attached to her house at a ninety degree angle. The store's double front doors faced Appleton Street, which joined Persimmon Lane and took travelers straight to Ocean Boulevard/North Carolina Highway 12. The highway ran from Corolla south to Kitty Hawk, where Lynne lived with the kids when they weren't in the condo in Virginia Beach, and where Adir lived all the time over

Lynne's garage.

Lynne's BMW SUV was parked in its usual place next to the side of the shop and away from the modest parking lot. Lynne drove the BMW because her husband had hauled away the ancient Dodge minivan and forced the new vehicle upon Lynne, the kids, and Adir, who was usually along for the half-hour drive from Kitty Hawk to Corolla. Lynne still cursed Ron for taking away "the baby" that had been held together in its last years by bumper stickers and memories of concerts past. She'd begun to make headway on the white Beamer, though. The COEXIST bumper sticker was proudly displayed next to ones about honors kids, supporting the military, just saying no to drugs and football, and, Hydee's favorite: "Where are we going and why are we in this handbasket?"

The Silver Fox's main-level bay windows were clean and currently completely empty of their usual displays. Music blared from the wide-open front doors, and the mist had dampened the heart-pine floorboards. Empty metal stands and one set of hand-painted purple shelves stood on the porch. Even the wind chimes that typically hung from dozens of hooks from the overhang of the second floor's balcony were gone, taken inside to be rearranged.

Lynne and Adir must have gotten there at the crack of dawn. At seven a.m, it was still chilly bordering on cold, and when Hydee walked into her shop, she was grateful that the gas fire was lit in the stone, see-through fireplace at the rear of the store. It was a vast improvement over the curtain that had hung there for years.

For a moment, the bright, updated interior was gone, and Hydee was standing in the store as it had been some sixteen years ago when her father, Halloway Fox, had bought it. The main floor's boards weren't wide planks with gleaming polyurethane; they were patchy wood covered in mouse droppings, mattresses, and candle wax. The stairs leading to the second-story landing weren't carpeted in a chic black rug patterned with suns, moons, and stars; they didn't even exist except as an echo of functionality, they had so many holes. The upper landing wasn't outlined in a green banister railing, the windows didn't have broad white sills with stenciled designs, and the second-floor balcony wasn't a cozy outdoor spot with rocking chairs and garden merchandise; the second floor was missing railings altogether, the windows were fractured eyes with broken panes, and the balcony was wrecked, nothing more than old, molded tar over creaky pine.

Now The Silver Fox was a symbol of the community. Back then, it had been an eyesore that the town had wanted demolished.

The odd, empty shop with its attached run-down Victorian had been Hal's latest money scheme when Hydee had turned fifteen. Hal and Hydee's mother had never married, but Hal had managed to make sure Hydee was given a suitably hippie name—Hyacinth Silver Fox—before going where the warm breeze of fate would take him. He'd been in and out of Hydee's life when she'd been a kid, but he'd come to stay for what Hydee had hoped would be for good when she was in her mid-teens. He'd bought the house and the store, moving into the first and turning the latter into a hodgepodge of As Seen On TV items and car parts. It had smelled like somebody's garage storage closet, and now when Hydee went to get her oil changed at the Quik Service Center, it reminded her of those early days when The Silver Fox had been Hal's Emporium.

For three years, Hydee had spent every day after school and every weekend helping her father fix up the place and then, when it was as fixed up as their shoestring budget would allow, she'd helped him run the cash register and keep the books. Hal had always been miserable with numbers. Hydee, as it had turned out, had been excellent with them so long as they came with dollar signs attached.

Hydee had known since she'd laid eyes on the place that it had been part of her destiny. She'd also known that her father wasn't going to have much part of that destiny.

Sure enough, for Hydee's eighteenth birthday, her father had vanished but left her the shop and the house. Despite seeing it coming even before she had found the keys and the deeds, Hydee had cried. Crazy and vagrant as he was, Hydee missed her dad when he was on walkabout.

There hadn't been much time for tears, though, because customers had shown up that very day. When word got out that Hal was gone and Hydee was on her own, everyone had thought she was crazy: eighteen and running her own business. Hydee's aunt, though, had thought it wonderful. She was an accountant and helped Hydee with the taxes. Hydee's mother, who had worked multiple jobs all Hydee's life, had no time and had wanted nothing to do with her ex's project, so Hydee's best friend since kindergarten, Lynne Crossgrove, had signed on for a very modest salary of zip, zilch, and nada. Lynne's parents were well off, and by then Lynne's engagement to her high school sweetheart, Ron Hart, was official. Lynne had no more interest in college than she had in the academic side of high school. Ron, however, had gone on to college and law school. That had suited Lynne just fine. She'd had Cecelia and Victor in that order, and eventually had changed her mind about education. It'd been a strange kind of education, but it'd been perfect for Lynne, and having a certified medium on staff did have certain advantages. Lynne had what she called The Luck. She always landed on her feet, won every contest she ever entered, and she could share The Luck with others under the right circumstances. Hydee didn't know what she would do without Lynne.

Despite the naysayers, the shop prospered, and soon Hydee had been able to pay her employee with funds left over. Lynne had worked on the spiritual angle, giving card and life readings to customers. She was great with people. It'd been Lynne who had found Adir Flies With Ravens. Adir used to answer to a different name, but he'd gone on a Name Finding Journey and afterward had legally changed it. He'd shown up one day, had claimed to have seen the store and the two women in a vision during the journey, and he'd moved east like his vision had told him to do. Such a story would have been farfetched to some, but not Lynne or Hydee. Lynne had hired Adir practically before the kid was over the threshold. She and Adir got along like cake and icing, and Hydee was the ice cream, as they liked to say.

The present-day office door upstairs opened, and Adir flew onto the second landing. He was twenty-five going on a hundred and five, tall, willowy, and had long black hair and deep green eyes. He tended to dress in rich flannels and ripped jeans, which went with his Native American complexion beautifully. Though calling Adir or anything about him Native "American" was likely to get one a lecture on how full-blooded Indians such as himself identified more with a tribal nation than the country at large. His people were Blackfeet, from Montana, though his parents and siblings had escaped the reservation and disavowed their history. They lived in Texas. Adir never went home, and he rarely spoke about any family except his grandparents, who were still on the res.

Adir saw Hydee and grinned. He sang along in perfect pitch with the candlestick's solo from *Beauty and the Beast* and grabbed a round stand heavy with hats and scarves. On the beat, he began tossing clothing down to Hydee one by one. Hydee dropped her cell phone and charger onto the front counter and dutifully tried to catch the falling apparel.

"So nice of you to join us," Lynne called loudly, rolling a cart full of books by Hydee and onto the front porch. Lynne's ample behind was covered by a patchwork skirt, and her curly dark brown hair was bundled into a knot on top of her head.

"It's barely seven," Hydee protested. Adir sang louder and dumped an entire box of hand-woven handbags onto Hydee's head. "Hey!" she yelled.

"It's Changing Day," Lynne bellowed. She started helping Hydee pick up Adir's mess. "You're usually here at five a.m. and have half the damned store rearranged before

I'm even—Adir, cut that shit out!"

Adir laughed and put all the hats he'd not thrown down to Hydee and Lynne onto his head. He balanced them perfectly while picking up the empty rack and maneuvering it to the stairs.

"I swear, that man and his Disney fetish. Talking animals just *do* something to him," Lynne muttered.

"You mean like enhance his musical qualities?" Hydee asked innocently.

"I mean being more a pain in the ass than usual."

"Like I said…"

"You say it nicer."

"Part of the job." Hydee turned to a set of shelves that had held jewelry for the last three months. The hats would fit on the pink-and-green shelves perfectly. She started arranging them. "I'm the nice one at the front counter, and you're the weird gypsy in the back with the crystal ball."

"More like the sleep-deprived mother with the Alka-Seltzer."

"Uh-oh," Hydee said. Adir came over with the empty stand and bent so Hydee could start adding his headwear to her shelves. "Ceecee?" Hydee asked Lynne.

"Zombie nightmares again." Lynne shook her head. "I don't know where she gets the ideas in her head, but she's telling me at three a.m. about how zombies are made through a blood-borne disease that the government's going to release, and somewhere in there, I went for the wine."

"Did you give her some?" Hydee asked. Lynne tossed her a look. "What? Works like a charm when I do it."

Lynne wagged a finger at Hydee. "Stop encouraging my daughter's alcoholism, Hy-Ho. If she's going to get it from anybody, it's going to be from me."

Adir swept by them, pausing midtwirl to say, "The ladies with the jams and jellies are pulling into the parking lot." He walked backward with a flamboyant bow and fled up the stairs.

"Still afraid of them, I see," Hydee said.

"I would kill to watch Mrs. Adcock put Adir's hair in pigtails again," Lynne mused, heading toward the front door. "To be continued?"

Hydee nodded. "Adir! Turn it down!" she cried in the general direction of the office. Seconds later, Angela Lansbury was singing at a volume not threatening to rupture eardrums. Hydee finished the hats and went upstairs to help Adir move the furniture around.

For the next two hours, Hydee barely had time to think. Vendors came and went, dropping off merchandise. Hydee stocked a range of merchandise from mainstream sellers, but the more interesting items came from the locals. The Myrtles brought their turtles, dozens of ceramic figurines that Hydee elected to put in the front window. Felix Crass brought two more rocking chairs that went on the second-floor balcony. Harmony Wilcox parked, and Hydee yelled at Adir to help her unload her metal sculptures, which she swore would be fine on the porch. "If I couldn't hurt 'em while I was makin' 'em, nothin' but God's gonna bother 'em," she said to Hydee.

Normally, Hydee would be right there, arranging and chatting with Harmony in the misty rain that was threatening to get serious, but today, Hydee had merely admired and gone back to sorting jewelry in the front display cases. She told herself the tight feeling low in her belly was nothing. She had no reason to worry and no cause for anxiety. She was tired, hadn't slept well, and besides, Jane Featherall would be in that afternoon with the latest of her stone-and-wire creations, along with Lily Wexley with her Mother Goddess necklaces. Those things were enormous. Hydee couldn't waste her entire Changing Day socializing. She had to make room.

Around ten, Brenda Cameron and her two grandkids, ages eight months and five, brought in an entire crate of homemade coffee cakes, cookies in every flavor of the rainbow, and two huge warming carafes of Russian tea. "Hello, dears," she said, bouncing the baby in a sling. "Set up in the usual spot?"

"We've got the porch all ready for you," Lynne answered, helping herself to a free sample from a plastic container. "Here, let me give you a hand."

While Lynne and Mrs. Cameron set up outside, Hydee retreated to the second floor and hid in peace for half an hour. Adir wasn't the only one who could pull a vanishing act. "Good crowd," Lynne said when she found Hydee reorganizing peasant skirts.

"Always is for spring Changing Day," Hydee said. One of the skirts was steel gray, and it reminded Hydee of stone steps. The pit in her stomach that had nothing to do with hunger deepened. She was dizzy for a few seconds, and then it passed. "Did I ever say thank you?"

"For what?"

"For everything." Hydee shook her head to make herself stop replaying her dream for the tenth time that hour. "For starting all this. Changing Day."

Lynne leaned against the wall next to Hydee with her arms crossed. "I didn't do anything. We were drunk because you were upset about *him*, again, and we started wrecking the store at four a.m. the day before our vendors were going to show up. When they got here, they thought it was a thing that the crazy psychic and the mystical shop lady did when they got bored." Lynne blew a piece of hair away from her mouth. "Thank goodness we only do this four times a year now, and not every month. My back couldn't take it."

"Yeah." Hydee fingered the skirt. "Dreams."

"Hmm?"

"I'd had one of the bad dreams the day we first rearranged the inventory. That's why I was upset."

"Yeah, I know. I'd seen it before."

The dreams weren't always sunshine and giggles. Hydee could remember fights and pain and deaths too. "Yeah. You've seen me dealing with them for a long time."

"Mmm-hmm." Lynne nodded. "Did you have one last night? A bad dream?"

"No." Hydee turned to face Lynne. "Why?"

"You're acting odder than usual."

Hydee shrugged. She felt odder than usual. Like she still wanted to be curled up and hiding under her red blanket with her cat and the rain outside and nothing else for days on end. Maybe weeks. "Don't know. I'm just tired."

"Yeah, I can tell." Lynne studied her. "And that's what's weird. You're usually the one with the fire under your ass. Today bothering you more than usual?"

"Changing Day, you mean?" Hydee asked.

"Yeah. Nothing like reorganizing your entire life's work to clean out the emotional leftovers."

Hydee snorted. "Nah, I'm used to it."

"Then what gives?"

"Don't know. Maybe I had the zombie dreams too and just don't remember." Hydee smiled at Tommy, their FedEx delivery man, who stomped up the steps and came over holding out an electronic clipboard for her signature. "You get a cookie out front?" she asked him, scrawling her name.

"Not yet, ma'am."

"Well, grab a few on your way out."

Tommy's eyes swept over Hydee in the assessing, familiar way that spoke of appreciation and interest without wandering into the land of rude. "Will do. Thank you, Ms. Fox."

He lingered, and Hydee was swept away by the memory of warmth on her shoulders, of a body so near hers, of how happy she'd been… About how she could never be that way when she was awake. "No problem," Hydee almost whispered.

"Ma'am?" Tommy gestured to Hydee, and she realized she was holding his clipboard hostage.

"Sorry." She passed the board back to him. He smiled at her, looking as though he wanted to say more or maybe was waiting for her to speak. When neither of them did, he nodded and left.

Hydee sighed and discovered Lynne staring at her with a dangerous and familiar lift of eyebrows. "What?" Hydee asked. Lynne didn't answer.

"Oh, don't do that thing with me," Hydee said, stalking away from Lynne and toward the stairs. She could see the stack of boxes Tommy had left sitting in front of the main counter.

"Do what thing?" Lynne asked innocently, following.

"You know what."

"I'm utterly clueless, I swear."

Hydee grabbed a box cutter off the front display case. "The reading-me-without-permission thing."

"I don't have to use my otherworldly powers to see that something's up, Hy."

Usually, being transparent to Lynne made Hydee feel better, not exposed. "The I'm-going-to-stare-you-down-until-you-crack thing hasn't worked on me since the fourth grade." Hydee crouched and savagely opened a box. "Save it for the customers."

"Okay."

"And don't do *that* either," Hydee said with more irritation than she thought she had in her.

"Now what?" Lynne asked.

"The patronizing thing."

"Okay. What the hell crawled up your skirt and died, Hy-Ho?"

Hydee slapped the box cutter on the floor. "That nickname's not been funny since we were six. You know that, right?"

Lynne put her hands on her hips, likely about to launch into a lecture on how Hydee was allowed bad days like anybody else, but could she kindly keep her snark to herself, but Adir walked in arm in arm with a tall woman whose hair was so blonde the white streaks in it looked like highlights. Her pale eyes were almost colorless. She wore slacks and a dress shirt, and when Adir made her laugh, it sounded like sandpaper rubbing against itself. Hydee cringed.

"Hi, sweetheart," Hydee's mother said.

"Hi, Mom." Hydee struggled to get up, her legs weaker than normal. Lynne held out a hand, and Hydee took it. Lynne squeezed, still giving Hydee the All-Seeing Stare, and Hydee dodged the penetrative glance and swept behind the front counter.

"Glenda," Adir said, kissing Hydee's mother's hand.

"Oh you…" Glenda wheezed a laugh. She'd smoked two packs a day for years, only quitting when she'd suffered a thankfully mild heart attack a couple of years ago.

Adir wandered away, picking up a FedEx box full of inventory and carrying it to its new home. "He's just precious, that man." Glenda set her bag on the counter and drummed her nails on the glass. "Why can't you find somebody like him to date, Hyacinth?"

Hydee and Lynne exchanged a glance. "I'm…not his type, Mom."

"Oh, I know, I know, he's… Well, you know."

"Yeah. I think I do," Hydee said.

Glenda's smile was thin. She looked at Lynne. "How're the kids?"

"Ceecee's having nightmares."

"Oh no."

"Speaking of," Hydee said. "Do you want me to talk to her again? About dreams and what their symbols mean?"

"Might need to, yeah."

"No problem. Just say when."

"That's my Hyacinth." Glenda patted Hydee's hand. "Always fixing everybody else."

The compliment was strained and awkward, but Hydee gave her mom points for trying. The woman had never been comfortable giving affection. That had been Hydee's father's area of expertise. Hydee knew now that she reminded her mom of her father, whom Glenda had never understood. Hal was a whimsical, flighty man with big ideas and the Zen-like acceptance that if they never came to fruition, they were still good ideas. Glenda had never agreed with Hal's philosophy.

"What brings you by, Mom?"

"I wanted to see you on Changing Day. The place is always so alive." Glenda sighed. "I wish your father could see you now."

"He knows about the shop, Mom." Hydee treaded carefully. Though Hydee considered it ancient history, Glenda had taken it as an insult that Hal had left the shop and house to Hydee. She never could quite tell if Glenda had wanted the place for herself or if she'd interpreted Hal's gift as a way of saying Glenda could never provide for Hydee what Hal could and did. Maybe it was some of both, but whatever the reasoning, it was a touchy subject.

"Have you heard from him?" Glenda asked.

"Dad? Yeah, he wrote me a letter a couple weeks ago."

"And where is your father now?"

"He was in Thailand, heading for Borneo."

"What on earth is he going to do there?"

"I don't think he's going to *do* anything, Mom. He's just going to see it."

Glenda shook her head, aghast at the sheer insanity that was touring the world for fun. "Well, power to the man. At least he writes you."

"He does. He asks about you. Says to tell you hello."

Glenda rolled her eyes, and Hydee was bracing for a barrage about responsibility and fanciful ideas and how Glenda was grateful Hydee had at least some of her mother's better sense, when Lynne nudged Hydee's arm with one elbow.

A tiny woman hugging a mailing tube had entered the shop. Georgiana Glover was four feet five and ninety-three years old. She walked three miles every day and had snow-white hair pulled into a bun that emphasized her pointed ears and bright brown eyes. She looked like an attractive brownie, a renegade member of the wee folk. "Mrs. Glover," Hydee said. "So nice to see you."

Mrs. Glover smiled, and her entire face animated with it. She wore a skirt, silk shirt, jacket, hose, and bright white tennis shoes. "Good morning," she said to the three of them. "Oh my, I've caught you in the middle of something."

"No, no, it's okay." Hydee tried not to sound too desperate for a distraction. "What can I do for you?"

"Nothing for me. I brought you something, dear." Mrs. Glover held up the cylindrical shipping tube. "My granddaughter sent it to me, and I just don't think it's going to go with my decor. But I immediately thought of you."

"Oh boy," Lynne said, too softly for Mrs. Glover's hearing aid to pick it up. All three women exchanged nervously amused looks over Mrs. Glover's head.

Mrs. Glover's granddaughter was forty and a former actress of the triple-X kind. The last time Mrs. Glover had thought of Hydee, it'd been to give her a poster of marching dildos in various military uniforms. Adir had fallen in love with it immediately and had taken it home to hang it proudly on his wall.

Hydee rolled the tube closer. "You really shouldn't have."

"It's quite all right. You do so much for the community here, with your store." Mrs. Glover beamed and set her purse down on the case across from Hydee and Lynne. "She does so much," she said to Glenda, and didn't let Glenda get a word in edgewise. "I just don't think you know what you mean to us, Hydee dear. You're our little hot spot. Do you know I saw Mrs. Cameron and her grandbabies out front talking to those two gentlemen who own that ribs place down the street? She was flirting, if you can believe that. Those men are young enough to be her sons."

"Shameful," Lynne said with a mock leer.

"Hardly, dear." Mrs. Glover winked. "It's the most action the old bat's seen outside her kitchen in years."

Glenda laughed, and Hydee got the tube's top free of tape. She tugged out the white plug. Inside was a poster, and Hydee gently removed it, holding her breath. Together, she and Lynne unfurled the thing on the countertop.

"Oh…my…" Lynne said.

"Good Lord," Glenda added.

"I know how you like him," Mrs. Glover said to Hydee proudly. "I always appreciate that poster in the ladies' room."

"Adir's idea," Hydee murmured.

Theo Monk smiled invitingly at them from where he was lounging on a pool chair. His bathing suit left absolutely nothing to the imagination. He was perfect, the man who haunted Hydee's dreams in all his incarnations, but the thing that struck Hydee hardest was the brilliance of the sunlight on his skin. Theo was tan in the picture, a nutty brown, and the sun shone in water drops highlighted by the shadows thrown by the turn of his body. His fingers were above his head laced into the chair back's slats, and a hundred visions poured into Hydee's mind about rope and rhythm and mouths forming moans.

Hydee shook her head, attempting to sling the memories from the front of her mind to its rear. A flash of anger struck like lightning, but Hydee doused it. Wherever it had come from, it had nothing to do with Mrs. Glover, who was sweet and sincere and an excellent customer. Hydee let go of the poster so it snapped into its roll. She formed her mouth into a smile. "Thank you so much. This'll go great next to the other one, don't you think?"

"I did think," Mrs. Glover replied happily. She picked up her purse and hugged it. "It's not much, but I thought you should have it."

"Thank you," Hydee repeated.

"Hydee can't ever have too much Theo," Lynne said.

The anger crackled again, and Hydee forced her shoulders to relax. Honestly, what was the matter with her today?

Lynne beckoned to Adir, who had floated down the steps and headed their way when he saw Mrs. Glover. "Look what we've got."

"Oooh, if it's from Georgiana, then it's got to be good." Adir swept over to them, and though he did his usual flirtatious banter with Mrs. Glover and the woman ate it with a spoon, to Hydee, their voices started to grow distant. She was hot all over.

"Earth to Hy-Ho?" Lynne said.

"Mmm?" Hydee steadied herself on the counter. The weight of Lynne's gaze was heavy on Hydee's shoulders, but she didn't look at her friend. "I'm sorry, what did you say?"

Mrs. Glover chuckled and covered Hydee's hand on the counter with her own. "They can be so distracting, can't they?"

"What?"

"The objects of our desire, dear."

Hydee blushed. Glenda squirmed. This discussion needed to be cut short before temptation overwhelmed Glenda and the woman had to speak her mind. "Do you have time to stay for a while, Mrs. Glover?" Hydee asked. "The Myrtles brought over a fresh batch of turtles today."

"Oh! Yes. I'll go and have a look." She glanced sidelong at Adir. "You ladies have a good day."

"We will," Adir promised. "I love her," he said when Mrs. Glover had gone about her way.

"Honestly," Glenda huffed. She poked at the poster. "How do you stand it, Hyacinth?"

"Stand what?" Hydee asked. She was a weed in the garden about to be plucked by her mother's indelicate hands.

"The entire town knowing about your ridiculous obsession with this movie star. I'd be so embarrassed."

"Why should she be embarrassed?" Adir asked with an edge to his tone.

"It's a hobby, Glenda, like anything else," Lynne said mildly.

"I wish it were just that, but we all know it isn't."

The storm inside Hydee was getting worse. "Mom, please. Not today, okay?"

"I'm sorry, honey." Glenda paused, and for a moment,

Hydee thought that might actually be it.

Wishful thinking. "I hate to see you throwing your good years down the drain is all," Glenda said. "I do not understand why you spend so much time mooning over this ridiculous movie star when you could be out there finding yourself a real man."

Hydee didn't reply, and Lynne shifted closer to her side. Adir bit his lip. "Honestly," Glenda said. "I blame your father. He had all these obsessions too. Still does, apparently. Borneo. For pity's sake." She sighed and smiled sadly at her only child. "I gave up hoping for your father to see the light a long time ago, but I still hope someday you'll realize you're not a child anymore and you'll, I don't know. Get over your little crush. Be the woman I know you can be."

The dam of tolerance inside Hydee broke. The ground began to crumble beneath Hydee's feet. Her ears rang. Her breath echoed inside her skull. She stood and seethed at her mother, and for each second that Hydee remained silent, the light of hope in her mother's eyes faded bit by bit. And that was the worst of all.

Lynne and Adir were quiet too, and at long last, Glenda nodded. "I've upset you. I'm sorry, dear. But that awful poster—"

Hydee turned to Lynne. "Watch the shop, okay?"

"Hyacinth…" Glenda tried.

"Have a good day, Mom. Excuse me." Hydee bolted around the counter and out the front door. She turned down a plate of coffee cake and trudged around her home as though slogging through quicksand. She thought she might split down the middle in angry anguish, and she hugged herself tightly. The breeze kicked up, and Hydee imagined it peeling off her clothes and layers of metaphoric skin and blowing them out to sea. It'd be such a relief, to fall to pieces and float on the water.

The wind scraped and scraped, stripping Hydee emotionally bare as she worked the doorknob and shoved into her living room. Oscar rose from a chair, took one look at Hydee, and fled up the stairs. Hydee stood still for a moment, hands in fists, and then she went to her sofa. She picked up a pillow. She squeezed it.

"Little crush," she said, raising the pillow and hurling it at the wall. "Little." Another pillow flew. "Stupid." The next pillow knocked a picture down with a crash. "Crush!"

Hydee choked on rage and landed on her knees. She pressed the heels of her hands into her eye sockets. Immediately, the dream flashed in her mind. The stone steps…the warmth…the hand in hers…his smile…

With a cry, Hydee rose, chucked another pillow, spun, and landed in a heap. She fell against the side of the couch, shaking and seeing red. She didn't understand. She didn't get angry. Not like this. She didn't have breakdowns and throw shit and make a fool of herself. Not over her mother's opinion. Hydee had reconciled her mother's practical disbelief with Hydee's inexplicable dream curse a long time ago. This was not the first time her mother had said those things. It wouldn't be the last. But today, Hydee simply couldn't take it. It was too hard. Waking up every day…smiling…carrying on… She couldn't keep going on like this. She might never be able to get up off the floor again. Her mother had found an old, worn thread, plucked it at exactly the wrong time, and Hydee was coming unraveled.

Behind Hydee, the side door opened. Seconds later, Lynne's presence was a comforting warmth along Hydee's back. Lynne hugged her, and Hydee clasped Lynne's hand at her waist with a desperation that Hydee observed from outside herself.

"I'm so sorry, Hy," Lynne said.

"It's… I…" Hydee shakily inhaled. "It's not…only…"

"Not just your mom?"

"No."

"I know. What is it?"

The Hydee with Her Shit Together watched the Hydee Completely Unhinged, and neither version of herself understood the other. "I don't know," Hydee said helplessly.

"Well, we'll be right here until you do." Lynne nosed Hydee's shoulder, echoing Hydee's own words. Years and years ago, there'd been a night when Lynne took a test and it came back positive. She'd wanted kids. She'd loved Ron. She'd wanted a life in the Outer Banks where she could be a wife and mother and near her family and best friend. But when that circle had appeared on that stick, suddenly it'd all gotten very real very fast. Lynne had sat on Hydee's bed, and it'd been Hydee doing the hugging and the asking, "How do you feel?" and when Lynne had answered, "I don't know," Hydee had told her that she'd be there until Lynne did.

"Thank you," Hydee whispered, and Lynne hugged her tighter.

Adir's sweet cologne filled Hydee's nose, and he sat down cross-legged next to her and Lynne. He held out a glass of Bailey's: two fingers of drink with three ice cubes, precisely as Hydee liked it. Hydee accepted it and sipped.

"Talking is in order?" Adir asked. He took Hydee's hand.

"We're worried about you," Lynne added.

Hydee held the chocolaty-sweet liquid on her tongue until she couldn't taste it anymore. She swallowed. "I'm just… I can't…" She floundered.

"Which dream was it?" Lynne asked gently. "That you had last night?"

"The one where we're on the steps." Hydee sniffed and wiped her nose on her arm.

"Holding hands?" Lynne asked.

"Yeah," Hydee answered.

"That's a good one."

"A really fucking good one."

"Usually the happy ones don't—"

"I know." Hydee took a deep breath. She counted to ten. She breathed and started over. She often said that emotions left inside too long got bottled and the pent-up angst would make an unrelated situation far worse than it needed to be. "Let emotions flow through you as they appear on your horizon," she would say. That was the whole philosophy behind Changing Day, after all. Clear the shop of accumulated juju and other people's energies. Shake up the routine. Let the emotions flow out the windows and the doors so everybody and everything could breathe easier. Hydee tried to live by her own advice, but right now, she couldn't help but wonder what she'd been letting gather inside her with no outlet in sight.

"A crush," Hydee said. "A little…stupid—"

"Your mother doesn't know what she's talking about," Lynne said. "She never has."

Hydee stared at the pile of pillows at the base of her wall. "I remember the first time I dreamed of him."

Lynne and Adir inched closer. "Yeah?" Lynne said. "Tell us."

"You've heard it before."

"I like the dream stories," Adir said.

Hydee drew a long breath and blew an even longer sigh. "It's not the earliest life on our timeline, but it's the first one I remember seeing. I think we were in Africa, and it was a long time ago. In the dream, we met as kids. We were part of the same village by the water. Everyone fished, and he was showing me how he could stab one in the water with the spear his father had made him. We were small and thin and hungry. We wouldn't live past our early twenties, but I would live those years with him. We had children of our own, and he made our son a spear." Hydee drank and tried to center herself. "The first time I had that dream, I didn't even know it was Theo Monk."

"I know," Lynne said. "Your mom called him your little dream boy."

"Oh yeah. Harmless, those dreams. No big deal." Hydee felt herself smile without mirth. "Then one day Mom and I were in the living room…" Hydee trailed off because she'd recounted this story so many times, she wasn't sure she could get through it again.

"Go on," Lynne said when she knew Hydee's will was

faltering.

Hydee closed her eyes. "I was nine, and I was drawing in a notebook and sitting on the floor. Mom was at the table by the front door, smoking next to the open window. It was raining. The TV was on. We had a little thirteen-inch thing that picked up four channels on good days and one on bad days. It was a bad day. So Mom was watching a soap opera."

"*The Dawning Light*," Lynne said.

"Yeah, and then he was there. The person in my dreams knocked on the door to some woman's house on the show, and she opened it, and I knew him."

"It's the eyes," Lynne said softly. "You say it really is something about the eyes."

Hydee nodded. "The soul looking at me through them is always the same."

Lynne picked up the story. "So then you did what any kid would do. You pointed at the screen and said, 'Mama, look! It's the man I'm going to marry.' And Glenda's like"— Lynne mimed taking a drag off a smoke and rasped in a two-pack-a-day voice—"'Yeah, honey. Me fuckin' too.'"

Adir laughed a little, as though he wasn't sure he should, and Hydee ran her hands over her face. "It's always been way more than a crush."

"That's because it *is* more than a crush," Lynne pointed out. "You bound your soul to another soul in some magic ritual of the gods some ten bazillion years ago or whatever, and now you dream about you and your soul mate together in every lifetime you've ever lived. That's not a crush, that's destiny."

In the earliest lifetime Hydee dreamed about, she was priestess in a temple built to worship the gods of the earth. Part of that worship involved a fertility ritual. A male consort was to drink some potion so the god of the earth could embody him, and then he and the chosen priestess were to get it on so they could make more priestesses for the temples or sons to sacrifice to the gods and make the earth stronger.

In that dream, Theo was the consort, one of the

village sons, and he and his family had a touch of the same magic coveted by the temple. When he'd confessed he'd seen priestess Hydee on festival days and had fallen in love with her, she had agreed to do the equivalent of a marriage ritual so he'd feel better about having sex with a random priestess and hopefully knocking her up.

Lynne was convinced the ritual worked and now they were fated to be together for the rest of their lives. She even thought the reason Hydee always knew her soul mate but not the other way around was because Hydee had been the one who had actually performed the ceremony. Hydee didn't doubt her friend's theory, but it was Lynne who needed such explanations. Hydee wasn't sure she did. To her, it mattered less when or why or how she was bound to Theo than what to do about it in this life.

Or that what she had tried and was doing wasn't getting her anywhere. Hydee made a fist, opened it, and flexed her fingers. She could sit there and make her hand obey her mind all day but at night, she was helpless. The dreams took control. Anger was on her horizon again. "So where do the dreams end and I begin?"

"I think you've found that balance," Adir said. "Or seem to have found it, to me, anyway."

"Yeah, see, I'm not so sure, anymore." Hydee got up and went into her kitchen, but when she got there, she couldn't remember why she'd gone in the first place. She stood in the middle and slowly spun, eying the coffeemaker, the fridge, the counter, the cutting board…

"Hyacinth?" Lynne and Adir had followed her, and Lynne sounded truly concerned. They both were. Hydee couldn't help but think they should be. Beneath the frozen lake of false calm where she was trapped, Hydee was starting to panic.

"Do you know I kiss him good night and good morning?" Hydee couldn't face her friends, so she spoke to the greeting cards stuck to the refrigerator. "I've kissed dozens of men in my life, but none of them feel as real as stupid pieces of paper. The men who've shared my bed haven't been as real to me as the man I've only known in photographs."

"Real is relative," Adir said.

"No," Hydee said firmly and matter-of-fact. She spun and put her glass on the counter. "*Real* is you and me, flesh and blood, bone and bodies. Real is getting to date and wondering if it'll work out to be better than you ever imagined, not eating dinner with a guy you know is never going to measure up because he's not in your head every night catching you fucking fish in a village that's been dead for hundreds of years." Mania bubbled in Hydee's bloodstream, and she started to shake. Lynne began to come closer, but Hydee held up a hand.

"She thinks I don't try," Hydee said, her heart thudding so hard it made her chest rattle. "But she's wrong. I do try. I have. But I've only ever had bad dates. I've only ever had relationships that I knew would never work. Because I don't have fantasies, I have memories. I remember what he's tasted like for thousands of years. I could draw you how he looks when he's sad and how he smiles when he's laughing. I've seen the same expressions on hundreds of faces, and those moments, those dreams, are the only times I've ever felt whole. Ever."

It was Adir's turn to try. "Silver, why don't you come over to the couch and we can—"

"I don't want the fucking couch." Hydee scratched at her arm. She rubbed her neck and tugged her braid. She felt solid, but at any moment, she would disintegrate into atoms and scatter all over the house like so much unwanted dust. "I want to stop being so fucking sad. What I do, who I am, it's… I'm…" Hydee met Lynne's eyes. "I used to look at him and see the man I love. But now…now do you know what I see when I look at him?"

Lynne shook her head.

"I see happiness I can never touch. The real, honest-to-whatever-is-listening kind of happiness. The sort you could build a life on top of and know it'll stand through the storms. I see a man whom I rationally have no business thinking I know, but who feels, and who always has felt, like a part of me." Hydee lifted her arm, reaching for an invisible dark-skinned man on stone steps. He wasn't there, never would be, and she let her arm fall. "And I can't be with him."

"We don't know that for sure," Lynne said.

"There must be something else to do or try," Adir said. "Maybe the timing was wrong before, but now it's right. Lynne could use her Luck, maybe figure out a way to meet—"

"We've done that," Hydee said, her voice heavy and cold. "We've tried that. We've tried everything. I've done all I can think to do to meet him and have a shot of getting to know him, but nothing's worked." Hydee laughed, and for a horrible second, she thought she might not be able to stop. She put a fist to her lips and pressed so hard her front teeth hurt. "It's not like our lives have always worked out." Hydee wrung her hands. "There've been lives where it's gone catastrophically wrong. But when I'm a woman and he's a man and we have the chance to meet and talk, we figure out a way to be together, even if it's only for a little while. Even if it means risking our lives or our reputations or everything we've got. The Universe always has our paths cross, and it's up to us to make it work, despite families or disease or even war.

"But I've met him, and you know what happened? Nothing. I mean, I've seen us fail for reasonable but tragic reasons. I could handle something like that. Like he up and dies in a car wreck and there I am, in mourning. Or maybe I'm in India in an arranged marriage, or we're dirt poor on different continents. That shit? That shit I could see.

"But no. This time? This stupid fucking time? I can't know him because he's a fucking oblivious, untouchable movie star. A day job and we're done. It's got to be some sort of fucking joke. Any day now, the Universe is going to be like, 'Just kidding!' and make it right. I want to believe that!" Hydee realized she was yelling and smacked her lips shut. She picked up her drink and drained the last of it.

"It can," Adir said. "It will happen."

Hydee pressed her hands to her heart. "I'm just… I'm not sure anymore. I feel like all I do, everything I am… It's delusional. I'm insane."

"No, you're—"

Hydee overrode Lynne. "What I do, what I think, what I believe… It's not right. It's not normal. It never has been, and it never will be. I know how strange it is. I know how I sound when I try to explain that I'm this woman who has been in love with the same man for hundreds if not thousands of years. I see him. I know him. I remember him." Tears erupted from Hydee's eyes and burned hot trails down her cheeks. She hated the tears as much as she hated knowing she needed to let them go.

"When I go to sleep at night, I go to this place where I'm one fragment of a million pieces, each one a life and each one me." Hydee's chest heaved, and pure grief tried to wring the life out of her. "I'm there, and it's real. I believe it with my eyes closed and have to fight myself from not keeping them closed all the time. Because I don't dream of some exotic lover. I dream about a living, breathing human being who has always existed and still exists and does it best when he's with me. It's like he's alive at night, but in the morning…when I wake up…a version of him dies. I bury a version of my lover every single day. My graveyard's the size of Montana." Hydee looked at Lynne with blurred vision. "Do you have any idea how hard it is to *wake up*?"

"Oh, honey." Lynne was crying too, and Adir had bowed his head.

"But I do wake up," Hydee said around a sob. "Every day. Because I know I have to keep going. Because there might be a fucking chance, and this isn't only about *me*. I know *him*. I know what he needs to be happy. It's tricky and complex. He's not a simple man. But I've made him happy for eons and could do it now, but I'm stuck here, alone and unable to do for him what I've always done. You have no idea how hard it is to be here knowing he's there and being unable to do anything. Being with him… It's not a whim. It's not a longing. It's what gives me meaning.

"But what if…" Hydee could barely speak. "What if me longing for him is somehow hurting him? Like, he feels the pull and the drive but doesn't know what it is or where to go? I know for a fact that it's happened before. If you believe the dreams. If you believe me. If I even fucking believe… And I just…" Hydee looked at her friends, the two people in the world who understood her and who would be the most disappointed in her if she gave up. "I'm sorry," Hydee croaked in a small, weak voice. "I'm so sorry. But I don't think I can do it anymore. I think I have to let him go. I can't… There's so little to hang on to and…I just… I *can't*."

Lynne and Adir rushed in and held her. The three of them collapsed onto the floor, and Hydee cried until she thought she might turn inside out. She had no idea when she'd started thinking maybe this life wouldn't work out for her and Theo, but now that she'd recognized it as a possibility, she wept for every second of every day of every week and month and year they'd not been together.

"We're here," Lynne whispered.

"Love you, Silver," Adir said.

At some point the tears began to abate, and Hydee could think again. She took incredible comfort from her friends, who believed in her even though her fixation with Theo Monk could easily be seen as hand-me-the-straitjacket-please kind of bonkers. The ugly, unspeakable truth, though, was that they spent most of their time not thinking about it. Hydee understood it; they weren't in her head all the time and by no means should be thinking of the dreams and lives as much as Hydee. Sometimes Hydee even forgot that everybody else went about their business without being plagued by dreams of their lover who had been with them for, oh, a few thousand years. It was surprisingly easy to do: forget that people managed to live life, fully and happily, without knowing they were intrinsically connected to people across space, lives, and time. For Hydee, it'd been a reality she'd worked to understand since she was eight. For other people, it was a reality they were often too scared or too skeptical to admit.

Hydee didn't blame them. And if she was being completely honest, she'd say that there were plenty of times when she wondered if everybody else was right and she really was off her damned rocker. During those moments, the only comfort she had was that she wasn't hurting anyone with her Theo thing.

Except herself.

She'd always had such faith in the Universe. When somebody remembered all she did and knew all she knew to be true, wasn't it her job to believe? To trust in the unknown and the invisible? She had thought so, and she'd tried so damn hard. What did she have to show for it? Dozens of scrapbooks about somebody else's life that didn't and wouldn't include her, and dreams that made her want to go to sleep and never wake up.

It wasn't a question of fairness or duty anymore. It hadn't been for a long time. It had become a question of choice. Did she want to live like this? Hoping for someone who simply couldn't be with her?

Hydee rested against Adir's chest. He'd resettled them against the pillows and wall next to the kitchen. "I'm sorry," Hydee said.

"Don't be," Adir answered.

"I know I've had my moments before about Theo and the dreams, when Mom said exactly the wrong thing to get me going."

"This is different, though," Lynne said. "I've never heard you like this. I've heard you pissed, I've heard you depressed, but you've never once said you couldn't handle it."

"That's because I always thought I should. Handle it, I mean. I didn't think I had a choice." Hydee tried to breathe, couldn't, and Lynne got up to get her a paper towel. Hydee blew her nose. "Leave it to the happy dreams to make me crack, right?"

"You do have a certain dedication to being different," Lynne teased.

"Ha. Yeah."

"What are you going to do?" Adir asked.

"I don't know." Hydee sighed. "I think I'm done trying to reach out to him. Short of selling the shop and moving out West, my life be damned, I don't know what else I could do that we've not tried. Besides, I don't have the energy to try to explain myself to him and sound like an un-crazy person."

"Your story is sane if you hear all of it," Adir said. "I'm sure he'd think so."

"No," Hydee replied dully. "He wouldn't. I've done that in dreams and seen what happens. He gets freaked out, runs away, or, as it happened in one memorable life, has me arrested and put in an asylum."

"Oh yes. That life." Adir kissed her hair. "Sorry, I'd forgotten."

"It's all right. Honestly, if I were him, I'm not sure I would do anything short of calling the people with the white coats if somebody told a story like mine to me."

"That's just not true," Lynne said. "Adrienne Kerr's story was definitely more off the wall."

"Pfft." Hydee waved one hand dismissively. "So she thought her father was still alive and living with her. So what?"

Adir cocked his head, birdlike, and peered down at her. "So she makes him dinner and eats the meal twice so he can"—Adir held up fingers and quoted the air—"clean his plate."

"You were the one who got her to see how weighing six hundred pounds was not going to make her father happy," Lynne said.

"And since then she's lost like, fifty pounds, and now her dead father is encouraging her to go to the gym," said Adir. "She has found the slightly less crazy skinny person within."

Hydee gave a weak laugh. "To me, it doesn't compare. I've been screwed up all my life."

"Well, what about Dan Blair?" Lynne asked.

Hydee shot Lynne a look. "Now you're being unfair to Dan."

"I don't think so. His mama dug heroin. He was born addicted. He's fought addiction all his life. It's ruined relationships, it's had him in and out of clinics, he's been on every medication in the book, and yet, when he walked into Silver Fox and was like, 'I think I'm having dreams about my grandfather whom I never met but who apparently was an alcoholic,' you listened to him, you gave him books to read on past lives and spirit guides, and you didn't even make him pay for the merch or the time."

"You're a one-woman forgiveness and spiritual-guidance machine, Silver," Adir added. "Go-go gadget guru superpowers."

Hydee's laugh was stronger the second time around. "I don't see it like you do, I guess."

"Perspective's a bitch," Lynne agreed.

"It is." Hydee slowly sat up and straightened her hair. "And until I sort mine out, I think I'm… I think I'm done. I'm done kissing his picture. I'm done collecting the magazines. I'm done with scrapbooks and romance and everything Theo Monk. I don't even want to hear his name."

"We can help with that," Lynne said. "But what are you going to do about the—" Lynne's eyes got wide. "You're not thinking of doing what I think you're thinking, are you?"

"I don't see any other way," Hydee answered.

"What are we thinking of thinking?" Adir asked.

"She can ban the man and lock up scrapbooks, but

that won't do anything about the…" Lynne trailed off.

"You've got it." Hydee sighed and petted a piece of Adir's long hair. "If I want to stop dreaming, the only thing that works is the medication."

"What medicine is this?" Adir asked.

Hydee shrugged. "Sleeping pills at night. Antidepressants during the day."

"But you're not depressed."

"No, I'm delusional. It's more complicated but thankfully still affected by the good drugs."

"Don't talk about yourself that way." Adir scowled. Nobody scowled like Adir, with his thick eyebrows that touched over his wide nose. "You're not delusional. You've in love."

"I'm connected. There's a difference."

"I know. That's what I mean. You're special and different for it."

"Am I?" Hydee asked. "I don't feel special. I feel like another woman in love with somebody she can't have. I just happen to know more about the object of my affection than most. And what I know about him currently isn't that great. Maybe I'd hate him this time around, and that's why the Universe is keeping us apart."

After a long moment of silence, Adir took Hydee's hand in his, imploring her with his gaze. "You have to keep the faith. You must."

Hydee wanted nothing more than a nice long nap with Oscar. "Adir, I appreciate that, but look, if this were any other woman's situation, we'd tell her to move on and to stop wanting the impossible and embrace what she could have."

"Other women are not you, Silver," Adir insisted.

Hydee really couldn't argue the point. She wanted to, but she couldn't. Crazy or not, whether she believed in the dreams or didn't, at the end of the day, she was different. At best, she knew a secret of the universe. At worst, her mind did not work like everyone else's. "I'm so tired," she confessed, and Adir pulled her into a hug.

"I know," Adir said softly in Hydee's ear. "But please understand. Faith in the impossible dreams of others is the only thing that allows us to hope for ourselves."

"Adir," Hydee began, but he abruptly dropped a brotherly kiss to her mouth and stood.

"I should check on the ladies we left running the shop and make sure the coast is clear of your mother."

With that, Adir walked out the door. Hydee and Lynne stared at the space where he had been until finally Lynne got up as well. "I'll get you a washcloth for your face."

She headed in the direction of the downstairs bathroom, and Hydee thumped her head against the wall, trying to see a path that would get her through one more day.

Chapter Three

Interlude in Dreams

Hydee's Journal

I'm at a party in a house the size of a hotel. There must be a thousand people crammed into the lavish rooms. The men wear suits, and the women are in dresses and skirts and spangles with flamboyant hats or cute little caps over their bobs and pin curls. Some women even wear trousers and shirts without anything under them. Some men wear dresses and look better than the women. The air is full of smoke and decadence, and everyone is dancing. I'm watching them while I stand at a high counter littered with glasses, and a dark-skinned man asks me what I'll have. I tell him gin, and he starts to pour the last of the liquor into a crystal highball.

"Thank you so much." My accent is Southern and cultured, and the timbre of my voice is low and rich. It makes the men go crazy and the women hate me. I think of how they look at me when I'm on stage, and suddenly I'm blinded by the memory of spotlights, and my nose wrinkles at the smells of beer, sweat, and city. Then I'm sitting in a robe on a bench waiting for my costar and listening to the director yell for his assistant. I see a series of men's faces, I remember many a bruised cheek, and I think to myself that everybody is owned by somebody, even the lucky, the rich, and the glamorous. People never know what's good for them; they only know how to covet what they don't have.

I point to the gin bottle. "You almost out?"

"Yes, ma'am," the bartender says.

"Give it here, then, sugar." I reach for the bottle and the glass, and he hands both to me. My skin is milky white against his. My nails are short and blunt, and I've got dozens of bracelets on my left arm.

"Greed's gotten me everywhere I want to be in life," I tell the man, and we laugh. I turn, and for a while, I walk. It's aimless, just having fun, but soon I start to zig and zag down long hallways. There are portraits and paintings everywhere, the frames crowding the walls and touching in some places. The rugs are thick and lush, and I stagger more than once.

I pass young men with their ties undone. They're leaning next to a closed wooden door on either side of a brunette girl. One of the men slowly drags the strap of her dress down her arm and pets the top of her breast with the back of his finger. She giggles. They see me.

"Me oh my, you're so very fine," singsongs one of the men. His eyes are glassy green. I've found a kindred soul in the drink. Sweat dapples his forehead, and I like his smile. "Where you off to all alone in such a hurry with such a big bottle?"

"I've a date with an even bigger man," I say, and I'm impressed and proud of this version of myself. I'm brash and daring and fearless.

"You sure about that?" the second fellow asks, and he thrusts his groin at me. Beneath his slacks, he's hard and ready, and he is, I see, quite large.

"A baton when I want the bull." I laugh and spin, running for a short distance as they pretend to chase me. They catcall in Spanish, cries to the bull from the matador, but I find a set of stairs. I run up them. They spiral, and I get dizzy. For a moment, I think bombs are going off outside, and this makes me think of war and dead bodies. I'm terrified and then relieved, because a girl yells, "Firecrackers!" and she and her half-naked john run past me.

I turn again. All this spinning is making the dreaming me a little seasick, but the past-life me is fine. I like the way my head swims, and I like the tall, narrow windows beyond the banister with a view of the south lawn. I see paper lanterns and bursts of color in the night sky, and for a second I almost run outside, but I hear a crash in the room behind me.

Unafraid, I clasp the door's handle and shove open the door. It's a parlor of some sort, with chairs and tables and desks. Heavy curtains let in slim streams of moonlight, but otherwise it's dim. It's the movement of the figures next to the desk that helps me to see them. I grope blindly and find a lamp out of pure luck. I pull the chain, and in the yellow glow, I see two men. One is as slim as me with brown curls and an expensive tuxedo. He's gazing at another man, who is broader but not taller. For a moment, I think the slender man is threatening the larger one, and then I see a slim-fingered palm caressing the front of the larger man's pants. When the bigger man sees me, he retreats from the touch. The slender guy, however, lets his hand linger in midair for a few seconds more.

"Well, hello there," says the slim man. He's got a wicked smile and kohl around his dark eyes. They practically jump out of his face at me. "Are you lost, little fawn?"

"Hardly," I say. I shut the door with my hip and hold up the bottle for them to see. "Looking for a private party to disturb."

"Excuse me," says the broader man, and he tries to leave, but Slim stops him.

"Don't go, sweetheart. We were just having a good time. The lady understands a good time, don't you, fawn?"

"Sure thing," I agree, but Big and Irritated shakes Slim and Persuasive off. When he leaves the room, I follow without a second thought. I don't much care for crooked men, mostly because their crooked ways don't lead to me, but I like the look of the bigger gentleman. His wide shoulders sway with the length of his stride, and I chase him into darker recesses of the house. I realize he doesn't know I'm following him when he enters a room and tries to shut the door on me.

"I beg your pardon," he says, and I laugh. I shut us into the room. Low lights are on in here, and I count six billiard tables in front of the massive floor to ceiling window that's overlooking the outdoor show. I smell smoke and hear giggling nearby. I put my finger to my lips, throw the bolt on the main door and find a side door to lock. I return to him with a dancing girl's prowl, and he stares at the sway of my hips.

"I apologize for what you saw in there," the man says with dignity.

I take a swig from the bottle. "Nothing I've not seen a thousand times."

He's hesitant and unsure, and would be caustic if he weren't blushing like a boy. "What is it you think you saw?"

"Pleasure." I shrug. "The hunt for it, anyway."

His eyes narrow. "I know you, don't I?"

"You like the theatre? Or the pictures?" I ask. "I'm in those."

"An actress?"

"A singer, a comedian, an anything and everything but especially a whore for the camera." I laugh at his darkening blush, and in that instant, I know him.

Everything that is the essence of him rushes at me across time and space, and I think I might pass out. "You," I say, and I nearly drop the bottle. The world's gone truly sideways. It's him. It's the man I always find. The man from my dreams. All my dreams.

"Me?" he asks, tilting his head. He's so real and so near and so handsome I can hardly breathe. I close the remaining distance between us, and then I do drop the bottle, uncaring of its contents. He watches it spill, chuckling, and I run my hands under his lapels. His pupils change, and his lips part. On reflex, he reaches and encloses each of my narrow wrists with his hands. He doesn't push me away.

"You don't like men," I say. I don't make it a question, but he takes it as one.

"Certainly not." His blush spreads to his throat, and I know he's not telling the whole truth just like I know we'll have a lot of fun discovering that truth together.

"You want to know what I like?" I ask.

"Very much," he murmurs, studying my face. I'm as tall as he is in my heels.

"I like a man who knows what he likes and isn't ashamed of it." I wrap my arms around his neck. His hands drop to my waist. Silk and cotton rub over my skin beneath his grasp. "You liked that he was pretty, didn't you?"

"Who?" he asks, and I smirk at him. I know him. He cannot fool me. He drops the act. "He's not as pretty as you," he says. "No one at this party is." The awe in his voice sends shivers up and down my spine.

I push fingers into his hair and squeeze. His gasp blows over my lips. "Do you like what the pretty ones can do to you?"

"I like this."

I smile. "What's your name, handsome?"

"Randal." He's close enough to taste me, but he won't without permission. He never has and he never will. "And yours?"

"Clara." The name goes well with Randal, and I picture place cards with our names stacked on top of each other. "Shall we see what I can do to you, Randal?"

He makes a soft sound and pulls me closer. The fireworks boom and the windowpanes tremble. Or maybe that's just me. "Please," he whispers.

And so we do.

Chapter Four

The rental's GPS was trying to drown him. Theo kept his speed under twenty-five and poked at the outdated map in his Subaru Outback. It had been the nicest car available to rent that the airport in Norfolk, Virginia could provide during the morning rush hour. Theo hadn't cared, so long as he was the one doing the driving and his chariot of choice had five wheels and an engine, but it would have been nice to know that the GPS was collecting sacrifices to Poseidon.

"*Turn left, then turn left, then make a U-turn.*"

"That's still the water, jackass," Theo growled.

"*Turn left.*"

"Fuck you, lady," Theo said to the jaunty British woman instructing him to turn in circles for the tenth time that day. He pulled into the parking lot of a liquor store slash gas station and tried taking another pass south.

"*When possible, make a U-turn.*"

Theo bellowed in frustration and stabbed at the machine until it shut off. It shouldn't be so damned hard to navigate these fucking islands. There was essentially only one road, and that was Ocean Boulevard or Highway Twelve. Granted, it had about twenty names, but it wasn't one way, made of sand or rocks, or so narrow one could only fit a single car at a time. It was the actual road, in other words. The rest of these dirt paths had no business calling themselves streets.

Theo smacked his own cheek to wake himself up. He had landed in Virginia after taking the redeye from San Diego. Security had been mildly concerned as to why a grown man was traveling cross-country with only a bottle of Xanax, a phone, a pen, and some keys in his possession, but Theo had told them the truth. His girlfriend was on the warpath, and he'd suddenly decided he needed a vacation. As far away from the bitch as possible. The man who'd been considering doing the anal probe had just gone through a divorce. He'd sent Theo through with his blessing and a comment about how he'd wished he'd been able to vacate dozens of times.

Once on board, Theo'd swallowed his Xanax with gin and tonics and had curled up in his first-class seat and slept most of the way. When he'd landed at nine a.m., he'd not even bothered turning on his phone. Screw airplane mode, he'd shut the thing off. The messages were getting threatening and the battery getting low.

"Clump of bushes, scraggly trees…" Theo muttered, straining to see beyond the beach foliage that blocked his view. Somewhere around here was the realty office where he had to check in and get a key. A fact that hadn't occurred to him until after he'd driven all the way to his rental property and realized, as he sat in the driveway in front of the enormous house, that he had no way to get in. He'd considered breaking a window and paying the damages, but he was trying to keep a low profile, not make a criminal one.

The realty office where he had to check in was in Corolla, for some ungodly reason, which was a good stretch north of his house in the Southern Shores area. He'd done a study of the OBX while waiting in line at the airport, and he'd remembered he'd once filmed a movie supposedly set in Duck, but they'd not filmed any of it even close to the actual town. Corolla was the northernmost town of any size, though it and Currituck occupied some of the same space, at least on maps. There was a lighthouse at Currituck, and much of the northern part of the Outer Banks was nature and wildlife preserve. Theo knew this because he'd somehow missed the rental office and had turned around when he had hit marsh.

Spotting houses beyond the trees, Theo took a chance and turned onto Persimmon Lane. He had to make an immediate left onto Appleton, and he saw a line of shops and historic buildings that were bustling with tourists. His windows were rolled down, and he could hear the singing of wind chimes and the call of gulls. Theo pulled off the strip of pavement calling itself a lane and turned the GPS on again. His phone would be more accurate, but he didn't want to face the roar of jilted personnel just yet. While he waited for the maps to load, he glanced around at the stores. It looked like the typical clothing boutiques with a smattering of kites and jewelry. He was parked right next to a sign for something called The Silver Fox. It sold art, books, tea, and treasures, in that order, according to the script on the white sign topped with wooden scrollwork. Theo studied the sign and the shop. It seemed familiar, somehow. He must have seen it advertised as a local attraction on the rental company's page.

From the looks of things, the press was working. The place was busy. People lingered by the steps and in the parking lot. One tall teenager with long pale purple hair was helping a dark-haired woman load a table into the back of an SUV. Old men sat in the rockers on the second-floor balcony. The wind chimes tinkled where they dangled from the porch's overhang, and there was a woman out front next to a table loaded with what looked like cookies. His stomach growled. He couldn't remember the last time he had eaten, much less the last time he had read a book for pleasure. Maybe he could do that while he was pulling his vanishing act. Read, buy some art supplies, paint for once. Fly a kite.

Walk on water. Cure cancer. Win the Nobel Prize.

Relaxing was somebody else's daydream. He'd be lucky if he didn't land himself in the ER in less than forty-eight hours. It didn't matter that he knew in his mind that nothing was wrong with him. His body thought differently and made his mind question its commitment to sanity.

Theo punched buttons on the GPS. *"Drive one hundred fifty yards and turn left."*

Theo stared at the road directly in front of him and the dense trees just beyond that and rolled his eyes.

* * * *

The lock on the big blue house turned out to be electronic. He opened the folding card the woman at the realty office had given him and punched in a six-digit code. The box chirped, and the locks clicked. Theo walked inside, punched in numbers again, and listened with a sense of satisfied safety to the bolts slide into action.

He was safe here.

Theo passed through the entry area, went by the stairs leading both up and down, and entered a den with a big screen and furniture that would have made his decorator weep over fake leather and burnt-orange accents. The rear wall was all windows with an overlook of the wooden gazebo that was a pit stop on the private pier to the beach. A door off the den led onto the mid-level porch, which was screened. He found three bedrooms with king beds and decent linens on the main floor.

It was so quiet.

Theo's shoes barely made a sound on the carpet. He returned to the entryway with its bright wooden panels and stucco, and he headed downstairs. He found a pool table, an arcade, a couple more bedrooms, and doors leading onto the private pool. There was a hot tub with a bright red cover, and a machine was sweeping the bottom of the pool. He was pleased to see the sliding door was also on the alarm system. He didn't bother opening it. Instead, he retraced his steps and headed up the stairs all the way to the top floor. There he found the kitchen, dining, and great rooms. Fifteen feet of sparkling clean windows showed him the water under the late-afternoon sun. There was a metal sculpture sitting on the narrow ledge of the apex window. The word ESCAPE was carved in dull silver and flanked by mermaids. Theo imagined the dozens, if not hundreds, of other people who had stood where he now did, grinning at the water and being grateful for a vacation. There'd be children running amok, maybe a grandmother yelling about dinner, a wife sliding a hand into a husband's with a knowing look that suggested they should try out the master shower before doing anything else.

He was alone.

Swallowing on a suddenly thick throat, Theo wandered around touching fake wood and plastic picture frames. He checked the fridge: empty. He checked the freezer: also empty. He turned the sink's faucet on and off. He walked to the door on the leftmost wall of the great room and discovered the top-level master suite. There was another big-screen TV, a bathroom with a huge shower and soaking tub, and a sliding door onto a private deck.

For a few minutes, he merely stood next to the glass, listening to the hum of the central air. He shivered in the clothes he'd been wearing for two days. It'd been getting cool outside when he'd walked from his car up the fifteen narrow stairs to the front door of his temporary home. He'd only been here for half an hour, tops, and already he liked it more than the empty, cold palace waiting for him in California.

Theo threw open the sliding door with more force than he'd intended, and it banged into the frame. He stepped over the threshold and got hit in the face with a chilly ocean breeze. There were rocking chairs and a lounge with a table on this porch, but he ignored them and went to the railing. His mind was pleasantly numb, though the faint stirrings of panic were waking up in the reptilian fight-or-flight center at the base of his skull. Voices were beginning to whisper. What was he thinking, coming out here all by himself? What if he fell? What if he had a heart attack? What if he died in stinking, wrinkled clothes on this very porch?

Who would give a shit if something horrible happened to him? Would he even mind if he winked out of existence? Theo didn't know. He'd made so many terrible decisions; one of them was bound to lead him to his ultimate doom.

He started to pull his cell phone out of his side pocket but reached into the rear one instead, retrieving his wallet. He flipped it open and fished behind the cards to tug out a piece of paper. It was soft with handling over the years. The folds were deep cracks in the stationary's surface. He'd lost the envelope years ago, and these days Theo rarely opened the page, fearing it would tear.

Theo stroked his thumb across the letter's worn edge. He carried this touchstone with him everywhere. It was a reminder, though of what, exactly, Theo couldn't say. The letter was one of the first Theo had ever gotten from a fan. It'd been when he was on that awful soap, though despite the script writing and the way he'd been worked to death, Theo remained proud of that role. He'd gotten the part on his own volition, unlike the commercials and theatre work that had come at the hands of his parents' influence, and he'd done a decent job. He must have. The letters had started coming in, and Theo had tried to answer some of them personally. He'd been writing a reply to the letter in his wallet one night while staying in a hotel room. It'd been the night before a press function of some sort. Theo didn't remember precisely what, now. He'd never made it.

Theo had started answering the letter, but he'd kept fucking it up. He had a sculpture of crumpled hotel stationary in the waste basket when the phone had rung. It'd been one of his transient friends who said they'd been heading for a great time downtown and did Theo want to come? Theo had agreed, frustrated with his lack of skill with the written word. He'd gone with his friend, and they'd met more friends, and later that night, Theo had punched a cop.

Theo had no memory before the punching or what had led to the incident itself. His friends had said he had been raving about his mother outside a club and an officer standing nearby had made a remark about being respectful of his elders. Theo had gone for the man's throat. He'd been arrested, released, and they'd settled out of court. His people had been pissed at first, but the media had started calling Theo the new bad boy in town, and suddenly Theo's stock had skyrocketed. He'd landed his first movie role soon after the headlines had aired, and more had followed.

At the time, Theo had joked that he needed to punch people more often. Later he wondered if he had stayed in that hotel room and had managed to answer that letter, would he have ever made it as an actor? Would he have limped through a half-ass career on daytime soaps and genital herpes commercials until quitting at age thirty and doing something else with his life?

No one would ever know, least of all Theo. He'd made his bed and had been sleeping fitfully in it ever since.

As up to facing the discordant music as he was going to get, Theo tucked the letter into his wallet, pulled his cell phone out of his pocket, and turned it on. The instant it powered up, hoards of alerts buzzed and blinked at him. Text message after text message appeared on the screen:

Where are you?

Fucker where did you go?

Why are you doing this to me?

Mr. Monk please call at your earliest convenience.

Theo scrolled and found: *Theodore? It's Merrykind. I've heard you're missing. I hope you're all right. Let me know?*

Theo tapped on Merrykind's message and replied: *Took your advice. Got away. Am okay. Tell them not to look for me for a few weeks. Need to think. Sorry to ask. Thank you.* He hit Send, and a splash of water fell on the screen. Theo glanced up at the clear blue sky. He blinked. It burned. He touched his face and then stared at the water drop on the tip of his index finger. He was crying. Actually crying. Why in the fuck was he standing on a deck at the beach, sobbing?

His phone buzzed twice, and he saw Merrykind's first: *Thank God. Will pass on messages. Take care of yourself, son. Find some peace.*

The second message was from Brooke: *IF YOU DON'T ANSWER ME IN FIFTEEN MINUTES, YOUR LIFE AS YOU KNOW IT IS FUCKING OVER, ASSHOLE.*

Theo started to laugh, and he didn't know why he was doing that any more than he understood his tears. He didn't even want to try to conjure the energy to figure it out. The only thing for certain was that something about Merrykind's texts gave him the strength to hate Brooke's. He yanked the SIM card out of the phone, dropped the phone, and brought his size-12 Italian loafer down onto the plastic shell. It cracked with a terribly satisfying crunch. He picked up the carcass and stared at the ocean. The brochure for the house had boasted the property was forty yards to the water. In his younger years, Theo could have thrown a ball for fifty yards without breaking a sweat. He rolled his shoulder, reared, and threw the busted cell phone as hard as he could. Of course he couldn't be sure, but he swore he heard a splash. He imagined Brooke's watery screeching, and he was still laughing and crying when he stripped out of his clothes and crawled under the covers with the door open and the daylight beginning to dim.

Theo sighed and fell fast asleep.

* * * *

"I'll take it all," Theo said to the curvy woman with dreads done up in a tower on her head. Even in a store that charged nearly a hundred bucks for a T-shirt, nobody could forget this was a beach town.

"You will?" the girl asked, eying the pile of linen, silk, and cotton that Theo had dumped on her counter.

"Yes, I will, and I'll be wearing these out." Theo gestured to the army-green linen pants and the muted blue, short-sleeve shirt.

"Fantastic." She grinned at him and waved over an associate to help her fold. He'd just done some serious damage to Baxter Chagall's Linen Boutique's men's section. Theo had no idea who Mr. Chagall was, but he needed clothes, and this was the first store he'd found in the upscale Beach Comber shopping district. All the shops had white picket fencing outside and anchors in their windows. Theo had wanted quaint, and he'd found it.

Twenty minutes later, Theo carted his shopping bags to the Outback. He tossed them in along with the toiletries he'd found at Walgreens and the gourmet coffee he'd found in The Green Bean next door to the clothing store. In the backseat was a new laptop courtesy of Best Buy, and he'd bought a prepaid cell phone. He just wasn't ready to commit to anything more than limited minutes.

Behind the wheel, Theo popped a Xanax. This was only his second one today, and it'd been over six hours since his last. Maybe Merrykind had been on to something; Theo needed rest. He'd slept for over fourteen hours in total. When he'd finally gotten out of the bed, he'd been hungry enough to eat his own leg, but he'd settled for the bakery, which was within walking distance of his rental. When the fruit-and-soy yogurt hadn't cut it, he bought a half dozen gluten-free blueberry muffins. He reached into the white sack in his passenger seat and plucked off a hunk of pastry. He chewed and pointed the car toward that bookstore he'd seen the day before.

It'd been the strangest thing, but he'd dreamed of The Silver Fox. He'd awoken around five a.m. to piss like a racehorse, and when his head had hit the pillow again, his mind had been filled with images of bookstore. He'd chased that girl with the purple hair all over the place, passing by racks of books and clothes and, possibly strangest of all, rows of stuffed ravens and growling bulldogs. He'd have thought the dream would have left him feeling frustrated, but when he'd roused from it, all he'd wanted to do was try to sleep more and return to chasing the girl.

So weird. But then, he'd been cutting down on the meds in the last forty-eight hours. Maybe there were side effects.

Less jetlagged and refreshed by food and retail therapy, Theo could enjoy the scenery as he drove north on Ocean Boulevard. The temperature had crept into the low sixties by lunch, and the cool wind was bliss as it floated through the car's open windows. He'd found jazz on satellite radio and listened to the horns scat. So far today, nobody had recognized him. He'd mostly been paying with cash, but with his three-day beard and ball cap, people didn't give him a second glance even when he handed over plastic. He felt positively normal in his nondescript car with his perfectly mundane schedule of eat, shop, and buy groceries. If he didn't know any better, he'd think the strange bubbling sensation rolling around his midsection was what regular people called contentment.

Theo found Persimmon easily enough and made the correct turns that led him past the scrolling sign and into The Silver Fox's parking lot. He pulled in next to a big white Beamer with a bumper full of stickers, and he tucked his Xanax into the glove compartment before climbing out and strolling across the gravel lot. There appeared to be a house attached to the rear of the store. The railing needed a new coat of paint, but other than that, it was in great shape for a structure that had survived a host of hurricane seasons.

A woman with white hair and a cane was climbing down the front steps as Theo was walking up them, and she paused to stare at him. He nodded, hoping he'd not been made. For the first time that day, nerves flared. Icy tendrils shot down his arms and legs, and Theo remembered to breathe. He paused at the top of the steps and rang a set of chimes, casually glancing back at the woman. She'd already moved on. Theo let out a sigh of relief. Thank God for a few more hours of blissful anonymity. He crossed the wide porch and reached for the door handle. He froze, hand extended and his shock reflected at him in the glass.

Most stores he'd encountered today had a standard sign in their windows explaining that customers needed shoes and shirts to enter. Some also outlined that no skateboards or skates or scooters were to be used on the planks outside the stores or on the handicapped ramps. Pretty normal stuff, so far as Theo was concerned.

The Silver Fox also had a sign. It took up an entire pane of one door and was impossible to miss. It read, "The Silver Fox asks customers to wear shoes and comfy clothes. Please no outside food or drink. We have plenty inside that are free for you to sample. No skateboards, no surfboards, no politics, no religion. Indian/First Nations/Native Personage on premises. All terms accepted. Psychic on board. Skepticism welcome but check your negativity at the door. Vendors use side entrance and ring bell except on Changing Day. Have a great day and welcome!"

Theo had seen stranger, but it wasn't the printed text that stopped him dead in his tracks. It was what was handwritten below, scrawled in black magic marker in block letters: NO THEO MONK ALLOWED. PLEASE DO NOT INQUIRE WITHIN.

To date, Theo had been stalked, had managed death threats and avoided their cruel ends, so far, anyway, and he'd been the object of one too many schoolgirl and boy crushes. He'd been banned from restaurants or merely asked to leave. He'd been told somewhere else might serve him better, and he'd had very kind people suggest he use the back door or private entrance. Until that moment, however, Theo had never been told via a shop window to get the fuck away and stay there, please and thanks.

His first thought was, *What the hell did I do to these people?* His second thought was to leave. His third one, though, was to go inside and damned well inquire as to why he, out of all of Hollywood and the rest of the crazies out there, wasn't allowed over the threshold. The third instinct won, and Theo went inside The Silver Fox with a scowl on his face that was making his eyebrow twitch.

The shop was pleasantly cool. Soothing music played over a sound system, and Theo could smell incense. Immediately to Theo's right was a long, L-shaped counter displaying jewelry and more expensive art pieces. A gorgeous stone fireplace with pale pink and lavender rocks took up most of one rear wall. On the other side of the cold hearth appeared to be a private home. Somebody had taste, that was for sure, and it ran toward the eclectic. The shelves were painted shades of magenta, purple, blue, and black, and they were deep, stuffed with items and eye candy. The books were over to the far right, the jams, jellies, and baked goods on the far left, and in the middle were an assortment of art, trays of marbles and stones, bath stuff, and one long hanging rack of vinyl records. Upstairs were tiers of clothing and an office with glass windows overlooking the store.

It was cozy, warm, and inviting. Theo felt like he'd just come home for Christmas. If his home had actually been happy and inhabited by people Theo would have helped if they were being actively mauled by a bear in front of him. He took a few tentative steps deeper into the shop, waiting for… He wasn't sure. Alarm bells to sound or a siren to go off or a mechanical voice to yell *Theo Monk alert!* or something. Nothing happened, but Theo did see that around the corner and beyond the end of the front counter was another office of sorts. This one was tucked underneath the second floor's ledge. The table was surrounded by swaths of hanging silks, and a woman with long curly hair was sitting at her makeshift desk, poking at a laptop.

"Ahm, excuse—" Theo began, but he was interrupted by a crash. Theo jumped about ten feet in the air, and his sunglasses dropped off his head and went skittering across the wooden floor. His heart leaped into his throat. He looked up and saw a tall, thin kid with long black hair standing at the banister on the second floor. He was gaping down at Theo, and Theo saw the liquid that had been in the guy's shattered coffee mug start to drip from the top floor to the lower one.

"A dear?" the woman in the silk tent office yelled. She was up and out in a blink. When her eyes landed on Theo, there was no instant recognition. Theo saw confusion flit across her features and then what Theo could only interpret as outright hostility widened her eyes and drew her mouth into a thin line. "A dear?" she called again, and Theo realized she was saying the guy's name. Adir, not "a dear." "What'd you break?"

"Mug," the kid answered, still slack-jawed.

"You cut?"

"Dunno."

"Well, check, would you? And clean it up."

"Sure." Adir sounded dreamy and didn't move. The woman didn't take her eyes off Theo while barking questions and orders.

"Good afternoon?" Theo said, irritated when it sounded like a question not a statement. "I was looking for a book or maybe…" He glanced around, trying to appear casual. "Maybe some tea?"

The woman's eyes narrowed. "You don't like tea."

A strange mixture of surprise and trepidation ricocheted through Theo. "How do you know I don't like tea?"

"I read it."

"Oh." Theo made an attempt to paste his professional smile on his face. "You a fan, then?"

"Not exactly. What are you doing here?"

"Lynne," Adir said, and Theo jumped again. Had the kid freakin' levitated or something? Adir was an arm's length away from Theo, and he hadn't heard the other man walk down the stairs or cross the shop. Adir put his hands on his narrow hips. "He's a customer, and we're always happy to see customers, right?"

"No," Lynne said.

"Welcome to The Silver Fox," Adir said at volume. His smile was wide and seemingly genuine. His eyes flashed green. "I'm Adir Flies With Ravens, and the bulldog is Lynne Crossgrove-Hart."

"Bulldog," Theo muttered, trying to remember an image that was just beyond his mental grasp. It fluttered with the flick of butterfly wings and was gone too fast for Theo to catch it.

"Term of endearment," Adir assured Theo.

"Of course." Theo cleared his throat. "You must be the Indian-First Nations-Native Personage-all-terms-accepted on premises?"

Adir's smile wavered. "You saw the sign."

"I did." Theo pried a chuckle out of his lungs. "Did my evil twin stop by and break all the merchandise or something?"

"Oh God… no," Adir said slowly. "It's just that… Um?" He looked to Lynne.

"Movie," Lynne grumped, arms crossed and shoulders squared.

"Right! Yes. You made that movie that was set here…"

"*Water's Call*," Lynne provided.

"That's it, yeah." Adir laughed a funny little high-pitched laugh. "You've been quite the, ah—"

"Person of note," Lynne filled in.

"—ever since," Adir finished.

"Even before that, really," Lynne added.

Theo swung his gaze from Lynne to Adir and back again, waiting to see if they were done. He bent to pick up his fallen sunglasses and used it as an excuse to back away a few steps. "Yeah. That one was shot on set in LA, mostly."

"We know," Lynne said.

"Was it?" Adir asked.

"Eyah. Too bad, really. This is a gorgeous place."

"It is," Adir agreed, nodding.

"Why are you in it?" Lynne asked.

"Beg your pardon?" Theo countered. At any moment, this woman was going to pull out a massive fly swatter and squash him.

"She means what brings you to the Outer Banks?"

"No, what she means is I didn't expect this to happen. Ever." Whereas Lynne's former statements would have been easy to hear from next door, this one was almost inaudible.

Theo glanced at the tent, remembered the sign, and got it. The psychic was pissed that she'd not foreseen a movie star coming into the shop. If she'd seen it in her crystal ball or whatever, she could have had a place set up for him to sign autographs. Theo had dealt with these sorts of crazies before, and they always believed their skills to be real.

In fact, the more preposterous the skill, the more they believed. Theo hoped he didn't visibly slump in what could correctly be assumed was defeat. "It was a spur-of-the-moment decision, I promise." He tried to smile. "No reason for it to be in the cards until this very second, really. I only got in yesterday."

"Changing Day." Now Adir had joined the muttering party. At least he appeared happy about it. Lynne appeared confused.

"What?" she asked.

"I just mean don't worry," Theo said. "Your crystals wouldn't have known to point west or whatever." He wheezed a dry laugh. Lynne wasn't smiling.

"My *crystals*?" Lynne said, the disbelief dripping along with Adir's spilled coffee.

"Oh boy," Adir sighed. "Lynne, he clearly doesn't know a thing about—"

"Oh, you're right. He clearly knows nothing." Lynne squinted at Theo. He would need some antlers and a spotlight to act out his part if she kept it up. "That's what worries me."

"I meant no offense," Theo said, backing away again. "I'm sure the tarot things work for—"

"Things?" Lynne repeated, advancing faster than Theo was retreating. He bumped into the edge of the front counter and inched his way around it.

"The little cards or whatever they're—"

"*Little?*"

"Okay, that's enough." Adir got between Lynne and Theo. "Down, girl, down."

Lynne ignored Adir. "If you think I would waste my time and energy reading some douchebag Hollywood actor trying to determine his whereabouts—"

"You mean like you thought about doing last night after dinner?" Adir deadpanned.

"Shut up, Tonto." She stepped around Adir, and all five-feet nothing of her glared at Theo. "See, some of us are finally getting over the mania surrounding you. Some of us are sick of hearing about you and how you continually make poor career and locational choices." Theo thought of his house crisis back home, and his mouth went dry.

"Some of us are worried that your timing is going to make everything worse around here, not better or magical like some"—Lynne shot a pointed look at Adir—"would like to think. So perhaps, Mr. Monk, it'd be wise for you to go the hell home."

Once, years ago, Theo had been doing a red-carpet event for his second starring role in a romantic drama. In the movie, he'd played an asshole who'd had one of those life-affirming moments wherein he completely and mystically changed so that he could forever be with the sweet, small-town girl and, in all likelihood, make her life miserable until the inevitable divorce that was never shown on screen.

As Theo'd been about to enter the building for the screening, a young man had shouted his name. Theo had turned, and the man had spit on him, right in the face. The kid had screamed that Theo was an asshole for what he'd done to the actress who'd played opposite Theo. Naturally the kid had been hauled off, though Theo declined to press charges.

So this certainly wasn't the first time Theo had faced down insane people who had their own ideas about what Theo had or hadn't done in the fiction they believed to be reality.

"I see," Theo said with a slippery smile that was more teeth than lip. "Well, that might be a bit of a problem. You see, I'm in between homes right now, and I've been looking at this lovely property just south of here." He put his hands behind his back, feigning interest. "Might invest in real estate. Start my own business." He stared Lynne down. "Buy out somebody else's and run it better. That sort of thing."

"You. Fucking. Bas—"

"Now, if you'll excuse me?" Theo interrupted the spluttering woman. "I'll go buy books at some conglomerate

whose goal in life is putting the little guys out of business.
Have a nice day."

Face on fire, Theo pivoted and stalked out the front
door. He had no idea what he'd been thinking, flying out
here like this. He was unprotected and exposed. He never
should have left the house. These islands were chock-full of
well-off tourists; surely there were delivery services.
Throwing enough money at a problem almost always made it
go away or made the answer come right to one's front door.
He could have had clothes and books and groceries
delivered. What on earth had possessed him to tempt fate
like this? People were everywhere. They couldn't be avoided.
And, as it turned out, even if Theo didn't know them
personally, they could still find reasons to string him up in
the middle of the historic town square.

Breath out of his control, Theo climbed into his rental
and locked the driver's door. He instantly felt cramped in the
car, and he shoved the front seat as far back as it would go.
His hands shook as he reached for his bottle of pills, and he
cursed black and blue while getting the cap undone. He
swallowed one dry, and maybe it was the anxiety attack or
maybe it was the smell of the blueberry muffins, but he
thought for several serious seconds that he was going to
vomit up the medicine and breakfast and possibly dinner
from two nights ago. He curled his spine and put his head
between his knees and hands over the back of his neck.
When he heard the polite taps on the window, he thought
about ignoring them. Let the person knocking think Theo
was preparing for the incoming nuclear blast that the person
outside the car didn't know about.

When the tapping came again, Theo decided the
intruder was going to be all persistent about interrupting
Theo's self-deprecating party. He slowly sat up using the
steering wheel to steady himself, and he had to remember to
turn on the car to roll down the window.

Adir crouched next to the car and put his hand and
chin on the window ledge. "You're really not all right, are

you?"

Theo wanted to answer with any number of snappy comebacks ranging from *What tipped you off?* to *Man, those First Nations skills are good!* But all Theo managed was something like, "Mmuhnghst."

"Yeah, she's not either." Adir sighed.

"You mean that harpy in a skirt?" Theo rasped.

Adir's expression didn't change, but his voice lowered in temperature. "Take care when speaking of my friends."

"No offense? But your friends should have a care when speaking to me." Theo cleared his throat, reached for his bottle of water, and realized he was empty.

"You were unexpected." Adir handed Theo a thermos with a raven in flight on the side. Theo took it and had another one of those half thoughts that made his back teeth itch. If he could just remember the other half, he would know why a raven was significant.

"Clearly," Theo muttered.

"Lynne is resilient," Adir continued. "She'll be over this inside a week or two."

"Thanks. I will sleep better tonight."

Adir didn't seem affected by the sarcasm. "I was not speaking of her when I said someone was unwell."

Theo raised his eyebrows at Adir. He uncapped the thermos and took a sip. It was water-based and sweet, whatever it was. "Who did you mean?"

Adir looked toward the shop. The wind blew around his hair, which was tied in a low tail at the nape of his neck. When he turned to Theo again, a chill raced along Theo's spine. "I meant the owner of the shop."

It took a second for Theo to shake off the irrational sensation of significance. "The owner's not all right?"

"No. She's not."

"What's wrong with her?"

"She's having a bit of a crisis of the faith."

"I'm...sorry?"

Adir tilted his head. It was remarkably birdlike. "You

really *don't* know who I mean, do you?"

The insistence confused Theo. "Why would I know the owner?" His mind flipped through the possibilities. "Was she in the business? Movies, I mean? TV?"

"No." Adir shook his head, and sadness so obvious that even Theo recognized it danced across the guy's face. Theo started to apologize for something, anything, but Adir sucked in a sharp breath. "Her name's Hyacinth. She has lavender hair. She's sort of famous around here, to us."

"Oh yeah, I think I saw her." Theo sipped at the water again before recapping it and handing it over.

"When?" Adir asked.

Theo would give the man this much: Adir could do an intense gaze like nobody's business. "Yesterday. I was lost. I drove by, turned around in your lot, and I saw a girl with purple hair. I thought she was a kid."

"Definitely not a kid. Don't think she ever was." Adir smirked. "I also don't think you were so lost."

Another chill arced through Theo, and he really wished the Xanax would kick in already. "What do you mean?"

Adir licked his lips, and his eyes lit up. It made Theo incredibly nervous. Or maybe that was the day he was having. The *life* he was having.

"I mean, Hydee's famous not just for the store. She helps people."

"How so?" Theo asked.

"You've heard of life coaching?"

"I'm from California."

"Then you get it," Adir said without missing a beat. "Hydee coaches, and Lynne and I, we help. I handle the reading list, Lynne does the spiritual angle, and Hydee does the communicating and planning. It's not official or anything. Not yet. Though I was playing around with something." Adir set aside the thermos and dug into his pocket. He retrieved a duct tape wallet and a business card.

"FRB Life Counseling?" Theo read.

"Fox, Raven, Bulldog."

The information he'd been struggling to recall broke free of its bonds and punched Theo in the gut. He saw himself standing in the store and staring at a row of stuffed ravens and bulldogs. "A dream," he said. "I had a dream."

"Hills and valleys being exalted and all men being equal in the eyes of the nation and God?" Adir asked.

"What?"

"Never mind. What was it?"

"About stuffed ravens and bulldogs in that store, and I was chasing…" Theo leaned back in the seat. "I was chasing a girl with purple hair."

"Like I said, Mr. Monk." Adir smiled. "Not so lost."

Chapter Five

"How are you, Mrs. Hardacre?" Hydee asked the woman sharing the supermarket aisle with her.

"Fine, dear, thank you."

Hydee smiled at one of her regular customers and tossed a can of chickpeas into her cart. She scratched the item off the list and headed for the next row. She liked to organize her grocery list by aisles and take her time with the shopping. The orderly sea of food was calming, and Hydee needed to unwind.

The breakdown yesterday had helped Hydee see herself and her life clearly for possibly the first time. She'd ruminated over choices and decisions while finishing Changing Day and restoring the shop to its new version of order. When they were done for the day, Lynne had lingered next to her BMW. The parking lot was lit by two safety lights. It was dark and still misting, and they were shivering under their raincoats. Adir was already in the car. He didn't like getting his feathers wet.

"So…" Lynne had said.

"Yeah." Hydee had jabbed the toe of her boot into the gravel and kicked a rock away from them.

"You need anything?"

"No. I think I'll be all right."

"You know you can always call."

"I know."

Lynne had made no move to get into the Beamer. "So you're going to take the pills."

"Yeah. I am."

"The last time…" Lynne stalled out.

"Was after you won that second big contest for me, yeah." Hydee had tried to meet Theo more than once. After writing letters that were never answered, Lynne had used her Luck to win Hydee contests. Once, she'd been able to shake his hand and get an autograph on the red carpet. He'd barely looked at her. Another time, she'd been able to attend a film shoot. Theo's assistant had been there to escort Hydee and the other four winners around. They'd gotten free T-shirts and hats and glossy photos of the cast. The signature on that Theo Monk photo had looked nothing like the one Theo had signed for Hydee.

It'd been soul crushing, getting that close and not getting anywhere at all. The hope that he would look into her eyes and see memory and love there instead of a vacuum of fanaticism had been too much to take.

"For a while after that, it was too hard to see him, even at night, when we were other people, together, and happy. So I took the pills for a few months. But then I decided to love him from afar and keep records, because God knows he won't remember, so somebody should be writing this shit down."

"So what have you decided this time?" Lynne had asked.

"I'm not sure. I think I'll need time without him to see my options clearly. I think…" Hydee had gotten distracted watching insects fly toward the beacons of light that illuminated her house, her store, and, really, all the things and people who mattered most. "I think hope makes one weird wound. Every time you try to bury hope, you feel like you'll die. But every time you resurrect it, you tear yourself open again. You have to bleed for hope. It won't stick around any other way." Hydee had smiled at Lynne, who had tears standing in her eyes. "The dreams are the last bastion of hope that one day, Theo and I will be together. I love them, but they're killing a piece of me every single night."

"So this time…" Lynne had begun.

"…is for good, yeah." When Hydee had spoken the words, she could have sworn she heard the sound of a door slamming, and all that followed in her mind was silence.

Lynne had hugged her and had left, and Hydee had gone inside. She'd made her favorite comfort food—spaghetti and meatballs—and had skipped the glass and drank straight from the red wine bottle. She'd wandered through her home, taking down Theo Monk posters and propping them up backward against the wall, beneath where they'd hung for years. She'd turned all the DVD cases of his movies around so the black edges showed, not the titles. She'd taken down the portrait she kissed good morning and good night, and somewhere around one a.m., Hydee had found a cardboard box and begun packing up her journals.

When she'd hidden enough Theo to satisfy herself, Hydee had crawled into bed with a sleeping pill. She'd stared at it, unable to put it on her tongue and wash it down. After fifteen minutes of deliberation, Hydee had picked up her cell phone.

Lynne had answered on the second ring, told her to hold on, and Hydee heard her say that Ron should go back to sleep. Hydee had waited while Lynne had walked from her house to Adir's apartment over the garage, where Lynne always went when Hydee called in the middle of the night. "Okay," Lynne had said. "What's up?"

"I'm staring at the pill."

"And?"

Hydee had taken a moment to consider. She was happy, now. Life was good. The only source of unhappiness came from wanting something she knew she couldn't have. But even if she was ready to give up her lifelong Theo Monk project, she couldn't picture what that meant. Burning down the house and shop and maybe the rest of the Outer Banks and moving to Alaska occurred to her, but that was the wine talking. "I have no idea what I want to do."

"You said earlier that if you were any other woman, you'd tell her to move on."

"Yeah?"

"Well, what else would you tell a younger or different you?"

"I'd…" Hydee had wished she'd had another bottle of wine. "I'd say get rid of that which brings you nothing but misery." It had been a rote answer, one that Hydee had often counseled, but it seemed to apply. "Throw it away, burn it, divorce yourself from it, quit it, but put it out of your life."

"Go on."

Hydee had shut her eyes and seen a teenage version of herself standing on the customer side of the front counter. "I'd say that we're here for a blink; our lives are a scant glance from the Universe's busy eye. But we're here for particular reasons, and it's hard to get anything done in abject misery."

"Good."

Hydee had stared at the ceiling. "If you've done all the right things, done all you can think to do to nurture someone or to fix a problem, and something or someone hurts you more than helps you grow, holds you back instead of urges you forward, then put it or them out of your life."

"And then I'd lecture them on the use of red cloth to contain fear, cleansing herbs, and how you have to destroy items because you can't give bad juju to someone else without it coming back on yourself."

"Mmm-hmm," Hydee had said. "And Adir would be standing there with six books on how to start over after ending a relationship or getting away from addiction or whatever."

Lynne had chuckled. "Yeah. He fucking would."

"He's there with you, isn't he?"

"Couldn't pry him off me with a crowbar. We're worried about you." Lynne's voice had dropped like it always did when she was reading someone and being serious about what she saw. "You're on a precipice of change. You've been on this path heading toward this moment for years, and now that you're finally here, there are choices to be made and things to be done, and none of them are going to be easy."

"Tell me about it." Hydee had held up the pill. "Okay. Go back to bed."

"For what it's worth, we both think you're brave, giving up something like this that's been with you for so long."

"Adir doesn't think I'm brave. Adir thinks I'm an idiot."

"He'll come around."

"Are we talking about the same Adir?"

"Love you, Hy."

"Love you too."

Hydee had taken the sleeping pill. The things were way out of date, but she'd still slept through her alarm butler's urgings until ten, had nearly died of shock when she saw the time, and had raced to the store. Lynne and Adir were there. Adir refused to come out of the office, but Lynne had come out of her silk sheet tent.

"How'd it go?" Lynne had asked.

"I'm on the road to sanity."

"Long damned road," Lynne had said drily. "Did you dream?"

"No," Hydee had answered, and it'd been a sad sort of relief. "Not a thing."

Lynne had patted Hydee's hand, and they'd spent the rest of the morning cataloging inventory. It'd been business as usual with the added bonus of Hydee feeling rested for the first time in years.

Hydee dropped a brick of white cheddar into her cart and marked the final item off her grocery list. She pushed her cart to the front and got into a line. Theo Monk's face stared seductively at her from more than one magazine cover. His police drama was wrapping up this season, and everyone wanted to know what he was going to do next. The Hydee of forty-eight hours ago would have grabbed every magazine with him on it and read them, cutting out pictures afterward and brainstorming with Lynne about what Theo would, in fact, do.

It was amazing what a difference a couple of days could make. Hydee snorted at her old self, and the new

Hydee trying to move on walked by the racks, resolutely not picking up a single magazine. She dug out her wallet while the clerk scanned her items.

"Oh," the clerk, Samantha, said. "Did you not see this one?" She flashed a cover with Theo in full police uniform.

Hydee gave Sam a tight smile. "Already got it, thanks."

"No problem." She grinned. "He is awfully cute, isn't he? I totally see why you crush on him so hard."

"Mmm," Hydee managed. Moving on, she thought, was going to be one hell of a bitch.

It was cool outside and muggy. Hydee squinted at the clouds and thought an evening sitting with Oscar and reading a book while it rained sounded perfect. With a few glasses of wine in her, she'd be able to tape up the box of journals. She envisioned herself carrying the box to the shed in a downpour. It would be appropriate, somehow. She'd let the rain wash everything away.

Hydee opened the rear of her RAV4, and she tossed in the drugstore bags containing her medicine first. Her doctor had no problem prescribing the medication again, so long as Hydee had agreed to a checkup. She started unloading her grocery bags, and the clouds parted above her. Sunlight splashed around her in rays, and Hydee looked up to discover the widest and most brilliant rainbow she'd seen since she was a little girl. The thing was practically on top of the parking lot in full color glory backlit by stormy clouds. Hydee gasped, shading her eyes and staring.

"Pretty," said a man's voice.

Hydee glanced back at the tall man standing near the Subaru two spaces down from her. "Yeah!" she laughed. "It's gorgeous!"

"Think we should look for the gold?" he asked.

"Probably!" Hydee laughed again. She was lighter and more carefree than she had been in so many years. Maybe it was the restful sleep, the choice to change, or the rainbow, but pure happiness bubbled in her throat and actually brought tears to her eyes. "I've never been at the end of a rainbow before."

"Me either. I imagined more leprechauns."

Hydee tore her gaze off the sky and heard a hissing sound. She and the man had enough time to turn in sync before a wash of misty rain streaked across the parking lot like a rippling curtain closing across a stage. Cries went up from the far side of the lot, along with a gale of little-girl giggles, and when the rain passed over Hydee, she cried out in shock. "Oh, that's cold!"

"What the hell?" the stranger asked, staring down at his damp clothes.

"Sun-shower," Hydee called. The mist pattered, grew heavier, and the heavens ripped open to dump water on everything below. Hydee heard herself laughing, and she spun around with her arms open wide. Maybe this wasn't the end of the rainbow. Maybe this was the beginning.

Nearby, the man stood with his back to Hydee, his hands in his linen pants pockets. Hydee was happy for the company. In a matter of moments, though, the rain ceased entirely, leaving puddles and glistening cars and Hydee's hair dripping down in her face. She brushed the strands aside, chuckling. "They happen sometimes when the wind comes off the water just right." She walked closer to the man, who was bent and shaking out his shaggy dark brown hair. "I've got tissues," Hydee said, digging in her purse and holding out the pack. "Here, take…"

Hydee froze as though she slammed into an invisible wall. Theodore David Monk stood up straight, smiling his million-dollar movie-star smile. He tossed his head and slung his arms, shaking off the water before casually rolling up his sleeves. He was so close that Hydee could see his huge eyes were nearly black, they were so deeply brown. His cheekbones had been cut out of stone, and the dip in his chin was highlighted by a day or two's growth of dark stubble. The years since she had seen him in the flesh had been entirely kind. Hydee blinked, trying to make the hallucination go away, but it stubbornly persisted. In fact, it reached for the tissues and took them from her hand.

"Thanks," the illusion said.

"No problem." Hydee didn't know she was falling until her butt abruptly met the floor of the RAV4's cargo hold. She sat there, feet dangling, while Theo blotted his face. She groped for her own arm and pinched the skin until it burned.

He was still there.

She tugged at her hair until the roots ached.

Still there.

Which meant that he probably wasn't a side effect of the pills.

Probably.

Theo wadded up the used tissue and shoved it in his pocket. Hydee crazily wanted to remind him to take that out before he did laundry. But then she remembered this was Theo Monk. He probably had laundry people to do his laundry. Then again, he was standing in a Food Lion parking lot. So maybe he did more than Hydee thought. Like drive and brush his teeth and walk over to where she sat so he could brace on the car to take off his shoe. He tapped it against his thigh, slinging water, and God, but he had perfect feet.

"So you know me, huh?" Theo asked in a voice that sounded much richer and lower in person than it did on screen.

Of course she knew him. She knew every inch of him in a thousand different bodies. Her head swam, and her vision tunneled. Her spirit felt stretched over eons, scattered across a timeline that was continuous despite its ebbs and flows, and Hydee had to grab on to the edge of the car. She'd dreamed of meeting him. She'd seen her dream self cope with the sensation of being many people at once, in multiple times and places, but she'd not felt it firsthand.

Hydee thought she might throw up. She put her head between her knees.

"Should I take that as a yes?" Theo asked.

Hyde had envisioned this meeting a hundred thousand times. She'd planned what she would do, and what she would say, and all those things tried to happen and come out of her mouth at the same damned time. "Nnngarlgh," Hydee croaked. The world was still spinning.

"Are you all right?" Theo asked, and he seemed about to come closer, to touch her or help her somehow, and Hydee panicked. She frantically waved an arm in his general direction. "Okay, no problem." Theo backed up, and Hydee let go of an explosive breath she hadn't realized she held.

"He said you weren't feeling well," Theo said conversationally.

Who would say such a thing? Who the hell would talk to this man without warning her first? The blasted teenager at the grocery store's cash register knew she adored Theo Monk and somehow someone had neglected to mention the man himself was in town? How did that even happen? And how could he just stand there being calm and reasonable when clearly the parking lot was getting eaten by a big gray blanket?

"Here, sip this." A water bottle appeared in front of Hydee's face. Theo had evidently yanked it out of the pallet Hydee had bought. She blinked and realized she'd slumped over against the side of the Toyota's cargo hold.

"Believe me," Theo said grimly. "I understand."

What did he understand? That they were destiny embodied? That if one looked up the word "soul mate" in the dictionary, their picture circa 6000 BC would magically be there? Hydee wanted to ask and to be eloquent, but she grunted like a Neanderthal agreeing that fire would be an awesome thing to have around. She took the water and twisted the cap. Her skirt and shirt clung to her in a soggy mess of cotton and silk, and the water was warm, but at least the gray blanket had stopped chewing up the fabric of reality.

"I get these attacks. All the time, actually." Theo wheezed a little laugh. "It's why I'm here. Stalking you in the parking lot, I mean."

Hydee shoved her hair out of her face. Nothing the man said made a lick of sense. "Huh?" she managed.

Without asking, Theo plucked the water out of Hydee's hand and drank. He passed it over to her when he was done. "Do you know that I never eat or drink after anyone, and I've done it twice today so far?"

Hydee was pretty sure she shook her head. She was also positive that she was having an out-of-body experience and she was watching the two of them sitting in the back of her car next to a soaked cart of groceries. God, she looked like a sick, drowned, purple rat.

"The other time was with that Native American guy at your store."

"Native," Hydee rasped. "He'd say he's just Native. And he's Adir."

Theo's eyebrows went up and down in a hypnotic dance. "Anyway, I told him about the dream I had about your store."

Hydee's heart launched itself into her mouth, and she choked. "What?" she coughed.

If Theo thought she was behaving oddly, he didn't show it. "I know. I sound crazy. I usually do, come to think of it."

"Mmm-hmm," Hydee hummed in the negative, shaking her head when the words wouldn't cooperate.

"No?" Theo laughed and nudged the bottle's bottom with a finger, urging her to drink. "I've been feeling pretty insane, lately." He frowned. "Maybe always. I flew in yesterday without so much as a spare change of underwear—"

Hydee coughed again, unable to stop the flood of images of how Theo looked in everything from a loincloth to French-cut briefs.

"I know. Nuts, right? But I had to get away from… Just everything, really. So I rented this house, slept well for the first time in I don't know when—"

Hydee wasn't going to make it through this

conversation. She was too hot, her chest and cheeks on fire.

"—and I dreamed about chasing this purple-haired girl through a store full of stuffed ravens and bulldogs."

Hydee made a fist and braced herself against the car's floor so she wouldn't topple over. "No…no way…"

Theo smiled at her, but it didn't touch his eyes. "I know. I swear I'm not a creep. Not that you could take my word for it, I realize. The Native – Adir? – and that other woman were not happy to see me, implied you would not welcome my company, and told me to get the fuck out of Dodge, pardon my language, but then Adir told me how you help people."

"I do what?"

"Help." Theo seemed confused, and a half smile tugged at the left side of his mouth. "There's not another purple-haired woman around here, is there? You *are* The Silver Fox's owner, right?"

"Hydee. I'm…Hydee." She wasn't so sure of that at the moment.

Theo sighed in exaggerated relief. "Oh good. He seemed to think that helping, ah, me, would help you out too somehow."

"Did he?"

"Yeah. He was pretty convincing, or I wouldn't be bothering you. He told me you'd gone shopping, and I needed groceries anyway, so…" Theo stared at the storefront, his face drawn. He was too thin, and the line of his shoulders was creeping toward his ears while Hydee watched.

"Let me try this again." Theo straightened and shook himself. He held out a hand. "Hi, I'm Theo Monk. I'm new in town. A friend of yours told me you'd be here, and that I should find you because I believe I'm in need of…help of some kind. Spiritual guidance, maybe?"

Dying in the focus of that megawatt smile, Hydee forced herself to take his hand and shake it. His palm was cool and his grip was firm. She didn't want to let go, but she made herself do that too. She chose and spoke her words deliberately. "Nice to meet you."

"Likewise." His gaze danced over her, and everywhere he looked, the very cells of Hydee's body came to life singing the "Hallelujah Chorus." "So how does this counseling business of yours work, exactly?" Theo asked.

Hydee cleared her throat. "Um. Well." She tried to think straight around the impossible situation sitting right in front of her. There was so much she needed to tell him, but she knew he'd never believe her. As of that morning, *she* had barely believed herself. Better to answer the question directly before her until she could regroup and freak the hell out. "I'm not sure what Adir told you, but the counseling's not a formal kind of thing. I don't have a degree in it or…what have you, but I'm good with people. Lynne and Adir are too. We each have a different, ah, skill set, as it were, and we've been known to listen to the, ah, stranger issues that face individuals in our, um, community. Here. Around here, I mean. Don't get a lot of, uh, you know. You."

Theo's eyes narrowed. "What kind of stranger issues have other people had?"

A warning bell clanged in Hydee's head. She understood that his privacy and personal information would need to be kept secret. Above and beyond his fame, he, personally, would need others to protect his life, value it. The question was a type of test, and she could see that as clearly as her own hand. The weird thing was knowing it to be true from the past as well as the present.

"I'd rather not say." Hydee tried to shrug casually, and the muscles in her neck and shoulders creaked. "We keep the details private."

The crease between Theo's eyes vanished. "Okay. Is it possible to deal only with you as opposed to you and your two employees?"

Dizzy. She was so dizzy. "Yes."

"Great. Good." Theo nodded. "Think I'd rather talk to you, if that's all right. Not sure that Lynne person likes me very much." He appeared sheepish. "I may have been an ass."

"Mmm." One part of Hydee was completely calm. It sweetly whispered that despite her bouts of idiotic doubt, she'd always known, somewhere inside herself, that this meeting would happen one day, and now it was, and everything would be okay. She needed to do what she always had done, and she would know what that meant on a moment-to-moment basis.

The other part of Hydee was running around in circles with her hair on fire, screaming like a teenage girl invited to dinner with Harry Potter, all the boys from all the bands, and Theo fucking Monk.

"We can work with that," Hydee said levelly.

"With me being an ass?" The smile had returned.

"You're not an ass."

"How do you know? You just met me."

Hydee laughed like a braying donkey. Theo jumped. "I, um. I'm a good judge of character, remember?"

Theo's smile affected only the lower part of his face. "Okay then, judge. What's next?"

"We should probably set up a meeting. Go over you—ah, your life, I mean, and what's going on in it and…see what we can do."

"All right. So long as that wouldn't be too much trouble?"

"I think I can handle it."

"Okay, then, when would work for you? I'm pretty free."

"Tonight? Dinner? I cook."

"Thank God. I don't." Theo smiled, and Hydee was beginning to think he was patronizing her, but in a kind sort of way. In a I've-dealt-with-a-million-sappy-fans-who-nearly-pass-out-at-the-sight-of-me kind of way.

Oh buddy, you have no idea, Hydee thought. She scrubbed her mouth with her hand so she wouldn't speak her mind. "My house is behind the store. Maybe come by around seven?"

"Sure. Can I bring anything?"

"Wine. Lots of wine."

Hydee winced, but Theo laughed and stood, shaking out his wrinkled pants. "White or red?"

"Yes?"

"Done." Theo's grin faded as fast as it'd appeared. He hesitated and shoved his hands in his pockets. "Thank you for considering this. I never do this kind of thing, ask strangers for…well. Anything. And I have to admit I don't put a lot of stock into…mysticism?"

Hydee knew he didn't. It was always one of their problems. She believed, he didn't, and it gave them something to fight about for entire lifetimes. "It's as good a word as any."

"I've tried everything else, though, and nothing's worked. Except the pills, but even those…" He shook his head, and Hydee had to dig her fingers into the cargo hold's floor mat to keep from running to him and holding him. In that instant he was the saddest man she'd ever seen, and a piece of her skepticism caught fire and burned to ashes.

"Anyway." Theo brightened. "Adir seemed to think you could do the trick, and at this point, I'm willing to try just about anything." He paused. "That didn't quite come out right."

"It's okay." Hydee would definitely let him try her. "I understood. I think we all get desperate enough to break down the walls of our comfort zone sooner or later."

"Exactly." Theo was at a loss until he spied her cart. "Let me help you with those."

"Oh, you don't have to do that…" Hydee protested weakly while Theo loaded the other two reusable bags into the RAV4. She didn't even get up when he pushed the cart to the return a few spaces over. She did wave when he climbed into the Outback, of all things.

Theo backed up until he could roll down the window to speak to her. "See you at seven. Your place. With wine."

"Okay," Hydee said. "Oh, hey, I should have asked: what seems to be the major issue in your life? The one we're going to work on?"

"Oh." Theo faced front and chewed his lower lip. Finally, he shrugged and squinted at her. "I guess it's my heart. I have all this anxiety because I think there's something wrong with my heart."

Hydee couldn't speak, so she nodded, and that seemed to work for Theo. He waved two fingers and drove away. Hydee wiped tears off her cheeks and wished she could have told him that they sold wine right there in the supermarket, and that thought, for whatever reason, sent her into a fit of giggles. She fell backward into the car and lay there, laughing and staring at the rainbow sky.

* * * *

The drive north from Food Lion to the unpaved grid of roads surrounding Hydee's shop seemed to go in slow motion. Even slower than the thirty-five-miles-per-hour speed limit would usually make it. She drove in a daze, and she passed Dwayne of the local police department on the side of the road standing next to his big Dodge truck. He'd pulled somebody over. Their tags were from out of state. Hydee smiled to herself. Dwayne loved irritating the tourists.

Hydee turned left and passed the signs directing people to the Currituck lighthouse. She wove around a gaggle of strolling people with cameras, pulled into her own parking lot, and drove around to the side porch, where she always parked to unload groceries. She killed the engine and tried to think about food. Tonight she needed to cook. For Theo Monk. Her long-lost lover who had stumbled, somehow, into her neck of the Outer Banks and who had found his way to her store and then to Adir and then to the grocery and…

The horn honked when Hydee's head hit the steering wheel. A moment later, the car door opened, and Hydee could feel eyes upon her.

"Yeah, I think he found her," Adir said.

"We texted you!" Lynne yelled.

Hydee, wincing, rolled her head to one side. She reached to the passenger seat and shoved her hand into her purse. She saw a dozen new text messages and missed calls. "Silent," Hydee said. "It was on silent."

"Fuck," Lynne said.

"This isn't a bad thing," Adir argued.

"He's an asshole."

"He's her soul mate!"

"Soul mate, schmole mate."

"But he's here! I told you he'd come! I told you!"

"He's fucking late." Lynne sighed. "Hydee? Honey? You in there?"

"No," Hydee said to her steering column.

"Can you tell us why you're damp?"

"Water falling from the sky," Hydee replied.

"Damn. If soul mates are this good in person, where can I get one of my own?" Adir asked.

"Mail order from Russia," Lynne said.

"My soul mate's Russian?"

"Would you hush?" Lynne snapped at Adir. "Did you get food?" she asked Hydee.

"Yeah. It's… He-he loaded the… I…" Hydee weakly gestured behind her.

"Okay." Lynne was all business. "Adir? Groceries. Hydee? I'm going to help you out of the car, now."

Hydee fell against Lynne and staggered on the sandy gravel. "I feel weird."

"One of the side effects of meeting your dreams face-to-face, I think." Lynne put Hydee's arm across her shoulders and shut the car door.

"It's so crazy." Hydee stared at her toes as she walked. "I mean, life's always been a little surreal, but nothing could have possibly prepared me for…" Hydee trailed off because a warning bell had sounded in her head.

"Well, that's why we've closed up the shop early today. You're going to go inside, have a nice mental breakdown, and tell us all about it."

Hydee stopped walking, the force of her frown making her head hurt. "I don't have time. I… He's…" The bell grew louder, and suddenly Hydee remembered that just that morning, she'd been packing. She'd put the journals away, sure, but the box was sitting smack in the middle of her office floor. There were still posters leaning against the walls, movies stacked on her entertainment center, and framed pictures from magazines on her nightstand and dresser. The autographed poster, the cards, the multiple copies she had of the first edition of his biography, one of which was signed; her entire home was decorated in Contemporary Theo.

"Oh God." Hydee flew up the steps and flailed for her keys.

"What's going on?" Adir called.

"Urge to vomit rising," Lynne said, but Hydee didn't have the spare focus to correct her. She raced into the house and stood in her living room like she was expecting the furniture to attack. She got to the entertainment center first and started grabbing DVDs.

"Are we burning those in effigy?" Lynne asked.

"No." Hydee stacked slim boxes in her arms. What had possessed her to get two of every movie?

"Are we building a new shrine?"

"No." Hydee dashed to the wall and grabbed the living room Theo Monk poster from where it leaned against the sofa.

"What are you doing, then?"

Hydee opened the coat closet. No way was it going to be big enough to store everything. She turned toward the stairs. If she put everything in her bedroom walk-in closet, he might see it. If he was in her bedroom. And looking around at her things. Hydee bit her lip.

"He's coming over," Adir singsonged, traipsing by with Hydee's bags on his way to the kitchen.

"What?" Lynne barked.

"It only makes sense," Adir said, unpacking groceries. "He met her, he needs her, he's madly in love, and now he's coming over for homemade brownies and a handjob."

Hydee whimpered.

"What?" Lynne repeated, glancing at Hydee, who nodded at her friend. "You're kidding me."

Hydee hesitated. "Well…maybe not the handjob."

"One can hope!" Adir yelled with his head in the fridge.

Lynne ignored him. "When is he…?"

"Tonight," Hydee croaked. "Seven. I'm cooking. He's bringing wine. He wants help." Hydee looked at Lynne with blurry vision. "He's got a problem with his heart he wants to discuss with me."

Lynne's eyes went wide. "He said that?"

"Oh yeah. Under a rainbow sky after a sun-shower."

Adir sang out like a one-man choir of angels from the kitchen, and Lynne sat right where she was on the floor. "Holy…"

"I know."

"Hyacinth…"

"I know."

"I mean, I always believed, don't get me wrong, but I never expected… I even told him that I hadn't seen this coming."

"Why would you?" Hydee asked, dreamily even to her own ears. "Your gift isn't the future. It's the present and the luck one can make in it."

"I know, I know. I… But this… He… This doesn't…"

Hydee hugged her armful of poster and DVDs. "Make any sense. I know. None of it does."

Adir came out of the kitchen. He glanced at each of them in turn and sighed, crossing his arms. "You white people: always talking a good spirit game but soiling yourselves when fate actually shows up to the party."

Lynne snorted. "Yes, ye wise Native who grew up in

blue-collar Texas. Teach me your ways."

"One cannot learn what is in another person's blood." Adir sniffed.

"Oh can it, pigeon feather," Lynne grumbled, getting to her feet. "This is serious."

"I never said it wasn't."

"You don't get it. What if he's dangerous?"

"Dangerous how?"

Lynne stiffened. "The last time I read him remotely—"

"—which I totally knew you had," Adir chimed in.

"—he was unstable and unhappy."

"That's what you said about him every time you checked in on him," Hydee pointed out.

"I know," Lynne said impatiently. "But it's been worse, lately. What if he's physically dangerous?"

Adir spluttered. "Are we talking about the same overgrown kicked puppy who showed up at the shop today? That man is more likely to break into ugly crying fits than fits of violence. He's probably not even a danger to himself. He's too paranoid he'd muck it up somehow, and we all know being a vegetable with a bullet in the brain is nobody's idea of a good time."

"You're impossible," Lynne chastised, giving up on arguing with Adir. "And this situation is insane."

"What'd you think this would be like? Besides"—Adir shrugged—"we've had weirder."

Lynne gave Adir a long look. "Despite all our former experiences with the strange and the unusual, we're in new territory now. This is Hydee."

"Who can hear you, by the way," Hydee managed to interject.

Lynne ignored her. "We've got to figure out what this means and what we're going to do."

"We?" Adir asked.

"Yes, *we*." Lynne glared.

Adir rolled his eyes dramatically. "Well then, listen up,

Miss Cleo."

"Excuse—"

Adir overrode Lynne. "'Cause the Native's going to learn you a thing. What this means is that Silver, here, was right all along, which we knew in our bones." Adir's dark green eyes flashed. "Didn't we?"

"I guess," Hydee agreed.

"Mmm-hmm." Adir's smug expression evaporated, and he sighed. "I don't know if you had to get to the breaking point for the spirits to take notice and send you Theo or what, exactly, but the stars aligned at long last. The lovers are united." He walked over to Hydee and squeezed her upper arm, which was covered in a colorful tattoo sleeve of a rendition of the Lovers from tarot depicted as humanoid birds sitting on tree branches and connected at the hearts by red strings of fate. Adir traced the butterfly above the upturned face of the girl bird and smiled at Hydee. "All is right in the world again, and it was your energy and your desire that carried you this far.

"Regarding what we're going to do?" Adir clasped his hands in front of his chest. "First, we're going to find out why Silver is removing all traces of Theo." He turned to Hydee, expectant.

Hydee cleared her throat. She stared at the picture's frame, petting it. "If dream experience serves correctly, then he's going to be uncomfortable enough tonight without seeing himself around every corner and thinking I'm some sort of..."

"Stalker?" Lynne provided.

"Knowing your other half as intimately as possible is different than languishing in hero worship," Adir pointed out with a cluck of his tongue.

"She keeps laminated copies of his magazine spreads in her bathroom," Lynne deadpanned.

Adir flapped a hand at her. "Well, what's a good love story without a wee bit of obsession? All the more reason to listen to the woman and help her hide the evidence of hope's past so as not to upset her soul twin's future."

Lynne cocked one hip. "Do you listen to yourself when you speak?"

"Me? You're the one who speaks Mumbo Jumbo Spirit Gumbo, not me."

"Then what the hell do you call what you just said?"

Adir studied his nails. "Truth."

"More like Hallmark for the universally challenged."

"Guys," Hydee tried to interrupt. It didn't work.

Adir put his hands on his hips. "At least I'm not so freaked out by completely missing the esoterically inevitable that I want to hide in my tent and tear up my tarot."

"I am not freaked out!"

"Right. Uh-huh. That's rational and sane froth around your mouth, then, huh?"

"Okay, enough." Hydee thunked the poster onto the floor. "I love the Adir and Lynne Fight for Fun Show as much as the next moron, but we've only got a few hours before he'll be here. Right *here*. Him. With me. Alone. With…food."

Lynne's irritation evaporated, and she lost her murderous expression. "Oh dear Lord, what the hell are you going to fix?"

"I have no idea." Hydee leaned against the wall, thoughts scattered like dandelion seeds on the wind.

"Yes, you do," Adir said patiently. "You know everything about this man. You have got to know what his favorite foods are."

Hydee took a deep breath. She thought of hundreds of articles and interviews. She remembered he preferred boxer briefs over anything else. The crowds on red carpets always made him nervous. She knew he had a freckle on the web of his left hand, between forefinger and thumb, and suddenly all the answers were there, exactly when she needed them. "Pasta. He likes pasta in garlic sauces. White wine, not red." Hydee stared longingly at her kitchen.

"See?" Adir asked softly.

Hydee did see, and for the first time in weeks, she began to feel sturdy on her feet. Maybe she really could do this. She'd done it before, after all, lots of times. She could remember plenty of success stories that involved their meeting and getting through the crazy parts to enjoy the being-together parts. She could do it again, get to know him in this life, and she was sure that the nauseating déjà vu feeling would eventually pass.

And if it didn't vanish completely tonight, she could always excuse herself to go hyperventilate in the bathroom.

Adir took the DVDs from Hydee. "How about we redecorate and you get showered, changed, and start cooking?"

Hydee blew a long sigh. "I… Thank you. I have no idea what I'd do without you guys."

"We know." Adir kissed Hydee's hair, and Lynne stepped over to Hydee and hugged her ferociously.

"Now get to making yourself even more beautiful," Adir said. "Oh, and where's your shovel?"

"In the toolshed by the garden, why?" Hydee asked.

"Just got a hole to dig." Adir took the poster and the DVDs. "Don't you worry your head about it."

Still dazed, Hydee was halfway up the stairs before she realized what Adir had said and its grave implications. "Adir?" Hydee bellowed, running down the steps. "Don't you dare!"

Chapter Six

Interlude in Dreams

Hydee's Journal

The fire in the hearth is roaring, but I'm shivering where I sit on the featherbed with the blankets drawn up to my chin. I'm wearing nothing but my silk undergown. Even my blonde hair is loose and flowing down my back, instead of braided and under a cap. I'm trying to be pretty, and I'm trying even harder to be good as I stare at the door, waiting for my new husband to appear.

The wedding had been awful.

My father arranged the marriage years ago, when I was only five and my mother was alive. I feel the grief of losing her all over again, both me as the dreamer and the version of me in the bed. I always wake up crying.

I am young, but not as young as my sister had been when my father married her off to a captain of the sea. My sister said the first night hurt more than she had ever thought possible, and she said that her husband kept coming back and doing it all over again, night after night, until finally he left on a voyage. My sister is only happy when her husband is gone. He has whores, and she is grateful, and her relief is horrifying to me.

I am older than my sister, but my marriage had to wait until my groom decided to return home. He is a wealthy first son, and he travels almost all the time. I'm not sure, either in the dream or otherwise, where he goes. Time and place are fuzzy in my dream self's head, as that version of me thinks of herself as a daughter of her father's family and anything or anyone beyond that doesn't matter. When I dream of other points in this life, I know I don't live very long, I know where I live is cold, and I believe it to be somewhere in Western Europe. I don't think it's Great Britain.

I do know I am educated, and I can read, but my life is narrowed to what my father allows, my maid's sharp looks and reprimands, and my wedding, which sealed my family to a greater family at quite the cost. It is up to me to bed and to please the man who had stood next to me for nearly two hours while the priest droned in Latin. It was hot, my dress was heavy, and my groom dozed on his feet more than once while the ceremony dragged on.

I, however, could not have thought of sleep, or the sweat pouring down my spine, or the way I grew faint from hunger. I was too captivated by seeing the real face of a man I'd seen in my dreams almost every night for all my life.

Before my wedding day, I had seen my betrothed only once, and I was too young to remember anything but his voice. As I walked down the aisle of the cathedral in full view of hundreds of noblemen and women, I could only stare as my dream lover's eyes came into focus. I spent most of the ceremony trying to decide if I had conjured my dreams based on the voice I had heard in our home's garden so many years ago. The voice had said I was a pretty child and would make a suitable wife. It had been a pleasant voice but without warmth. I had knelt next to my bridegroom and wondered if my desire for a happy life had created all the dreams of past lives spent with a man who was not my current groom but who also…was.

I am confused and scared when the door to my chamber opens. This will be the first time since the ceremony that I have seen him. Directly after our vows, we were loaded into carriages—separate ones. I rode with my maid all day and into the night until we finally arrived at my husband's estate. I was unloaded and ushered into a set of rooms with the finest furnishings, and the following day, I was excited and anxious for my husband to send for me.

When a manservant arrived to tell me and my maid that my husband would attend me that evening, my maid said it was an honor for him to come to me as opposed to me being summoned to his chambers. I, however, was hurt, though I did not let it show. It seemed to me that my husband came to me not out of respect or delight but because he didn't want me to see where he rested and lived while at home.

He shuts the door, and I see he wears only loose breeches and a rough shirt the color of candle tallow. I am thrilled for a moment, because I think he is beautiful, though I would dare not tell him such a thing. He is tall and broad and dark-haired and dark-eyed. His nose is crooked like a beak, and my sister told me many people say he is ugly, but I think the nose makes him distinguished. I want to ask who hit him, as his father's nose is perfectly shaped, and I think maybe it was the father who did the hitting, but then he is advancing upon the bed and me.

"Do you—" I start to say, but I stop when he slings the covers away from me. The motion is violent, and fear strangles me. I can't speak as he climbs onto the mattress and over me. He is a man years my senior and twice my size, and he moves my legs like they are kindling twigs and I am a sapling. It's not until he slaps my hands away that I realize I'm trying to cover myself and hold my gown. He shoves my silk up to my waist, but there is no time to be embarrassed, because I'm too busy being scared. He grabs my leg to stop me from scrambling away, and he reaches with his other hand to undo his lacings. I'm caught, my knees bent and body bare to him, and I see thick curls beneath his navel. I see him, his penis, which he takes in hand and begins to do things to it that I feel I should not watch but cannot help myself. I see him grow larger, and I have to blink because I think I'm seeing things that are not real. He grunts and gets even bigger, and all I can think is that this thing in his palm is a battering ram and I am the gate, and I remember how my sister still cries when she speaks of her pain.

I yank my leg out of his grip while he is distracted. I pull both my feet together, and I kick him in the center of the chest as hard as I can. He grunts, surprised, and I roll to the side. I hear him hit the floor as he falls off the edge of the bed, and with desperation beating in my skull, I grab a heavy, ornate candlestick holder. The lit candles spill to the floor, and I step on them with bare feet to snuff the flames. I don't even feel the heat. I'm gasping for breath, knowing I'll be beaten for this and disbelieving of my own behavior. It will be more than awful to be hit and bruised and still—it is difficult for me to think the word, but I do—fucked, but I think maybe I can make him bleed a little before he does it to me.

He grasps the footboard's post, and he hauls himself to his feet. He sees me, stares for a moment, and chuckles. "What are you going to do with that?" he asks, but I cannot answer him. My lips feel stuck together. I brandish the holder at him again when he takes a step closer. "Are you going to hit me, girl?" He smiles as if this brings him pleasure. "You are even more ferocious than last we met." He tucks himself into his pants. I try not to watch, and he snorts at me. He goes to a table where my maid left a pitcher of wine and another of ale. "Will my dangerous wife drink with me?" He asks the question while he pours, and he does not look at me.

"I hate ale," I manage to say.

"Have you had it?" he asks.

"Yes."

"Have you had mine?"

"No."

"Then you should taste it before you choose your wine." He holds out his gilded tankard to me. "Come here."

"The last time we met, I was a child," I say, blurting the words.

He lowers the tankard. "Yes. I remember. You kicked me in the shin."

"I did what?"

"Kicked me." He almost smiles. "I rode onto your land, and you saw me and demanded to know who I was and what my business might be. I told you I was there to make you my wife, and you kicked me in the shin. Rather hard, as I recall."

I'm aghast and then suspicious. "I would have been whipped until I could not move, and nothing of the sort happened that day."

"One tends to punish only those whom one catches." He takes a long drink. "I never told your father, and I suppose I can only blame myself for not being better prepared for our second private encounter."

I flush but straighten my shoulders. "As I said, I was a child then, my lord."

"And now you are…?"

"A woman grown." My arms are getting tired of holding the candelabrum, but I do not let it fall. "Your wife. And I will not be…" I struggle for the right wording. "I will not be punished like this."

His eyebrows rise. "Punished? I am punishing you, indulging in a husband's rights?"

I cannot tell if his tone is playful or dangerous. It occurs to me that I know little of this man and of what he is capable, despite the fact that my heart believes we've known one another a very long time. I think before I answer. "You are entitled to your rights, my lord, but I ask that you have a care about how you…take them."

"And I ask that you come here and drink this ale." His eyes flash. "Now, girl."

He reminds me of my father in that moment, and I obey, though I carry the holder with me. He is a full head and shoulders taller than me, but he makes no move to hurt me. I take the tankard from him, watching, and though both the tankard and the holder are heavy, I hold one in each hand. I drink, and it's a warm, bittersweet taste on my tongue. I return the tankard to him.

"Well?" he asks.

"It's not altogether horrid," I concede. He watches me, and I continue, "But I would still prefer wine."

Now his eyes are fixated on me, and I struggle to meet his gaze. He reaches for the wine and fills a silver cup. It should be me doing the pouring, as it should be me doing the submitting to my husband's will, and I am guilty, though attempting not to show it.

"So we are to be honest with one another, then?" he asks.

"I believe it is one of the better virtues, yes, my lord."

He smiles, but there is no joy in it. "She would have liked you."

"Who?" I ask.

"Levinia." He hands me the goblet.

"I will not be meeting this woman?"

"Not any time soon, one hopes."

He seems bitter, but I continue to question him. "Who is she?"

"She was my lover."

Misery steals though me, and I clutch the cup and the candle holder. "You are to have a mistress, then?"

He raises his eyebrows. "It may be prudent if my wife keeps kicking like a mule."

Heat burns my cheeks, but I sip my wine and say nothing. After a moment, he breaks the silence. "She's dead, Levinia, and she took with her the life of my son when she went to the grave."

"Childbirth?" I ask.

He shakes his head, and his eyes, lit by the remaining candles around the room, are haunted. "No. She drowned herself with my boy in her arms."

My instinct is to comfort him, but I don't know how. "Why would she do such a thing?"

"I am no devil, girl. I could not guess the notions they plant in us."

I set aside the candlestick holder, and I cling to the cup of wine with both hands. "When did this happen?"

"Two months ago."

I'm stricken, both with his honesty, which tells me he

never intended to love me as he loved Levinia, and with the horror of losing two people in such an atrocious manner. I struggle with myself, needing to hate him for being with another woman but needing to care for him because his grief is written in the lines around his frown and the downturn of his eyes. "I…I am sorry for you, my lord."

He sighs and drains his cup. He puts it down and faces me, effectively rendering me quiet with anticipation and the slivers of fear. "And I am sorry for my brutish behavior. I did not think I'd be capable of what is required of a husband with a young bride. A very pretty bride," he adds softly, "but a bride I do not love and who is merely money in my family's pocket."

The words and their tone cut me. "And I will not be so slighted by a man who is nothing but a chance for my father to regain his reputation and business."

Surprisingly, he laughs, and I put my back to him. "I do not love you either," I say, louder than a woman should ever speak. "What husband and wife begin in love? Such sentiment is for peasants, rutting in the dirt. I had not laid a grown woman's eyes on you until our wedding day, and you were cold and curt. I left behind all I've ever known to come to this place to be with a man who frightens me and tells me he grieves for a woman who was not his wife, and for his bastard son."

"Hard to be a bastard when you're dead."

I flinch but stand firm. "From my point of view, it is better to be a dead bastard than a living wife, my lord."

The tankard strikes the table when he sets it down. "Been a wife often, have you? Know all of the trials and duties therein?"

I'm so angry that I shake. How dare he scare me and tease me like this? I whirl to face him. "I know that men are beasts who understand drinking and whoring better than honor and kindness."

His nostrils flare. "And how do you know this?"

The room seems to tilt. "You just proved as much,

with your lover and your boy, and my sister—"

"Your sister?" he yells, and my back hits the bedpost as I retreat, and he advances. "Your sister, married to that creature not fit to lick my ass?"

I bring my hands up over my face, still holding the cup. He pauses. "What are you doing?"

"Wishing you would get the punishment done so that I might rest," I answer through gritted teeth.

"I'm not going to hit you."

I dare to lower the cup, but it's too difficult to meet his eyes. "Are you not?" I taunt.

"Do you wish me to?"

I swallow, once again finding myself unable to determine the meaning behind his tone. "I wish whatever my lord might—"

He makes a rude noise. "That's shit. Don't give me shit. Tell me what you think. You've been doing it all night. Why stop now?"

I glare at him. "I think you were better in my dreams."

Immediately, I regret my words, as his entire countenance changes to one of supreme interest. "Dreams?" he asks. "And what does a girl dream of a man?"

"We..." I swallow. "I..." He steps closer, watching me, and I press myself flat against the post. "A girl dreams of what a man should be and never will be."

"Oh?" he puts a hand on the post above my head. I can smell him, ale and hay and sweat. "Enlighten me."

I want to ball myself into a knot and hide, but I force my spine rigid and straight. "True and kind and faithful and...loving."

"You think I am not these things?" he asks, and doesn't give me a chance to answer. He's loud and close; his breath and drops of spittle flick my face. "You believe me to be incapable of a heart? Because your sister is with a monster, you believe I am one too? I, who have had nothing but patience with you this night? I, who waited until you were years older than your sister before forcing you to wed, despite your father's ravings? I, who kept my vow to you and your family even when I wanted to dash myself to pieces on the cliffs? I, who have tolerated violence and outbursts and who have not once raised my hand to you?"

"But you did," I retort, though my willpower is shrinking, shriveling, withering. "When you came to me, when you ripped away the covers, when you grabbed me and were going to…" I cannot finish the sentence.

"Going to what?" he asks, impossibly closer. "How do you know what I was going to do?"

I suddenly want to cry, but I refuse to let tears fall. "I didn't. You did not say."

"Oh, so I should say, should I?"

He doesn't move or speak again, and I wish for nothing more than for that tone, whatever it is, in his voice to be his version of gentleness. I would settle for it being pity. When he is still waiting a full moment later, I finally nod.

"Very well, then." He bends his knees, our faces aligned for a brief second. He takes away my cup of wine and tosses it aside, uncaring of the mess. "I'm going to pick you up and put you on the bed." His arms go around my waist, and he does as promised. My head rests on the pillows and my hands are clenched at my sides. "I'm going to climb over you." He does, settling directly to one side of me and resting against me. I'm holding my breath and then breathing too fast. I can't find a midpoint between my extremes. "I'm going to kiss your cheek." He leans in and does so, and one of my hands flies to hold on to his arm. I don't know what I think I will do with that hand, but I stare at it, hanging on to a man who feels like a stranger and a lover at the same time.

"What did I do in your dreams, girl?" he asks me, his low voice directly in my ear.

I shudder and am not sure why. "You… I saw us. You were…nice."

His chuckle this close feels like my own laughter rippling down my spine and in my belly. "Then tonight, I will try to learn what you mean by nice. I will show you my version of it, first." He kisses me in front of my ear, and I turn my head away, hoping he'll do it again. He does. "I've not done nice things to a wife, but I've done plenty of nice things for lovers and whores."

I tighten my grip on his arm, shoving him a little to show displeasure. "I am neither of those things to you."

"Ah yes," he says, while his hand traces my leg and pushes beneath my undergown to my hip. His hand is warm and carefully sure of itself. "But you don't like being a wife, do you?"

"No."

"Then what will you be?" He tilts to kiss my chest, and I let go of his arm to grab him by the shirt with both hands.

"Woman," I say, looking directly into his huge eyes over his crooked nose. "I will be a woman. Your woman. I am yours." I struggle to swallow on my suddenly dry throat. "And I think I want you to be mine." I stop myself from adding *again.*

A smile dances across his lips, but his expression turns serious and intent. He doesn't answer with his voice, but he pushes my gown higher. He kisses my belly, his eyes still on mine, and by the time I've figured out where he intends to kiss last and where he intends to linger, it is too late to stop him. He holds my legs open, the grip digging into the backs of my thighs. When I jerk and tremble, he kneads my skin, and he hums soft sounds of contentment, as though he greatly enjoys making a meal of me. His beard is rough against me, his lips warm and insistent on me between my legs, and I don't know what to do with how it feels, so I cling to his hair and fall back against the pillows. I think I mustn't tell my sister, because this will be a secret between my husband and me. I think it's dirty and wonderful, what he does, and as the dream fades, I wish it would last.

Because I believe I will learn to love his version of nice.

I will learn to love him.

Chapter Seven

Theo left the GPS at the condo and found Hydee's store and home without any left-turn-into-water incidents. He was early, so he pulled into the same spot where he'd parked previously that day. The shop's lights were off, but the house was well lit with a warm, orange glow. The storm shutters were lifted, revealing soft curtains billowing in the evening breeze. It looked and strangely felt like a safe haven; as if the home and the woman inside it were beckoning him, much as the East Coast had called to him when he'd needed an escape.

Turning off the car, Theo put his hand on the green wrap around the flowers he'd picked up along with the wine. He'd debated over the things for a full ten minutes. This wasn't a date, and Theo was profoundly uninterested in sex. Not that Hydee was anything less than beautiful; even the lavender hair worked for her. It was just that the evening had the air of a business meeting as opposed to anything more intimate. He was amazed that she'd agreed to meet him after he'd made such an ass out of himself in the Food Lion parking lot. He'd scared her; it'd been obvious. He'd kicked himself repeatedly for not waiting on her with Adir back at her store, where she would have been on familiar turf and not accosted unawares by some babbling lunatic in a freak rain storm. He wanted to be irritated with the Adir kid for telling him to go find Hydee at the grocery, but all Adir had said, really, was that Hydee was out shopping at the nearest Food Lion and that Theo should find her soon and talk. Theo hadn't even explained his particular ailments, but Adir had insisted that Hydee could help.

The stupid thing was Theo believing him. Theo had gotten all caught up in the bizarre coincidence of his dream and the symbols Adir had mentioned that went along with the Silver Fox's Life Counseling service. Theo had accepted that he'd dreamed of the store and the girl and the bulldogs and ravens for a reason, and he'd driven to the Food Lion without a second thought. Even his soggy and awkward plea for help hadn't disturbed the sense of fate's foregone conclusion. He'd been light on his feet during his conversation with Hydee, if embarrassed and anxious that at any moment, she'd yell at him to get the hell way from her. But she hadn't, and Theo had driven off with a stupid grin that wouldn't go away. He'd sung along to the radio, for fuck's sake, and he hated Top 40.

It wasn't until Theo had been debating over the flowers that the absurdity of the whole charade struck him between the eyes. He'd ended up buying the flowers because people had started to stare at him muttering to himself. He'd fetched the wine as promised, but he'd spent a couple of hours at his rental house thinking he should call Hydee and cancel. Not seeing her—no, the idea of disappointing her—had made him nauseated, but the idea of carrying through with the evening's plans had terrified him. He'd looked her up in the phone book that he'd found in a drawer, but it'd been the shop's number, not Hydee's home number. He'd never forgive himself for standing her up, though he wasn't sure why he was worried about it so much. Forget the fact that he'd stood up hundreds of people in his lifetime—dates, meetings, interviews, name it—surely Hydee was used to people getting the guts to ask for help and then losing the courage to follow through. She'd chalk him up as a coward, and she wouldn't be wrong. It wasn't like he had to see her ever again. He could cancel his rental reservation and go to a different town. He could go hide out in the Florida Keys for a while. Disappear without a trace, and nobody would be hurt or bothered.

At a quarter after six, though, Theo had wandered into the kitchen, picked up the wine and the bouquet, and he'd known he had to go. The second he'd understood that he was going to dinner, the seasick feeling had vanished. It'd been dreamlike, floating out the house and to the car. He'd been calm and sort of sleepy, as though he'd doubled up on the Xanax dose. And speaking of the meds, he'd been halfway to Hydee's before he realized he'd left his bottle on the nightstand. There'd been a spark of panic that had faded beneath the strange lull, which had helped him breathe deeply and get through the drive.

Theo couldn't explain it. He didn't understand it. Ever since he'd gone to the bookstore, he'd been exhibiting extremely un-Theo like behavior. The experience reminded him somewhat of religious types talking about the spirit of the Lord or whatever. He'd dated a girl who'd found Jesus in her Prada bag, and she'd spoken of the moment when she'd known she was connected to everyone and everything, including the Holy Spirit. She'd said she'd been light as a feather, happy, and at peace for the first time in her life, and she'd laughed and cried while dancing around in her living room.

While there was no urge to skip around naked on the seashore, Theo did feel remarkably…normal. Or, well, what he'd always envisioned normal feeling like, and even though he'd sooner cut off his own hand than admit to any sort of religion, be it purely spiritual or full up on the dude with the long beard and robes, Theo couldn't deny that the dream and the shop and the girl were awfully coincidental.

And it did feel nice to be sitting in his car wondering what Hydee had made for dinner. He hoped she could cook, but even if she couldn't, someone making him food was sweet. The flowers smelled good, and the seat was comfortable. He thought if he sat there long enough, he might doze off, which was a miracle in its own right. If he was this relaxed outside, what would it be like to sit inside with the woman in his dream? It couldn't hurt to try to get to know her and let her do her thing. She'd done this sort of guidance before, so she'd likely have an itinerary of sorts. If it started to go south, he could always leave. The rental house wasn't that far, after all, and again, if he chose to get away from the Outer Banks without so much as a good-bye or an explanation, it certainly wouldn't be the first time. He was making it a bit of a habit lately.

Besides, Theo thought while climbing out of the Outback, what if whatever it was she could do actually worked? So what if he had to lie on a bed of purple crystals or walk over fire or sit cross-legged while nude and balancing hot coals on his nuts? If it worked, it fucking worked, right? He'd apparently not given up entirely on a cure. He'd merely acknowledged that his cure was going to be more complicated than taking a pill and drinking prune juice. Being here and trying Hydee's methods didn't make him strange; it made him practical.

Juggling the wine bottles and the flowers, Theo jogged across the sandy lot and to the front stairs leading to Hydee's porch. It wrapped all the way around the side of the house, and Theo peered around the corner to see gardens and a rose trellis. So she gardened. Well, of course she did. Went with that whole Earth Mother Goddess thing she had going on, after all.

The house itself had pale purple shingles, just like the store and Hydee's hair. The chipped green porch boards creaked with Theo's weight. He tucked the bottles under one arm and paused before knocking to run a hand through his hair and to check his fly. This was as good as he was going to get for the moment. He pressed the bell and rapped on the screen door's wooden frame.

The door rattled, and Hydee answered not two seconds later, which meant she'd been waiting. She was a tall woman with an hourglass figure enhanced by the wide belt at her slim waist. Her white shirt was silky, and her skirt was rainbow hued and stopped a couple of inches off the ground. She was barefoot with shiny toenails. Her hair was in some kind of braid with tendrils falling against her cheeks, and she had an incredible smile, even if it was slightly wary. "Theo," she said. "You came."

"Hi there," Theo replied. He sounded like he was a radio DJ announcing his presence to the ocean nearly a full block away. He cleared his throat. "Nice to see you again," he said at a more reasonable volume.

"You too." She stepped back, pushing the screen door open with one hand. "Come in?"

"Thanks."

"Those are lovely," Hydee said, taking the flowers. She smelled them. "Thank you."

Some of Theo's anxiety dissipated with her casual attitude about the gift. "You're welcome."

"And I see you brought wine," Hydee said, and Theo handed over the bottles. "I'll chill the white?" Hydee asked.

"Yeah, that'd be great. I prefer it."

Hydee nodded and went around the corner into the kitchen. "I'll get the flowers in a vase first. They really are lovely!"

"Glad you think so." The interior of the house was lit with dozens of flameless candles and low-wattage wall lamps. It was easy on Theo's eyes, and the tension drained away from his spine. He handed Hydee his jacket when she returned and asked for it, and he watched her tuck it away in a coat closet in the small entryway. The room was a rich rose color, and the steps leading to the second floor had a hand-painted banister railing. The floors were shiny heart pine covered in area rugs that looked woven by hand. "Pretty place," he said.

"Thank you."

Theo followed Hydee into the living and dining room, which were chock-full of cozy furniture sprinkled with throw pillows. There were books on cases against the brightly colored walls. Magazines were stacked on the dining table, off to one side. Mail had been stuck to a board with tied ribbon pockets. He saw knickknacks and pictures of laughing children. The place was neat, tidy, and obviously loved and lived in. Theo wanted to curl up in the chair and bury himself in the knitted throw.

"Would you like some water?" Hydee asked.

"Yes. That'd be…yes."

Hydee gave him a curious smile, and she returned to the kitchen, which was tucked into its own nook off the living room. The space was divided by a breakfast bar, and she'd put the flowers in a blue vase on the counter. When she'd filled his glass, she set his ice water next to the vase, and he picked up his drink. Butterflies gnawed on his stomach lining, and he tried to think of something to say to break the crackling tension.

"That's a nice piece," Theo said, gesturing to the painting hanging above the sofa depicting a couple walking hand in hand in a rainbow galaxy.

"Thank you." Hydee gulped her water, and Theo watched her throat move up and down. She wiped her mouth with her sleeve with a nonchalance that Theo envied. "It was upstairs, but I've been doing a little redecorating."

"Did you paint it?" Theo asked.

"Oh no. A customer insisted on giving it to me." Hydee shrugged. "All I did was listen to her, but she wanted to repay me, and I love pictures of couples holding hands, so…" She shifted, and for the first time, Theo sensed her nerves. Oddly, knowing she was nervous eased Theo's urge to run, and he had to resist the temptation to reach over and squeeze her shoulder in what might pass as a friendly, nonsexually aggressive and possibly even comforting gesture.

God, Theo was so bad with people when he didn't have a script.

A timer dinged in the kitchen, and she all but ran away from him. "That's the shrimp. You eat shellfish, right?"

"Sure." Theo nodded. He pulled out a barstool and didn't bother to tell her that he'd not eaten any seafood since the nuclear meltdown in Japan because he was irrationally terrified of the next zit turning into a third arm.

"Good. I thought I'd read that somewhere." Hydee banged around in the kitchen, doing magical things with pots and pans and aluminum foil.

"You've read about me?" Theo asked, attempting for casual but genuinely interested.

Hydee paused, bent at the waist to put bread in the oven. Bread that Theo vowed he would eat, even if he'd not had gluten in over two years. "Ah, well, a little, yes. I'm a bit of a fan. Just around the edges, you know how it goes."

"Not really," Theo said before he could stop himself.

"Well, that's how it does go. With me." She stood and shut the door, gesturing to the oven. "Oh, and that's my bread. It's gluten free, and so's the pasta. I read about that decision somewhere too."

If Theo hadn't known better, he would swear that his relief about eating a dinner his body could handle was bordering on love for the contentious chef. "I've never been happier that my assistants really do tell all when it comes to my diet and exercise regimen."

"Your assistants?"

"Mmm-hmm. I have two. Call 'em the Detail Twins."

Hydee nodded, but it turned into a head shake of confusion. "You don't answer your own interview questions?"

"Sometimes I do," Theo admitted when Hydee's frown sent tendrils of malcontent through his middle. "There's just so many to handle, though, so when it's a stock Q-and-A, generally they deal with the press through the publicist's office or my agent's, depending on the venue. I do provide them the information, though."

"Oh." Hydee started pulling bowls out of the fridge. "That makes sense, I guess. There are dozens of articles a year, right? Even hundreds?"

"God, I hope not."

Hydee ignored his self-deprecating horror. "How could you pay attention to all of them?"

"Well, the premier ones I do," Theo answered quickly. "Anything about the films or the shows or upcoming…" Theo trailed off. He hadn't come here to talk shop. "Can I help you with anything?"

"Sure." Hydee tipped her head toward a knife block. "Grab one of those and cut up the peppers, would you?"

It took Theo a moment to respond. He always asked if he could help with dinner when he'd gone to someone's house and they were actually cooking, as opposed to having a meal catered or otherwise brought in, but he couldn't remember the last time somebody had taken him up on the offer. "No problem." Theo rounded the counter and selected a knife. He wasn't sure he'd ever cut a pepper in his life. His chef did all that and had done it for the last several years. Before the chef, Theo had eaten out practically every meal.

Theo picked up an orange vegetable and studied it. "Ah, I don't… How does one…?"

"Oh!" Hydee laughed in a remarkably inoffensive fashion. "You just cut out the top, scrape out seeds, and cut it into strips. Here." She took the knife and pepper from his hands, and Theo took a second to notice that both the food and Hydee smelled amazing. Hydee whipped the knife around the stem in a circle, removed the top of the pepper, and handed the rest and the knife back to him. "Now just get rid of seeds and chop. Simple."

"Sure." Theo turned to a cutting board and got to work. He was strangely satisfied. "It's so rare that I get to be useful."

"Oh, I don't know." Hydee fluffed fresh greens in a bowl. "I'm sure your fans think you're extremely valuable."

"Sure, all ten of them," Theo joked.

"Ten million, I think you mean," Hydee corrected, again not standing for the humble act he typically used with people not around the industry. It was…refreshing.

"You entertain people," Hydee continued. "You give them something to see and to do. Sometimes all we have is distraction to get us through a difficult situation."

Theo blinked at the white cabinet door with its stenciled butterflies. "I suppose that's one way of looking at it."

"I think so."

"I wouldn't have thought you'd feel that way about my so-called career."

"Why's that?"

"The sign on your shop door." Theo smiled over his shoulder to show no harm done. "No Theo Monk allowed?"

Hydee paused midstride again. It was impressive how someone with so much vitality could go so still. He wondered if she meditated and if she could show him the secret. "Oh. That. Yes. That must have been…strange."

"A little. Around the edges." Theo smiled, and it happened in a blink. Hydee stepped toward the fridge, crossing behind Theo, who at the same time spun sideways to throw a piece of the pepper into the garbage. He effectively clotheslined her, and she jerked away and so did Theo. He felt a fiery pain and didn't understand why until he saw that when he'd flailed and retracted his hand, he'd managed to slice his finger on the knife he held in the other hand. Blood didn't well from the wound; it poured. "Well, fuck," Theo said conversationally.

"Shit!" Hydee went for the sink. She slapped on the water. "I'm so sorry," she said, taking the knife away from Theo. She tossed it on the counter and grabbed his wrist, dragging him to the water and shoving his finger under the stream. He hissed. "Sorry, sorry," Hydee muttered. "God."

Theo tried to be a man about the fact that it felt like his finger was going to swell up and fall off. "It's okay. Really."

"I'm so sorry."

"You didn't do it. That was all me being a fucking klutz."

"No, no, it's a small kitchen, and I didn't think—"

"You zigged, I zagged, and now I bleed for it," Theo joked.

Hydee weakly laughed. "I'm so sorry."

"Really, it's all right. I've got nine other fingers, and it's a miracle they've all lasted this long." He hissed again when she poked at the edges of the wound. "But that does, ah, hurt. Yes."

"Stay here," Hydee ordered in a voice that did interesting things to Theo's groin, pain be damned. "I've got supplies upstairs, just"—she backed away and jabbed a finger at him—"don't move."

"Yes, ma'am," he said, and she ran—literally ran this time—out of the kitchen and thundered up the stairs. Well, at least they were getting the awkward parts of the evening out of the way. Theo chuckled to himself, but he cussed under his breath when he withdrew his finger from the stream and saw the cut. He'd raked it on the edge of the knife, all right. The sliver ran from under the first joint to above the second in a diagonal line that was bleeding like he'd tried to remove the whole finger.

"Son of a bitch," Theo sighed, and he heard Hydee return.

"Okay," she said as she set the full-size first-aid kit on the bar. It looked, for lack of a better term, professional. "That's going to bleed until further notice, so I'll use some of this superglue gunk to help it clot."

"You don't think it needs stitches?" Theo asked.

Hydee paused with a glass bottle and gauze packs in her hands. "Do you want me to take you to the hospital?" she asked with clear reluctance.

"No," Theo said, and the answer surprised him. "Not really. I was hoping to get through a few more days before I tried out the local facilities."

With a long glance of eyes so brilliantly green they'd make grass jealous, Hydee stepped closer again and began opening the gauze. "Do you have any medical issues?"

"Not real ones."

Hydee's lips played into a smile. "Any imaginary ones that would affect how fast you bleed out?"

"Well, I've always had a certain fondness for hemophilia, but I try to keep fantasy and reality as separate as possible."

Hydee actually laughed at the joke and cupped a pad in her palm. "We'll be thankful you've avoided a royal upbringing. This'll probably not feel great." She took his hand, removed the finger from the water, and wrapped the injury with the nonstick gauze. And squeezed. Theo grunted in what he hoped was a manly fashion.

"So about that—" Theo cut off abruptly when Hydee put her back to him and tucked his arm under hers, holding it steady against her side. She pushed his hand down so it was resting on more gauze on the countertop. Her hair smelled like citrus fruit, and that scent combined with the baking bread made Theo's mouth water.

"About what?" Hydee prompted. Her hand shook as she unscrewed the lid on the liquid bandage bottle.

"The sign in your shop's door," Theo said softly. He resisted the temptation to rest his cheek against the top of Hydee's head. He was bleeding. He was being manhandled by a strange woman with purple hair. He hadn't taken a Xanax in over four hours. He should be panicking and trying to climb the walls to escape and to be alone with his anxiety, but the sleepy-calm had descended again. He didn't even mind when Hydee started to work on his hand. The pressure and stinging weren't pleasant, but they weren't altogether bad either.

"I'm a pretty big fan of yours, actually," Hydee admitted. "I've followed your career since I was little, and the people around here, they know me. My dad left when I was young, was in and out and always causing havoc, and my mom had to work all the time. I think people wanted to help but weren't sure how. Some volunteer to paint my shop or repair my roof. Some insist on tipping me for retail service. Some bring me magazines with my favorite actor." Hydee shrugged a shoulder, and Theo would have been convinced she was being matter-of-fact, but this close, he could feel the heat pouring off her through her clothes and the hand holding his wrist steady was squeezing just a little too tight. "After a while, it got embarrassing. You know how people fixate.”

“Definitely,” Theo mumbled. She was painting the liquid bandage over the cut, utterly unperturbed by the blood, which was making Theo queasy.

“We’re a close-knit community.”

“I can tell.” Theo closed his eyes and focused on the give of her body where his arm rested against her. Unexpectedly, the image of a bulldog popped into his head. “Your employees definitely care about you.”

“We look out for one another.”

“I noticed.”

“There. That should hold back the dam and let it clot.” Hydee began wrapping the finger, and Theo opened his eyes to watch. “And, well, they’re more than employees; I’ve known Lynne all my life, and Adir insists that the three of us were destined to meet and accomplish great things.” She taped gauze and turned to face him. Theo counted six freckles in the splatter across the bridge of her narrow nose. “What about you?” she asked.

“Me, what?”

She peered up at him with a flutter of blonde eyelashes. “Family? Friends?”

“Don’t you already know?” Theo asked, not exactly meaning for the words to be so blunt.

“Maybe,” Hydee conceded. “Or maybe I only know what your publicist wants me to know. I’d rather hear the details from the source.”

It was difficult to speak beneath the intensity of her scrutiny. “I have people.”

“Yeah?”

“Yeah.”

“So, tell me about them?”

Theo sharply inhaled. “Mother, father, workaholics. One brother. Never see him. What’s for dinner?”

Hydee waited for a beat before beginning to clean up the bloody pepper and medical supplies. “Angel hair pasta. Garlic sauce. Side salad. Bread.” She stepped away from him.

"Plates are in that cabinet. Silverware's in that drawer. Why don't you set the table, and I'll finish the food?"

Theo stifled the urge to apologize and went for the cabinet feeling like he'd made a mistake somewhere. He hadn't meant to sound so defensive. He considered thanking her for bandaging him up, but when he said the words in his mind, they seemed like a half-assed attempt at heartfelt. Then he got angry about feeling like he'd fucked something up when all he'd done was try to avoid talking about shit that would make everyone uncomfortable, especially him. He watched Hydee from the corner of his eye. She didn't seem upset, but how would Theo know if she was?

Careful not to break anything, Theo took two plates and strode across the kitchen and living room to the dining table. There were four chairs, one of which was blocked by the stack of magazines. Should he set the plates at opposite ends of the table or side by side? Opposite ends would give them room, but side by side would make it easier to talk, and evidently, she wanted to talk. Was that part of the scheme? Was this some Freudian shit in disguise? Any second now, she'd tell him that he'd always wanted to sleep with his mother and therein was the root of all his issues.

Theo put the plates on either end of the table and went back for flatware. The garlic and oil were sizzling on the stove, and Hydee appeared to be concentrating. Theo's stomach rumbled, and he wanted to tell her the food would be incredible. The entire meal was his favorite, actually, from the pasta to the sauce, and he wasn't sure if that was coincidence or not. Would it be better if she had remembered everything about him or if she'd stumbled upon his favorites by accident? Why the hell did it matter?

On the third trip back to the kitchen, he wanted to ask how they'd gone from nearly holding each other while she glued him back together to unable to speak in less than five minutes. Theo wasn't used to silences when he was around women. They babbled constantly, about each other and their liposuction and the men they terrorized.

Hydee cooked, humming a little under her breath, and she seemed completely fine with that. "The wine's in the fridge," she said.

Theo, realizing he'd been standing and staring at her sautéing garlic, quickly got a move on. "Sure," he muttered.

"Glasses up there."

"Okay."

"Corkscrew in that drawer."

"Got it."

By the time Hydee was finished in the kitchen and bringing the pasta over to put it on Theo's plate, he had set the table, laid out the rest of the food, uncorked the wine, drunk an entire glass, and poured his second. His finger throbbed. He missed his Xanax, and he kept counting the panes of glass set in the side door.

"There we go," Hydee said, beginning to pile food on her own plate. "Dig in."

Theo forked a shrimp and chewed it while Hydee gracefully swept from table to kitchen and back again, finally sliding into her chair. "How is it?" she asked.

"This… All of this, it's"—Theo drank more wine—"it's exactly what I, ah, needed."

Hydee's smile lit up the room. "Good."

"Thank you," Theo said, and it sounded strained and stilted even to him.

"You're welcome. How's the finger?"

"Hurts."

"Want some Tylenol?"

"No." Theo twirled his pasta. "Yes."

"No problem." Hydee got up again, taking Theo's social fumbling in stride. If he'd been with his own nominal friends back in LA, their collective shaming about Theo being a graceless idiot and a wuss would have chased him out of the house by now. But Hydee was different. She was so forthright and casual and…capable that Theo caught himself relaxing, which was truly alarming.

Theo gaped at her retreating back and was still slack-jawed when she returned and handed him the pills. "Keep it to a quarter bottle of wine with those, all right?"

"Why?" Theo heard himself ask.

"Liver issues with Tylenol and drinking in excess." She laughed. "Lord, I sound like an overbearing mother with a medical license. I'm sorry."

"It's all right."

Hydee waved a hand. "No, you're a grown man. Do what you want. I'm too used to taking care of the kids."

"Kids?"

"Lynne's. She has two. Victor and Cecelia. I've been Auntie Hydee all their lives." She smiled fondly. "And, well, there's Adir. He's a kid even if he does act like a wizened octogenarian."

"Mmm." It was as though there were two Theos in the room: one was eating and interacting with Hydee, eager to learn more about her, and the other was sitting in the empty chair begging him to shut up and to leave immediately before he did something he'd regret. "Was that planned?"

"Adir?"

"No, the—"

"Kids. I know, and yeah, they were. Well, sort of. The first one was a bit of a surprise, but Lynne and Ron had been planning their lives since they were in middle school. I always envied them that."

The Chatting Theo made an affirmative sound, nodding. "My mother didn't want kids." The Regretting Theo hit his head on the table. Bringing up Mommy dearest was always a bad move.

To Hydee's credit, she barely missed a beat. "She didn't?"

"No." Regretting Theo screamed at him to change the subject, but Chatting Theo was determined to make an ass out of himself. "She thought we'd ruin her career."

"She writes, doesn't she?"

"Plays. Very good ones, from what I hear. My father, he's in set and sound design. That's how they met; he did one of her plays. Mother likes to micromanage, and Father used to like making her happy." Theo studied a nearby candle. Even though it wasn't real fire, the bulb flickered to give the desired effect. Theo couldn't help but think he was a whole hell of a lot like that plastic candle—all looks and no real substance or warmth. "My father, he…he would throw these parties while Mother was in London or New York. He mostly worked in LA, see, and he'd invite everyone to the house while she was away."

"Sounds exciting," Hydee said.

Maybe it was her tone that kept him talking. She wasn't demanding, she didn't sound judgmental, and she wasn't pressuring him. "My nannies would get me into bed, but sometimes I'd sneak down and more than once I caught the after-party show."

"What do you mean?"

"Sex. Drugs. Porn." Theo snorted. "God, could he have been more cliché?"

Hydee waved her fork. "Stereotypes come from somewhere, I suppose."

"Yeah." Theo nodded. "Yeah, they do, don't they?"

"Did your nannies catch you and haul you off to bed?"

"Most of the time. But there was this one night… Well, maybe more than one."

"Oh?"

"It's… I, um…" Theo couldn't tear his gaze off the candle or his head out of the past. "I was maybe six, and I'd sneaked down this curving staircase. That thing was straight out of the disco seventies. Hideous. So there I am, clinging to the banister railings, my ass numb from the marble, and I hear these noises that worry me and make me want to find their source. Like if you hear something in a dark room with a cracked door. You've got to push it open and see, right?"

"What did you see?"

"My father. Fucking this man and this woman on the entry rug in the foyer. They were this pile of noisy pink flesh.

I remember thinking the body parts didn't look like mine and didn't seem real. I thought I was seeing a live cartoon."

Hydee said nothing, and the weight of the silence squeezed more words out of Theo. "And you know, later, I'd hear my friends brag about seeing porn or the first time they got off or when they figured out what body part went where when it came to the nasty, and they were proud. Spreading the good cheer about fucking and thinking everybody would be on board, but mostly I remember being pissed. To me, sex was that ball of bodies that would roll around and break my mother's favorite vase and then lie later about how it had happened. My mother knew the truth, and she was even worse than Father. She started throwing revenge parties in New York. We'd get these phone calls, the boys who had the home number. They'd ask to speak to the woman they'd fucked the night or the week before.

"Now I wonder if that was my parents' foreplay, trying to one-up each other. I still don't know, but I do know they both fucked anybody, didn't care who saw or knew. Not even if it was their kid who was freaking out because what Father was doing in that foyer seemed private, like going to the bathroom was private, and yet these other people came out of the den and library and living room, just wandering past my fucking father. Slapping him on the shoulder, egging him on, making jokes about when the bitch was away the wolf would play. One man held my father's head back and put a joint to his lips so Dad could suck a little while getting blown. All I could think was, 'Fuck, someday that's going to have to be me. Someday, I'll have to want to do private things in front of everyone and let a man fuck me while I fuck his wife.'" Theo put down his fork. "And that was the first time little Theo tried to run away from home and this, my dear, is the shit that doesn't go in the interviews when they ask me what it was like growing up with famous parents in the industry."

"So you grew up in danger," Hydee said.

"Danger?" Theo asked, utterly derailed.

Hydee played with the stem of her wineglass. "Parents are supposed to protect kids, not expose them."

"I like to think they weren't exposing me deliberately. I sneaked down and saw everything for myself."

"Did your father ever see you? Watching?"

In a flash as blinding as noonday sun, Theo saw his father's eyes lock with his. Theo was older, that time, almost old enough to drive. That party had been for him, for Theo, but Dad was the one who scored the girls. Theo had stood in the kitchen watching Catherine Anne from biology sitting backward on his father's lap, bouncing up and down. Theo saw his father's heavy lids, the confused expression…the wave and the wink and the way he smacked her on the ass like she'd been a very bad girl. Theo's friends had thought it'd been awesome. Theo had seen himself in thirty years being the asshole who fucked his kid's underage classmates and had spent the next month drunk off his mother's gin supply. "Maybe once," Theo replied.

"Then that's exposing."

Theo had to order himself to stay calm and not raise his voice. He wasn't mad at Hydee; he was angry at his father. Thank you therapy and all you've taught me, Theo silently prayed. "Okay, maybe, but it wasn't dangerous. They weren't fucking me. Hell, they barely ever touched me." Theo's heart fluttered like a dying bird, and he rubbed his damp hands on his pants.

Hydee licked her lips and took a drink before speaking. "Lynne's little girl, Ceecee? She has nightmares about zombies. They're elaborate dreams that she has no business dreaming because she doesn't watch or read anything scary. But she still has them. They exist despite any rational reason to the contrary. So, Lynne asked me once to explain to Ceecee about dream symbolism. Lynne had tried, but you know how sometimes kids hear things better from people who aren't their parents. So, I sat down and explained to Ceecee that monsters in dreams mean other things. They aren't really zombies, they're the mean girls at school or the fear of coloring Hello Kitty the wrong color." Hydee paused. "She was five. I had to improvise."

"Zombie Hello Kitty. Got it."

Hydee's smile was a flicker of true warmth. "Well, even though we figured out that she was afraid of the kindergarten teacher's aide, she still had the zombie dreams. She was afraid of both the reality—the aide—and the zombies. So Lynne handled the woman, and I handled the zombies."

"How'd you do that?"

"I made Zombie Repellant Juice with Ceecee one day in the store. Adir got in on the action and blessed it, and we put the stuff in a spray bottle and squirted it on all the door frames and windows of Lynne's house and mine. Then I made this little antizombie charm thing and put it under her pillow."

"Sweet," Theo said.

"Yeah, but she's a smart kid." Hydee brushed her fingertips over her lips. "She kept telling me how zombies are immune to charms and that they're not like vampires, who hate Italian food."

"So it didn't work?"

"I think it did. Because even though she told me it wouldn't work, she still asks me to spray the room when she gets scared at night. I've seen her holding the charm under her pillow while she sleeps." Hydee rested her elbows on the table, and Theo got trapped by her gaze. "Parents and adults are supposed to protect kids from the real threats and from the ones in their heads. Because you can explain to a kid all day long that the things they see when their eyes are shut aren't real, but in the middle of the night, all that logic goes away. Darkness reminds kids, and adults too, for that matter, of the In Between."

"The what?"

"The place we go in between." Hydee cleared her throat. "I think kids are closer to Spirit than adults; they remember where they were before they were born, even if the memories are fuzzy. They believe in things adults have forgotten, they know things to be true that adults think are silly, so kids need the Indian-Blessed Zombie Spray because they need imaginary cures for so-called imaginary monsters."

Theo tried to digest all that and to see the connection to his own story, but he failed. "I'm pretty sure my father isn't imaginary, though one still has hopes he'll vanish someday."

Hydee's smile was sad. "Your father is real, what you saw was real, and the feeling of danger that what you witnessed created is also real. Lynne went to the school and told that teacher to back off and to apologize to her kid for something the teacher had said, which the teacher did. Lynne handled the reality, like any mom would, but you didn't have someone watching your back. Your mom wasn't there, your father lied to her, and you're a child barely out of diapers who's facing down terrifying and confusing reality without any filters. Nobody should see the naked, cold truth of life and loveless fucking at the age of six. Nobody needs to see that kind of desperation so young. Makes you feel like that's all there is and all you can hope for. That's partly why we as a culture decided children needed childhoods, for heaven's sake. Everybody deserves a few years of feeling like somebody cares enough and is powerful enough to keep you safe from the zombies."

"Neither of them gave a shit," Theo mused, more to himself than Hydee. Vaguely, he wanted to chastise himself for having this kind of conversation with this kind of woman, who was still all kinds of stranger, but he was too lost in the memory of his mother standing over him while he bled on the gravel. "I've been thinking about them a lot lately."

"Maybe you're trying to remember the last time you felt safe to be you."

A wave of pure discomfort struck Theo, and he had to hang on to the edge of the table to keep from bolting. Hydee must have sensed it, because she poured him another glass of wine while Theo worked up enough spit to unstick his tongue from the roof of his mouth. "What do you mean by that?"

"You said you keep thinking something's wrong with your heart."

"Yeah?"

"But you told me after you cut yourself that you didn't have any real medical issues."

"Yeah," Theo repeated.

Hydee shifted in her seat, elbows returning to the table. She had lovely hands: long fingers and short, even nails. No evidence of chewing in sight. "Energetically speaking, the heart is the symbol of emotional self. It's the reason we say 'He broke my heart' instead of 'He broke my head' or gut or any other organ that responds to stress and emotional pain. Wounds of an emotional nature hit here." She put her hand at her breast. "It's also the place where you allow yourself to feel so that you can move up the energy chain and vocalize who you are and your emotions"—she touched her throat—"and then think about what they mean and what to do about them"—she touched her forehead— "and then see how you interconnect with everything else." She made a loose fist that she unwound above her head like a tiny bomb exploding.

Theo squinted, trying to listen and not instantly disregard the new age crap. "I think my yoga teacher's talked about that. Chakras, right?"

"Yep. Energy theory put through a Hydee filter, as Lynne would say. It's how I see things, in other words. May or may not apply."

"Cancel any time, tip your waiters."

Hydee laughed quietly. "Exactly."

Theo contemplated and drank. "So, you think my heart energy's broken?"

"Stuck," Hydee corrected. She fidgeted with the end of her ponytail. "And I'm doing a lot of supposing here, but you just told me you got introduced to sex and violation of privacy and narcissism at a very young age. That kind of thing might get you stuck, energy-wise. You even said it yourself: it made you feel like meaninglessness was all you'd ever get to experience."

Theo thought of how he viewed sex and women and relationships and knew she was absolutely right. "So how do I unstick myself?"

Hydee's eyebrows went up and down. "Well, I'd probably start by acknowledging the experiences that hurt you and then figuring out the lessons while learning to let go of the pain and anger."

"Oh, well, thank God it's simple."

Hydee's eyes danced to show she got the joke, but she spoke seriously. "Not at all. Most people never make it through that part."

"That part?" he asked skeptically. "What comes after that?"

"You figure out what you want and what you'll do."

"Why?"

Hydee was unflappable. "Because that will determine who you are and who you'd like to be."

Theo stared at her for a moment and then threw his hands into the air in surrender. He flopped against the chair. Unexpectedly, he began to laugh.

"What?" Hydee asked.

"Oh, nothing." Theo rubbed the corners of his eyes with a thumb and forefinger. "It's just I've probably dropped a few hundred thousand dollars in therapy and seminars and books and alternative medicine, and none of it made as much condensed fucking sense as you did in half an hour."

"More evidence to my belief that we should have met and spoken earlier in life," Hydee said softly.

"Probably. Hell, you've known me for, what, collectively two hours and already have more insight than anyone else in my entire damned life."

Hydee scrubbed her mouth with her hand. "Maybe I just pay more attention to the details."

"Where did you learn all this, anyway?" Theo smirked. "Old Souls 'R' Us Academy?"

Hydee blanched as if she'd accidentally swallowed a cockroach, and a ringtone started to go off from the direction of the coffee table. "Excuse me," Hydee said, getting up to go answer.

Theo enjoyed the sway of her hips beneath the skirt as she went to the table and put a phone to her ear. She glanced at him and vanished into the entryway, out of sight.

Picking up his wine, Theo started to pour more, but remembered what Hydee said about livers and Tylenol. He'd hate for her to know how much Xanax was in his system. The Tylenol would have to get in line to do its damage. He put down the glass and thought about their chat, which was more personal than Theo had been with anyone possibly ever. He might have told his first shrink about catching his father in the act when he was six, but now he usually introduced his father into the conversation by saying the man was a sex addict. It worked.

God, how many shrinks had there been? A dozen? Theo regularly hit the same wall with therapists. They wanted him to cry and get angry and fucking journal, and he wanted to tell them it wouldn't matter if he did. He was forty, for Chrissakes. He'd not lived at home since he was seventeen, and he barely saw his parents once a year. He had a career and a life, such as it was. What the hell was the point in weeping over that boy in the foyer or the teenager with the gin bottle?

Theo got up and began to pace. Anger boiled beneath the surface of his skin, and he rubbed one arm, surprised when he didn't find blisters. He tugged at the collar of his shirt. Did Hydee really need to keep the house so hot? It was unbearable in here.

The side door's handle was in Theo's palm before he understood he'd walked over to it. He went out onto the porch and breathed. He could smell salt and beach and the garden. It was cool, the breeze sudden against him and making him shiver. He went to a rocking chair and sat, thinking his current setting looked remarkably like his place of inner Zen, the beach house next to the water.

Hydee pushed open the screen and came outside to join him. She sat in a matching chair on his right. She'd draped a shawl across her shoulders. "I'm sorry," she said after a few moments.

"For what?" Theo asked.

Hydee sighed. "I tend to talk about things that make people uncomfortable. I forget that the way I see the world and what I think is skewed based on my own experience."

"Isn't everybody that way, though?"

"Maybe," Hydee said. "But I think I might be more cockeyed than most."

Theo flexed his fingers over the rocking chair's smooth arms. "You weren't wrong."

"About what?"

"All of it."

"Okay."

"I've heard most of what you had to say before."

"You have?"

"Yeah, different vernacular, but basically you just told me what I've been hearing all my life."

"Which is?"

The chair creaked, the wind chimes rang, and for the first time since he'd gotten to the beach, he missed his crossword puzzles. "Know and learn to love thyself."

"Life's work is easier when it's somebody else's bumper sticker."

"It's easier when you know where to start," Theo said.

Hydee stopped rocking, and Theo glanced sideways at her. "Don't you?" she asked softly.

"Don't I what?" Theo mumbled. The soothing spell that had been broken inside by the cell phone was weaving itself again. Theo got lost in trying to identify the emotions dancing across Hydee's face. Hope, maybe, but something else too. Something Theo recognized as a feeling that visited him too often.

"Know where to start or…" Hydee swallowed, and her slow blink didn't break their connection. "That you already have?"

Words stuck in Theo's throat and made it hard to swallow. Hydee's hair floated around her face in the breeze, and Theo split into two people again. One of them rose, went to the woman who had dressed his wound and made him dinner and warned him about medication, bent, and kissed her. He lifted her out of the chair, mouth locked on hers, which was warm and eager against his. He dropped her shawl to the porch, tore the belt away from her waist, and lifted her shirt up and over her head. She slid her fingers up his spine, and they shoved and pushed clothing off and away until they were bare, skin to skin, cold on the sides that did not touch. He sat her on the railing, hands at her breasts before his mouth took over. Her fingers were in his hair, dragging across his shoulders, running down his arms, and he slipped a thumb between her legs and brushed her clit to hear her gasp. He locked eyes with hers and stayed there, circling and pressing and kissing and watching while her skin flushed, her kisses grew desperate and morphed into bites, and when she called out, he kept going because he wanted to see it all again. And again. Until they were numb with need and greed, and the world had fallen by the wayside, unimportant next to the reality they created and held between them.

The other Theo, the real one, didn't do anything at all. He watched the scene play out across his mind's eye, waiting until he felt as much like a whole human being as he ever did. He turned away from Hydee, exhausted and depressed. It took monumental effort to speak. "I should go."

"You didn't eat much."

"I'm not hungry."

"I could pack it up for you."

"You don't need to do that."

"You could stay."

Theo jerked to stare at Hydee, crazily thinking that his other, braver self had not been alone in fantasy land. Even crazier, it felt like he'd been here before, experiencing this exact sense of déjà vu. Vertigo made his ears ring, and suddenly he wasn't sure that he hadn't gone to her, kissed her…held her… And now it was the next day, and she was asking him to…

"What?" he asked, trying to reorient himself to space and time. How much wine had he drunk, anyway?

"You're tired." Hydee gestured to his hand. "And injured."

"It's nothing."

"It's something to me." Hydee frowned, and Theo actually leaned in his chair with the desire to kiss the corner of her mouth. Make her smile.

"You've done enough," Theo said.

"I've barely begun. We've barely begun."

"Is this part of what you…" Theo had to rest his head against the chair. It was like he was bobbing in the ocean and he was getting seasick. "Is this how you help people?"

"Everybody's different." Hydee rose and stood next to Theo's chair. Her eyes were the color of rainforest canopies at night.

"What if it doesn't work?" Theo practically whispered. He wanted to be angry at himself for acting like a scared child, but Hydee took his hand. It was cool and strong and confident. Everything Theo was not.

"You've already done the hard parts. You're here. You're trying."

Theo was no longer sure what they were discussing. "I couldn't impose on you like—"

"It's a bunk bed, but it's soft."

"The drive isn't that long," Theo said, though it seemed like the rental house was a continent away.

"I have a spare toothbrush."

Still divided, one Theo floated down the street to the edge of the Atlantic Ocean, which lapped and lured, calling to him. He could actually feel sand between his toes, and he could feel the water's spray against his cheeks. Standing there, he was so close to understanding some fundamental truth that would unlock the secrets of the universe that he could have reached out and dipped his fingertips in it. If he dove in, he would be immersed not in water, but in knowledge. He'd remember something…something important.

He tried to get himself together, to stop being an existential idiot and make a smart decision, but as he envisioned himself driving away from the safety of this house and the confidence the woman who lived there embodied, he went empty inside. An apple, cored; a tree trunk, hollowed; a man, soulless. When he thought about staying, sleeping here, and waking up to the sound of Hydee in the kitchen, he was no less unsettled, angry, or tired.

But he wasn't anxious. And he wasn't alone.

"I'll make you breakfast," Hydee promised.

"Sold," Theo replied, and he let Hydee hang on to his hand while he climbed out of the chair. As they went inside and up the stairs, he wanted to ask her how many people she had helped. How many had stayed here with her? A piece of him wanted to be the only one, and another piece could only find comfort in being one of many. But were they all this world weary and bitter? Was he beyond hope, or did he have a shot at figuring out himself and his life and where it was going? Where did Hydee fit into all that?

"Right down here," Hydee murmured. They passed closed doors on the second floor, and the rug under Theo's shoes was plush. He stared at the fall of her skirts and at the ends of her pale hair. Touching her hand wasn't nearly enough, and he slowed his pace in fear of pulling her to him. Did everyone want her as much as he did? Did they all want to hold her, bury their faces in her breasts and lap, never let go? Theo had never wanted to sleep with any of his therapists or instructors or doctors before. Hell, he couldn't really remember the last time he wanted someone in any way, shape, or form. Not like this. Was it that Hydee was different or that she was actually helping that made him want to break his pattern? Would the feeling be gone in the morning?

Theo supposed there was only one way to find out.

"This is the room." Hydee flipped a light switch, and a cheerful lamp came to life. There was a rainbow bunk bed set against one wall. The bedspreads were starry night skies showing constellations. "The bottom bunk's bigger, full size. I'd opt for that one. Bathroom's across the hall. Towels are in the closet in there, and the toothbrush is in the drawer by the sink." Hydee hesitated. "I'm right next door if you need anything."

"Thanks." Theo realized he was still holding her hand. He stared at their fingers wrapped around each other. "I'm sorry I'm cutting the evening so short. I'm just… Suddenly I'm ready to fall over."

Hydee touched Theo's wrist and drew a circle with the pad of her finger. "If every worry we have is a rock, and we carry those rocks with us, then eventually the weight wears us down. And when we shift the rocks, try to break them apart or hand them over or even drop them, we realize how heavy the things are in the first place. Sometimes the relief of letting go can be every bit as exhausting as the carrying."

It was too easy for Theo to envision himself buried beneath a mountain of boulders, resigned to his fate, and then seeing a ray of light for the first time. He'd probably convince himself it was a mirage, and Hydee would probably try to tell him to go and check it out. "I swear everything you say makes the strangest kind of sense."

Hydee lightly laughed and let go of Theo's hand. She appeared about to say something more, but instead she turned and went to the door. "Get some rest, and if you need anything…"

"Thanks."

Hydee nodded with a tight smile and disappeared from sight. Theo stood in the middle of the room, listening

to her footsteps on the stairs. He took three steps toward the
door, caught himself, and shut it instead of going through it.
With a long sigh, he undressed and crawled into bed.

Chapter Eight

Hydee dialed Lynne's number while staring at the entryway and huddled in a chair in the corner of the living room. Lynne answered on the second ring. "Well?" she asked, breathless.

"He's upstairs."

Adir squealed in the background, and Hydee covered her grin with one hand and glanced guiltily toward the second floor. "And you are…?" Lynne pressed.

"Downstairs."

"And?"

"And… I don't know."

"What do you mean 'you don't know'?" Lynne asked, exasperated.

"I didn't think he'd stay."

Adir was speaking, but Lynne shushed him. "Walk me through it?"

"Don't you mean 'us'?" Hydee said drolly.

"Hyacinth," Lynne spoke in her mom voice. "I call to check on you, make sure the crazy man is behaving himself, and you tell me in that floaty-dreamy voice you get when you're stoned or about to do something crazy that you're thinking of asking him to stay the night. You then proceed to hang up on your best, most trusted friend in the whole wide world without explaining what the hell that means. Then you call me not half an hour later and tell me he's still in your house but not with you. So, either you two had the fastest, dirtiest, most desperate sex ever and he's sleeping it off, or—"

"Oh God, no." Hydee laughed. "Nothing like that."

"Ask her why not something like that!" Adir shouted.

Lynne sighed. "Adir wants to know—"

"I heard, I heard." Hydee sighed and tucked her bare feet under the afghan. She honestly had no idea where to start. Her head was buzzing and her hand was still tingling from holding his. "It was the look in his eyes. It was what he said. And also how he said it. Like, he wasn't sure why he was here or talking but was too committed to back out."

"Uh-huh," Lynne encouraged.

"I just… I don't know. I couldn't." Hydee put her head on the chair's arm.

"You sound like you got hit in the face with a metaphysical crowbar."

Hydee groaned. "I think I did."

"Okay. Breathe."

Hydee obeyed, and six deep ones later, she was marginally more grounded. "I try so hard to balance the metaphysical chaos with the businesswoman and be levelheaded, you know?"

"I do."

"I run the store, I take care of people, and I love the kids," Hydee babbled. "I make my father write and tell someone where and how he is, and I check Mom's bank account when I think she's lying to me about being square. I remember everybody's birthday. I keep track of whose kid is allergic to peanuts when they come by the store and want brownies, but there's a whole other side of me who dreams about a man I've never really met and being with him over the last few eons. That Hydee believes in past lives, collects movie-star junk, and watches movies a thousand times to get a good cry going. I'm pretty sure the rational version of me never suspected that the dreaming version of me was anything less than psycho."

"The thing is, Hy, that's rational behavior in and of itself. You had to believe, but you also had to live your life without those beliefs completely running it."

"I get that. I do. But now, he's here." Hydee glanced at the steps and held her breath to make sure she hadn't summoned Theo by speaking of him. When all was quiet in the house, she continued. "I figured I'd be nervous. I understood that actually meeting him would be different in real life than how it went down in my head. But I guess I thought the dreams would somehow…that I'd be prepared to…"

"You weren't ready for him to be real."

"Exactly." Hydee sat up and crossed her legs. Her belt was trying to cut her in half, and she fumbled with the buckle one-handed.

Lynne hummed in the affirmative. "You've seen yourself as his leading lady in a hundred romantic comedies."

"And a couple Shakespearian tragedies, yeah."

"But this is behind-the-scenes shit."

"It is," Hydee agreed. "And the dreams, they're not…" Hydee made a frustrated noise. "I have no idea if it's genetic memory or what that makes me dream of us at night, and, really, I still don't know if any of the dreams are real."

"Hydee…"

"No, hear me out. Meeting him didn't prove to me that they were, because he's not connected to any of the dreams when he's sitting across from me at the table. He's not a memory. He's a living, breathing human being with a past and a history that I don't know and have to learn. In the dreams, I already know everything." Hydee tossed the belt to the floor and yanked the band off her entwined braids. "Or, well, I do eventually. Even if the particular dream self doesn't figure it out until I've had more dreams of that lifetime to… Oh God. I'm not making any sense."

"Sure you are. You thought that since you've met and known him all those times in your head that it would be easy to meet and know him again. The dreams would be your experience, and you'd know what to say and what to do, and it'd go smooth like lotion on a baby's butt."

"Yeah," Hydee answered absently. "I do feel like I know him, though. He's familiar even though he isn't and…" Hydee shook out her hair and rubbed her scalp. "God, I feel more insane, not less."

"I think you do know the essence of him. Even if you discount the dreams altogether, which I wouldn't, you would still understand the kind of person he is. There's something about him that makes sense to you. Maybe he reminds you of someone you know, maybe you just have an innate ability to understand his particular breed of bullshit, but you get him."

Hydee nodded even though Lynne couldn't see it. "Yeah. Okay. Makes sense."

"But you thought you'd understand him even more because you've been dreaming of him. The thing is, though, Hy, is that those people weren't him. They're echoes of him. They're like you said: memories. The gist of who he is might be similar, but he's not those people you've met before, because he didn't have those parents or those living circumstances—"

"Castles. Huts. Riverboats."

"Or those interests—"

"Collecting staves. Wearing too much war paint. And in one memorable lifetime, an addiction to prune juice."

"Seriously?"

"He was really into it, yeah."

"Right. Anyway. What you're talking about is reconciling the only reality you've known—the dreams and how those lifetimes worked out—with the one you're now facing, which is Theo Monk, actor and anxious douche bag."

"Lynne."

"He belittled what I do," Lynne grumbled in self-defense.

"That's because he doesn't believe in what you do. Or in what I do, for that matter. I tried to explain some energy ideas to him over dinner, and I thought his eyes would cross so hard they'd come out his ears."

"Figures."

"But in his defense, not everybody has read what we've read, studied what we've studied, or seen what we've seen. Same goes in reverse. He was telling me some stories from when he was a kid, and I had a seriously hard time believing people so selfish and uncaring could exist."

Lynne grunted. "Okay, back to you and your houseguest, who owes me an apology."

"And who is also sleeping in Ceecee's bed."

"So he owes her one too."

Hydee got up to pace. "I guess I thought I'd know what to do, but I felt like I was floundering around."

"Like any old regular first date?"

"It wasn't a date."

"Keep telling yourself that."

"It wasn't. He's…so not interested. Well, mostly, I think. There was this moment on the porch…" Hydee got lost recalling the need in Theo's gaze. The hunger there had seemed ready to pounce and devour her, and Hydee had been ready to let it.

"Oh?"

"Doesn't matter." Hydee shook off the memory. "He's wounded and exhausted and lost. And I feel like if I keep relying on the dreams to guide me, I might lose my mind or, worse, him. They're not helping me figure out what to do to help him like I thought they would."

"Okay, so, maybe you need to think of them differently."

"How so?"

"They've shown you the broad strokes of who each of you are. Even if the dreams aren't real, which, for the record, I think they are exactly what we think they are, memories of former lives, they've still given you an idea of what will work for each of you and what won't. Now you have to figure out the details of this version of him and yourself and how to make your relationship work. And even if you've not seen how this lifetime goes a billion times, you have been in relationships, dealt with strange people, and read a shit-ton of books on interpersonal psychology."

"So what you're saying is that if anybody can crack this egg…"

"It'll be you, Hy-Ho."

Hydee huffed a soft sound of disbelief. "Adir's being awfully quiet."

"He's pouting because I haven't asked if you've done anything interesting with Theo yet. And 'interesting' in Adir speak is—"

"Yeah, I know." Hydee studied her palm. "We held hands."

"Well, that's a step in the positive direction."

"It really is, especially considering I almost cut one of his fingers off."

"You did what?"

"Well, technically, he did the cutting himself, but I sort of accidentally encouraged." Hydee filled her friends in on the details of the evening, leaving out the specifics of what Theo had confided in her. An hour later, she was more relaxed, though she kept checking the entry and the stairs, expecting to see Theo wrapped in Ceecee's star quilt, leaning against the wall and listening. Despite the number of times she checked, however, the steps remained empty.

"You going to bed, then?" Lynne asked after a protracted silence, and Hydee heard her smack Adir when he asked which bed Hydee would go to.

"No. I don't think I could sleep now if someone paid and drugged me."

"Well, maybe that's for the best," Lynne said. "Spend some time enjoying the fact that the thing you've most wanted in your life is not only happening, but it's going well. Despite the blood loss."

"You think so?" Hydee whispered.

"He's there, isn't he? He believes enough in you to hear you and to stay under your roof."

"True."

"He could have run screaming down the beach, Hy-Ho."

"It's early, yet. Give it time."

"Give yourself time."

"To do what, exactly?"

"What you always do when you meet the other half of your soul, Hyacinth. You play it by ear until you know the way into his heart."

Hydee's chest constricted, and she rubbed her sternum. "Okay," she said, sounding altogether unsure of herself.

"It'll be all right. He'll likely just sleep tonight, anyway, and if not, we're here. I'm going to have to hit the hay, but Adir assures me that if you need anything at all, you can call him."

Hydee tipped back her head and addressed the ceiling. "If I need a refresher course on sensual massage, I'll be sure to phone ahead."

"Fuck massage, try—"

"Night, Hydee," Lynne said pointedly, cutting off Adir.

"Night." Hydee hung up, tiptoeing to the table by the couch to plug in her phone. Being as quiet as possible, Hydee began to clear the table and clean up the kitchen. She needed to keep herself busy, or she'd wind up sitting outside Theo's door listening to him breathe. She scrubbed counters. She cleaned out the fridge. She took out the garbage and decided the kitchen floors needed a mopping.

After drawing the line at reorganizing the spice cabinet, Hydee grabbed more wine and a glass and set them on the table. It was still early, relatively, and Hydee thought about TV or a movie. When she caught herself thinking she'd have to watch without sound in case she heard something from upstairs, Hydee rolled her eyes and mentally kicked herself.

Honestly, he was only a man.

A troubled, weary, complicated man with eyes like black water at night and a smile that was sweet even when he meant it to be a smirk.

Hydee rubbed her temples. Writing. She should try writing. Scribbling in her journal always made her feel better.

Besides, the journals were upstairs, which gave her a perfect excuse to sneak up the steps, avoiding the one that always creaked, and inch along the second floor's landing. Her grandmother's antique clock ticked from where it sat on a table near a front window, which cast the only light upstairs. Theo's door was shut, and the light was off. Hydee crept by it and dashed into her room, shutting the bedroom door behind her and locking it.

After convincing Adir that digging a grave in the backyard to bury all the Theo evidence was a terrible and time-consuming idea, Adir and Lynne agreed that the best place to hide the Theo Collection was in the attic. The access was in Hydee's bedroom closet. Thankfully, the inconspicuous panel with its slim, white cord looped around a hook was centered in the closet's ceiling, making it simple to pull the panel down and unfold the wooden steps. Adir had even thought to oil all the hinges so nothing creaked as Hydee climbed up three rungs and felt around for the cord that turned on the single bulb. When it came to life, she saw the pile of boxes, frames, file folders, and the crate with the photographs. She stared at the proof of her hope and obsession, and she steadied herself on the ladder.

Standing around and condemning herself about how much she had gathered and knew about Theo wouldn't do anybody any good. She had no reason to be so crippled by guilt. She'd not lied to Theo when he'd asked questions at dinner. She'd not exactly told the truth, but she'd not outright *lied* either.

Besides, if she'd told the complete truth, she'd likely never have had the chance to tell Theo anything ever again. He really would have run screaming for the nearest escape hatch, and Hydee would not have been able to blame him. It clearly took sincere effort and an internal battle for Theo to trust Hydee with what he had managed to say. He was a man hounded by fans and obligation and surrounded by people who didn't care about him, only about what he could do for them. In her heart of hearts, Hydee knew she wasn't like that. She cared for the right reasons, or at the very least wanted to, but her methods up until this juncture were a little…strange.

If she was lucky and Theo stuck around, Hydee would tell him the whole truth someday. Right now the thought of showing Theo the attic was horrifying, but at some point in the distant future, it might become funny. Maybe even endearing.

Give it fifty years and anything was possible, after all.

Hydee sighed and opened the lid on the box of journals. She took out the top one, resealed the container, turned off the light, and climbed down into her closet. She stored the ladder and stood for a full five minutes in her bedroom, waiting for the scene in the movie where the hero, who didn't fully trust the heroine because he couldn't know her true identity yet, would come barreling into the room demanding to know what she was doing.

The house remained completely still. Even the wind had calmed outside, and Hydee didn't hear a thing when she hovered outside Theo's door on her way downstairs. She made it to the table and collapsed into a chair. She drank deeply of the wine and opened her journal. She'd used everything from three-ring binders to composition books to fancy dream journals over the years, but these days she preferred ledgers. It was an oversized, plain, black book with a perfect binding and lined pages. She opened it to the next blank sheet and dated the entry. The other entries were her dreams, told through the eyes of whatever version of herself she had dreamed about, but Hydee couldn't write about meeting Theo as though it'd been a dream. Instead, she started with losing her mind in front of her best friends, and she had written four lines when she heard sounds from upstairs. Hydee dropped her pen and listened.

A dull *thud*, which might have been a large body climbing out of bed. More thuds, maybe somebody getting dressed in the dark. Silence followed by a soft click, which was definitely the door opening; Hydee was so attuned to listening for the kids leaving their room that she knew that noise by heart. That squeak was the board under the runner rug leading from Theo's room to the bathroom. More clicks; another door opening and closing. Hydee reminded herself to blink. Her eyes were so dry she had to dig her knuckles into them and rub to get them to stop burning. There was nothing for at least sixty beats of Hydee's rapid pulse, and then she heard water running through the pipes. Toilet flushing, sink running, and those sounds were followed by another soft click of the bathroom door. Would he come downstairs? Go back to bed? Hydee strained to hear, and her heart plummeted into her guts when she heard several soft knocks.

Theo was knocking on her bedroom door, he had to be, but Hydee wasn't in her bedroom. She was downstairs playing the part of seriously frazzled host with a midnight journal fetish. So she wasn't there to answer him. She wouldn't know what he needed. He could want company. He could be wondering where spare rolls of toilet paper might be. He might need mouthwash. He might need her.

Hydee slammed her journal shut and ran for the stairs. She tripped over her skirt, caught herself on a riser, and kept going. She hugged the banister rail at the top, and she made it in time to see Theo turn away from Hydee's bedroom and flinch in surprise to see her behind him. "Christ," he gasped.

"Sorry," Hydee panted.

"I was just—"

"Did you need—"

They both paused and then both started speaking at the same time again. "Mouthwash is—" Hydee said.

"I couldn't—" Theo began, but he frowned. "Mouthwash?"

"Yeah. I thought you might…need…" Hydee longed for a black hole to open beneath her toes and swallow her into nothingness. She was so tense she was queasy, and she was even more sick of herself. Who the hell was she kidding? She couldn't help this man, much less ever adequately explain that she may or may not have known him for a few thousand years. She could barely form coherent sentences when he was in the same room with her, for fuck's sake. Hydee slumped to the floor and leaned against the railing, knees bent and hands over her face.

"You all right?" Theo asked.

"Sure," Hydee said into her palms.

"I didn't mean to scare you."

"You didn't scare me. I scared you." *Give me half a chance, and I'll terrify and lose you,* Hydee added silently.

"Maybe," Theo said, and Hydee heard him walking over to her. She peeked through her fingers and saw him settling on the rug next to her. He was wearing the linen pants and nothing else. The light from the window above them struck his bare skin and made it glow. "I saw the light on, is all," Theo said.

"Light?" Hydee glanced at her bedroom and saw that she had, indeed, left a lamp on. She couldn't even remember doing that. "Oh. Yeah. I did…yeah."

"You sure you're okay?"

Hydee dropped her hands and heaved a sigh. "Honestly?"

"I hope so?"

"Then no. Not really."

Theo rested his arms on his knees. His hair was standing straight up on one side. "What's wrong?"

"I guess I'm worried," Hydee confessed.

"About?"

"You. Helping you." Hydee took a trembling breath. "I'm worried that I won't be able to…do whatever it is that you think I can do for you."

Theo's gaze danced across Hydee's face for one of the longest moments in Hydee's life. She would have decimated small villages to know what he was thinking, but she waited in silence, almost falling over in relief when he spoke. "Like you said, we've only started." Theo propelled himself closer using his hands, and he leaned on the railing next to her.

"And you've already helped. I was lying in there staring at the top bunk thinking about how you were exactly right about everything you said about my family. Nobody's ever put it to me that way, and it reminded me of this Thanksgiving when my brother came into town."

"Oh?" Hydee admired Theo's profile, the sharp nose and strong chin. Her blood was flowing too fast and too hot in her veins, and her internal organs were tumbling over themselves as though rolling down a hill, but all she wanted was for him to stay close and keep talking.

"More than one, really," Theo mused. "Thanksgiving, I mean. Christmas too, now that I think about it." He shook his head. "My brother, Frank, he used to have this occasional meth habit. He's older than me, and he's never done much with himself. No college, no career. In and out of rehab and clinics and on and off the road doing odd jobs and hitchhiking. It wouldn't be so bad if that made him happy, but he's one of the most miserable sons of bitches I know."

Hydee ached for Theo and his brother, but she didn't dare speak when Theo was working on what he wanted to say next. She'd learned that trick at dinner. Theo glanced at her and stared up and out the window. "When he'd come home for the family gatherings, he'd make scenes. Mother and Father would have all their friends over, the same ones who'd come to the parties, and me? I used to make a game out of seeing if I could tell which woman my father had been fucking. Usually it was the one clinging to her husband and avoiding eye contact with my mother, but not always.

"Anyway, Frank would come loaded for bear and drink until he couldn't stand. He'd end up yelling at them. Sometimes it was accusing them of not giving him money, sometimes it didn't make sense at all, but this one year, I remember, he climbed up on top of this catering table. All these champagne flutes crashed to the floor, and everybody shut up. He announced that he was eight months sober, and it was no thanks to anybody there. He said that he'd finally figured out what was wrong with him, after all those years of working on it, and he pointed right at my mother and said, 'I was born to a loveless hag and a selfish prick. A fuckin' million out of my trust fund if you figure out which one is which.'" Theo laughed softly. "He called them out on the cheating and the games and all of it, said that they never loved each other, much less their kids, and that he's fucked up because he has no idea what love is, thanks to them. They had to call in these big waiters to haul him off the table and out the door, and the whole time, he screamed, 'You never fucking loved anything!'" Too late, Theo seemed to realize he was yelling too, and he hit his head on the wooden rails of the banister, eyes closing.

"Sounds like he was on to something," Hydee said as gently as she could.

"He was," Theo agreed. "Thing is, I didn't think it at the time. I thought he was being a weak-ass douche bag. Everybody else had to suck it up and tolerate their shit. Why couldn't he?"

"And by 'everybody else' you mean…"

"Me." Theo smiled at her grimly. "Yeah. I'd forgotten about it, all those dinners. Or I'd forgotten what he would say. I must have told every shrink about my drug-addicted brother, but I don't think I've talked about why he was so upset or connected it to me in any way. Hell, I don't think about him or talk to him. Last I knew, he was clean and living in New Mexico, but that must have been…five or six years ago? My doctor brought him up the other day when I was at the ER, and then tonight I couldn't get him out of my head."

"The ER?" Hydee asked.

Theo scratched his chin. "Just a place I go to relax."

Hydee laughed and loved it when Theo studied her as though he'd never seen anybody laugh before. "Do you think you should call him?" Hydee asked.

"Frank?"

"Yeah?"

Theo shook his head. "I don't know. Maybe. Mostly I

was thinking about how I did everything to spite him. He let them get to him. He lost his shit, and I didn't want to be like that. I decided I wouldn't let my parents' fuck-ups rule my life, but instead of moving away and becoming, I don't know, something ridiculous in their eyes, like a painter or something, I went exactly where I was expected to go. I became an actor. I threw myself into it thinking I'd prove them and my brother wrong, when really all I was doing was what they wanted me to do."

"Well, it makes sense. You saw where your brother's path took him. He tried to get them to recognize their faults by throwing his in their faces. Brute force didn't work, and you recognized that, so you went the way of least resistance in order to get their approval."

Theo made a face. "Now you sound like the damned shrinks." He leaned away from her. "I don't think what I did was about approval."

"It's always about approval." Hydee sat up and turned toward him. "We always care about somebody, even if it's only ourselves. So there are always standards to meet and ways to fail. In a healthy world, our parents want the best for us and for us to be better than they were. We want to make them happy, so we try to live up to their expectations. But somewhere in there should be acceptance of who the kid *is*, not just what the kid can do, and that no matter what the kid ever *does*, they will always love him."

"I don't know," Theo said, dubious and closing in on himself. "If that's the way it's supposed to go, then they fucked up even more than I thought they could." Theo tried to laugh, but it came out raw and raspy. He had that wild look to his eyes that Hydee had seen at dinner. She was pretty sure it meant he was considering leaping out second-story windows.

"Want to go for a walk?" Hydee asked, mind working overtime.

"What?" Theo asked, taken by surprise.

"A walk. I'm not tired, are you?" Theo shook his head.

"So let's get out of here for a while," Hydee said.

"And go where?"

"I've got a place I go to relax."

"I'm not going to have to face Mecca and chant to Poseidon or something, am I?"

Hydee laughed. "Only if you feel inspired."

Theo frowned and chewed his lip, gaze roving everywhere but her. "All right. Sure. Let me get my shoes."

Wary and distracted, Theo rose and went to the bedroom. Hydee sat on the rug shaking all over for a second or two, and then she climbed to her feet. She thought about Mallory, the woman who had told Hydee about being abused when Mallory was only nine years old. Hydee had been the first person who had ever heard the story, and Hydee had listened and told Mallory that she wasn't alone and there were people who would understand and embrace her. Everyone had pain, and everyone needed help to manage it. After a few talks with Hydee, Mallory had called a therapist and in thanks had painted Hydee the picture of the couple holding hands and walking toward the light.

Hydee traced a vine on the banister railing. Maybe she needed a different perspective on more than the dreams. At the end of the day and in every life, Hydee understood that ultimately the only person who could help someone was the person themselves. Hydee could yell until she was rainbow colored in the face, but if Theo didn't want to listen or try something different, Hydee's enthusiasm would mean exactly jack shit. The same went for everybody, even her. She had been about to give up hope on ever meeting Theo, after all, despite Lynne and Adir saying it was still possible and she needed to find faith.

So, perhaps she was thinking about this helping business all wrong. She could tell he needed something, but the formal Life Coaching nonsense had been Adir's idea that had turned into Theo's excuse to speak to her and had become a ruse that Hydee had continued in order to get Theo into her house. It wasn't exactly her proudest moment, or her most honest. It'd been fueled by the fear she had of what would happen if the two of them didn't make it work this time around. Fear was never a positive motivator. Maybe the reason interacting with Theo once he'd arrived had become so strained was that she was trying too hard out of fear of doing something wrong. Maybe it wasn't about the doing at all. All she'd done for Mallory was exist and listen and encourage. It was all anybody could do for anyone, really, so maybe there was no right or wrong way, no path to helping or path to hurting. Maybe what Theo needed most was to be heard.

Theo came out of the bedroom wearing his shirt and shoes. "Ready."

"Cool." Hydee walked downstairs deep in thought. She found her sandals and grabbed her shawl. "It might be chilly," she warned.

"I'll live," Theo said with a shrug.

"Very well, I hope." Hydee smiled at Theo's surprised expression, and together they walked out the side door.

Chapter Nine

Interlude in Dreams

Hydee's Journal

I'm riding in a carriage, thinking there should be a better way to travel. The long drive is cobblestone and moss and canopied by willows and oak, but my backside is numb from the half-hour trek it took to get to the home of one of my wealthier patients, the Heisenburgs. It's also hot and humid, and I'm sweating beneath my suit, coat, gloves, and hat.

When I'm not eloquently gnashing my teeth over the loose rear wheel and how it hits every crook and cranny, I'm thinking of my mentor, Jon. A contemporary of Pasteur and an avid supporter of his crusade to explain how disease spreads, I am grateful beyond measure for the chance to learn from Jon and to support him and Pasteur's cause, which has lately been championed by the medical facilities in Paris and Vienna. Jon is a harsh man, entirely driven, and the best way to show appreciation and adoration is to do his good works with resolve and without complaint. I served as his apprentice and his student, doing any task he assigned while simultaneously excelling in my coursework. Upon its completion, I took a position in Jon's London office. I served the poorest parts of the city, attempting to instill the ideas of sanitation to those individuals who had not heard of or rather did not believe in its value. I am proud of the minds converted and the lives saved due to Pasteur, my mentor, and, I admit with no small amount of pride, myself.

Two years after my graduation and subsequent employ by Jon's practice, I was transitioned to an office in Bristol. I was given free rein to organize it as I saw fit, and, understanding that Jon's primary concerns were in desperate need of funds derived from other sources beyond private patrons and scholastic interest, I decided to structure the office as a group of outstanding physicians dedicated to attending the needs of Bristol and also of the transient tourist community in Bath. Many doctors in my employ still had the fire of humanitarian pursuits in their veins, a position which I found most admirable and worthy of encouragement, and thus I managed to achieve a balance between funds and outreach. Jon approved wholeheartedly, and I continued the work for another five years, greatly improving Jon's position in London as well as making my own way in the world.

It is my life and my destiny, I feel, being a doctor and a learned man, and it is a life I am considering giving up entirely as I travel through the entry gardens of the Heisenburg estate. I have reason to believe I am a fraud and possibly an evil individual, and as the carriage blessedly comes to a halt in front of the grand entrance, I am weary and longing for a stiff drink or even a draught of ether.

My driver opens the carriage door, and I gather my charm and my wits. I stride to the estate's door and am greeted by a servant who is followed closely by Madam Heisenburg, an attractive woman in a deep blue dress that manages modesty and fashion without strain.

"Doctor," Madam Heisenburg says. "Thank you for coming to us so quickly."

I take her hand and notice the drawn expression that tires her eyes and pulls at the corners of her mouth. I feel a brief stint of hope that she may care more for her daughter than for the embarrassment of having to call for a physician yet again. "While it is a delight to see you, madam, I feel I should attend the patient as soon as possible."

"Of course," Madam agrees, turning and gathering her skirts to ascend to the second floor of the estate. A host of servants follow in our wake, which I feel is rather dramatic but also entirely for Madam's benefit. "She is faring better today."

"You say she collapsed?" I ask.

"We were in the garden waiting on guests to arrive for a luncheon. All very mundane, I assure you. I know better than anyone that Grace's health has never been adequate or able to survive strenuous social activities." Madam is clearly saddened by this, and my hope for her appropriate concern for her daughter fades like a candle snuffed. "She is so unlike her sisters."

I barely listen, having heard this woman chatter on in every way possible that Grace Heisenburg is unfit for the family, a nuisance due to her ill health, which I believe their former physician worsened by his archaic beliefs and rough treatment. I have heard from Madam, in the most indirect terms, how wretched it is that Grace is so weak that the idea of marriage and the ensuing pregnancies are not viable options. She is the last unmarried daughter, a position that should be doted upon and cared for, considering her health, but has instead turned Grace into a pariah in her own home. Even in the mid-nineteenth century one finds such backward thinking lurking in the corners of great halls and crumbling homes.

It is in these moments that I wish to strangle Madam with my bare hands and demonstrate the weakness of all neck bones, even the ones not being trampled by high society's old-fashioned bootheels.

"I've had her girl in with her most of the night and morning," Madam tells me when we pause in front of Grace's gothic doorway. "They tell me there was quite a bit of…residue post her collapse."

Madam means blood, and I can do nothing but nod and flee into the unpretentious safety of Grace's chambers, which are dim, though thankfully open to the fresh country air. I have no doubt that Grace's mother believes this spell to be a misfortune of monthly cycle; a further sign of an ill-behaving body and not an omen of anything more dire. For this naïveté, I am also grateful.

I nod to the girl sitting near the foot of Grace's bed, and the girl smiles at me. She curtsies with what I know is real relief to see me. The girl and I have an understanding, and she leaves us alone together. I stand transfixed by the tiny figure Grace makes beneath the bedclothes. She is a tall girl, and slender with illness and, I believe, with bearing too much of the weight of her family and the world at large upon her narrow shoulders. Her hair is long and brown with hints of auburn in its curls, and when she opens her eyes, they are deep brown, wide and sweet.

"Philip," Grace says with a weak smile. "They sent for you."

I come round to her bedside and forgo the chair, choosing to sit next to her instead. I take her hand, and it is here in the dream that a kind of dizziness overcomes me. I know both as the dreamer and the man in the dream that I am myself—a woman and female soul—in a man's body, and I know that he—Grace, the girl in the bed—is in a similar predicament, only inverted. It is one of the few dreams where I feel very much like myself—like Hyacinth—instead of whomever it is I'm dreaming about. I also know him, despite the body, and it's the eyes. It's always the eyes. As both the dreamer and as the doctor in the lifetime, I think about eyes and windows and souls, about God and destiny and cruel twists of fate, and I want to tell him—her—that it is a mean joke, what this life has done to her and to me. This is one of my favorite lifetimes to dream about, because the eloquence and language I use to think about duality is so perfect and poetic. I can barely duplicate it in these pages, not matter how many times I try, but I see my soul mate as a beautiful entity trapped in a body weakened by circumstance, and I see myself as his and her savior. I feel unworthy of this, as though I have no right and no business to presume that I could help her in any way, and I am terrified of making her situation worse for my interference.

I sit on the bed in that dim room which smells of

French perfume and sweat and the lilacs in the spring garden, and I hold my beloved's hand and want to die of shame and fear. All the dreams, the analysis, the education, and all the experience in the universe could not make me worthy of such a fragile creature, and I want to weep and to kiss her, to take her in my arms and hold and protect her, but I feel even that is beyond my reach, because my restraint in such situations has proven to be weak. I am human, and I am a man, and I am horribly and miserably and ultimately in love. There is only her, there has always only been her, and I wish there to be none other. It is one of the few lifetimes in which I am sincerely grateful for all my memories, as they are all I have.

Much as my current lifetime seems to be.

"How do you feel?" I ask Grace.

"Tired." She smiles and shakes her head. "Tired and relieved."

I hesitate but bring her hand to my face. I shut my eyes and despise myself. "I am...I am ashamed and so terribly sorry, Grace. I do not know what came over me, and I am racked with guilt over how I left you last we met." I recall with vivid clarity the expression on Grace's face when she tells me she's called for me because she has news for my ears alone. At first I think, foolishly, that she wishes for a repeat performance of what happened the prior time we were together and alone, but her wan smile makes such base thoughts vanish. When she tells me she has missed a cycle, I am quick to tell her that such events happen with someone as frail as she is. But upon my examination of her, I realize what we have done; what we have made together in a moment of weakness. "There is no excuse for my actions. Please forgive—"

"Hush," she says. "Help me."

I assist her in arranging pillows so she can sit upright. She winces and holds her abdomen. "I should examine you," I say grimly.

"In time. I have news that should come first."

"News?" I ask.

She laughs at me. "Have heart, Philip. It is good news, this time, which I believe you will enjoy hearing."

I ease somewhat. "Then tell me."

"The recent discussion of my engagement to a certain gentleman not of my desire has ended." Her smile is broader now. "I used my temporary and illicit delicate situation to my full advantage. When faced with meeting the family of the man Mother hoped I would charm, I claimed I had been sick with displeasure over the prospect. A bit dramatic, perhaps, but Mother and my sister Aubrey have always been so fascinated by the notion of signs and portents that when I claimed I had a dream that showed my disastrous fate if the match should be made, they nearly dropped their tea." Grace giggles. "And then, out of fantastic fortune, my body picked that very moment to betray me, leaving me in a pile of soiled silk and sickly flesh."

"Good God," I cannot help but say, though I am entranced by her cunning and clear happiness over how the event unfolded.

"He is not merely good, but great." She covers our joined hands with her free one. "My family are all imbeciles, and we both know it to be true. I would have died had my former doctor not fallen ill and you come into my life. Your teachings and applications have strengthened me more than the prior ten years under that idiot's so-called care, and I am not the only one to notice. I have made the point more than once to my girl and to Mother, not to mention Aubrey and Patience. Over the last six months that you have attended me, I have been clear and repetitious when discussing the fact that your existence has strengthened my own."

"But also weakened," I interject, unable to help myself. "What happened... It was inexcusable."

Grace glares at me without restraint, and when she leans toward me to steal a kiss, it is equally unchecked. Again I am caught in a bizarre duality: I kiss her as Philip, the male physician, but also as myself, Hydee, the feminine soul, and

Philip believes it to be perilous and wrong but also genuinely right. All of me believes that being with him—the man trapped in Grace's body—is forevermore meant to be, no matter how it is accomplished.

"It was inevitable," Grace says. "I feel safe with you. I…I desire you, as I have desired none other. In truth, it was I who was the aggressor, though few but ourselves would believe such a thing." Her eyes twinkle despite the low light. "Me, the sickly weakling, the runt of the household, taking advantage of the strapping young doctor? It is a plot directly from one of the illicit novels my sister Patience loves to sneak past her husband in the post."

"I am not so modern as to believe that to be entirely true," I say. "As your doctor and as a man, I should never have allowed my baser instinct to overcome me in such a manner. Especially in the light of all I know of your condition." I shake my head, thoroughly ashamed in ways I cannot fathom, much less explain. "It was unconscionable, what went on, and it will not and cannot happen again."

"Unless we were to marry."

My spine straightens, and my mouth is dry. "But your family…"

"Is desperate to be rid of me."

"Your sisters all married—"

"Very well, indeed, and will keep my mother happy and my father suitably connected to the rising iron and oil interests growing here and abroad."

I still struggle with the concept, despite her unshakable resolve. "I am but a physician…"

"Which is one of the leading arenas of discovery and social interest, to say nothing of the kind of person who will champion men and women alike and allow us to lead fuller and longer lives free of disease."

My argument is weakening by the second, and I flounder for further excuses. "I am older than you by some years."

"And more stubborn by half, but if I can convince my

mother and sisters that all parties will be better served by our nuptials, then I have faith in my ability to convince you that being wed to me will not be such a chore."

"Grace," I say more sharply than I intend, but she is not affronted. A silence lingers between us until at last I speak. "I am unworthy of you, of this, in ways I do not know if I can properly describe. You do not know what is in my head every night, and I fear that if you did..."

She is unperturbed. "I know what is in your heart, my Physician Philip." She places a small hand to my breastbone. "Marriage will give me the rest of our lives to learn what is in your head and how to relieve you of any guilt over what I am sure are trivial concerns."

My dreams, my suspicions as to the nature of our souls, and my unchecked need of her are far from trivial. "I worry for your person, Grace. One encounter and it finds you with..." I have difficulty saying it. "With child." I cover my mouth, as the enormity of what we did and what we both have lost makes me weak. "I cannot... I do not want to..."

She shushes me, coming closer to hold me loosely in her arms. "I have been remiss in that I've not told you of my tears. I do not want you thinking I am a conniving, heartless beast who loses such gifts without considering their consequence. I have wept, Philip, and I grieve, but I have grieved all my life for my lack of normalcy. I am different. Too forward, too brazen, too masculine, but also too weak, too twisted, and too broken. I have been shamed, and I have been shunned. My mother does not know how I am her child, a daughter of hers, when I have ideas of traitorous individuality that undermine all she is and all she fears women will become. I cried for myself, for my mother's reaction to my sudden illness, and for the child I could not carry, much less birth and prepare for the coming age.

"When I woke in my bed and heard they had sent for you, it was as though a veil drew away from my eyes and hope grew again inside me. The only time I feel whole is when I am with you, no matter what it is we do or how we happen to meet. I feel I know you, and I do not fear your mind or what lurks there. Nor do I fear your body and what it might do to mine." Grace chuckles. "I rather enjoyed what it managed, as did you, if I recall."

I blush, and I am reminded that in some ways, I am not so different from her family. I am capable of being shocked, and Grace seems to know exactly how to gain a rise from me. A fact we revisit as she continues. "Besides," she says, "if there is anyone who could discover a way for us to be together as husband and wife without any lasting ill effects, I am confident it is you, Philip." She whispers then, in my ear. "I remember your hands being as skilled with pleasurable intent as they are with medical endeavors."

Struck by her bravery and bravado, I catch her face in my hands. I know then, as the dreamer and as Philip and a soul entwined with Grace's—with his—that he is braver than I am in so many ways. I am granted the boon of dreams. He braves the idea of togetherness without guide or map or memory. His existence is always a leap of faith. It is my job to show him the cliff, the surging wind, and the safe harbor he will find with me, who is lucky enough to be his counterpart. I may struggle to be worthy, but he struggles to find the courage to seek out me and the idea of us.

I love him. I love her. I kiss Grace, and in her ear, I whisper a single word.

That word is "Yes."

Chapter Ten

Theo shoved his hands in his pockets and listened to the crunch of gravel and sand beneath their shoes. It was a light night, the moon above them nearly full, and while it was brisk, Theo wasn't cold. He was too preoccupied with counting every time Hydee's arm brushed his to bother feeling chilly.

They walked together in the eerie quiet. The main road's noise had faded behind them as they had trekked across unpaved side roads that wound their way through a historic village. There were signs for a country club and bridge ahead, and there were larger signs with brightly painted arrows leading them toward a lighthouse. Hydee appeared to be following those. Theo matched his stride to hers, and when Hydee let go of her shawl with her left hand so it hung to her side, Theo took her hand. Without a word, they laced their fingers together and kept going.

With every step, Theo focused less on how much or how little anxiety he felt and more on the shape of Hydee's nose, the curve of her lower lip, and the way her hair was always in motion. Back at the house, he'd dozed for a while, but mostly he'd lain there thinking how absurd it was to feel so safe in a stranger's home. He'd never given much thought to safety, mental or physical. He'd grown up in a wealthy neighborhood, had attended good schools, and he'd always been in the presence of nannies or servants. He'd not been bullied, and he'd spent most of high school with tutors, not testosterone-laden classmates. His friends had been the kids of his parents' friends, and they'd all been like him: confused, lost, angry, and more than willing to distract themselves with anything available.

Until Hydee had mentioned it over dinner, Theo had never considered the people around him as safe or unsafe.

Nobody had been trying to hit or kill him, so he'd always thought he was okay. But in that bunk bed, Theo had realized that the real reason he'd wanted to stay the night had more to do with safety of the emotional kind. He wasn't that drunk. The drive wasn't that long. He wasn't angling to get Hydee into bed. There was nothing he wanted here, other than more of the peace he'd found when he'd crossed the threshold.

When they'd left on their walk, Theo had expected to be flooded with dread, but the lulling spell that had made Theo relax on his initial drive to her house and that made him want to tell Hydee about his father and about his hatred of overcooked green beans and about how his favorite nanny smelled like tangerines, hadn't vanished once they were outside the house. Which, of course, meant that the feeling of safety was coming from Hydee. She infused it into her home, put it into the very food she made, and exuded it with every glance, every step, every nervous gesture. Theo had no idea how someone who was clearly struggling so hard to do the right thing made Theo feel so restful, but it was a magic Theo was loath to leave. She cared—about Theo, about everybody, probably—and caring that didn't come with a human sacrifice was beyond rare.

Theo still wasn't sure if the caring and sense of calm were why he wanted her. Well, okay, that and the curves and the smile and the eyes. Figuring out where his head was might have been easier if it was a purely physical attraction. It might be a sign that he'd had one too many shrinks in his life, but he didn't much like the idea of Hydee being safe and therefore desirable only because of that trait. It was logical and yet left a bad taste in his mouth. Was liking Hydee for the way she made him feel an abuse of her and of power or the way affection was supposed to work? There were all those variations of that line in all those damned movies: "She makes me want to be a better man." Theo wasn't sure if that was what was going on here or if it was merely gratitude that somebody gave enough of a shit to ask the right questions.

"So if you only became an actor because that's what was expected of you, then what did you actually want to be?"

Theo almost laughed. Good timing had nothing on Hydee. "I don't know."

"Oh come on," Hydee said. "You're a little boy, it's a good day, and you're thinking about what you want to be when you grow up. What was in your head?"

"Probably nothing," Theo said, and Hydee deliberately bumped into him. "I was a slow kid, what can I say?"

"Well, what about what you said at dinner? Being a painter to spite them?"

Theo snorted. "That was only for example."

"Do you paint?"

"Anyone ever mentioned that you're relentless?"

Once again, Theo was concerned he'd been too blunt, but Hydee laughed, loud and full. "Maybe once or twice." She threw Theo a look that cut completely through his bullshit and studied his innermost parts. "It's helped more than it's hurt me." She shook his arm. "Now come on. Answer me?"

"I'm thinking, I'm thinking." They turned left onto a wider gravel road that transformed into a paved pathway marked by more arrows. Ahead of them, Theo saw the lighthouse shooting high above a canopy of trees. Clouds rolled past it and the moonlight struck the brick, casting shadows and creating highlights. It'd been more than a decade since Theo had tried to take the images out of his mind and put them onto paper. The hobby had fallen by the wayside when he'd started to deal with the anxiety. Suddenly anything he tried to do wasn't good enough for his inner critic, and though he'd disappointed his mentors, who claimed he had promise, he'd stored the brushes and taken up crossword puzzles.

Now Theo envisioned what it'd be like to snap a picture of the lighthouse on his phone and how he'd put it on canvas. The image of himself as a boy with finger paints was so clear, it was as though they walked past him along the side of the street. The vision of himself as a young man in his early twenties asking his mentor questions was equally as real. He could smell oil and thinner, and he could feel the way the brush would slide over stretched linen. "A little," Theo finally admitted. "I used to paint a little. Where are we?"

"Currituck Lighthouse," Hydee replied leading him to a sidewalk that looped around a courtyard dotted with historic buildings and at least one home with a PRIVATE PROPERTY sign staked in front of it. "Don't worry; the caretakers know me. I sometimes walk over here and sit when all the tourists have gone back to their condos and hotels." She pointed across the manicured lawn and its landscaped beds. "My favorite bench is over there. Come on."

They wandered around the circle and came to a stop at a bench set off the path in the grass. In the daytime, it'd be in the shade of two tall trees, and as they sat, he could see the lighthouse, the flowers, and the closed, darkened tourist shop with its wide front porch and rocking chairs. "It's a good place to think," Hydee said, settling and hugging her shawl around her shoulders. She'd taken off her belt at some point, and the blouse was loose over her skirt. She looked comfortable and at ease. It was infectious. Theo sat beside her, one arm resting on the back of the bench behind Hydee.

"The whole of the Outer Banks is good for thinking."

"I've always thought so, yeah," Hydee agreed. "How long are you here?"

"I've got the house rented for a few weeks, but"— Theo shrugged—"I don't have any definite plans."

"Good," Hydee pronounced. "Give yourself time to figure out where you're going next." Her expression grew sly. "Like to the art supply store with me tomorrow."

Theo tensed, ill at ease. "I don't know if that's a good idea."

"Why not?"

"Because," Theo said slowly, stalling while he tried to figure out a way to tell Hydee he wasn't sure if he'd be able to leave the house tomorrow. Doing as much as he had today with as little medication as he'd ingested was a series of miracles. The familiar constriction around his heart returned. He missed his pills. "I might be recognized."

"We'll put you in some of Adir's clothes. You'd never wear them. Those and a hat with that beard, I don't think anybody would see Theo Monk. We'll go inland too, so that people won't recognize me either. Or I could not go at all," she added quickly. "I was thinking of offering you company, but if you want to go yourself…"

Theo had to order his jaw to unclench. "Hydee…"

"What is it?" she asked gently, moving closer on the bench. "What's—"

Hydee jerked a look over her shoulder, and Theo followed her gaze. When he heard a series of sounds—crunching, scraping—he thought he'd climb over the back of the bench and make a break for it. It took every ounce of control Theo had to stay put. "Did you hear—"

A warm hand covered Theo's mouth, and surprise kicked his anxiety in the nuts. Hydee was so close he could smell soap and sweat and vanilla. Hydee extended a finger toward one of the sheds that had, if Theo was reading the sign correctly at this distance, once been the lighthouse keeper's home. Theo squinted, struggling to make sense of the shadows. A tall, broad shadow dipped lower, and a fainter, thin shadow spread across the shed's wall. Soon enough, Theo recognized a moan followed by the *thud* of a body against the boards.

"Caretaker," Hydee murmured. A woman's gasp and laugh reached Theo's ears. "Don't know who she is," Hydee added.

Not ten seconds earlier, Theo had been ready to vacate his skin, but Hydee's simple touch had sent his panic scrambling to its deep, dark corner. It was the distraction aspect, had to be, much like the crosswords made him think and long drives helped him unwind. He slowly exhaled into Hydee's palm, and she turned toward him. Her eyes were wide, and she caught her breath. With a brief frown, she mouthed *sorry* and started to withdraw.

Theo swiftly brought his hand up to cover Hydee's so they both rested on his cheek. Hydee's eyes got impossibly bigger, and her tongue darted to wet her lips. Theo could do nothing but stare at her, fascinated and searching her face as though answers were buried beneath the soft planes of her cheeks or hidden in the sweep of her eyelashes.

There was something about this woman. Just this one. Only her. He had no idea why she was different, couldn't decide if it was right or wrong, impulse or strategy, good or bad. Two things, however, were certain: he wanted more, and he wasn't the one who made the first move.

Hydee kissed him. A brief brush of lips to lips, and it was over, but a kiss it was, nonetheless. Hydee looked thoroughly stunned, as if she hadn't known she was going to do that either, and even in the dim light, Theo saw her blush. Theo's heart thudded strong and steady, if faster than normal, and time slowed. Hydee covered her mouth and ducked her chin. "God, Theo, I'm—" she began, but when Theo kissed her forehead, she stopped. He put his lips to the bridge of her nose, gentle and light as though she were breakable. When he reached her mouth, though, he wrapped an arm around her and pulled her toward him as though she was life's necessity. In that instant, for him, she absolutely was. Hydee gasped, and Theo made a quiet sound, encouraging and satisfied. Hydee grabbed his shoulder, and he sank fingers into her thick hair. Soft, she was so soft; her hair was silken, wound around his fingers, her skin was smooth beneath his mouth, her body was malleable to his arms' direction, and Theo didn't remember moving from her mouth to her neck and ear, but her shudder and breathy sounds woke him from his daze.

They stayed like that, as though someone had hit the Pause button: Theo, with his lips grazing the baby-soft,

damp hair behind Hydee's ear, and Hydee with one fist
bunching his shirt and a leg hooked across his thigh. Theo
nosed Hydee's throat. "Should I stop?" he asked.

Hydee swallowed. "No."

Theo felt her muscles tense under his hands, and he
leaned back against the bench while Hydee straddled his lap
so she faced him. She darted down to his mouth, sucking at
his lower lip with a soft, soft moan. When she grazed his
mouth with her teeth, a spark of current shot down Theo's
spine to his groin. He pushed one hand up her shirt to span
between her shoulder blades, urging her down and closer.
He was hard and getting harder, and he rocked against her.
Hydee made a sound trapped somewhere between a cry and
a growl. Theo panted, not sure if he'd ever heard anything so
honest and sensual in his life. He stared into her wild eyes,
decided he needed her to make that noise again, and he
shoved his other hand up her skirt. As he traced the bend of
her knee and the muscular swell of her thigh, Hydee's kisses
grew urgent and deeper, their tongues rubbing against one
another. Theo stayed on the outside of Hydee's leg, reaching
to cup and grip one perfectly shaped ass cheek. The give of
it pulled a groan out of his lungs. Theo squeezed and rocked
against her with enough force that a warning rang in his head
about hurting her, but Hydee tore away from his mouth to
speak in his ear.

"Touch me," Hydee ordered, huskily and with
demand dripping from her words.

Theo didn't need to be told twice. He followed the
line of her panties around and between her legs. She was
scorching and wet beneath the fabric, and Theo cursed
under his breath as he shoved her underwear out of the way.
He cupped all of her with his palm, fumbling for a better
angle, and Hydee shifted up and to one side. "Oh God," she
gasped in a hushed whisper as he dragged fingers over her to
slick them. He grunted with the desire to be inside her, but it
was trumped by the urge to get her off like this, with her

over him and pressed to him and trembling from his exploring touch.

Hydee's hips rolled. "In me, in me," she whisper-chanted. When Theo complied, sinking two fingers into her, Hydee clutched the bench and attacked his throat with kisses to muffle her hitching groan. She moved herself on his hand, and he caught the rhythm, matching it. "God, Theo, yes." Hydee hissed the word, and Theo stroked his thumb over her clit. Her movement ceased to be strictly up and down and started to circle, and Theo took over with his thumb, keeping the pace she set and letting her sink to find the pressure she needed.

Theo turned to repay favors to Hydee's throat, holding her where he wanted her by the hair. "Move for me," he breathed.

"Mmph." Hydee's sharp exhale was through her nose, and then she held her breath. Theo tugged Hydee closer, experimentally tightening his hand against her scalp by fractions of degrees. Hydee's cry was small and frantic.

"Like that?" Theo murmured, wanting her to enjoy it. Needing her to. He throbbed hot and protectively aggressive from head to toe, and he worked his thumb faster. Hydee called out unchecked, and he kept moving exactly…like…that, as Hydee shook and flexed around his fingers. She was slippery and warm and snug, and Theo knew he'd never get enough.

"Close?" Theo asked, and Hydee's answer was a soft, inarticulate sound of need. "Come on, sweetheart," Theo said tenderly. "Do this all night if you need it. Won't stop till you want me to. "

Hydee raked a hand through Theo's hair, gripping it. Her breath reached a frenetic, broken pace, and Theo crooked his fingers on their next plunge inside her. Hydee froze, Theo made sure he moved with that rhythm, that pressure, that depth, and Theo held his breath with her. He kissed and sucked at her skin, practically willing her pleasure, and Hydee buried her face against his shoulder. She was silent when her body began to flex around his fingers in a telling, pulsing rhythm, and when she remembered to breathe, she whispered, "Oh God, oh fuck," over and over in time to her body's clenches.

When Hydee shakily sighed, Theo slowed and slipped out of her. He was so aroused he could barely remember his name. He loosened his grip in her hair and wrapped both arms around her. He could feel sweat cooling on his forehead, and he thought he could stay exactly like this all night.

Finally Hydee pulled at the resistance of his arms, and he let her sit up. Her hair framed her face, and her teeth gleamed when she smiled. "Your turn," she said, sliding off his lap and taking his hand. "Come on."

Chapter Eleven

The walk out of the lighthouse garden was a blur. Hydee was with Theo—her Theo. She had his hand in hers. She could still feel his fingers inside her and his mouth on her lips and her neck and whispering in her ear. A million dreams didn't add up to this reality. The elation consumed her, swallowed her whole until she couldn't remember ever feeling this good. She was so sure she would wake up soon that she broke into a jog once they reached the gravel road heading toward the bookstore. Theo didn't complain. He huffed a laugh and kept up, and that made her run faster. He chased her, caught her, and spun her around, kissing her more breathless than she already was. His eyes danced when he pulled away. He was so full of life, full of the kind of focus that made her squirm and her body tighten in anticipation. She playfully licked the tip of his nose before breaking free and making a mad dash toward the house. She was five and glorying in the thrill of getting chased by a boy on the playground. She was fifteen again, running away from the school group taking a field trip so she could kiss Michael Wesson in the woods. Michael had looked like a young Theo, and now Hydee had the man himself pounding up the porch steps, hot on her heels. Hydee's hand shook getting the door open, and she didn't turn around until she stood in the middle of the living room.

Theo stood by the door, breathing fast through an openmouthed half smile. He shut the door with a deliberate push of his hand. He threw the lock and advanced upon her. Intent on staring at Theo, sweaty and eager, Hydee retreated, trying to memorize the image. She rounded the corner of the entryway, and Theo caught up to her. He smelled like sex and night air. His breath carried a hint of stale wine and faded toothpaste. Hydee could barely think and didn't want to blink. He'd vanish. This would end. It'd be over.

"Hydee?" Theo murmured, but when he reached for her, Hydee grabbed him by the shirt and waistband and yanked. She turned them, not knowing what she intended to do until his back met the wall by the front door. His arm knocked a coat off the rack, and an umbrella went toppling to the floor with a clatter. Hydee watched Theo watching her, and she undid the button fly on his linen pants. She peeled it back, revealing dark blue underwear, and Theo grabbed his own shirttail and pulled off his shirt. He slowly lowered his arms, letting the shirt slip from his fingers, and still they stared at one another. Theo's chest rose and fell, a sheen of sweat on his warm skin. Dark brown curls salted with a sprinkle of white spread from his breastbone and shot downward in a perfect highlight of abdominal contours. When he lifted his hands again, Hydee watched the tendons and muscles at the front of his shoulders shift under his skin. It took multiple commands from her brain to make her body obey and move, and she leaned forward to kiss his collarbone. She licked a line to his shoulder, smeared her mouth over the smooth curve of it, and drew away with one finger touching his chest.

"Don't move," she whispered. Theo froze in place. His fingers dragged along her shirt as Hydee stepped backward. He didn't lower his arms as Hydee stepped out of her skirt and started unbuttoning her shirt. All she could think was that he was here, really here. They were doing this. She could kiss him. Hold him. Touch him. She fought a brief battle within herself. One side wanted to grab him and drag him to the floor, make it fast, dirty, practically brutal. The other side wanted to take time, caress the body she'd been admiring for most of her life, get to know him, feel him, and see if the tricks that made the Theo in her dreams turn into a feral creature also worked on this version of him.

The side begging for experimentation in the name of orgasmic satisfaction won. Leaving her shirt on but undone,

Hydee pressed close to Theo. He sighed at her, the breath tinged with relief and want, and he loosely held her. She cupped him through his underwear, and he mashed his lips together to stifle a soft grunt. He tried to kiss her, but she stayed out of range, feeling along his hardening shaft and learning its width and length. His eyelids lowered to half-mast, and he wadded a handful of her shirt in a fist.

"So hard for me," Hydee observed, and he nodded soundlessly, his forehead touching hers. Hydee shoved her other hand lower, covering his balls, and Theo's low moan sent rippling shivers through Hydee's insides. When she stroked him with a shift of fabric, Theo darted forward like a snake striking. He trapped her lower lip with both of his, sucking at it, and Hydee closed her eyes for the long lashing of tongues and mingling of quickening breaths.

Memory beat in time to Hydee's rapid pulse. She saw what he liked and what turned him on, and she desperately wanted him that way. "Put your hands behind your head." She spoke against his chin and made sure her voice was soft and the demand gentle, but she did not say please. Theo's eyes widened, and he tilted his head at her, curious, but he lifted his arms and did as she asked.

Hydee hummed in approval. She kissed along his jaw, brushing against the grain of scratchy stubble. She moved to his ear, and he dipped his chin to give her more access. Heat poured off Theo's body and mingled with Hydee's. His breath stuttered when she traced the shell of his ear with her tongue. All the while, she continued stroking his cock through the cotton, shivering when the fabric stretched over the tip grew damp. She kissed down his throat. She lingered at his pulse, sucking at the skin, and the muscles in his arms jumped. She moved south, mouthing his chest until she reached his nipple. She bit at it before licking along his ribs.

"Ah…" Theo's exhale carried the syllable of want, and he rocked his hips toward her. He drew in breath to say something, maybe ask what she was doing, but Hydee rose and nipped at the tender skin on the underside of his raised arm. Theo was usually ticklish, but so long as she kept the pressure firm, he typically loved being kissed, bitten, and marked there. A mixture of nerves and greed urged Hydee onward, and she sucked at Theo's skin, gently using teeth and savoring the taste and the tense-flex of his body.

As Hydee explored, Theo grew more and more rigid. His hands made fists where they rested on the wall above his head. When she lazily returned to his nipple, sucking at it, Theo let out an explosive breath. Goose bumps marched across Theo's skin. "Holy shit," he muttered in a husky whisper while Hydee moved to do the other nipple before paying attention to the other underarm. "*Ungh*," Theo grunted, and Hydee stopped stroking his balls so she could trace her mouth's path with one hand while she dragged teeth over his triceps.

Theo chuckled throatily and spoke like a man lost in his cups. "How do you even… How are you doing that? No one ever does…"

"Does what, this?" Hydee grabbed Theo's wrists and pinned them. She kissed Theo like she wanted them both to drown. Then she dragged her touch and her body down his until she knelt before him. She looked up at him and kissed next to his navel with a tenderness at odds with the wrench she gave the fabric of his pants, drawing them lower. Hydee traced Theo through his underwear with the tip of her tongue, and she felt the length of him jerk in anticipation.

"Yeah," Theo said. "Oh yeah."

"Want it?" she asked, mouthing him.

"Fuck, yes." Theo's smile was dazed, and he stayed still while Hydee explored every inch of him within reach of her mouth or hands. Finally Theo shook his head. "You're killing me here."

When he began to lower his arms, Hydee stood. She tugged him away from the wall by the open fly with their mouths locked on one another's. His hands were everywhere, searing her wherever they touched, and Hydee's heartbeat pounded in her ears to the rhythm of *want him, want him*. They spun in an unsteady circle, each of them trying to start up the stairs, and Hydee heard the *thump* of Theo's heel against a stair riser the instant before he started to fall. Hydee lunged for him, laughing, but Theo caught himself with his hands. He sat hard on one step with his arms and legs sprawled across the others, and Hydee lowered herself on top of him. She put one arm on either side of his head and a knee between his spread legs. They kissed and ground against one another. Hydee wasn't aware of Theo undoing her bra's clasp until it came undone, and he slid to a lower step to make angles work. His hands and mouth were on her breasts in quick succession, and Hydee didn't know who sighed, who moaned, or how long they stayed like that, Theo tasting her and Hydee fisting Theo's hair, encouraging him closer.

Time wavered, and over and over Hydee remembered this was Theo in her arms, under her on the stairs, pulling her closer and groaning from what she was doing to him, with him, for him. Hydee grew dizzy and feverish. Sweat broke across her forehead and along her spine, and white noise punctuated by breath and sighs filled her mind. She heard her own soft cry when he brushed her nipples again and again in exactly the way that trapped her in a sensation of too much and too little. When he shifted to kiss beneath the swell of her breast, Hydee reached between them and freed him from his underwear. Theo braced an arm across Hydee's back and used the other hand to help her get him undressed, kicking and squirming until his clothing pooled around one ankle. Hydee grasped his cock, and Theo's hold on her tightened.

"Mmph, yeah." Theo strained his neck to meet Hydee for a kiss. "God, yeah," he said against her lips. His lower body rolled, urging Hydee faster, and he was reaching between her legs when she broke off and knelt between his spread knees. The need to pleasure him was tangled up in years of unrequited desire and lifetimes of taking care of him so he could take care of her so the cycle could continue forever. She felt as she often did in her dreams, as though she occupied many timelines at once, and she moaned with disorientation and from the first taste of him on her tongue. She lapped up the underside, flicking her tongue beneath the head, and Theo trapped a sound of pure need behind his teeth. He hiss-sigh-moaned when she covered him with a tight seal of lips and suction, and Hydee's universe narrowed to slickening slides, up and down and up and down, with a twisting stroke of her hand always following her lips' retreat.

"Oh. My. God." Theo groaned, voice loud and clear in Hydee's ears. He squeezed her arm and clasped her hair in his hand, but then abruptly let go. He flailed at the wall and found the banister, gripping it with violence that made the wood creak. The other palm landed on the stairs and clung to an edge. "Fuh… Hy…" Theo swallowed around his rushed breathing. "That's… Oh fuck. Good…"

Hydee hummed, a thrill dancing through her body and setting off sparks of triumph. She listened to his gritty snarls, and she stayed with the rhythm and pattern until Theo's thighs shook. She came off him to duck lower, licking his balls, and Theo's moan rattled off the walls. He spread his legs even wider, and he shifted to the edge of the stair so she could get to any and all of him she wanted. His ass clenched, knocking his cock against his belly, and when Hydee licked upward again, she tasted precum with a greedy little suck to the head.

Theo's spine arched. "Shit. Christ… *mmph*…"

Hydee threw herself into a personal challenge to take all of him into her throat with each downward glide. Theo's upper body twisted every single time she succeeded, and Hydee rewarded the reactions by petting his tightening balls with the backs of her fingers.

"Oh…*nnnah*… I'm close," Theo panted in warning after long moments lost in the give and take of physical bliss. Hydee gripped the underside of Theo's leg, and once again, she was pulled across lives and time. She was in a featherbed with him sliding into her mouth. She was in a cave on top of him, straddling his face, their mouths trading favors. She was on a throne telling him how to touch himself.

He came free of her mouth with a wet sound, and Theo's inarticulate noises became punctuated with question marks. Hydee rolled her eyes to meet his, and she put two fingers in her mouth, wetting them. His eyebrows danced, and he reached for her, caressing her breast. He didn't just stare at her; he drank in every detail. He pursed his lips, a frown marring his face, but Hydee didn't pause to explain.

Still looking at him, Hydee lowered her mouth to him again, licking a tease around the crown while she steadied him at the base. With her other hand she cupped his balls and sought behind them. The light of understanding didn't glimmer in Theo's eyes until her plan was already underway. Hydee petted the ring of muscle in light circles before breaching it with care.

"Wha…?" Theo sat up and curled in on himself. He clapped a hand on her arm with a bruising grip. His eyes were screwed shut, and he shook like a leaf.

"Breathe," Hydee intoned, and Theo gasped for air. His body gave, and Hydee let it tug and invite her fingers deeper into hot, flexing warmth.

"Ah, nah, wha…" Theo gasped in rapid fire. He shook his head, and he slowly lowered himself backward and onto the steps. "What are you doing?" The question was almost a sleepy afterthought, as though he knew the answer but had to ask anyway.

"I'm getting you off," Hydee replied. She bent to him again, sliding over him and swallowing all of him while her fingers pressed and beckoned inside him.

"Holy…fucking…sh-*shit!*" Theo's knuckles banged on the banister before he found his grip on it again, and Hydee's knuckles met Theo's body. She came up for air and deliberately slowed her mouth's pace before matching it with small thrusts of her hand.

"God… Hy… God… fu…Christ…" Theo's head rolled side to side, and his face contorted in pained prelude to imminent endgame. A dozen different Theos begged in Hydee's mind. They cursed and pleaded and whimpered. They came undone, unraveled, and the present one strained against the stairs, echoing his former selves. There was nothing but Theo for Hydee, his voice, taste, feel, smell. He plunged into her mouth, ground against her hand, and when he called out, sharp and high and loud, Hydee shuddered in satisfaction as Theo shook in his release. She swallowed all he gave her, and she withdrew first from within him and then off him when he was done.

Theo rested, blinking dazedly at the ceiling, and Hydee gently chuckled at him. It took some doing, but she lay next to him on her side, propped on an elbow. "You okay?" she asked.

With a grunt, Theo took her hand and put it on his chest, holding it. "I'm good. I'm surprised, but I'm good."

Hydee laughed and kissed his cheek. "Should I apologize or promise to do it again?"

"Maybe both?" Theo sloppily grinned at her.

"Then I'm sorry and until next time," Hydee said.

Theo snorted but grew serious, eyes searching her face. "I've never told anyone that sometimes I…"

"Yeah?" Hydee asked when Theo was quiet for too long.

Theo's scowl was brief. "Do you do that with everyone?"

"No," Hydee said honestly.

"How'd you know I'd like it?"

Theo's expression woke up a nexus of nervous déjà vu in Hydee's core. "I guessed," Hydee replied, being as honest as she could. She had the sense that Theo's issue wasn't as simple as fingers in his ass during sex. He narrowed his eyes, gaze calculating.

"Sometimes…sometimes it's like I know you," Theo said softly. "I get these flashes like I've…done this before. And it's as though you know me. More than you could from magazines. Like we've met. Made out. Something." He licked his lips. "Is that stupid?"

"No," Hydee answered at once. Her heart had swelled until it was too big for her chest. "I…feel the same way."

Theo nodded, relaxing on the stairs and watching her for a long moment. "Have we?" he asked in a low voice.

"Met?"

"Yeah?"

Hydee couldn't remember how to swallow. "We… I… Yes."

Ferocious intensity came to life in his eyes. "When?"

"At one of your movie premieres. I was in the VIP section beside the red carpet. You signed a picture for me. And then again when I won a tour around a set you were working on, though I barely saw you in person that time."

Theo petted her wrist, and Hydee suffered through a lengthy silence. "That's not meeting me," Theo said at last. "That's just seeing me in my public disguise."

"I know." Hydee inched closer. "But I'm getting to know the real you here and now."

Theo nodded, clearly mulling things over in his mind. When he sat up, it was sudden and his kiss to her lips was swift. He planted a fainter kiss between her eyebrows. "Shower?"

"Yeah," Hydee agreed.

"Good." Theo's smile turned devious. "'Cause I think it's your turn again."

Chapter Twelve

Interlude in Dreams

Hydee's Journal

I'm lounging on a reclining couch in the peristylium, or indoor Roman household garden. It's one of many Roman words I know because this dream is one that I have often and is a favorite for so many reasons. I thought it was worth the research.

The dream version of me turns a page in my book, and Laelia, my favorite servant, dashes in to say that my lover, the captain of my personal guard, has returned to the estate.

"Why are you out of breath?" I ask Laelia, closing my book and setting it aside. I had been weaving, but had grown tired of it. I pick up a basket of multicolored yarn and fuss with it.

Laelia is young but smart, and she chooses her words carefully. "Master Tadius is stern today, Mistress."

"Stern?" I repeat with a frown. My Tadius is not by nature cruel or vicious with his words, and he typically causes harm only in the name of defense. "Rest assured I am more stern. You told him I require an audience?"

"Yes, Mistress."

"Then off you go."

The girl bows and flees. I wait and listen to the sound of birds perched on the red clay edges of the open ceiling. Fully grown indoor trees block the light of the sun, which is warm today but not blistering. I think for a moment of what it'd be like in Rome proper on a day like this: stuffy and stifling with the scent of sweat intermingled with unbearable perfume and overtaxed waste management. The baths would be overflowing, and I wonder if my sisters are there. I think of each of them in turn, one pale and fair with reddish-blonde hair and the other darker with light brown curls. One is married to a senator, the other is married to a man who owns one of the largest shipping companies in all of Rome.

I am the eldest sister. There are no brothers. A family with three children, all girls, would have been a heavy burden on anyone with fewer means than my father. Our family can trace its roots to the beginning of civilization. It is only this history and its expansiveness, along with my good fortune to be born at a time when Rome endowed its women with many of the same powers as its men, that allow me to live as I do. I was married to a man who preferred cock to what rests between my legs, though he was dutiful enough to father children upon me. My son and daughter are with their Aunt Candra—the one with the reddish-blonde hair and the senator for a husband. She's the youngest and the one most interested in children. She is a simple, pretty girl, upon whom my father doted.

My other sister Leta and I were always more stimulated by business. It was the desire for such stimulation that led me to taking over much of my father's brickmaking company. Leta preferred pipeworks and lead and has made a success of herself accordingly, particularly once her husband understood her mind and made use of it in his own business affairs. My father always did have an eye for men who would appreciate his daughters and their unique gifts. For this, I am grateful and also wistful, as my father died some years ago.

When my father fell ill, I took over almost every aspect of the business and began grooming individuals to help me manage it. My husband died of brain fever before my father passed on, thus encouraging my father to leave me with his brother's estate. My uncle had a series of marriages that never lasted. He gave up after the third wife, and instead of a new woman, he acquired a beautiful piece of property in one of the provinces. It's on a hill with a stream and orchards, and the house is decadent. With not one but two floors and an atrium the size of some entire city houses and tiled in exquisite mosaics, my uncle's home is the envy of anyone with enough brains to appreciate the country as opposed to the close-quarter conditions of the city. While most citizens think one has to live perched on top of the pulse of chaos, I've found plenty of action in the country.

The estate is located conveniently between the main brickyards that make up my industry and the city wherein they are sold and shipped. I moved in upon my father's death, and my sister Leta acquired our family home. The arrangement suited all of us, though there was much talk of my remarrying for my own safety, being a woman alone in the provinces.

After my experiences with an ineffectual husband, I answered their concerns by employing my own household guard. They have proven to be ever so much more effective than a simple husband, in all aspects.

The captain of my guard came with recommendations from citizenry both high and low born. His father had been a legionary until an injury forced him to retire. He taught his son how to use a sword, and when that son grew to be two heads taller than the father, the son joined a privately funded fraternity dedicated to policing the streets in their section of the city. The legionaries are so often overtaxed with public works and campaigns that we rely on these brotherhoods to manage petty crime. As one of their leaders, my captain gained a reputation for loyalty to personage and coin, and he often served as a bodyguard. Leta's dear friend had employed him to guard her family as they traveled many times, and it was this word of mouth that persuaded me. I arranged a meeting, and when I saw him in person, I expected no less than the tall, broad, scarred man who walked into my home office, but what I didn't expect was to know him.

Since I was a girl, I'd seen a man in my dreams and known him intimately in dozens of different ways, from the mundane to the mystical. Unlike in other lifetimes when I am usually concerned for my own sanity and typically scared of admitting my dreams or considering what they mean, in this life, I instantly understand my dreams to be a sign from the gods. I don't put much faith in the gods, though I honor them as tradition demands, but when I see Marcianus Tadius, I know I will love him, and he will love me, and it is destiny. This version of myself finds it all to be quite simple and straightforward, and I told Marcianus when we met that I believed we would do well by one another.

He agreed, and we've had a socially mismatched but intimately fulfilling relationship ever since. It would never do for a woman of my status to marry him, but we entered into a sort of concubinage. I tease him that he makes a beautiful concubine to the master of the house, and he teases me about how disappointed my former husband must have been to encounter a woman with a man's mind but without the other physical parts to please.

Our relationship has its fair share of intensity, and I suspect, as I hear Marcianus's forceful footfalls approaching, that today may prove intense indeed.

Marcianus stalks around the painted wooden screen separating this room from the former and descends two steps to enter the garden. Lilies brush his tanned, heavily muscled arms, and he must duck beneath the branches of the shade trees. He has a wide face, a flat nose, and strikingly light brown eyes. His hair is short and brown, and today he wears a simple white wool tunic and belt. He could be a peasant were it not for his elaborate sandals, which are hand tooled by a master craftsman. Marcianus once told me he became a mercenary instead of a soldier because he wanted enough coin to buy the best shoes. He makes much of taking care of his feet. I believe they might be the second most fragile part of him, the first being his heart.

I remind myself of my love of all this man's parts as he takes a knee before me. I remind myself of the days spent teaching Marcianus to read, as he only had a rudimentary education from his father. I remember that Marcianus loves poetry even more than I do, that he is a gentle beast in times of peace and a ferocious wolf when facing an enemy, and I do my best to channel my irritation with him into curiosity.

"My gift," I say, using my pet name for him, "you have returned to me."

He can barely speak around his scowl. "My lady," he greets me without further comment.

"I cannot help but note my gift is without his armor," I say.

He flexes his jaw. "It is being cleaned." He huffs a sigh. I know he hates implying he'd have anyone serve him, and I wait for his correction. "I have set it aside to be cleaned."

"You are not a man limited to one breastplate," I point out drolly.

"I have done enough in armor today, my lady."

"And what was it you did that required you to leave me for two days and two nights without my permission and with only your second and third in command—"

"Who would answer to me should anything happen to—"

"Do not interrupt me, servant mine," I say with a roll of thunder in my voice. "I am in no mood."

Again his jaw dances and his eyes bored holes into the tiles beneath my couch. He says nothing. "You leave without permission," I say. "You take provisions. You take men. Not enough to leave me wanting or to endanger me." I hold up a hand when I sense he's about to disobey me. Again. "I am cognizant of my safety and its risks and what will defend it, Marcianus, but I am not aware of what could be so urgent that you do not tell me of your plans." I pause and sweep my legs over the side of the couch. I sit up and put my hands in my lap. I'm wearing the stola he likes so much, the one dyed red to match my hair. I remember a dream I had wherein I was in a position similar to this, only I was a priestess and he my consort. I'm momentarily sickened, and then the Roman version of me continues. "I worried for you, my gift. Where were you?"

"I was called away suddenly, my lady," Marcianus answers roughly. "It could not be helped." At long last, he raises his eyes to mine. They are honey gold with dark flecks, and I am in love with them all over again. "I made certain of your safety before I left. I did not violate my duty. There were extra men on watch and—"

I rise and walk to him. I put a finger beneath his chin and hold his gaze. I wonder for a moment if this is part of a game. We play games, Marcianus and I. We both understand I am master and he servant only in name and tradition. I trust him to keep myself and my home and my business safe. He trusts me to care for him and the men he and I choose to employ. When I fell ill with a cough and fever last winter, he stayed by my bedside, nursing me as much as the servants. When his knees or shoulders ache, I rub the sore spots until he sighs and relaxes. As my lover and advisor and a man now of his own means, he could easily and proudly stand in my presence. Most times he does. He kneels for me because we both enjoy it, or he kneels for me when he wishes to signal to me what kind of enjoyment he would like.

I stare at him. His eyes never waver, and it is his steadiness and his weariness and lack of armor that convince me this is no ploy for me to flex my control over him in a game of power and lust. His submission today is about something altogether different. I see fear in his eyes, and perhaps angry shame. "You forget how I know you," I say quietly, still holding his chin. "Tell me where you were and why you have the look of a man seeking forgiveness."

He struggles for what to say. "I received word from a member of my family."

I cannot hide my shock. "Family? The family you claim not to have?"

He tries to look away, but I hold him firm. "I have not lied to you, my lady. My family is dead."

"Not entirely, it seems."

He sighs and shakes free of me. I gesture to a stool, but he continues to kneel. When he speaks, it is blunt and cold. "There was a woman once. She had a child. It was a girl. There would be no marriage."

It is my turn to interrupt. "Why?"

"Her father objected, and then she died."

Now I think to my current self that he has too much misfortune when it comes to dead spouses. "What of the child?" the Roman me asks.

"Raised by her grandparents in one of the worst districts. However, it was known I was the girl's father, and I would greatly object to anyone who harmed her."

I smile into my hand so he cannot see my pride. "What happened?"

His stare is distant and the curve of his lips sends chills along my spine. "I had to object."

"Did you do so legally?" I ask calmly.

"I did. But he resisted my rightful citizen's arrest."

"Then you have retaliation rights." I reach for a cup of wine sitting on a small side table. "What was his punishment?" I ask before I drink.

"I made him an example of what happens to people who harm those I protect and who defy the laws that citizens and soldiers enforce to keep the city and its provinces safe."

"And that involved…?"

His mouth twists. "His head on a pike staked outside the bar where he forced himself upon her."

The malevolence in his voice only partially hides the pain. "Is she well, your daughter?"

It takes him some time to answer. "She will recover."

"Why have you not intervened in her life until now?"

"She was married," he says defensively.

"Was?" I ask.

"He was killed."

"And what has become of his killer?"

"He occupies a pike next to the violator."

I cannot help but chuckle. Though Marcianus does not believe in my dreams or in the gods, he often does agree that when he met me, his life changed. His focus narrowed, his desires grew, and he became more of the man he was meant to be. He credits me for this, and I credit both of us. Before him, I was lonely and lost. Now I am paired with a man willing to kill for his family. For me, for us, for the life we live together, he would sunder the world, and I would help him do it. I am gripped by pride and need of him, and he kisses me back when I bend to take his mouth with mine.

Marcianus tastes the remnants of my kiss with a slow lick of his tongue. His eyes glitter gold. "I was careful."

"You always are."

"I trust the men who were with me, and there were no witnesses. People know who did the deed, but no one saw it enacted."

I shake my head at him. "If it is in the district I think it to be, the legionaries and the common citizens will only be grateful that two miscreants are no longer a worry."

"I know, but..." His scowl returns with a vengeance, and I cannot fathom what bothers him about the situation.

"You were doing your job," I say, and I manage to speak the words that are the key to unlock his grief.

"I was not," he growls in reply. "My job is here. I protect you. I had to choose. I did not like having to choose."

I make no comment about his hatred of decisions. They are not easy for him when he must make them for his own purposes. Decisions for my Marcianus are only simple when he makes them in my name. Beneath his scars and his brawn and his calculating mind is a man who finds peace in serving one whom he loves. In such service, he finds the will to be ferocious in his duties and in the choices he makes. It is a delicate, tricky balance that I manage because I understand him and have known him for lifetimes. The gods have given me my wisdom to ensure this man lives his life to its full potential. In return, I am granted a lover unmatched by any other.

I love this dream because it reminds me that my role is simple: love him in the ways he needs so that he can become the man we both want him to be.

"Then you shall have to choose no more," I say.

"My lady?"

"I will send for your daughter. She will live here. Though these grandparents will not, else they prove their loyalty to you. I desire no one under my roof who does not respect you and thusly me. You are my strong right arm."

Marcianus becomes a man carved of stone, he is so still. In that instant I see the love he has for me cease its war with the love he has for his daughter. His eyes shine with emotion, but his voice is steady as always. "You would do this?"

"My gift, it is done." I set my empty cup on its table and pick up a brass bell next to it. Laelia appears soon thereafter. She bows. "See that the captain's armor is cleaned and that none disturb us until our business is concluded. No interruptions, no exceptions."

"Yes, my lady."

"And once the captain emerges, you will find men to spare to return to the city tomorrow and bring home a young woman recovering from injury. Make preparations in the spare rooms."

"Yes, my lady."

"That is all."

Laelia bows and takes her leave, and I sit on the edge of the couch. "I have missed you, my gift. Come here."

Marcianus rises to his towering full height, and he approaches. He stops with our toes nearly touching, looming over me as I lift my hands and rub the hem of his tunic. "Did you not tell me of your plans in fear of my objection?" I ask.

"Yes," he answers.

I reward his honesty by caressing the outside of his knees. His skin is warm and dusty with travel grit. "Are your fears alleviated?"

"I fear nothing when I am with you."

His voice is rough and rich. I slide my hands up his thighs, and without me asking, he widens his stance and puts his hands behind his back. "Remember that, then, the next time you think of not telling me a piece of information," I chide, though not unkindly. "I would have you fearless when you defend myself and our extended family."

"Yes, my lady," he replies.

"In this house, I am father and mother and guardian," I say. "You and yours are mine."

"Yes," he answers simply and softly. His eyes are tender.

I undo his loincloth's belt and let both drop to the ground. "Apologize for the worry you caused me," I order.

"You have my deepest regrets and most humble apologies, my lady," he says. I encircle his length with my hand and begin to stroke him. His chest swells with a hitching breath. "Such transgression will not happen again."

"No," I say. "It will not. But the question of the moment is not what I will do should you disobey me once more, for that will not happen." I cup his balls with a rough grip. He grunts. "It is what I will do to you for keeping secrets from me."

His eyes close briefly, and I think he may be done with the game, until his lashes flutter and he stares down at me with unchecked hunger. "I submit to my lady's commands."

"Yes, you do." I slowly stroke him from base to crown with the full of my fist. He swells until my fingers cannot meet around him. "Are you hiding anything else from me, my gift?"

His body begins to move with my touch, but he answers me readily. "No, my lady."

"Mmm," I hum in skepticism. "I cannot be sure unless all of you is open to me. I know your heart, but it has been days since I have known your body."

"It is true," he agrees. He is eager. I love him this way.

"The basket with the yarn," I say. "Search it and show me what you find."

Without moving away from me or my touch, Marcianus bends at the waist and picks up the basket. When he finds my present, his eyes widen and his lips quirk at the edges in the beginning of a smile. I have teased him about making him such a thing for months. "I had planned on showing you this treasure the morning I awoke and found you had left me without explanation."

Marcianus drops the basket and holds the smooth phallus made of bone in one hand. I had it made to resemble his own shape. "I see, my lady," he says.

I let one of my hands wander between his ass cheeks and caress him there. The cock in my hand throbs. "Does it intimidate you, my new toy?" I ask.

"No, my lady."

I lightly laugh. "Liar."

He smiles at me, showing teeth. "I will endure whatever my lady asks."

"Oh, I had not thought to ask." I stand and encircle the base of his balls with a thumb and forefinger. "I had thought to be gentle, though, to savor the first time with our new toy." With my free hand, I brush my thumb across his mouth. He catches it with his lips and sucks, and his eyes are like onyx ringed in jasper. "I would fill your mouth with it. See how you enjoy such pleasures when they are turned upon you. I would tell you to wet it well, and I would tease your holes with toys and fingers until I had my fill."

A low sound rumbles in his chest, a feral snarl, and he clasps my waist with one hand. I allow it. "I would have you on your back," I say, tipping my head backward when his face lowers to mine. I speak merely a breath away from his parted lips. We steam the air with words and respiration. "I would want to see your face, as you love to see mine. I would push it inside you." He wrenches me closer, and a fast hand steals beneath my stolla and undoes my loincloth. "I would be slow. I would be careful. As you were with me; as you are with me when I wish it." He wraps an arm around me, and he draws up my skirts. He steps closer and puts the length of his cock between my legs and against my sex. I gasp when he begins to move back and forth, not entering, but sliding his shaft along my lips, sending surge after surge of desire through me.

"Or perhaps," I say, though I'm breathless, and he is kissing my jaw and making his way to my ear. "Perhaps I would not use it on you at all. Perhaps I would use it instead of you."

The sound he makes is possessive, and he throws the toy into the basket with violence. He bites my neck exactly the way I love it done, and I call out before regaining enough sense to speak. "No, then?" I ask. I put a hand around the front of his throat and catch his short hair with my other fist. I draw his head away from mine so I can see his eyes gleam. "Then tell me what you do wish, my gift."

His answer is immediate and like stones grinding against one another. "I wish to fuck you, my lady."

"Then, my gift…" I kiss him with a barely there brush of lips. "My Marcianus." Another kiss, and he is waiting…waiting… I am on the edge already with his faster, furious friction between my legs and his willingness to play like this so readily on display.

I speak into the warm cavern of his mouth. "You may."

He slams me onto the couch, and he is on me, in me, encompassing me as I envelope him. We are as united when so joined as we are when clothed and commanding our lives. I hold him, and I urge him, but my eyes are on the sky above us. He is whispering in my ear, and I am calling out like a beast being sated in her heat, but my gaze is on the treetops. I see the clouds and the high branches and the birds perching. Our ending cries send them screeching in a flurry of wings. As the pleasure wanes, we cradle one another until we are soft and languid and the sky begins to darken.

Chapter Thirteen

Theo woke up with a crushing weight on his chest. Before Theo could panic, however, the weight began to purr.

"Morning, Oscar," Theo mumbled to Hydee's cat. The animal flicked its tail at him and stood, digging four pointy feet of death into Theo's chest. Theo braced, and Oscar strolled toward the nightstand to be in petting range of Theo's free hand, which was resting by his head on the pillow. Theo obliged the Grouch, scratching between Oscar's ears. At first the beast hadn't been too sure of Theo and had stayed hidden. But once Oscar had realized he fit perfectly in Theo's lap, they'd become the best of friends.

Theo sighed and turned his head. His other hand was attached to the arm shoved under Hydee's head and pillow. The shop was closed today, so Hydee was still asleep, and he watched a piece of her hair flutter with her deep, even breathing. He had to stop and think for a moment of exactly how many days he'd been there, because he'd lost track. There'd never been a conversation about him staying, exactly, or for how long he could. She just kept making him coffee in the morning and dinner at night, and it was getting easier and easier to forget anything had existed before her.

They'd spent the rest of the lighthouse night in and on each other. The shower, the bed, the floor, the couch… Theo had made it a personal goal to learn every inch of Hydee with fingertips and tongue. He'd traced her tattoos: the owl in flight between her shoulders, the butterflies wrapped around her left ankle, the birds in human clothing on the tattoo sleeve. She'd similarly explored him, and the sun had risen with them in bed and Hydee's head resting on Theo's leg. They'd been tangled in her sheets, and she'd been telling him about her father and the shop. One of the most incredible things about Hydee was the lack of secrecy and pretense. He'd ask her a question—what was life like in the third grade, what was her favorite color, who was the first boy she'd kissed—and she'd answer. Simple. No games. No playing coy. No making it worth her while. Theo was in heaven listening to her talk with such straightforward passion about her life, and they'd never made it to the art store. Instead, she'd made him coffee exactly the way he liked it and left him in the house with books and Netflix. She'd gone to work right next door, and he could hear her working thanks to the see-through fireplace. He'd felt a little guilty as he'd listened to her drag her friends upstairs when they'd started asking questions in that caustically friendly way of theirs, but whatever she'd said had shut them up.

Though Adir did tend to wander close to the back of the store and make casual suggestions to the shelves next to the hearth of what to watch on Netflix. Theo had to admit the kid had taste. It tended to run toward the man-on-man action, but Theo was excellent with the skip button.

The first day had been surreally peaceful. Hydee's voice and her laugh had been comforts as he had figured out where she kept everything in her kitchen and had started catching up on a decade of fiction. Theo had forgotten how much he liked to read.

At lunch, she had returned. They'd made love in the kitchen with the window open to the backyard, her bending over the sink and Theo behind her. They couldn't be seen by anyone, but they had to be quiet, and God it had been hot watching Hydee muffle pleasure in her hand and arm and even the dish towel. It'd become a favorite spot of theirs, the kitchen, and Theo was beginning to develop a Pavlovian association between the smell of herb garden and orgasm. Yesterday, he'd weeded her raised flower beds and gotten hard as a rock breathing in the scent of thyme and sage.

They'd ended his second night with takeout and a movie. They'd fallen asleep cuddled on the couch, and Theo had carried Hydee upstairs to bed. They'd begun the next day with coffee and sex, and Theo hadn't even had the concentration to read for the hours he'd been by himself in the house. He'd been too busy thinking that life couldn't possibly be so simple.

Adir had joined them for lunch the third day. He was a hilarious kid, if a little fixated on Hydee and Theo's relationship. "I'm so happy you're finally here," Adir had whispered to Theo when Hydee was out of earshot.

"You say that like you were waiting on me or something," Theo had answered.

Adir's smile had given Theo chills. "Of course we were."

Other than the minor creepy factor and the irrational belief in divine intervention, Adir was all right, though Theo had spent the rest of that afternoon contemplating life choices. While he wanted to be grateful that he was there at all and had met Hydee when he did, he couldn't help but wonder what life would have been like if he'd met her years ago. He hadn't been able to shake the feeling that he'd done something wrong, and that night, Theo had been stricken with anxiety. He'd met Hydee at the door when she'd come home from work. "I...I need my pills," Theo had said.

Hydee hadn't batted an eye. She'd grabbed her keys and shawl. "We'll go right now." She'd held his hand and breathed with him on the drive to the rental house, and it'd been her suggestion to stay there that night, not his.

"It took a lot for you to get here," Hydee had said, sitting next to Theo on the bed in the master suite. "Let's give the medicine a chance to do its work."

Theo had felt so small and helpless, but there was no belittling with Hydee, no shame or humiliation. Theo had followed her in muted awe into the bathroom. She'd drawn him a bath, helped him undress, and gotten in with him. When the tub was full, Hydee had ducked under the water. "Wash my hair?" she'd asked when she'd come up for air.

Hydee had sat in front of Theo, and he'd been working lather into the length of Hydee's hair when he'd started talking about his dog. "His name was Fetch. We got him from the pound when I was nine, and that was the name they'd given him. Didn't seem right to change it since he was used to it." Theo had toyed with the ends of Hydee's hair. "I loved that dog. He came with me everywhere, auditions, errands, even school. We got him admitted as a service dog." Theo had laughed with forgotten irony. "He supposedly helped me avoid panic attacks. And he did, I guess. He was always there."

"What happened?" Hydee had asked.

"I was filming *Dawning Light*. I'd just started, only gotten there, and I was living in this hotel. No pets allowed. It was only going to be a few days, though, until I could get home, get my shit and my best friend, and then find a place for both of us. But when I came home, Fetch was gone."

"Gone?"

Theo hadn't been able to breathe, but it hadn't been panic. Hydee had turned and put a hand on his chest. "She told me he'd been sick, that she took him to the vet. She said he'd been terminal. She said there'd been no need for me to know or for him to suffer. She killed him without saying anything to me until it was too late. No good-bye, no…no nothing. And when I asked her… When I asked her why the hell she hadn't thought to call me about the creature who'd been with me for half my life, my mother said, 'He was only an animal, Theo.' She didn't understand. She couldn't. She didn't even try."

"I'm sorry," Hydee had whispered.

"The thing is, I can understand where she was coming from. I see her side. He was a dog. But the other half of the story is that Fetch was the only thing in the entire world that actually cared about me. I'd never experienced affection and loyalty and just…love like I got from that animal. No human being ever came close. He made me happy. He gave me something to look forward to. And she…killed him. I think she killed him for it. I think if she could, she'd kill anything that did that for me."

"But you won't let her."

"No. Never. I never lived at home again. I only visited on holidays. I've never taken anyone I even remotely liked to see her."

Hydee's smile had been sad. "You learned. You got away. That's what matters. It's horrible, but it's what matters. You can never let people who want to use and destroy who you are or what makes you happy rule any part of your life."

Theo had taken Hydee's hand, and his words had felt like an oath. "I won't."

Hydee had kissed him, sealing the vow. "I know."

They'd swum naked in the pool that night. He'd gotten her off with his mouth while she sat on the edge, and then they'd wrapped up in towels and walked along the private pier to the ocean. Theo had stood shivering next to Hydee on the sand watching the play of the ocean waves. When he'd taken her hand, it had felt like hanging on to hope.

The next day, they'd packed up what few possessions Theo had and had moved them to Hydee's house. It'd been the most natural progression in the world, the only logical thing to do. The second week, Lynne had joined Adir, Hydee, and Theo for lunch, and Theo had gotten his chance to apologize.

"I'm used to people hating me after I've given them a reason," Theo had said to Lynne, talking about the sign on the door. "We got the order wrong."

Lynne had snorted. "You've got some timing. There I am, terrified that you'll never—"She had come up short when Adir had launched into a coughing fit and flailed to steady himself on Lynne's arm.

"God, sorry," Adir had said. "Feather stuck in my throat."

Adir took some getting used to. "You were saying?" Theo had prompted Lynne.

"Nothing. I want Hydee happy. We'd all about given up on the idea, especially her. It was breaking my heart."

She'd stepped closer and murmured, "Which is why I will still break you if you hurt her. Me and my little tarot things."

"Got it."

Hydee had walked into the dining area. "Lynne, stop threatening people and eat."

Adir had laughed, the tension had broken, and Lynne and Theo were several days into an uneasy truce. The truth was, though, that Theo was terrified of hurting Hydee too. The time he'd spent with her was the most profound of Theo's life. He loved their pattern: breakfast, then Hydee went next door and Theo cleaned, read, and dozed. He was more rested than he'd ever been. At night, they ate with Adir and Lynne or by themselves, and then they went for walks. They talked.

"I'm sorry I've been such a homebody," Theo had said one night while they stood on the country club bridge facing the ocean and the golf course along its edge.

"Why?" Hydee had asked.

Theo had shrugged. "I suppose I keep thinking you'll want me to work on who I want to be. Get to the art store or whatever."

"How many pills have you taken today?"

Theo had thought about it. "None," he'd said, surprised and even more shocked that he hadn't immediately fallen into a panic over it.

Hydee had smiled mysteriously at the water below the bridge. "You're working on it. Figuring out who you are and being that person, it takes time. Work. Patience. It's the hardest thing you'll ever do."

"I guess so, yeah. Maybe that's why I chose acting. It was easier to pretend to be someone else."

"It always is."

Lying next to Hydee in bed, Theo wondered if that was true. Being the man he was with her was simple. But that was only because Hydee's nature allowed it to be and, Theo supposed, because for her, he was willing to try.

Hydee stirred in her sleep, mumbling to herself. She

dreamed more than anyone Theo knew, and he watched her brow dance, her lips move, and finally her eyes open.

"Mmm, hey," she said, smiling and inching closer to Theo.

"Hey." Theo tucked Hydee against his side and chest. She curled her long, bare body around him, and Theo hugged her. "What was this one about?"

She drew lines on Theo's chest and belly with her fingertips. "Mmm, I was a wealthy Roman woman."

"Oh yeah?"

"Mmm-hmm, and the captain of my personal guard had been a bad boy."

Theo chuckled. "What had he done?"

"Left me alone so he could avenge his daughter and his daughter's husband."

"This is your dream, right? Not a novel you're writing?"

Hydee sat up and grabbed a tin of mints off the nightstand. Hydee loved morning sex but not morning breath. She stuck her tongue out at him. "I do write them down, the dreams."

"Really?"

"Yeah." Hydee popped two mints into her mouth. "I keep journals."

"Can I read them?"

Hydee went still, and she thoughtfully sucked peppermint. "You'd want to?"

"Sure. If they're all Roman ladies punishing their bad, bad soldiers." Theo lightly tickled Hydee's side and copped a feel, and she giggled, grabbing his hand and squirming to get on top of him.

"Maybe someday, if *you're* a good boy." Hydee bent and offered her tongue and a mint to Theo. He took both.

"Mmm." Theo stroked Hydee's smooth, bare legs. "Oh, but you'd have to tell me how to be good, my lady."

Hydee gaped at him and sat up, straddling Theo. The heat coming from between her legs was distracting, but he paid attention when she asked, "What did you call me?"

"My lady." Theo took both her hands and kissed her fingers. "Why? You like it?"

"It's what the Roman soldier called me in my dream."

"Oh ho." Theo drew her closer. Her weight shifted pleasantly across his torso. "And what, exactly, did you do to this soldier?"

"I could show you," Hydee offered breathlessly.

"Will I like it?" Theo teased.

"Oh…I think there's a decent chance. We're going to need lots of lube, though."

The hint stoked the dual fires of trepidation and want. Fresh flames licked through him, curiosity laced in their warm tendrils. Theo dragged Hydee to him and rolled, pinning her to the bed. "You're on," he said and bent to kiss the place on her neck that made her breath catch. She smelled like linens and sleep and the personal blend of essential oil, soap, and coconut shampoo that was just Hydee. She tasted faintly salty, and her fingers threading through his hair squeezed with the pressure he fucking loved. His scalp tingled, and he slid down her body to mouth her breasts. Hydee had wide, pink nipples that matched the color of the roses growing on her garden trellis. Each slippery, tender nipple hardened under his tongue as he licked and sucked it.

Hydee's sigh morphed into a throaty chuckle, which meant she was about to do something to change things up. A second later, Theo was on his back again, and Hydee's mouth found his for an eager play of tongues. He fisted her thick hair and ran his free hand up and down the length of her body. He cupped her ass and urged her to press flush against him. She blew a harsher breath through her nose when her pussy met his shaft, and he rocked against her. God, how sweet it would be to get hard like this and slip into her. He'd slide and grind, slide and enter, and the echoing memory of Hydee's moan and the sensation of her tight walls around him shot a shiver down Theo's spine. Sheer want erased the rest of world, and there was only Hydee's tongue, Hydee's body, and Hydee's slickening heat astride him.

When Hydee broke the kiss, it was sudden, as though she remembered she had something else to do. Her green eyes were hazy as they blinked at his, and Theo kissed her chin, more than willing to let her lead.

However, as Hydee sat up and went for a nightstand drawer to pull out a toy that Theo had heard about in theory but not actually used himself, he began to have second thoughts about where exactly Hydee wanted to go. His cock, self-serving bastard it was, was eager to go along with this idea. It liked the idea of the anal plug up his ass, and his dick throbbed and filled while Hydee retrieved a bottle of lube.

Theo's brain, however, wasn't entirely convinced, and it was hard as hell to think with his heart pounding in his throat. He eyed the toy skeptically. It wasn't some enormous phallic thing, but a reasonable sort of plug with interesting bumps and swells that would probably feel pretty damned good. Probably.

He reminded himself that the last time he'd tried this kind of thing hadn't gone badly. At least, he was pretty sure it hadn't. It'd been a couple of decades ago with a woman who was not only nameless but faceless because Theo'd been drunk. Very, very drunk.

At the moment, Theo was entirely sober and willing, but he couldn't wrap his head around how this was supposed to go or what he was supposed to do. He licked his lips with a dry tongue. "You just…had that lying around?" he attempted to joke.

Hydee shrugged one shoulder and put the toy and lube on the bed near Theo's knee. "Lynne went through a sex-toy-selling phase, and I like anal toys."

"You do?" Theo blurted, strangely needing this confirmation. Fingers up the ass during a blowjob were one thing. Toys were in a different category of awkward.

Hydee nodded. "She had a buy-one-get-one sale one week, and so…" Hydee's sweet smile was also mischievous, but her playful attitude and casual tone dialed Theo's concern down a few notches. It was almost as impossible for Theo to be ashamed around Hydee as it was for him to be anxious. She had a way of making anything from ice cream for dinner to anal plugs first thing in the morning seem positively normal.

"Don't worry," Hydee murmured. She caught his hand and put it on her breast and settled on top of him again. "By the time the toy gets involved, you won't be thinking this much."

"Oh yeah?" Theo challenged, pinching one of her nipples between thumb and forefinger and wondering how long he could keep up the banter before he begged to be inside her. "How you going to go about that?"

Hydee's smile widened into a wicked grin. "Like this."

With the grace of a dancer, Hydee flipped herself around. One bent leg went to either side of Theo's head, and she rested on all fours. The smell and sight of Hydee's pussy and ass eradicated any other urge except to taste and to feel, and Theo was straining his neck to meet her as Hydee lowered herself to his face. She remained curled so Theo was able to reach and cup the swell of her breasts.

"Oooh…" Hydee's moan dragged on in time to Theo's lazy lick from taint to clit. Hydee tasted like a penny soaked in lime juice with just the right amount of sweat and skin flavor. The longer he lingered between her legs, the more citrus he tasted. Going down on her was like drinking his favorite martini to savor the aftertaste he'd get once it was done, and Theo took his time tracing every line of her anatomy. She shaved everything below her mound, which was covered with pale blonde curls that trapped her scent. The assault on his senses was fucking delicious, and Theo's eyes rolled in his head. He sucked gently on her inner labia, explored the creases between inner and outer, and circled her entrance, tasting her wetness when it began to flow.

"Fuck, Theo." Hydee arched her back. She rocked herself to align her clit with his tongue, and with that signal,

Theo wasted no time stiffening his tongue and flicking her. He followed the flick up with a lick using the underside of his tongue, knowing it'd be a softer sensation, and Hydee shivered with a breathy little whimper that heated Theo's blood to boiling. Hydee stayed still long enough for Theo to find a slow, even rhythm on her clit beneath its hood, but the second her legs began to tremble, Hydee shifted. Theo felt her fist around his cock half a second before the warm, wet, sucking heat of her mouth covered his head, and just like that, the race for her orgasm and his delay began. Sex was like tug-of-war with a bungee cord: use all his strength to get his partner across the line, and the instant she was over, stop resisting, snap to her, and cross the line himself.

Nobody had apparently taught Hydee how to play this game fairly, however, because she sucked all of him down into her throat. Though she made no sound, Theo felt her gag, and Theo dug his heels into the bed, bucking his hips as he involuntarily sought more. "Christ," he slurred.

Hydee came up with a satisfied hum. "Like that?" she asked rhetorically while licking around his crown before going all the way down on him again.

"Unngh, yeah… Fuck, yeah." Theo tensed his lower body and matched her rhythm. He held on to her, arms around her waist and feet leveraging his weight off the bed. Theo could do little more than cling and rock into the constricting friction while she let him fuck her face in agonizingly good slow motion. Pleasure rolled through Theo, tightening his belly and force-flexing his thighs. Soon his sounds were echoing off the walls, startling him, and he growled against her.

Determined, Theo gave the pace back to Hydee, tonguing her clit in sync with Hydee's dives. Thrills coursed through him when she gasped through her nose and shuddered. Her breathing ratcheted, and she couldn't take him all in. Theo drew back from an edge he was dangerously close to meeting, and he focused on running his hands over Hydee's legs, ass, back, and anywhere within reach. Sweat rolled off both of them, slickening Theo's grip and making the sheets stick to his back and legs.

Just when Theo thought he had her, had gotten his flick-suck-circle just right, Hydee started to add a twist of her hand and a counter-twist of lips around the head of Theo's dick. She cupped his balls, tugging them exactly right, and Theo tossed back his head for a helpless gasp of air.

"God…damn…" Theo mumbled. He groaned when Hydee twist-sucked him at speed, and he wrapped his arms around her thighs so he could add fingers to his tongue's play. He danced a single finger around the swollen mound of her clit before slipping it into her. He pressed forward, finding the rougher patch defining her G-spot and massaging it. Hydee immediately came off him with an inarticulate cry and resorted to stroking his cock. Theo quickly swapped one finger for two. She was soaking wet with arousal and Theo's spit, and Theo watched himself finger her, dying for it to be his dick dipping into her, teasing, pressing, and finally seeking as deeply as he could go.

"God, Hydee. Wanna be inside you," Theo murmured in a rumble that Hydee answered with a sweet, high moan. She teased the head of his dick with a lick, and Theo chased the sensation, lifting his hips on reflex. It was an action he'd likely not have noticed, but the second he shifted, something cool and slippery pressed against his asshole.

Theo froze, equally afraid the sensation would retreat or increase if he moved. Hydee lowered her body to his mouth to the point of near suffocation, and Theo dug his fingers into the supple flesh of Hydee's ass. Trapped by the cage of Hydee's legs and sex, Theo could only hold his breath when the pressure at his hole circled, nudged, and eased inside. The instant the toy breached him, Theo had to get a stranglehold on the urge to come. If Hydee had been sucking him or stroking, he was pretty sure he would have. The chaos of needing to get off thrummed through him and made his dick throb and balls tighten, but he didn't spill.

"Nngh… ah… fu… guh…" Theo tried and failed for

words. Hydee paused, and Theo made a desperate noise.

"More?"

When Theo could translate Hydee's question, he groaned his need. Hydee's grip around the base of his cock tightened, and she coaxed the toy deeper into his ass. Theo called out when she met resistance, and he heard soothing words that made no real sense. The toy went from seeking depth to shallowly fucking him, nudging and pressing and *turning* inside him. Fuck all, but he wasn't going to come. He was going to fall apart and get remade into whatever shape Hydee wanted. Anything she wanted. She could have… He would do…anything as long as she kept making him feel like this. Close to her and crazy for her and out of his mind over what that meant and how that felt.

Hydee's hot touch lightly stroked his shaft. "Good? Is it good?"

Her voice sounded as shaky as Theo felt. "Y-yeah. It's…it's…"

Hydee interrupted with a broken moan. "Theo…" She dragged herself across his face and rocked backward on his fingers while keeping her rhythm with the toy. She mouthed his balls, and when she spoke again, the words vibrated against his nuts. "Theo, please. Fuck…I'm close. Get me off, baby, please…"

Theo saw flashes of white behind his closed lids. He dove for her clit and her G-spot, vaguely remembering to go faster on the first and slower on the second. Because that was what got Hydee off. That was what he'd done last night, and he wanted her to tremble like that again. He wanted her to shake, to gasp his name, to call out at a volume that bordered on scream. If she came, then he could, and oh Christ God Almighty, he needed to. The toy was deeper, *sliding* in and out of him, and Hydee was stroking him, so *damned* slow, and it was too fucking good, so fucking perfect, so…very…

Hydee came with a bellow that sent shockwaves through Theo. She pulsed around his fingers, and the scent and taste of her climax rendered Theo dizzy drunk. Hydee's hips stuttered, and Theo steadied her with one arm. When she shied away from his mouth and hand, Theo withdrew, relaxing onto the pillows. At the exact same time, the toy sank home inside him, deep and full and driving the breath out of Theo in a wheezing exhale. He blinked, and suddenly Hydee was no longer straddling his face. She was over him, hovering above him, hands on his chest and nails digging into his skin. Her hair stuck to her face and floated around her in messy snarls. Her skin was flushed across her cheeks and throat and breasts. Her eyes were full of a hazy sort of intensity that called directly to Theo's arousal, and she sank onto his cock with a swiftness that leveraged Theo's torso off the bed.

When they locked eyes, Theo was helpless to look away. He saw her shoulders shake when he was seated in her. He saw her eyelids lower, lift, and saw the focus of her gaze fixated upon him as she started to move. Theo's ass clenched around the toy, and the sensation shoved noises out of his mouth that added up to *oh God, please*. Her ride was short and brutal, and Theo had no idea what he did or actually said; he had no idea how loud he was being or if that should be a concern. He came harder than he could remember in recent memory. He pumped and poured into Hydee as though her body demanded every ounce he could give her, and she rode him through aftershocks until he had to grab her to hold her still. It was too much, and he'd go out of his mind if she kept going for even one more nanosecond.

Hydee lifted herself off him and fell to one side. "Fuck," she said in quiet bewilderment.

"Mmm-hmm," Theo agreed, not quite up to forming actual words just yet.

They lay next to one another as their panting subsided into more normal respiration. Theo wiped his forehead and face on his arm, and when he turned his head to look at Hydee, she was smiling at him. Without another word, she reached for his hand and intertwined their fingers.

Theo couldn't imagine a moment in any universe more perfect.

* * * *

The walk across the parking lot was more challenging than it should have been. Theo adjusted his gait to accommodate his tingling ass. Who knew that spatulas made such mean paddles?

"You know, I'm beginning to wonder if any of the historical peoples in your dreams *weren't* kinky."

Hydee giggled wickedly. "Is that right?"

"The Romans, the Russians, the Romanians. I'm learning to fear the R groups of this world."

Now Hydee laughed. "Well, maybe you should."

Theo glanced at Hydee archly, questioning, not for the first time, which of Hydee's bedroom fantasies were dreams and which dreams were fantasies. "Not that I dislike playing naughty Russian charge to his nanny mistress, but…"

Hydee attempted a nonchalant tone. "You didn't seem to mind at the time."

"I didn't. At the time." He tugged her hand and bent to whisper in her ear as, after weeks of seclusion, they finally walked through the automatic doors of the art supply store. "And you won't either, when I pay you back later in kind."

Hydee waggled eyebrows at him. "Promise?"

"I've got this dirty-nurse-and-a-sponge-bath idea."

"Ooh, how traditional of you." Hydee's eyes flashed. "It's a date."

If Theo wasn't careful, he was going to fall for this woman.

Maybe it was far too late to be careful.

"Okay," Hydee said, all business as she hooked an empty shopping basket over her forearm. She pulled a list from her purse and unfolded it. Theo noticed the stationary matched The Silver Fox's sign. The paper had a fox curled around the name of her store at the top, and below that was a list more organized than the Library of Congress. "This place won't have everything you need, but it'll have enough to get you started. And if you like returning to canvas, we'll get more serious about supplies and a place for you to work."

"We will?" Theo asked, following Hydee up a center aisle.

"Well, I mean…" Hydee flushed. "If you want to stick around here, there are spaces you can rent or buy if you want a studio. I could clear out some of the storage shed for you in the short term, maybe, but you might want more privacy. I do have a home office upstairs that I…ah, probably won't be using much, anymore. I mostly used it to…scrapbook, but I'm not sure I'll be doing that anymore."

"Lost your enthusiasm for it?" Theo asked.

Hydee's cheeks went bright pink. "Yeah, kind of." She paused at an end cap and fiddled with pipe cleaners. "Anyway, the light up there in the office isn't bad. You don't have to take me up on any of this, obviously. I was only thinking about next steps."

"Apparently," Theo said, carefully teasing. He leaned in to kiss her and tell her that he loved the idea of setting up shop in her home, but Hydee choked. "What's the…?"

Theo didn't get to finish. Hydee shoved Theo into a side aisle full of feathers and beads. He was about to protest, but from the next aisle over, he heard a woman with a smoker's rasp say, "Well, look who it is."

"Hi, Mom," Hydee said, and Theo put his back to the end of the aisle and grabbed a craft book. Which was completely inconspicuous. He was just a grown man wearing old flannel and sporting a bushman's beard reading about making Harlequin masks and feather boas. Nothing to see here.

"I've been calling you for days," Hydee's mother said.

"What are you doing all the way over here on the mainland?" Hydee asked.

"Shopping. You all right? You look overheated."

"I'm fine."

"You've not come down with that sinus thing going around, have you?"

"No, Mom, I don't have a sinus thing. What are you looking for?"

"Oh, googly eyes and kits for the Sunday school class. I went by that store in Nags Head, and they didn't have anything good. Did you get my messages?"

"Messages?" Hydee asked. They'd both been avoiding their phones, both the landline and their cells.

"Yes." Hydee's mother made an exasperated sound. "I've been hearing crazy things."

"More than usual, you mean?"

A cart wheel squeaked, and Hydee's mother's voice grew clearer. "I heard you were with some man one night near the lighthouse."

"You're kidding?" Hydee asked, and Theo could tell she was somewhat relieved, but Theo chewed on the inside of his cheek.

"I don't know. Am I?"

"Who told you that?"

"Maryanne at church said that her sister, Diane, was with Jeremiah the groundskeeper having a little outdoor fun, if you know what I mean."

"Uh-huh."

"And Maryanne said that Diane said that she saw a woman with purple hair enjoying herself with a tall man on a certain bench." Hydee's mother sounded very pleased with herself. "Something you want to tell me, Hyacinth?"

"I, uhm, well," Hydee stammered. "I'm not really ready to talk about that. Him. I mean. I'm not ready to talk about him."

"But there *is* a him to talk about?"

Hydee's voice was higher pitched than normal. "Oh, I think he qualifies, yeah."

Hydee's mother hummed excitedly. "That's wonderful! You've not been with a man in ages. Not since that last fellow, the one who did all that work with leather…"

"Mom. Not here, okay?"

"Fine, fine. So tell me, was this a blind date? A friend of Lynne's? How'd you meet him?"

"All that would qualify as talking about him, yes. Which I just said I'm not—"

"—ready to do, yes, yes," Hydee's mother finished. "Be that way, then."

"Thanks, I will. It was good to see—"

"We can talk about Theo Monk, instead," Hydee's mother interjected, and Theo cringed. He went down on one knee in the aisle, hoping that maybe if he wadded himself up into a knot, the woman would stop talking about him.

"What about him?" Hydee asked, and Theo had to give her points for sounding so calm.

"He's missing."

"He's what?" Hydee asked.

Oh hell, Theo thought. Brooke. What had she been doing? They'd been watching movies, not TV, and he'd not so much as opened his new laptop.

"I saw it on that Hollywood news channel. Theo Monk checked himself in and out of a hospital near San Diego and then vanished. Nobody knows where he is."

"Wow. That's, um… Wow."

"I thought if anyone would have heard this news first, it'd be you." Hydee's mother laughed. "You always keep such a close eye on your dream—"

"Do they suspect foul play or anything?" Hydee asked hurriedly.

"Well, not that I heard. There was some blonde woman heading up a search on that Tweety Bird website—"

"Twitter?" Hydee suggested.

"That's the one. She seemed very concerned and was asking for any information to be e-mailed to her. FindTheoMonk at Google com or something like that. There's been supposed sightings of him in airports on the East Coast, so police aren't taking her seriously."

"Well, maybe he went on vacation and didn't want anybody to know where he went."

"Funny you say that, actually. The reporter did say that a source indicated they'd been in contact with Theo, and the source seemed to think Theo was taking a breather after that cop show finished, but they didn't have any other information. Goodness, I can't believe I remember all this. I couldn't remember half my grocery list earlier. But I had to tell you. I left messages."

Theo put the book down and rubbed his face. He wanted to believe Brooke was legitimately concerned about him, but it was far more likely that she merely hated being in the dark. She was like a bat that had lost its sonar ping directing it toward a food source.

"When did you see the news report?" Hydee asked.

"Oh, a couple of days ago. You really hadn't heard all this?"

"No, I really haven't."

"Does that have something to do with the sign on your shop door?"

"Sign?" Hydee practically whimpered.

"The No Theo Monk sign in your shop window."

"Is that still up?"

"It was when I went by the store yesterday, and those posters of him weren't in the ladies' room anymore either."

"I had a bad day."

"Well, I'm proud of you. This is definitely for the best, honey. It's high time you—"

"I didn't see you, though," Hydee interrupted. "Yesterday?"

"Well, when I asked, Lynne and Adir said you'd left. I asked why your car was still there, and they said a friend had picked you up early and you'd gone off with them." Hydee's mom lowered her voice. "That friend wasn't a certain man from the lighthouse encounter, was he?"

"Yeah," Hydee said wearily. "That was the guy."

"Good for you. You know I always hoped you'd

finally figure out that hanging around and waiting for—"

"Mom," Hydee said sharply, cutting the woman off. "I've really got to run."

"But we've not talked in—"

"No, I mean really run. To the bathroom, run. I don't feel well all of a sudden."

"Oh, honey…"

"They're at the front of the store, right? The bathrooms?" Hydee asked, and Theo, hearing the hint in Hydee's voice, slowly stood.

"I think so. Next to the exit, if I remember."

"Thanks. Think I'll head that way. Probably go home and lie down."

"I hope it's not that sinus thing."

Hydee's mother continued speaking, but Theo was dashing down the aisle, away from the end cap where Hydee stood. He went right, tugging his ball cap lower over his eyes and shoving his hands in his pockets. He all but ran toward the front of the store and zipped out the entrance. A series of wide brick columns held up the storefront overhang, and Theo hid behind one so he couldn't be seen from the entrance or exit, but he could see Hydee's RAV4 in the parking lot. His guts churned like choppy seas. He was going to have to deal with Brooke and the mess he'd left in California. He hated confrontation, absolutely hated it, and for a brief second, he wondered what Hydee would think about moving to Europe.

Theo kept his head down until Hydee emerged from the store. He waited until she was almost at the car and chased after her. As soon as Hydee unlocked the car doors, he raced around to the passenger side and got in.

Hydee shoved the key in the ignition. "Holy shit."

"You have posters of me in your store's bathroom?" Theo blurted.

Hydee glared at him. "Not exactly the most important part of that conversation, now was it?"

"Sorry," Theo apologized while Hydee drummed her

fingers on the steering wheel.

"You really did leave without a word to anyone, didn't you?" Hydee asked.

"I told my doctor. Well. I texted him, anyway. He's a family friend, and he knows I'm safe."

"Well, who doesn't know you're safe who would be staging a manhunt?"

Theo's thoughts turned bleak. "Oh, I have a few ideas."

Feeling Hydee's soul-searching gaze, Theo tried to smile at her reassuringly. "I'll take care of it. I've been avoiding too much as it is. I'll make some calls and get it all sorted."

Hydee continued to stare. "Anything you need to tell me?"

Theo swallowed and shoved Brooke, the housing fiasco, and every other part of his West Coast life out of his mind. Hydee didn't need to be bothered with any more of his personal messes. She'd done enough for him on good faith already. He wished he could be half as honest as Hydee, but she wasn't the fucked-up variable in this equation, and if he spilled any more of his guts, he was afraid she'd get tired of carrying his emotional baggage and send him packing. "No. We're good. I'll handle it."

"Okay," Hydee said after a long silence. She twisted her body to see behind them and backed out of the parking space.

"Anything you want to tell me?" Theo asked, replaying the mother-daughter chat in his mind.

Hydee hit the brakes. She mashed her lips together. She sighed through her nose. "When I was little, I thought we'd end up married."

"Really?" Theo asked.

"Really." Hydee threw the car into drive with a little more force than necessary. "And the idea of us being together may have persisted beyond my childhood."

"How far beyond?"

"A while. A while beyond."

"What's a while?"

"I don't know. Say"—Hydee gestured with one hand, palm up—"up until about a month ago?"

Theo couldn't help it. He laughed. Of all the people in the world, Hydee was the only one whose crush didn't bother him in the least. Quite the opposite, really. He relaxed in the passenger seat. "That's kind of adorable."

Theo loved how easily Hydee blushed. "Hush," she said. "It's only cute because you know me now. Before, it was just crazy."

"I like your crazy."

Hydee waggled a finger at him. "You think you do, but you couldn't handle all of it."

"Wanna bet?" Theo challenged.

When Hydee arched an eyebrow at him, Theo was reminded of Adir. "I am already making that bet," Hydee said. "I al…ready…am." She stared wistfully out the windshield, took Theo's hand, and they spent the rest of the ride home in contemplative silence.

Chapter Fourteen

Theo stood at the kitchen island and fluffed the salad greens with a wooden spoon and fork. Hydee stood at the fridge. Cold wafted out of the open refrigerator door, and Theo glanced at Hydee, giving her a tentative grin. "What?" he asked, gesturing with the utensils. "There's no knives involved. I should be safe."

"Just keeping an eye on you." Hydee grabbed the salad dressings and potato salad. "I have plans for those hands later."

Theo chuckled wickedly, and when Hydee brushed by him on the way to the table, he kissed her neck. Hydee sighed, leaning against him for a fraction of a second before forcing herself to set the table.

Most of the time these days, Hydee wandered around in a pleasant fog. It was as though all the collective happiness of all their lives together blurred into one great big cloud, and Hydee floated on it through her daily routine. Her feet hadn't touched the ground in weeks, and she could always see rainbows out of the corner of her eye.

There were moments, though, when Theo did or said something that woke Hydee up out of her daydream and into the sharpened clarity of *this* reality and *this* life they were starting to live together, and Hydee tried to hang on to those precious bits of the present. They'd happen at the strangest times, like when Theo was turning a page in a book or flossing his teeth or fluffing salad greens. Hydee got reminded that he was there, with her and next to her and sleeping behind her, and all Hydee could do was thank the Universe, wipe away the occasional furtive tear, and carry on.

She knew there was still plenty of hard road to travel. They'd barely scratched the surface of Theo's anxiety, and that was a demon that would hound Theo in some way, shape, or form all his life. He needed a therapist, he needed stability, and they really couldn't address those needs until he faced the life he'd left in California. He had staff he'd need to manage and probably a house to sell or rent. Hydee adored living in their bubble, but the Universe had done them a favor today by crossing their path with her mother's. It's been awkward bordering on terminally embarrassing, but they couldn't live in seclusion the rest of their lives. People in town would eventually discover that a movie star was among them and living with Hydee, just like people from the life Theo was trying to leave behind would want a place in his new one.

Nothing could be avoided forever. Eventually it would end up on the doorstep whispering that sooner or later, it would find a way in.

As though on cue, someone knocked on Hydee's side door. Her heart fluttered, and she laughed at herself. "That's them." A timer went off. "And that's the pie. Can you…?"

"Got it," Theo said, snatching up oven mitts while Hydee jogged to the side door and opened it.

Lynne marched inside first. "Girl, you are in trouble," she said, kissing Hydee's cheek on her way to the kitchen.

"What did I do?" Hydee asked Adir, who shut the door behind him.

"What didn't you do, you bad girl." He flicked her arm without real force and grinned down at her. "That's for never telling me you were a closet exhibitionist."

"I'm a what?" Hydee asked with a sinking feeling.

"Mostly, you're a busy woman," Lynne said, grabbing tongs to serve her homemade fried chicken.

"Very busy," Adir said, solemnly taking plates to the table.

"What's happened?" Theo asked from behind the kitchen bar.

"Hydee's sleeping with Dwayne the policeman," Adir informed him.

"Or maybe Tommy the FedEx man," Lynne added.

"Or possibly both?" Adir suggested.

"One right after the other," Lynne said.

"And outdoors, even," Adir finished.

"I *am* busy." Hydee viciously stirred the iced tea.

"I hope you charged them what you charge me," Theo joked.

"I just hope she remembers I'm a kind and loving pimp who needs his cut," Adir said.

"Not likely, friend," Theo said.

Hydee stopped next to Lynne. "So I take it the town's heard that Theo and I…"

Lynne's jaw dropped. "Did you…really?"

"Um."

"On the…?"

Hydee nodded. "Bench by the—"

"—lighthouse." Lynne cackled and whacked Hydee with a potholder. "Good God, Hy-Ho. What are you going to do next? Get a neon sign to hang out front? 'I FUCK THEO MONK HERE'?"

"We don't need a sign," Theo said smugly before Hydee could choke out a reply. "Voices carry."

"Oooooh," Adir crooned, snatching up the bottles of wine he'd finished opening. "But they don't carry far enough. Perhaps you'd be willing to reenact what your side of the conversation sounded like?" He chased Theo into the living room.

"So it's business as usual. He's shameless, and the rumors are flying," Lynne observed.

"I know." Hydee filled both Lynne and Adir in on the conversation she'd had with her mother.

"At least we know how the rumor mill went from grinding to steamrolling," Adir said as they all took their places at the table for family dinner.

"I love your mom, Hy," Lynne said, "but she can't keep her mouth shut to save her life."

"I know," Hydee agreed. "We were going to have to

face reality eventually.”

“Sounds like reality is facing you,” Adir said. “Who’s out to get you from California?” he asked Theo.

“Who isn’t?” Theo grumbled, and Hydee didn’t press him. With Lynne sitting right there, Hydee didn’t need to.

“What’s that supposed to mean?” Lynne asked.

“I pissed some people off before I left.”

“You?” Lynne said. “Make people angry? No…”

“Lynne,” Hydee cautioned.

“No, it’s okay,” Theo said. “Sarcasm is Lynne’s favorite defense mechanism. Don’t take that away from her.”

“Oh, fuck you, Freud.” Lynne said, and she and Theo grinned at each other.

“But seriously,” Adir said, gesturing with a forkful of potato. “Why would people you pissed off be staging this media manhunt?”

“I don’t know that they are,” Theo said, eyes shifting rapidly from side to side, which meant he wasn’t telling them everything.

“Then what do you know?” Lynne asked.

“According to you? Jack all.”

Lynne contemplated the ceiling. “Well, I’m not wrong.”

“It doesn’t make any sense,” Adir continued. Someone knocked on the door, and Hydee rose, throwing Lynne a confused glance. Lynne shrugged at Hydee as if saying she didn’t know who was knocking either, and they were damned rude to be doing it during dinner.

“I get that you left in a hurry, but you’ve been keeping in touch with someone, right?” Adir was saying as Hydee went to the front door. She struggled with the stubborn lock. “You didn’t leave them all hanging; you told somebody you were all right and are still okay, yes?”

“You do remember you’re a movie star, right?” Lynne asked. “People hate misplacing their commodities.”

“Tell me about it,” Theo said.

Hydee shook her head at her friends and yanked open

the door. She blinked at a large-framed man with a buzz cut and sheepish expression. "Dwayne—ah, Officer Ascott?"

"Hi, Hydee," Dwayne said casually. He hooked thumbs in his belt and waited until she opened the screen. "I'm sorry to bother you."

"It's okay." Hydee flapped a hand at the invasion of moths attacking the porch lights. "What's going on?"

"Well, we've been getting some interesting calls at the station. Seems there's this actor who's gone missing, and I wouldn't have paid attention to it, but the actor is that fellow you like so much. What's his name… Ted… Terry?"

A rock landed in the pit of Hydee's stomach. "Theo. Theo Monk."

Dwayne nodded. "That's the one. And even with the phone calls, I still would never think to bother you, but I had a woman show up with a…a committee, I guess. Sort of a posse, really, and she claims he's being held against his will. Now"—Dwayne threw his hands up—"I know that's likely a bunch of bull, but we're sort of supposed to check this kind of thing out if it's reported with cause, and she's got pages of information from these Twitter accounts of local folks saying they've seen you with a man who matches the description of the, ah…kidnappee."

The few bites of dinner Hydee had managed were rebelling. "You're… You've got to be…"

A warm hand touched Hydee's lower back. Dwayne's eyes went wide. "Officer, I assure you the reports of my detainment have been greatly exaggerated," Theo said. He smiled that Oscar-winner smile. "I asked her to use the handcuffs and rope. All very consensual."

Dwayne cracked a smile and rubbed the back of his head. "Well, that's more or less a relief, sir, but—"

"That's him!" The voice cut through the night like a razor dragged across metal. Dwayne and Theo flinched. "That's my Theo."

Vaguely, Hydee saw a person walking awkwardly across the grass. When she got to the bottom of the porch steps, she came into the light and focus, and she had to steady herself on the railing to regain balance in her four-inch heels. She had blonde hair, a pointy chin, enormous breasts in a push-up bra to show ample cleavage beneath her formfitting green dress, and though her smile was wide, her eyes were positively manic. She was also oddly familiar.

"Theo," the blonde said. "I've found you."

"Brooke," Theo said.

"Brooke," Hydee repeated. Visions of gossip columns flickered through her mind. "Brooke…Hutton?"

"The very same." Brooke's smile got impossibly wider.

Dwayne's expression was stuck halfway between annoyed and exhausted. He looked at Theo. "Sir, if you could confirm for me that Ms. Hutton is, indeed, your fiancée and that you are not, in fact, being held against your will by Ms. Fox, I'm perfectly happy to let you sort this out, as I neither see it now nor do I wish to see it ever as a concern for the local PD."

The title banged around inside Hydee's mind. She slowly swiveled her head to see Theo's jaw clench and flex. "She's not my fiancée."

"Then what is she?"

"Nobody's been able to figure that out, least of all me."

Brooke laughed like china breaking. "Oh, Theo, don't try to joke. I've been so desperate."

"Ma'am," Dwayne said. "He seems not to—"

"Oh, we've been fussing, Officer. But it's real. Here's the ring, see?" She held out her left hand, and sitting on the ring finger was a huge, colorful ring of the diamond-and-gemstone persuasion. Hydee returned to her study of Theo's jaw. Her mind and body were going numb. Voices were clamoring for her attention, some mental and some physical and coming from behind her, but all she could think was that she'd done most of the talking over the last few weeks and that might have been a huge mistake.

"Do know this woman?" Dwayne roughly asked

Theo.

"Yes, Officer, I do."

"Are you here of your own free will?"

"I am."

"Excellent." Dwayne tipped his hat. "Evening, everyone. And Hydee?" He glanced at Theo, Brooke, and then Hydee in turn. "Good luck."

"Thanks," Hydee croaked.

Dwayne descended the porch stairs as two more figures emerged from the twilight. "I see you brought the Detail Twins," Theo said dully.

Brooke flinched as though startled by Theo's words. "I didn't bring them. They're not luggage. They were concerned about your disappearance, and they came with me to find you."

Theo's face hardened like setting cement. "I'd appreciate it if you'd leave."

"Leave?" Brooke put a hand to her breast. She took a moment, gathering herself. "Theo. I've been going crazy. That doctor wouldn't tell me anything useful, and you've been acting so unlike yourself. I've been so worried."

"Worried?" Theo raised his voice. "Those text messages saying my fucking life would be fucking over as I fucking know it didn't exactly scream worry to me."

Brooke fidgeted with one diamond earring. "I admit I might have said some things out of anger and fear, but I promise you—"

"You *promise* me?" Theo left Hydee's side and stalked forward. Brooke and the two assistants at the bottom of the stairs took a collective step backward, and Hydee had suddenly seen enough. She turned and went inside to find Adir and Lynne waiting anxiously next to a window, watching.

"Who is that?" Lynne asked.

"Brooke Hutton," Hydee replied, her voice sounding very far away. Adir put his arm around her and walked with her to a chair. "She's a social media mogul." Hydee collapsed in the chair. "And an actress. She dated Theo."

"I thought that was a long time ago," Lynne said.

"Me too."

"She's not his fiancée," Adir said, kneeling in front of Hydee. "There's no way."

Hydee had to excavate the words out of her throat. "She has a ring."

"I'm sure there's an explanation."

Hydee was sure there was, and she was equally sure the explanation wouldn't be good. Hydee was familiar with Brooke and Theo's relationship. They'd been on the brink of marriage more than once, if one could believe the entertainment news. She'd obviously been looking for him, so clearly there was something still between them. Why…why, God, *why* hadn't she made Theo answer more questions? Screw letting him work things out on his own time and in his own way; Hydee made everyone who came to her for help talk about their current circumstances. Theo should have been no different. Sure, maybe he would have caught her up if they'd had another week or two, but shouldn't the honesty have come before the Hollywood cavalry had shown up on her doorstep? Especially if one of the search parties claimed to be Theo's…his…

Dear God. All those talks about the difference between what the public knew and what was real, and she'd never thought to ask him something as simple as, "Are you with someone right now?" She'd just assumed he wasn't when he'd kissed her back. When he'd… and they'd…

Hydee had never cheated on anyone in her life. She never would have done anything had she thought he was somebody else's partner. She'd been trying to help him, for Pete's sake, not dig him deeper into amorality. And instead of asking and getting answers, there'd she'd been, thinking about how he could move in, set up a damned easel, *start over?* What the devil had she been thinking? A few weeks did not mean a lifetime together. Even if in the dreams…

Hydee put her face in her hands. Oh, the goddamned

dreams. The *fucking* dreams. Was she this far out of her mind? Not twenty-four hours before Theo had shown up, she was ready never to speak his name again, and then, what? She somehow thought the universe was finally doing her a favor? Putting them together at long, ever-loving last? Not likely. Nothing about this lifetime of her attempting to reach out to him had gone easily or according to plan. Hydee didn't want to be cynical, but with Brooke, Dwayne, and Theo arguing on the front porch, Hydee finally understood she'd been waiting for the other shoe to drop. It'd been too easy, and Hydee had known it.

Chest aching and bile gurgling, Hydee put her head between her knees. She heard the door bang and watched several pairs of feet stalk into her living room.

"Oh. Well. I see I've caught you at a bad—" Brooke stepped in front of Hydee's chair. Hydee stared at Brooke's shoes. "I'm Brooke Hutton. I understand you are the owner of The Silver Fox Bookstore?"

"She is," Lynne said.

Brooke remained pleasant. "I see. And you are?"

"Lynne Crossgrove-Hart. I work with Hydee."

"Ah. You must be the psychic?" Brooke might as well have asked if Lynne was Napoleon Bonaparte. Hydee slowly sat up. At that moment, Hydee couldn't blame the woman for her skepticism.

Lynne stiffened. "I read people and help them with spiritual matters, yes."

Brooke's slow smile made a glacier cuddly by comparison. "All right, then."

Brooke stood near Hydee's chair, in front of the love seat. Two other women, the assistants, stood near the table. Adir was next to the coffee table, arms crossed and glower in place. Lynne was closer to the kitchen, also glaring. Theo came to stand next to Hydee's chair, and Brooke gracefully sat on the love seat, long legs crossing at the knees and spine straight. "I hope you don't mind if I sit down," Brooke said. "It's been a long few weeks."

"What are you doing here?" Theo demanded.

"I don't suppose there's any way for us to speak privately?"

"No," Theo said.

"This is as private as it gets," Adir added.

Brooke adjusted her hemline. "Okay, then, well… Theo, I'm here to encourage you to come home with me."

"Allow me to make myself very clear," Theo said. "Any place, no… Any state that you call your residence is no home of mine." He implored Hydee with his eyes. "She is not my fiancée. We are not together. It's been over for years."

"Oh my," Brooke said with a small sigh. She spoke to Hydee. "I take it you and Theo have a romantic relationship?"

Hydee's face went hot, and Brooke waved a hand. The ring sparkled. "Don't worry. It's happened before. It will happen again, and I've accepted this. Theo occasionally has these…bouts of sincere self-doubt—"

"What the fuck are you talking about?" Theo fumed.

"And in these bouts," Brooke said loudly, "he tends to abandon his responsibilities and temporarily create a new life for himself."

A drop of cold, pure horror spilled into Hydee's belly and spread to her limbs in a flash freeze. "What?" she whispered, a dozen dreams of Theo out of his mind with grief and anxiety and loss zipping through her mind like so much unspoken evidence.

"That is…complete…utter…bullshit!" Theo bellowed.

"Is it?" Brooke replied without looking at Theo, her tone smooth as glass. "Did he tell you we live together in California?"

"We do not," Theo denied.

"We practically do. Did he tell you he's been in therapy and seeing doctors for months for what everyone agrees is a sincere case of paranoia and hypochondria?"

"She knows that! It's why I'm here!"

Brooke blinked, the only sign her patience was wearing thin. "Did he tell you he bought me this ring in Canada, where he was filming his last season of *In Force* and thinking of marrying me when it was done?"

Theo stalked forward, hands in fists at his sides. He never raised them, but Adir put a hand on Theo's chest. "Easy, friend," Adir said.

"I bought that fucking ring in La Jolla after I got home to make you shut the fuck up about moving into that damned palace you want me to buy for you." He whirled to Lynne. "You can call and confirm that."

"Okay," Lynne agreed with a nod. "What's the name of the—"

"Wait." Brooke stood. "You did what?"

Theo ran his hands through his hair and snarled in frustration. Adir stepped aside, putting a hand on Hydee's shoulder. She watched the people crammed into her house like they were performers and she was the audience. She was floating, distant and dreamlike. She was the eye in the center of their storm. She was the balance in which both sides of the supposed truth were being weighed. It would have taken too much effort to speak.

"Look," Theo said, "these people don't need to be involved in your shit, Brooke. They don't know what you do, how you try to ruin lives and think it's the best high there is. I know that I'm at fault here. I should have told Hydee about you so I could warn her. I should have told her—"

"That we were fucking the night before you flew out here to run into her pretty little arms?" Brooke asked.

"Brooke—" Theo began.

"What?" Lynne barked.

"Who cares?" Adir cried. Everybody looked at him like they'd forgotten he was there.

"I'm sorry, who are you again?" Brooke asked.

"I don't give my name to forces of evil," Adir said.

"Excuse me?" Brooke demanded with an incredulous

laugh.

Adir turned to Hydee. "Who cares who he was with before he was with you? He hasn't been with her since he's been here, right?"

Hydee shook her head, mute and feeling as though she was encased in Jell-O. She didn't know how to say that the problem had nothing to do with whether he'd been with Brooke or not or when. It was that he'd not said a word. Her Theo would have told her. He always told her the truth. Or, well, she thought he did. The dreams always showed him telling her the… God. The dreams again. The stupid, miserable, fucking…

Adir crouched next to her chair and touched her hand, which Hydee realized was gripping the chair arm so hard her knuckles were white. "Silver, it's going to be okay. You're not crazy. He is the one. He's the guy. We've all felt it over the past week, I swear. You can't give up now."

"What the hell is he talking about?" Brooke asked mildly.

"I know you're tired." Adir gently moved Hydee's chin so she'd look at him. Hydee was immediately swallowed in two pools of deep green. "I know you've only gotten a glimpse of happiness, and it's not enough to make up for the years you had to wait. I know you're tired of fighting, of trying to figure out what's real and what's not and how much anything matters, but you have to believe, Silver."

"I'm trying," Hydee whispered.

"Oh fantastic, Theo, you've found a nest of crazy people this time." Brooke sighed and waved a hand as though encouraging Theo to move ahead. "You want to tell me what he means? Go on, I'm game. Let's hear it."

"Actually, I'm not sure," Theo admitted. He was looking right at Hydee, but she couldn't make her lungs and vocal chords and tongue work to speak. It was beyond her, as impossible as flying in that moment.

"Hydee?" Theo asked, and Hydee could tell he was growing tired of the confrontation. He'd be worried about her and slightly panicked that she would believe Brooke, not Theo. Hydee empathized. She wanted to go to sleep. She wanted to get up, kiss Theo stupid, and tell Brooke to take a hike. She wanted Theo to be the person Hydee knew he could be, knew he had been, but she wasn't sure he was ready to become. She wasn't sure if it was fair to ask him to hurry. She wasn't sure about anything at all.

"He means that Hydee was waiting on Theo," Lynne said. Hydee jerked her head to shake it at Lynne, silently beseeching her friend.

"He was going to find out, Hydee," Lynne said gently. "You couldn't keep it from him forever."

Hydee hadn't planned on that. She had been going to tell him. Slowly and in a way that wouldn't overwhelm him. Hydee turned to Theo, whose expression was darkening with confusion, and Hydee knew he'd never buy what Lynne had to say. He'd never believe it. A part of him might want to, but he'd be terrified of that part and want to shove it deep within himself and run from anyone or anything that made him examine it.

"Nn," Hydee tried, but Lynne stepped away from the kitchen's bar. Hydee saw it as though Lynne moved in slow motion, and Hydee sucked a sharp breath.

"Keep what from me?" Theo asked.

"Hyacinth knows you, Theo Monk," Lynne said in her power voice, the one she used to make proclamations to clients and the one she used to command the attention of her children, her husband, and anyone who needed to hear her. "She has dreamed of some incarnation of you every night for practically all of her life."

"Incarnation?" Theo repeated.

"I think she means past life," Brooke supplied. She crossed one arm at her waist and the other hand covered her mouth and nose like she smelled something foul and didn't want to say anything about it yet.

"Lynne," Hydee croaked.

"Past... Wait, what?" Theo asked. He shook his head

at Lynne and took two steps toward Hydee. The trust in the motion broke Hydee's heart. She saw all their lives like a movie on fast-forward in her mind. In a moment of clarity, Hydee realized she'd been avoiding telling Theo about their metaphysics just as much as Theo had likely been avoiding telling her about Brooke. They'd been keeping the truth from each other, and Hydee realized she wasn't upset about Theo and Brooke at all. She wasn't even mad at herself for believing in the dreams or for having them.

She had been and continued to be terrified of losing Theo, who was already so scared and conflicted. And if he found out the source of her so-called wisdom about him came from lifetimes of knowing him, he'd be within his rights to declare her crazy and walk out.

Theo's and Hydee's eyes met, and though Lynne kept speaking—explaining about the lives, the journey, all of it—to Hydee it seemed as though Lynne's voice faded to nothing. White noise filled her ears. She mentally groped for the place in her soul that dreamed, and she tried to follow the connection to Theo like the connection was a rope she could use to climb up the stone wall of Theo's lack of memory. Hydee tingled all over. Her hair stood on end. And she reached for her lover with everything she had.

Hydee saw Theo raise one arm, and then the living room disappeared.

Hydee exhaled.

Was she awake?

Was this a dream?

Hydee heard gulls crying over the ocean, even though that was impossible at this distance, and for some reason, she thought Theo heard them too. She thought Theo might even be sending her the images. It was as though he had sought out the safety of the water at night, and Hydee had followed and found him there, on the shore with his toes in the surf and moonlight in his hair. He blinked at her standing beside him, his lips parting and his head tilting ever so slightly to the right. He didn't speak, but Hydee could hear him wondering.

"What does Lynne mean?"

And Hydee replied, *"I've not been entirely honest with you either."*

Theo frowned. *"What is she talking about? How did you get to my place of peace?"*

"Theo…I've loved you for a long time."

The version of Theo standing in front of her softened. His eyes shone with emotion, and maybe he saw the truth in the answers in her eyes. Maybe the real version of him heard her, somehow. He'd seen her in a dream about the store. She'd seen him in dozens of stores, in thousands of dreams. They were linked. They were tied by silver thread that could not be broken. The Theo standing next to the water glanced down and touched his chest, exactly where Hydee imagined the silver cord that bound them would be. She touched her arm, where she'd tattooed the Lovers forever connected by the shimmering ropes of fate. Theo looked at her hand on her arm and then back into her eyes. In that suspended second, anything was possible. Of course they existed in every lifetime, and they were all happening at the same time. Of course they were both in the house and also in Theo's safe haven by the water. Of course they were together. They were meant to be.

"Please don't be afraid."

Hydee ached with the hope of hundreds of lifetimes and thousands of years. She sent him wave after wave of silent supplication:

"I'm right here. I've always been right here."

Theo frowned and his shoulders shifted, as though he were a man about to run.

"You know me. I know you. Please."

Hydee could sense a breeze on her skin like nighttime winds. Chills crested along her spine and danced over her body. She reached toward the Theo next to the water. They were standing in it now. Waves were breaking against their thighs. It was warm and playful, the water, so soothing in comparison to the winter of the night, of being alone. Theo reached back. His fingertips hovered over hers, and the electricity of their souls sparked between them.

"Take my hand. I'll lead the way. I know where to go."

When her arm began to itch, Hydee could sense the birds of her tattoo ready to take flight. She felt the owl at her back ready to soar. The butterflies tattooed on Hydee's ankle fluttered. They were ready to go, ready to grow, ready to see.

"Come with me."

Hydee thought of a priestess, a doctor, a Roman woman, an actress, a girl on stone stairs, a young woman in a fishing village, and collectively, they held out their hands to their version of Theo.

"It's our souls' journey."

For the first time, Hydee could clearly see her existence from a vantage point high above herself. Though she'd made a life and friends and a family out of her community, the truth was she'd been incomplete with Theo. She always would be. As he could only become all of whom he was meant to be with her, so too did she need him.

"This way… It's this way."

There was power in their link, and Hydee called upon it as she never had before. He'd never been so lost, and she'd never been so alone, but Hydee was poised to hold on to Theo with him hanging on to her, and together, they'd make for the horizon, her watching for signs and him waiting to see what would come next. Together, they could make this life into what it should be and all it could be. It was *right*, him holding her and her seeking ahead. It was as it always was. It was foretold and wonderful and safe and—

Fingers snapped in front of Theo's face, and he and Hydee both jumped. Theo had been a mere foot away from Hydee, beginning to crouch, but he rose and stumbled backward.

"Excuse me. Are we boring you?" Brooke asked.

The ocean vanished. The awareness fled. Hydee was herself, again, a single entity sitting in her chair.

"That woman left when I was clearly talking to her. Did you see that?" Brooke fumed. "No one leaves when I'm speaking to them. No one." She had to be referring to Lynne, who was no longer in the room. Adir seemed to be praying, his head bowed. One of the assistants was against the wall, and the other girl stood behind the love seat, staring openly at Hydee with her jaw dropped.

Brooke made an impatient sound and snapped her fingers again. Theo dug his palms into his eyes. "What is wrong with you?" Brooke asked. Despite her irritation, though, even she sounded shaken, and the look she threw Hydee was revulsion wrapped in fear.

"What…what?" Theo stammered.

"You were standing there like a mentally deficient person while that woman spewed her nonsense. You could have at least stood up for yourself. Or me."

"I…didn't?"

"No," Brooke answered.

"I…don't remember what…" Theo swayed on his feet and patted his chest as though searching for something.

"Is it an attack?" Brooke asked.

"No." Theo scowled. "It's… No."

"Then what is it?"

"The lights were flickering," the assistant behind the couch murmured. "Did anyone else see that the lights were flickering?"

"Of course we did," Brooke snapped as she steadied Theo. "We were all here."

"That's not entirely accurate," Adir said.

"Why were they flickering? There's no storm," the girl asked.

"For pity's sake, it's an island," Brooke stated as though this explained everything instead of exactly nothing.

"And the windows are closed," the assistant pointed out.

"So what?"

"So how did the moths get in?" As the girl asked the

question, a moth streaked past Hydee's nose. One had landed on Adir's hair, and there were more congregating around the lamps.

"Who the hell cares?" Brooke asked.

"I'm sorry," Theo said, and though he spoke to the room, Hydee knew he was really speaking only to her. "I'm so sorry," he said again, and the guillotine blade fell and cut the cord of hope she'd been desperately weaving between them.

Theo's eyes were full of fear, and his face was drawn tight with nerves. "I just… I can't."

Hydee sank into her chair. "I know," she said. She couldn't will him into acceptance.

He never believed. He never remembered her. Not even in the dreams.

Adir stood tall, hand once again on Hydee's shoulder. "What does it take to make a blind man see?"

"It takes surgery, asshole," Brooke replied. She whirled at all of them, hands on her hips. "Good fucking God, but you're all acting nuts." She narrowed her eyes at Adir. "Some of you might not be acting."

Lynne thumped down the stairs, but Hydee couldn't make herself look up when her friend rejoined them. Adir, however, nodded in Lynne's direction.

"Okay." Brooke smoothed her clothes. She went to Theo and clasped his arm. "Theo? I know you think these people have wisdom or knowledge or something else you believe you need, but we've got people like this back home in California. Dozens of them. Hundreds. We can find whomever you want to do whatever you need, but you have to know, you have to *see* that you need to come home and manage your affairs. Or at least tell me and the girls what you want to do about the house and your belongings and the offer of a lifetime your agent has for you."

"I'm sorry," he said to Hydee one last time, and when he turned to Brooke, Hydee knew she'd lost. "Did you say offer?" Theo asked Brooke, who smiled.

Hydee had done all she could, and in the end, Theo's fears and his disbelief had triumphed. If he left her now, Hydee would have to hope the Universe would guide him home and never had Hydee's faith in the Universe been so small.

"We've been trying to get in touch with you," Brooke said sweetly to Theo.

"I threw my phone into the ocean," Theo said in a sleepy monotone. Hydee knew that voice. He was inundated and confused and falling into old patterns. When he was stressed and anxious, he always trusted the familiar, even if it was poisoning him. He always had. Apparently, he always would.

Brooke laughed and linked her arm through Theo's. "You ridiculous man. Don't worry. We'll get you a new one. For now, we need to get to our flight."

"Flight?" Theo asked.

"Of course. I had Carla book one as soon as I saw it was you in this house. There are things to be done and papers to be signed and plans to put in place, Theo." She kissed his cheek. "I want the best for you."

"Bullshit," Adir said, screwing himself up for a speech, but Lynne beat him to it.

"Wait," she said. Lynne held out a stack of notebooks, and Hydee did a double take when she realized Lynne was offering Theo her journals. "Take these."

Hydee tried to stand, but she didn't have the energy. She was worn out as though she'd run two marathons back to back. "Lynne, what are you doing?"

Lynne stared at Theo and didn't look at Hydee. She smiled out of the corner of her mouth. "I'm trying my Luck."

"What are they?" Theo asked.

"They're some of Hydee's journals. You should read them."

Brooke made an unpleasant scoffing sound but otherwise didn't protest as Theo took the journals carefully from Lynne's hands. "Are these…the ones you mentioned?" Theo asked, raising his head to meet Hydee's gaze.

"Yes," Hydee answered.

Theo nodded. "I'll get them back to you. I promise."

"Okay," Hydee said.

"There now," Brooke said, ushering Theo toward the door. "We'll be sure to mail those, absolutely. Is there anything else here that you can't do without, Theo, love? We really do need to get that plane."

"Hydee," Adir rumbled. "He needs Hydee."

"He needs his therapist, his doctor, his medicine, and the people who've known him for years, not weeks," Brooke said, and Hydee had to admit, she made her argument sound completely rational. Hydee couldn't fault it. He would have needed all that if he'd stayed with her too.

"He does need to take care of his shit," Lynne said reasonably, glaring headlong at Brooke. "That's for damned sure."

Brooke sneered. "You people will be lucky if he doesn't sue for false advertising and coercion and anything else our lawyers can throw at you."

Lynne showed her teeth. "Oh, I'm plenty lucky. Too bad you won't be."

"Oh my, is that a threat?"

"Enough," Hydee said, her voice a clarion bell that silenced the room. "Enough, Lynne. Adir. We've done enough."

"I'm so glad you see it that way," Brooke agreed. "Thank you."

Brooke, Theo, and the assistants began walking toward the door, but Theo stopped in his tracks, halting everyone's progression. He looked over his shoulder at Hydee. "I…need some time to think, Hydee. I'll… I've got to…"

"It's okay," Hydee told him. "You'll be okay."

"Thank you for what you did for me so far. I'll… I don't know what it all means. I don't know what happened or why I'm…" Theo's brow furrowed in frustration.

"Just go. Take care of yourself. I'll see you when I see you."

Lynne rubbed her forehead with one hand. Adir sighed and squeezed Hydee's shoulder.

And Brooke led Theo out the door and out of Hydee's life.

Chapter Fifteen

Interlude in Dreams

Hydee's Journal

There is a wagon train on Main Street, and the oxen are shitting the morning air foul. The wagons have stopped outside General Goods. They're stocking up for the rest of the journey westward, and I think, not for the first time, that maybe I should head that way too.

A boy runs off the covered porch lining the street. He's got a shovel and an old sack, and he's cleaning the streets in front of shops for a few coins. I think that's Hansom's boy, the butcher's kid. He certainly wouldn't be bothered by shit after being surrounded by entrails.

I am sad. I am alone. I am lost.

West. I could always go West, I think to myself. I like my tavern here in the Louisiana Territory. I think of the interlocking timbers and of building the place by hand. I think of how I've built such buildings half a dozen times. I started back east, near where I was born, but I wanted nothing to do with the war. None of them. War was my brother's game.

My brother. The outlaw. The killer. The wanted man.

Who has the eyes that haunt my dreams.

I shake my head and pour more whiskey. It's barely dawn, but I didn't sleep, so who gives an oxen shit if I'm a man drinking away his morning when it's still technically his night? I'm sitting at the window on the second floor of my tavern. I live there, in a wide, open room that has a bed, a stove, a chair, a table, and not much else. Some woman I used to fuck. I try to think of her name. Eloise? Elsie?

Something with an E, but she had bought me lace curtains.
Lace, of all things. They're over the windows, though, and
I'm looking through them at the oxen, the travelers, the boy
cleaning shit, and I'm thinking of how I kept moving west to
get away from dying men. I figured out a long time ago that
cowards survive. I like surviving. Or I did. Now I can't
remember why.

Because my brother is sitting behind bars in the jail
down the street, and I'm pretty sure they're going to hang
him. Maybe just shoot him. It's a toss-up as to what's more
valuable: the rope or the bullet. They'll use whichever one
costs them the least. And people can always reuse rope.

I drink. I think that if I'd slept, I would have dreamed,
and I couldn't deal with that. My dreams are full of a woman
I can never have and a man I can never be. When I was little,
I used to think the man was my brother. The eyes—they're
the same, somehow. And sometimes I'd think the woman
was more me than the man I actually am. I used to think
everybody dreamed of their brothers being with women who
might or might not have been themselves. Then I realized I
was cursed. Then I discovered that drink shut it all down.

So I drink.

The real version of myself, the one who is dreaming of
a man thinking of dreaming, understands that this man—this
version of myself—does not know he is seeing himself in a
woman's body in the dreams he has. He does not connect
the dreams to anything in his life, and when he does, he is
profoundly disturbed by them. He doesn't understand
himself, his brother, or anything in his existence. The more
he tries, the more fear he feels, and that fear was only abated
by speaking to his brother. With the brother not around, that
left the alcohol.

It is horribly lonely. He is… I am…terrifyingly cold.

The dual awareness makes me seasick, but the dream
continues. In it, I reach down and squeeze my dick. I can
feel it, and that's a good thing. It responds, and that's better.
I'm not so far gone that I should stay in the room all day. I

don't have all day to waste.

I get dressed in brown pants and a dirty cream-colored shirt. I hook suspenders over my shoulders and shove my feet into old boots. I scratch my beard and splash my face with water. I'm sure I stink, but the streets are worse, and no one will really mind or notice. When I get downstairs, I make a stop in the water closet. I built it for my tavern myself, just a box shelf with a hole under it that I dug deep. It'll take another ten years for enough people's shit to pile high enough to make me seal it off.

I won't be around in another ten years. I'll be lucky to last another two. The pains in my belly don't go away anymore. It's the drink. It's killing me, but it's all I've got, so I let it.

Before I leave, I grab my coat though it's shaping up to be another hot one. I pluck a fresh bottle of rye from behind the bar and take my hat off its peg near the front door. With my hat pulled over my eyes and my head down, nobody says much to me as I lock and leave my business and head along the covered walk. This town was a French and Indian fur trading outpost that got bigger and bigger as the game dried up farther north. Most people here speak French, as do I, but there's also English, Spanish, and Dutch. I think to myself that I'm technically a French citizen, and it makes me laugh, because I've been a British citizen and an immigrant on Spanish territory and finally I'm a Frenchie. Now, though, I'm about to be an American. The big men back East, they're looking to get themselves more room to expand because those dying boys…they won the war. Though now I hear they're fighting Indians and Brits up along the northern border because nobody knows exactly where that border is anymore.

I don't want anything to do with land or wars.

My brother, though… My goddamned brother…

I'm angry enough that I want to wake up, but the dream goes on. I pass the butcher's, the barber's, and reach the jail. It's just another building stuck in a line of buildings, though the jail's got bars on its narrow windows. There'd be hell to pay if there was a fire. As I reach for the door to go inside, I see her face in my mind. It's the woman's face that changes in my dreams but is oddly always the same.

Then I see Caroline's face, and I almost don't go into the jail. I almost go home and try to kill myself faster with the liquor.

Edward sees me, though, through the window, and he waves at me. Edward is a deputy, which means he's a regular at my establishment. He's not French. He's Dutch. I wonder if anybody is who and where they're supposed to be. I go in.

Edward is polishing his pistol. He's very proud of the flintlock piece with its worn ivory handle. He's told me it's a bitch to reload and that he prefers his rapier, which he has leaning next to him in its scabbard. When he grins, I see the eight teeth he's got left. "Who'd you kill?" he asks.

"Nobody yet. It's early."

"Never too early to start off right."

"I guess." I take off my hat. "I hear you've got a guest in suite one."

"Mean son of a whore." Edward spits. He stands. He points to a poster on the wall. It's my brother's face. I recognize the scar zigzagging from his hairline to his chin. I wonder how many people would have thought my brother's picture was me if it weren't for that scar and my constantly shaved head. "Answers to Keeper. Keeper Dawes."

He answers to Keeper because that's what our mother nicknamed him. Our father had named him Culpepper. He had named me Barrington. The last person who'd called me Barry had been my brother. That'd been fifteen years ago, give or take.

"Can I see him?" I ask Edward.

"Why would you want to do that?"

I shrug. I take out the bottle of rye and set it on Edward's desk next to the oilcloth. "We have a history."

Edward leans back in his chair as though he's considering what we both know he's already decided to do.

He points at the rye. "You remembered."

"It's a thing I do." I smile. "Remember details."

"Like what people do to you before they end up in cells?" Edward asks. I don't answer. I know my eyes. They're long dead. I know what they must look like. Edward visibly shudders. Finally, he nods. "You armed?"

"No."

Edward grunts. He pulls open a drawer and tosses me a knife in its sheath. "If you kill him? Make it quick and quiet, would you?" He tosses me an iron key on a ring. It jangles when I catch it. "I like to drink in peace." He flashes gums at me again.

I put the knife and key ring into my pockets and tip an invisible hat. I think of how little anybody cares about life. If it's not war, it's the pox or the fevers or the drink. If it's not the British trying to skewer us on bayonets, it's the Indians trying to shoot us full of shafts and arrowheads. And if none of the people manage to do the job, the weather in the middle of this godforsaken country will fry a man crazy or freeze a man to scraps.

I'm wondering how anyone lives past the cradle or why anyone would want to when I walk through a door between the front of the building and the back of it. The door's heavy oak, and though I take care, it slams behind me. I'm in a hallway running beside two cells. The windows are high, small, and barred. There's a rear entrance with another heavy oak door braced by metal. I grab a stool that's sitting derelict next to the rear entrance. I move it to sit in front of the first cell.

The lump of worn leather and wool that's facing away from me on the cot doesn't move. A black hat's covering the lump's head, and there are holes in the gray socks on the lump's feet.

"You're awake," I say, easing onto the stool and listening to my bones creak. I feel like I might throw up or shit myself, but I figure if I do either, nobody will care. Least of all me. "I could always tell, you know. Back when we were kids and you'd get sick of listening to me and pretend to sleep."

My brother doesn't say a word, but I see he's holding his breath. So I let mine go in a long sigh. "I heard they caught you last night. Well, I heard last night. Don't know when they caught you. I own the tavern here, see. I kept that up. It's harder running the places alone, but every post or town or shit stop likes a tavern. People need drink and whores and tables to play cards and talk about the assholes they've killed."

I pause. He's still not breathing, so I carry on.

"So I heard you got caught the same way I heard you'd lived. Good thing you pissed so many people off. Otherwise I guess I'd think you were singing with the angels like Mama always said we'd do when we died."

Keeper finally sighs, his whole body sagging on the cot. He rolls onto his back, the hat still on his face. He doesn't talk, but I find I've got a lot to say.

"They've got you for what, killing Indians? Trading them too much alcohol? Desertion? Treason? Violating how many countries' laws about how we're supposed to handle ourselves over here?" I snort. "Murder. They got that on your poster too. Who else'd you kill? Other than the woman I loved, I mean."

The hat is off Keeper's face, and he's sitting up in a blur of motion too quick for me to follow. It's like I blink and he's done it, and I wonder if he's that good or if I had one more drink than I thought I had before I left the house. The scar's ugly on his face. His hair's thinning. His skin's been tanned by the sun into rawhide. His eyes are two black holes, and they're burning with a dull fury as he looks at me. "I didn't kill her."

I shake my head and take out the flask that's always in my coat pocket. I unscrew it, drink from it, and smack my lips. "No, no, you didn't kill her. The fire did, right? That beam that fell on her crushed her. That son of a bitch killed Caroline. Not you. Not the man she followed to bed that night. Not the fucking wrong brother." I should be shouting, but I'm not. I'm too tired and sad and sick.

"Goddamn it, Barry," Keeper curses.

"It's Michael now. I'm French."

"Fuck your French."

"You're the fucking expert."

Now Keeper's up and at the bars. He doesn't prowl, doesn't shift or move; he stands there barely inches from me, staring me down. "What do you want from me?"

I don't stand. I lean back and smile. I know the smile is like my eyes, but Keeper doesn't flinch. "I want to talk about the night I gave you that scar."

Keeper snarls and puts his back to me. "Then talk," he says, walking over to the cot and sitting on it. "Talk all you goddamned want. Get it over with fast, though. They're gonna hang me."

I take the knife Edward gave me out of my coat pocket and put it on my leg. "They won't hang you before I'm done." I take another drink. "I used to think about that night a lot. I'd think about walking into the tavern we'd built. I'd think of my pride in it and how I loved my little brother. I'd think about all them poor sons of whores who'd died, but how we were smarter. We were the ones who got out, were making something of ourselves, who had a good in with the Indian tribes and a good coin to be made selling drink and trapping. I'd think of Caroline. Of how I loved her. Of how you knew I loved her. And yet when I walked in that day, you were fucking her blind."

Keeper growls, but I ignore him. "I know, I know. You loved her too. You loved her first, you told me, and I was always drunk. I was a fucking drunk, that's what you said, wasn't it? Probably couldn't get it up even if she'd given me half the chance. I said some shit. You said some more. You threw a bottle at me. I broke it and cut you up. You went into the back room, and Caroline, she's screaming at the two of us. I left. I couldn't even tell you now where I went, but I left, and I didn't come back until I saw the smoke. I got back, and she's dead, and you're bleeding, and I told you the next time I saw you, I'd kill you."

We look at one another, Keeper's face hard with his thin lips turned down. His eyes, though. I can never get away from those eyes.

I drink more. We sit for a while. "You know what I think about more than the night of the fire?" I wait until Keeper shakes his head. It's a little shake, barely anything, but it's enough. "I think of two things more. First I think about how when we were little, we'd kiss."

"Oh fuck me." Keeper squirms on his cot and crosses his arms. It's nice to see that he's got nowhere to go, for once. I like that a lot.

"Mama kissed us on the mouth all the time. Daddy kissed Mama on the lips. And before we'd go to sleep, I'd kiss you. I know you remember. I know you remember, because when Daddy caught us, he beat us so bad we couldn't get out of bed for a week."

"The fuck is this about?" Keeper asks.

I pet the smooth deerskin knife sheath. "It's about how it didn't mean anything except affection, but Daddy saw something more. Mama too, maybe. She let our father beat us half to death. And it's about how later, when I told you about the dreams, you asked me if they were the reason I used to kiss you."

"You tell me you dream about a guy who isn't me but is me and a woman that guy is with every fucking night. And sometimes you think you might be the woman. What the hell kind of..." Keeper scrubs his face with his hands. "If it's all the same to you, brother, I'd like to die without hearing this shit again. Because this? This conversation happening right now? It's why Caroline didn't love you and why you've always been fucked in the head."

"I know," I say, and I'm amazed at how calm I sound and feel. "It's also why you're going to leave here today. Alive."

Keeper goes still. "What?"

I drain the flask. "I'm dying. That's the other thing I think about more."

"What?" The second time Keeper says it, he's even more unsure than the first.

"It's the drink. My profession, my salvation, my sanity's downfall, all in one." I rasp a chuckle. "I drink 'cause I don't want to dream and don't want to remember, and I'm tired of that, Keeper. I'm very, very tired of it. I couldn't stop now even if I wanted to. You, though, you're the survivor between us. You're the soldier, the commander, the guy who can get things done. You were the one who got us away from home in the first place. It was your idea to build a tavern. It was even you who introduced me to Caroline. I may be older, but I'm smaller in every way."

"You're shorter too," Keeper says, but quiet.

"I know." I pluck the knife off my leg, stand up, and lean on the bars. "I used to wonder what kind of wisdom I should have found in the dreams. I think I was supposed to figure that out. I think I was supposed to pass it on to you. You needed an older brother, but what you got was a burden. I think whatever job I was destined to do this time around just didn't work out the way God wanted it to. I wasn't cut out for it.

"You, though, you're strong. In a way, knowing you've been out there being strong and giving everyone hell was the thing that kept me going. Didn't want to admit it, but..." I shrug. "When we were kids, looking out for you gave me strength. Seeing you able to do anything you wanted made me think I had purpose figured out. I supported you so you could conquer the world. But then the fire...the scars...the fucking dreams." I shake my head. "I'm used up and ready to go, but you're not, Keeper. Whatever comes next, it's not ready for you yet."

"How do you know?" Keeper asks, his voice hoarse.

"Because the good Lord or whatever bastard's up there and in charge put you in this town and in this jail with a deputy I can buy with a jar of rye." I toss the knife and the key ring into the cell. "Go on. Get out of here."

I start to go, but Keeper grabs my arm through the bars. "What are you going to do?" he asks. His eyes are wild, and I realize I'm watching a man figure out life and family and the meaning in between. It's the realization that keeps my voice gentle for my baby brother.

"What I need to do."

"They'll hang you if I get loose."

I smile. "Brother, they won't get the chance."

Understanding makes Keeper's jaw drop. He snaps it shut at once, teeth clacking. "No. Come with me."

"Where?"

"New Orleans."

"Keeper…"

"It's hot as seven hells, but they're freer down there than anywhere else. There's no winter to kill you, and when the assholes in power buy this land, New Orleans will be part of it. Trade's good down there. They've got boats. Ships. We could leave."

"Where would we go?"

"Anywhere we wanted. I've got plenty of cash stashed in places nobody will find it but me."

"Keeper, I wouldn't last the journey."

"You don't know that."

"Yes, I do."

Keeper's stubborn. He juts his chin at me. "Goddamn you, Barry. I didn't spend the last fifteen years hating your guts to see you die to let me go free."

"I'm not dying to see you go free. I'm dying because I'm dying."

"Fuck that. You don't decide fate."

"No, it does, and it's a mean bitch." I shake free of Keeper's hold. "It's over, Keeper. I'm done." I grab the front of his throat and squeeze with a hand that could break him if I wanted it to. "Don't let me see you again."

I let him go and yank open the door into the front part of the jail. Edward is snoring behind his desk. I walk over and pick up the shiny pistol. I think I'll borrow it, as it'll do the job cleaner than a knife to my wrists would. I'll write a note with an apology for the mess and the bother, and Edward will have his pistol back when it's done this one job for me.

I don't know how I miss the door opening behind me, and I don't know what Keeper hits me with, but I go down hard. I see stars.

I think he's a royal bastard. I should have cut his throat when I had the chance.

I think I hear him say neither of us is ready for what comes next.

I think I feel him kiss me.

And then everything goes black.

Chapter Sixteen

"Kinsey, call the flight coordinator and tell him we'll be there in less than half an hour," Brooke said from the driver's seat. Kinsey dutifully picked up her phone and began dialing numbers. Brooke glanced in the rearview mirror at Theo in the backseat. "Are we getting close, dear?"

Theo glanced around, and his brain had trouble comprehending the simple landscape of dune, street, and water. He was having trouble grasping all sorts of things at the moment, really, and he'd been staring at the stack of closed journals in his lap. There were all sorts of them: spiral-bound notebooks, fancy dream scrapbooks, and even ledgers. "It's…it's up here somewhere," he muttered, frowning out the window.

Brooke sighed her short, irritated sigh. "Kinsey?" Brooke asked, and while Kinsey spoke into a hands-free mic in her ear, she began pressing more buttons on the tablet in her lap, searching, no doubt, for the rental office where they had to return Theo's keys. Kinsey's Detail Twin was in Theo's rental car headed for the airport return. Carla would be taking a commercial flight home from there. Theo, Brooke, and Kinsey were headed for a private airport in Elizabeth City after they dropped off the keys.

Theo wasn't sure what he was doing in the Escalade's backseat. He couldn't quite remember getting from Hydee's living room to the vehicle. The last thing he did remember clearly was feeling like he was inside Hydee and she was inside him. Or maybe it was as though part of Theo was Hydee, both parts lived within Theo, and for a moment back there, the opposite parts had turned inside Theo to examine one another. He'd staggered away from the experience like a man who'd eaten a gallon of ice cream and then gone on every roller coaster in the park. Twice.

"It's a few miles ahead," Kinsey said to Brooke, who settled in her seat like an anaconda digesting a field of mice.

Theo didn't want to be here, but he wasn't sure he wanted to be at Hydee's either. Whatever had happened there had scared him. Actually, the moment Brooke showed up, Theo realized that every event from getting on the plane out of San Diego almost two weeks ago up to the present moment unsettled him. He was pretty sure the discontent had more to do with explaining himself to Brooke than anything Hydee or her friends might have done. He just wished he could get himself together enough to think. The icy edges of anxiety were scraping the edges of his awareness. His head ached, and he had a belly full of fire. He was ashamed of himself for not telling Hydee about Brooke, but he was even angrier at himself for not dealing with Brooke sooner. He should have…dealt. Somehow. People like Brooke didn't vanish without a fight. Theo knew better.

He was so tired, but it wasn't the kind of exhaustion that sleep would fix. Theo tried to ignore the bells and buzzes coming in through Kinsey's tablet and her quiet voice speaking into the earpiece and the smug looks Brooke kept casting his way. He shut his eyes and attempted to get his thoughts in order.

All that dream stuff… Theo kept remembering scraps of the monologue Lynne had given about Hydee, and the question that kept playing over and over in Theo's mind was simple: who was crazy? Somebody had to be. Was it Lynne? Was she crazy just for telling him about the lifetime dream stuff, or had she somehow made the whole thing…

Theo petted the top journal's cover. Okay, so she couldn't have made it all up and managed to produce the evidence so fast. So Lynne thought she was telling the truth. So did that mean Hydee was insane for actually believing that she did dream of past lives? Was the concept really that absurd? Given everything else that had happened in Theo's life and all that he knew of Hydee's, were Roman dildo

dreams really that off the mark? And if they weren't, then
was Theo the ludicrous one for getting involved with people
who believed in such things as past lives and prophetic
dreams?

If he could only figure out who was deranged here,
Theo thought he might be able to figure out what he was
actually supposed to do. Maybe the looney tunes winner was
Brooke for hunting him down, though she did have a point
about returning to California. There were loose ends to tie
up. He'd known he wouldn't be able to run away indefinitely.
Maybe Brooke was even right. Maybe he did go off on his
own and submerge himself in a different life to escape his
own. It seemed like a pretty reasonable definition of "acting"
after all. He couldn't remember ever doing it in his personal
life before, but right now he was having a hard time
remembering anything other than Hydee's eyes and the way
she looked while sleeping and the sound of her voice…

"I've loved you for a long time."

"Turn here," Kinsey announced, and Brooke
smoothly guided the behemoth into the rental company's
parking lot. The office was a bright yellow building situated
between a surf shop and a gas station. Surprisingly, it was
still open.

"Kinsey, could you—" Brooke began, but Kinsey held
up a finger.

"Mr. Watersworth? Yes, this is Kinsey Aims. I work
for Theo Monk?"

Brooke pouted in the seat before finally turning to
Theo. "I'll be right back." She patted his knee. He blinked at
his leg where she'd touched him, wondering if it'd go up in
flames or begin to melt. He was going to have to get away
from Brooke. It had been the entire point of flying east in
the first place, hadn't it? Theo thought so. He had to
remember she was a manipulative bitch not to be trusted. It
was harder to remember that when she was around. Maybe it
was her perfume. The way her tits looked under the dress.
The smooth, confident manner in which she spoke and

convinced him to go from point A to point B.

Maybe she was just the devil he knew. So, devils be damned. He'd go back to California, take care of business, sell his house, and return to Hydee. She was safe. She was *good*. Maybe one brick shy of a load, but so was Theo. He could go back to the lavender house with the green porch and figure more of himself out. Right? That was… Was that what he was supposed to be?

Theo sighed. He was missing something. An important something. A very obvious something.

There wasn't any more time to think about what it could be. The instant Brooke was out of the vehicle, Kinsey locked the doors and yanked the headset out of her ear. In her summer suit, she crawled to straddle the console and braced herself on the driver's seat with one hand. "Sir? We need to talk."

Theo rapidly blinked. "Ah…"

"We don't have a lot of time."

"Um?" Theo said, staring at the girl, half wondering what she was on and half wondering how he managed to get himself into these situations.

"Sir? I quit."

"You what?"

Kinsey swallowed. "I quit, Mr. Monk. I quit because I need to tell you some things, and I can't do that if I'm still your employee."

"Kinsey, what the hell are you——"

"Sir? Please shut up and listen to me. She'll be back any second."

Theo's hands clutched the journals. "Oh…okay."

Kinsey squinted at him and then reached to pinch the blue fuck out of his arm. "Ow!" Theo yelped. "What the hell?"

Kinsey's eyes were still narrow. "Okay. You're more here than you were. Are you stoned?"

"No!"

"You look stoned."

"If anything, I'm too fucking sober."

"Fine." Kinsey eyeballed him. "Just listen to me, okay? Brooke… Sir, Brooke is a bitch."

A laugh escaped Theo. "Ah yes. I had noticed."

"No, I don't think you really have. She hunted you like a wild animal, sir. She found you using a social media manhunt. She didn't need the cops or to triangulate your cell phone's GPS signal or anything like that. She found you through fanatical followers and rumor. Well, and she followed up with a credit card trail that ended here. She bragged the entire time that no matter what you did, you couldn't escape her. She said over and over that you weren't allowed to leave her. If you hadn't come with us willingly, she had an entire media plan ready to launch to try and ruin your career by making you out as crazy."

"Wouldn't be far off the mark," Theo muttered.

Kinsey scowled. "This is serious, Theo. This is criminal blackmail. You know Brooke. She has ties to every major entertainment station, tabloid, Twitter feed, and magazine. She was going to say you're having some sort of mental breakdown, and she had plans to commit you to an institution for observation."

Though still skeptical and disembodied, a sliver of icy fear wormed through Theo's guts. "She couldn't just do that. She'd need probable cause."

"I know that," Kinsey said impatiently. "She had us convinced she had it. Until I saw you tonight, I thought you'd gone off the deep end and we'd find you living under a bridge. She's got some doctor back home ready to sign paperwork saying you're a danger to yourself."

"Not Merrykind?"

"No. Your shrink."

Theo slumped in his seat. "The one Brooke recommended I see."

"Of course she did. And of course you agreed to see him. It's very difficult to say no to Brooke. The shrink's completely under her spell. She's got him convinced that you've got paranoid tendencies."

"I'm pretty sure I can provide plenty of fodder for that cannon all on my…" Theo sighed. "It wouldn't work, Kinsey. It couldn't. Brooke gets out of her mind when—"

"I know. That's precisely what I'm trying to say. She is, as we speak, out of her damned… Look, it isn't about what she could actually do. The mileage on that's going to vary. It's about what she *wants* to do—what she'll try to do—if you don't obey her. She's crazy, sir."

Theo's temples throbbed. The weariness he hadn't felt since he'd been in California returned. "If she's so crazy, why are you still here?"

"Because I want to bring her down, sir. I don't like what she does to people. I definitely don't like how she's treated you since we got back from Canada. But what I'm going to do isn't the point here."

"Oh? Then what is?"

"It's—" Kinsey paused. "Fuck." Brooke had returned from the rental office and was quickly walking around the front of the truck. She tried the handle.

"What's going on in there?" Brooke asked, peering through the tinted glass.

"Sir, there's no movie deal," Kinsey said, trying to remain calm but clearly faltering.

Some of Theo's confusion cleared. "What?"

"That was a lie she said to entice you to come with her."

"How do you know she was lying? There could have been something you didn't—"

"She told us as much." Kinsey watched Brooke prowl around the car. "She said she might have to resort to extreme measures because you'd be too far gone and we'd be unable to reach you any other way."

"But what was she going to do when I got home and realized there was no offer on the table?"

"Tell you she never said such a thing and, if necessary, use your faulty memory as another reason to lock you up."

"But that's… I'm not crazy."

"I know. She is. This is what I've been trying to tell you, sir. She hunted you like an animal, and she planned to cage you up like one too. She had all her documents and her witnesses in place, and she had us write up the entire takedown plan, and Carla's ready to launch it. But I wrote up some things of my own." Kinsey's brown eyes were desperate on Theo's. "You have to understand: my hate-on with Brooke had nothing to do with you in the beginning. I figured you'd be collateral damage, and I didn't start feeling really bad about that until Canada, but after what I saw in that house back there? It's become about you."

"Kinsey? Unlock the door." Brooke banged on the window.

"Why…" Theo could not shake the feeling of exhaustion and numbness. He had to fight the urge to lie down in the floorboards and hide. He was beginning to shake. "Why is it about…"

"Because you don't belong mixed up with her. You never wanted to be in the first place. You don't even belong in fucking California. You told me as much in Canada, remember? The night you kept sending me to buy beer and then told me to stay to make sure you didn't die in your sleep?"

"I did that?"

"More than once, sir."

"Oh. Fantastic."

"It was, in its own way, sir."

"Kinsey!" Brooke bellowed.

Kinsey spoke faster. "It was human. Very human. Very real. I've lived in California and worked in the industry practically all my life. Real is a rare fucking thing, sir. So rare that I'd begun to think it was a myth. Until I got to know you, and until I met those people in that house. You should know, I don't believe in anything. Not God, not the devil, not anything. I think life's pretty much a cosmic joke, but whatever happened with that woman with the purple hair?

With the lights and the damned butterfly things? *That* was real. I felt it." Kinsey paused to breathe. "Felt something, anyway. That woman… There's something about her, sir. Something altogether solid. I've never met anybody like her."

"Me either."

"And you, sir? You looked like an entirely different person in that house, with that woman and her friends. You looked… Well, sir, you looked whole."

Brooke swept around to the passenger side of the truck and tried that handle. "You let me in right now, goddammit!"

Kinsey gulped. "I'm sorry to do this to you here and now, but I couldn't keep going without telling you. Not after meeting those people and seeing you with them. I get that you don't have to believe me. I understand you don't even really like me or have any reason to trust me." She picked up her tablet and handed it to Theo. "Here. The passcode is 82665. The files are all there. The ones she wanted me to write and the ones I want to publish. I believe that if I launch first, her campaign against you will completely lose steam. I think I could even leverage it to discredit her entirely. You'll see that what I want to do could ruin me as much as she wants to ruin you. Take your time and look it over, sir. Think about what you want to do. Don't let her in until you're done." Kinsey touched Theo's wrist. "You don't have to do what she says, sir. You don't have to do what anybody says. You"—Kinsey's smile was small and ironic—"are Theo fucking Monk."

With that, Kinsey turned, opened the door, and nearly knocked Brooke over on her way out of the truck. Kinsey flipped the locking mechanism before she slammed the door. Theo was safely trapped inside the Escalade, and Kinsey grabbed Brooke's arm. The assistant was speaking ninety miles an hour, and Theo couldn't do much more than stare at the pair of them for long, slow minutes.

It was official. Something about these islands made

people lose their minds.

Theo glanced at the tablet. He swiped it to light up the screen. He punched in the code. He flipped through neatly organized files and tapped on one labeled THEO MONK FINDS LOVE. At the top of it was a list of flash media sites, the kind that took information bites and flooded the globe with them, and below the list was a short paragraph about how Theo had left California on a quest to find his long-lost love. His ex-girlfriend and entourage didn't encourage the journey, but Theo had been brave and persevered, and he'd found her, his love, in the Outer Banks.

"Hydee," Theo whispered. There was an itch in his mind. A memory was doing its damndest to resurface. It was so close. Right there. At the surface and breaking through the dirt. "Hyacinth," Theo said to himself. "Hyacinth Silver."

The name was so unique. Theo knew if he'd ever heard it before, he would have certainly remembered it. But he hadn't known it before he'd seen Hydee's sign, met Hydee in person, and put the shop name together with Hydee's full one. She'd laughed when she'd told him… When they had been wrapped up in one another…talking… What had she said?

"My dad. He's a total wanderer, you know? But he had to give me this name before he left. After his favorite flower, his favorite color, and, well…I think he digs foxes. Always nice when the spirit animal's in your actual name, huh?"

Theo dug his fingers into the corners of his eyes. His head hurt. The air-conditioning in the truck was running full blast, and he shivered. He tossed the tablet aside. He didn't care what Kinsey did or even what Brooke did. He wasn't sure he wanted to act ever again. He wasn't sure what in the hell he wanted to do. Whenever he got like that, to the place where he had no further fucks to give, he went along with whatever somebody else said was a good idea. He had to look no farther than the Escalade to see that was true. He hadn't been sure he'd wanted to stay with Hydee, so he'd agreed to go with Brooke because she was familiar and

seemed to have a plan that might give Theo time. He'd
wanted to clear his head and focus. He still wanted answers.
He needed to know what was true.

One of the journals fell off his lap, and Theo bent to
pick it up. He flipped through the pages full of Hydee's neat
handwriting. She wrote in blue ink. He touched the letters
and felt the dent the pen had made in the paper. Even her
writing was sure of itself. He skimmed the text detailing a
dream, and when he got to the bottom of the page, his heart
tripped over itself in his chest.

Theo stared, breathless. The world stopped spinning.
Sound faded to nothing. His surroundings evaporated. There
was only the journal and Theo. Every second of every
moment of the last few days replayed in his mind in fast-
forward.

"I'm right here."

What were the chances? Of running away to the very
place he needed to be to meet the people he needed to meet
to get the answers to questions he didn't even know how to
ask to find the faith that would be the difference between a
life lived in anxiety and a life lived in hope? One in a billion?
One in a gazillion?

Once for every life he chose to live?

"I've always been right here."

It was all there. Everything he needed to know
summed up in a few strokes of a blue pen. Suddenly it wasn't
about figuring out who was nuts. It wasn't about believing or
not believing in the impossible.

It was about seeing what was right in front of his face.
Because ignoring it, not paying attention to the biggest sign
of his life, would be the most batshit-crazy-stupid thing
Theo had ever done.

Theo shut the journal. He grabbed the rest of the
notebooks, fumbled with the lock and the door, and
staggered out of the truck. "Theo?" Brooke asked, rushing
over to him as fast as her wicked-witch heels would carry
her. "Are you all right?"

Ignoring Brooke, Theo clasped Kinsey's arm with care. "You're right. About everything. Do what you need to do, with my blessing, and afterward, if you want a job? You know where to find me."

Kinsey's eyes went wide, and they were wet as she nodded. "Yes, sir."

"What's going—"

"And you," Theo said to Brooke, cutting her off. He stepped close and loomed over her. It was gratifying when she shrank. "I'm going to say this clearly and exactly once. I never want to see you again."

"Theo," Brooke sounded pained.

"Get out of my life."

Brooke's eyes went from earnest to aggravated. "Baby, please—"

"Stay away from all that is mine. Don't call. Don't text. Don't fucking tweet."

"Don't you dare presume to order—"

"Shut. The fuck. Up." Theo thought he heard his voice bounce off the sides of the rental office, and Brooke's lips smacked shut. Theo put a finger in her face. "If you get within a thousand yards of me or mine again, I will get the most public restraining order you've ever seen. If you try to smear my name, if you so much as aggravate me in the media, I will make it my secondary life purpose to destroy you."

Brooke bared her teeth. "You wouldn't even know how!"

"Oh yeah?" Theo gave Kinsey a knowing little smile. "Try us."

Brooke whirled on Kinsey, and Theo stepped in front of Brooke, bringing his face directly in front of hers. "Leave. Me. Alone."

Fear and pain flashed in Brooke's eyes, and that was enough for Theo. He turned on his heel and walked away. "You don't get to fucking leave me!" Brooke screamed after him. "Nobody fucking leaves me, dickhead! Not you, not anybody! Get back here!"

Theo gritted his teeth and kept walking across the parking lot. Ocean Boulevard roared with traffic. Anxiety tickled his insides when he wondered how he was going to get to Hydee, but it calmed down when he told it that he knew the way. He had two good feet. He could walk. Walking had taken him away from a poisonous land once; it could do it again.

But when a white BMW SUV with too many bumper stickers ignored the curb and the grass trying to grow there and bounced to a stop right in front of Theo, he wasn't surprised. No more surprised than he'd been by his assistant turning around, pinching him, and telling him what to do when he had been desperately asking the universe for answers. No more than he'd been when he needed a sign about what to believe, and he'd been given one, plain as the sky was blue. If he was lucky enough to spend more time with Hydee, he might really begin to believe in the idea that if he found his path and followed it, the universe would show him where to go when he got lost in the weeds.

Theo didn't break stride as he walked up to the car, opened the door, and climbed in. "How, white man," Adir said. "Seen the light?"

"Been blinded by it."

Adir grinned. "About damned time."

Theo fastened his seat belt. "Drive."

Adir threw the Beamer into gear and steered Theo onto the right roads home.

Chapter Seventeen

It was hot under the sea of red blanket, but Hydee couldn't find the strength to crawl out from under it. Lynne hugged her from behind. Her best friend was right there with her, in bed under the stifling covers. Hydee squeezed Lynne's hand.

"He's going to come back."

Hydee wanted to believe Lynne. She had wanted to believe Adir when he'd fled out the door to chase Theo and Brooke and the California crew. He'd said he was going to find Theo and bring Theo home. Unconscious and in a sack if necessary.

"It's the Luck, Hy. It's going to work." Lynne snuggled closer. "Can't you feel it?"

There was too much to feel to sort out one emotion from another. Loss, despair, and anguish were all present and accounted for and ready to pounce on her. Hope was holding them at bay, but the defenses were dwindling with every second that the house remained silent.

"Tell me a good dream," Lynne said, and when Hydee didn't respond, she added, "Please?"

Images of Theo in rough leather in a jail cell were hard to push from her mind, but Hydee managed. She shut her eyes. She prayed. And then she answered: "It's a really long time ago. I live in a cave with a mud hut in front of it. I've got a child, a little boy. He looks just like his father, who has gone on a hunt. I'm the one with the bow-and-arrow skills, but I've been sick. I think I'm pregnant again, and I'm thinking about the next baby and staring at the elk hide that's also our front door. It's getting dark. I'm beginning to worry and be scared, and I hate that in myself. I'm never afraid, because I met my husband when we were children, and we've… We've hung on to each other…" Hydee caught her breath and rubbed her cheek on her tear-soaked pillow. "We've held each other all our lives."

"What happens next?" Lynne asked.

Hydee stifled a sob. It was stupid, her feeling this way. He was going to California and then he'd be back. That was what he'd said. She had to believe him. She had to believe *in* him. It was the only way the magic would have the chance to work. She'd believed all her life. A few more days… Surely she could believe for a few more days.

"I make dinner," Hydee said. "I feed our son. I wait. I make a burned offering to a goddess who I know will watch over me and my unborn child, and when my husband finally does come through the elk skin… I…I'm… I can't…"

"Shh, sweetie." Lynne hugged her tighter. "It's going to be okay."

Hydee willed Lynne to be right, and she willed herself to doze. She held on to the picture of Theo as he'd been in the dream of the cave: small-framed with dark hair and tanned skin and eyes the color of dark emeralds. She clung to how she'd felt, a mother protecting her child, both born and unborn, who was grateful for the meat her partner had brought home. Seeing him and holding him was salvation. It was life. Living. All the goodness in the world…

Dreaming, Hydee was confused when she heard the slamming door. Elk hide did not slam. It was hot in the dark cave with her lover wrapped around her, so when cool air struck her face and arms, she fought to keep it. Hydee woke when she was sitting upright in her bed with Theo kneeling to the side of it. Lynne quietly slipped out of the room, and Hydee felt the burning tracks of fresh tears.

"Am I dreaming?" Hydee asked.

Theo slowly shook his head. His eyes sparkled, filled, and it took clear effort to tear his gaze from her and down to something he held in his hands. He wiped his cheek on one shoulder, and then he slowly unfolded a letter written in faded blue ink on rose-and-rainbow stationary. He laid the letter flat on the bed so it faced Hydee. Then he picked up one of Hydee's earliest journals that Lynne had given him and opened it to the first page. He set the journal next to the letter, and he pointed to the foxes at the bottom of the pages.

The blue fox on the journal's page was a tidier version of the blue fox on the letter, but both were clearly the fox that had been part of Hydee's signature since she was a little girl. It was the same one that had been the inspiration for her Silver Fox Bookstore logo.

"It was you," Theo said in a husky voice. "It was you all along."

Hydee bit her lip and caressed the first letter she'd ever written to her lover in this lifetime. "You…you kept it?"

Theo looked at Hydee. He swallowed. "'Dear Mr. Theo Monk,'" Theo said, searching Hydee's eyes while he recited her letter to him by heart. "'I hope you're okay. Actually, I hope a lot of things about you and for you. I see you've been working hard on your TV show, which is where I first saw you. Since then, I've read articles about you in magazines and watched your interviews at my friend's house. (She gets cable and records them for me. She's a good friend. I hope you have one of those too. A good friend, not a VCR or cable. I guess you'd have those).'"

Hydee groped for Theo's hand, and he took hers. He lifted her fingers to his lips, and he brushed kisses to her knuckles. "'You seem smart and funny and are very good at what you do, but you also seem a little sad. I hope you're not, but if you are, I hope this letter helps. I'm thinking of you, and I know I'm just one person, but I still think it matters. I hope work is good. I hope you're happy. I hope your family and the people closest to you know how to love you. It's important, the knowing how to love somebody. Because everybody is different. My father told me that. I hope your father told you something like that too. If he didn't, then I can and just did.'" Theo's chin trembled.

"'I can also tell you that I'm different,'" Hydee recited, prompting Theo.

"'You don't have to believe me,'" Theo said. "'It's okay.'"

"'But I'm not just a fan,'" Hydee said.

"'Though I'm sure that's what all the serious fans would say,'" Theo continued.

"'I dream about you,'" Hydee whispered.

Theo's throat worked as he clearly struggled to gulp down emotion. "'I'm sure a lot of people do, but not a lot of people would tell you that the dreams I love the most are the ones where you're smiling.'"

When Theo's voice broke, Hydee continued. "'I had to write you to tell you that. I had to try to see if you were all right. I'm sure you're very busy, but if there's any way you could tell me you're happy and doing okay, I would really appreciate it. I know it's asking a lot, and I wouldn't normally ask somebody for anything, but I know my life will be better if I know you're doing well. The address on the front of the letter is a P.O. Box, but it will get to me. I promise. I also promise that even if you don't write back, I'll still hope you're all right.'"

"'I will keep dreaming,'" Theo recited. "'I will keep loving the ones where you're smiling. I will keep hoping things for you. The good stuff. I want you to have the good stuff.'"

"'To prove I'm not a crazy fan,'" Hydee said, "'I won't even tell you my name. It's not important for you to know me. It's only important that I know you. I think that's how it's always been.'"

"'Best of everything, Mr. Theo Monk. I hope the world for you is kind.'" Theo smiled, tears streaming, and for a moment, Hydee was crying so hard herself that he wobbled in and out of focus. "'P.S.,'" Theo said with a small laugh. "'Do you mind if I call you Theodore?'"

Hydee wiped her nose with one hand. "Well, do you?"

"No." Theo kissed her palm. "You can call me anything you want so long as I can call us 'together.'"

Hydee put her hands over her mouth, and Theo pushed the faded letter and the journal aside so he could sit next to her. He took her face in his hands and tipped her head back so their foreheads could meet. "I don't know a lot, and I'm not sure what to believe, but I do know you tried to save me once, with that letter. I think this time, if it's okay with you, I'll let you."

Their kiss was ferocious and salty, and when they finally broke apart, Hydee made sure her punch to Theo's arm was gentle. "Don't you ever leave me again, you jerk."

"I swear." Theo leaned against the headboard and pulled Hydee's legs across his lap so he could hold her. She fit perfectly against his chest and right under his chin. She listened to his heartbeat and felt her own pulse slowing to match his. The light quality in the room changed as dusk faded into darkness. Lynne must have left the windows open, because when it started to rain, Hydee could hear it against the storm shutters and the windowsill.

After long moments of simply being together, Theo took a deep breath. "Though you do know what this means?"

Hydee hummed sleepily. "You're going to need that space to paint?"

"Oh, definitely. And?"

"We're going to need a bigger house?" Hydee asked. She saw a beautiful beach Victorian in her mind with a big garden and a view of the water. She could swear she heard children laughing.

"Yes," Theo confirmed. "And?"

Hydee tipped her head and frowned at Theo, trying to puzzle out what he wanted her to figure out. "We're...going to have to go to California, which means taking Adir because he loves to travel, and California will never, ever be the same?"

Theo chuckled. "Mmm-hmm. And?"

Hydee thought of pills and counselors and how the clerk at Food Lion was going to die on the spot when she got a load of Theo in the flesh. "I don't know," Hydee said, knowing they'd figure out those details along the way to spending the rest of their lives with one another. "What?"

"Eventually"—Theo sighed dramatically—"someone's going to have to tell your mother."

"Not it!" Adir shouted from the other side of the closed bedroom door. "Ow! Fucking hell, woman!"

"Idiot!" Lynne said in a harsh whisper.

"Sadist!"

Theo took off his shoe and threw it at the door. Their friends scattered like two startled animals, and laughter bubbled from Hydee's middle to spill out her mouth in gales. She laced her fingers through Theo's. "This," she said, "is most definitely the good stuff."

Postlude in Dreams

Theo's Journal

I need to tell you about my dream.

I've had it every night ever since your mother passed away the same way she lived: with grace, in peace, and surrounded by the people whom she loved and who loved her. I need to tell you about the dream because I'll be gone soon too, and you two, my beautiful children, will finally get to make good on your threat to read the journals your mom kept and that she made me try to keep.

She's been gone a couple of months now, but I still feel her. I don't think I'll stop feeling her. It's one of the reasons I know I'll follow her soon. I always follow her. She sees the path and leads me. I'll get to see her, tell her I missed her, and apologize for being so late.

I'm always late to her party.

I hope I get to see Merrykind too. I need to tell him he was right. I really did outlive 'em all.

Anyway, I know she would want me to try to write this down. I don't have the way she had with words. I'll do my best.

Your mother saved my life by showing me that the path to happiness is through my own choices, and that I can always make those choices. Because of her, I let go of fear, and in return, I got to paint, to see the world, and to share it all with people who reminded me every day that there are joys in this life that cannot be measured.

The greatest gift Hydee ever gave me, other than her love and you two, was the assurance that none of us ever ends. It's not in our nature to cease to be. Nothing in nature does. While I never found quite the faith your mom had, I did and do have complete faith in her. So when she told me where she'd meet me right before she left us, I paid attention. I figured it was the least I could do. Maybe that's why I'm dreaming; it's me making sure I remember.

In the dream, I'm walking down a hallway. It's long and narrow but not uncomfortable. There's a white wall on my right and a mirror on my left. It reflects me and the wall, but somehow I know that on the other side of that mirror are people, and some of those people are watching me walk. It's not a bad thing. It's comforting.

There's no doorway at the end of the hall. It simply stops. I step from the sterile hallway into a rich field. I think that field is why Hydee loved her garden. Every flower in the world is in that field, and on the edges of it is every tree. It's spring and warm and there's a breeze, and I walk and walk until I see the fence and the gate.

The gate's wide open and the glittering fence touches the sky and stretches so far in both directions that I get dizzy trying to see if and where it ends. There are hundreds of thousands of gates, maybe millions, and they all open onto that garden. Beyond the fence is pure light and gossamer fog. When I see it, I understand I can linger as long as I want in the garden. The fence, the gate, and what is beyond will be there.

In the garden, I see shapes that I know are people. They're picking flowers. They're holding hands. They're the ones going to the two-way mirror to watch the living. It's at that moment in the dream that I know I'm dead.

Except I don't feel dead. I feel very much alive. Young and refreshed like I just woke up from the best sleep of my life. I'm twenty-five again, and I get distracted for a moment thinking that I want to paint this garden. I think in my life I've tried to paint a thousand gardens, and some of them even turned out okay, but if I painted this garden, I'd finally get "garden" right.

And then I hear it. It's faint at first, but it gets louder.

I hear my Hydee calling my name. It's not Theo or Theodore, as she preferred, but my real name. Suddenly, I don't want to paint anymore. I only want to go to her, because I know she's been waiting, and I know I promised to meet her.

When I reach the gate, I run my hands over the shimmering bars. They're wonderfully warm. Through the open gate, standing with her toes in the swirling light and fog, I see a girl with lavender hair. She's wearing a rainbow dress that picks up the light and reflects all the colors. Then I see it's not a dress at all, but her. I call out to her, she speaks my name, and when she begins to turn, I wake up.

This gate is as real as I am, sitting here writing you about it. The gate stands between our world and the next world, where we go to wait with people we love and are connected to until the next life comes along that we want to try.

I want you to know that's where your mother and I will be. We'll watch through the mirrored hallway as you become all you can be, and then, when you're ready…

We'll meet you at the gates.

I love you with all my heart and soul.

—Dad

P.S.

Marco—I expect nothing less than the cure for all the rest of the diseases out of you, young man. But, of course, anything short of that will be miraculous too, as all things you do are miracles. I love you, Doctor Marcianus Monk.

Clara—Keep your brother in line. It's a full-time job, but somebody has to do it, so in between saving all those other souls in your many congregations, find some time for him. And never fear, daughter mine: you'll find your someone. Your mother had to wait thirty years for me to come around. Thank God you inherited her patience. I love you more than the stars.

Adir—I know you're reading this too, you wonderful bastard, and you'd better be at the gate party too. Meanwhile, in addition to making sure Lynne doesn't try to resurrect a rock band so she can be the world's oldest groupie and taking care of your doting husband, all the grandkids, and the shop, would you mind looking after Hydee's gardens for us? I spent more time building those than anybody ever did building our house, which, as I'm sure you've figured out, is going to you and all our remaining family.

Hydee loved this place and all of you. And you know, I can feel her holding my hand as I sit here under our tree on this wooden bench with a view of the water. You know the one. We had it made to match the first one.

We always did like to sit on our bench and hold hands while the sun set on another day.

Postlude in Dreams

Hydee's Journal – First Entry

I need to tell you about him.

I have to write it down as close to how it happened as I can. I have to remember. There are so many details, and so many of them are lost on me, a child of the here and now, but a dreamer of the there and then.

I dream every night, and we're together. The landscape and the era swap out behind us like scenery in a play. Our names change, and so do our bodies and faces and circumstances, but intrinsically we're the same.

And we remain.

We're old friends, lovers, parents, and sometimes siblings. We're enemies, competitors, saviors, slaves, kings and queens. Occasionally, I'm the man, but usually he is. I believe this is an agreement we make in the time we spend In Between.

I've spoken a thousand languages and understood them all while my eyes are shut, but I confess, Dear Journal, that I record the meanings in these pages and not the actual diction. I wish I could convey the way his voice sounds when he speaks to me in French, Russian, Italian or in languages old and dead and long gone. Perhaps especially those. I've been keeping journals all my life, but I don't think I'll ever find the words to express the emotional marks he's made on my heart.

Him. He. His. Mine. But I can't remember his real name, the one we use In Between. Maybe one day, these writings will jar my memory, and I'll recall it. But even if that never happens, I know it, and I will speak his name on the far side of the gates between the living and the In

Between, and he will answer.

He always answers.

I know him, but he only knows me after we've met in the dreams of lives long gone. Maybe that was part of the spell. All magic has its drawbacks. I often wonder if it was magic, the kind that I like to think existed long, long ago, that linked our fates. But that's only a guess and maybe a silly one. In truth, I don't know how we were joined, but I do know the dream about the first lifetime we met. I've dreamt of it so often that I've memorized every look, every nuance, every texture beneath my fingertips.

I dreamt of it again last night.

It's a long time ago. So long that there are no gods, only the sky above, under which we are born and die, the animals, who are our friends or our enemies if we anger them, and the ground on which we walk and live. We build temples to honor the air, animals, and earth.

I don't know what happens to the women in the air or animal temples, as I am never allowed to see them except on festival days, and then only from afar, but the priestesses in the Earth Temples are treated as nobles because they make sacred life in their bellies. Once a year, men are chosen from the surrounding villages and sent to the temples for the rites. In them, the spirits of the land possess the men and sow their seed in the priestesses. If the rites produce female children, then those girls are raised as future priestesses. If the rites produce male children, the potential strength in their baby bones is sacrificed unto the earth to appease the land.

The land must have its sons to make it strong, and the people must have its priestesses to bear those sons and more women to do the laboring. As far as I know when I am the priestess in the dream, it has always been this way. My mother was a priestess, and her mother before her, and now it's my turn to take the herbal brew made by the eldest priestess. I have to drink it for three days, and it makes my insides unbearably warm. She takes a different herbal paste and rubs it onto my skin all over my body. My nipples grow sensitive and my sex feels swollen. The elder tells me this is the way of the rite, and that I am to endure and wait.

I'm not alone. There are four other girls who are of age who are going to undergo the rite for the first time. I'm not afraid, exactly, but I'm anxious and nervous that the spirit of the land who will possess my chosen boy will not like me. I'm worried about displeasing the elder, who is quick to strike me with her bamboo cane when I do not do as I should or as I am told. I am not concerned about the boy, for he can be no crueler than the elder with her mean fingers and her beatings.

I also understand that the boy will drink a special herbal tea, too, so that the spirit may enter him, and it comforts me in a strange kind of camaraderie to know I'm not the only one being taken by another.

I know all this as I sit in my chamber in the temple on the night of the ritual. The rooms fan out from the central atrium and are long and narrow. They have half walls at the back so that the earth spirit may freely come and go. The field beyond the temple is silent and still. The sky is cloudy, and the stars are hidden. I'm nervous because it feels like I've been waiting for a long time. It's also chilly, and I'm naked, though that's not unusual. Typically I only wear clothing when the blood is upon me. My hair has never been cut, and it falls to my knees. It's pale, which the elder tells me is a sign of purity. My little girls will be very blessed. The elder tells me I will have four girls and two strong boys for the altar knife. She hit me when I wept for my sons. She hit me again when I asked why I would only have six children if I was to participate in the rite for the next ten years, as was common. I think it means I will die after the sixth child is born. I think it sounds like a very long life if I keep getting hit every time I ask a question.

There are voices in the next room, and I walk to the end of the straw bed that's been made up with blankets sewn with special symbols to encourage the rite. There's a table at the foot of the bed with the herbal tea for my consort. There's also food and drink. The only other furniture is a single chair. I have enough time to wonder if I should be sitting in it while I wait before the drapery whisks aside and a boy steps into the chamber.

My first feeling is relief when I see he's not much older than me. He has dark hair and eyes and is wearing nothing but a loin cloth. His chest is wide but thin, and his arms and legs are long but skinny. He watches me for a long time and doesn't say anything.

"Hello," I say.

"Greetings, priestess. I am Erdohl, third son of my father." He frowns at the floor. He won't look at me.

"What is it?" I ask.

"There was more I am to say, but I can't remember it."

"Oh." I pluck a berry off the table and chew it, considering him. "You are the third son?"

He bristles and now he does look up. "Yes."

"And they picked you?"

"Yes." He doesn't like me asking, which makes me smile.

"Why?"

"I'm the tallest."

I laugh, and after a moment, he chuckles too. I don't hear laughter from the chambers to either side of mine. Somewhere, somebody is weeping. The elder will not like that.

"Did you want to get chosen?" he asks, and he's come closer as I've listened to my sister cry in the darkness. His voice is gentle and soft, and I know he can hear her too.

"I did not get chosen. I became old enough for the rite." I pick up the herbal tea. "You are supposed to drink this."

He reaches out for the cup but doesn't take it, pulling back at the last second. "My cousin said it made him sick."

"Your cousin did the rite as well?"

"Most of the men in my family have." He shrugs as if

this is simply a fact of his life and not a rare honor. "The women in our line have the gifts, and some of the men do too."

"Boys are not blessed with gifts," I argue.

He smiles at me, and I'm reminded of the salve that the elder applied before she left me to wait for Erdohl. My skin tingles. "Is that what you are told, here?"

"Of course it is. And it is the only truth."

He bows slightly at the waist. "If you say it is so, then I will believe it."

I push the cup to his chest. He really is very tall. "Drink it."

"What happens if I do not?" he asks.

The elder's timing is perfect. From next door, we hear the crack of a cane again stone and then the dull thud of it against flesh. My sister cries out, gets hit again, and then all is quiet. I flinch, and he jumps with each of the strikes.

"I will drink it," he says, and then does. He drains it in thick gulps that move the front of his throat up and down. When he's done, he makes a face. "That is awful."

"I know. So was mine."

"You had to drink it as well?"

"A different drink. They rubbed me with potion too."

He swallows again, and though the light from the candles in the corners is dim, I can see him blush. He glances down at me before meeting my eyes. "Where did they rub you?"

A thrill tickles my spine. I step closer to him. "Everywhere."

He looks at me one more time, but then steps around me to put the cup on the table. He keeps his back to me. "I saw you. Last festival day."

"Everyone did."

"You were nude and painted in gold and red."

"I always am." I walk to the bed and sit on it. I'm right in front of him, but he won't look at me. I wonder how long it will take for the spirit to inhabit him so he'll stop being shy. "Come sit by me."

"No."

The refusal hurts. "Why not?" I demand. "Do I displease you?"

He frowns, even deeper than he did before, and he turns on his heel. He's heading for the tapestry, and I jump to my feet. "Where are you going?" I ask in a hushed whisper, chasing after him and grabbing him by the arm.

"They should have chosen my brother. He could do this."

"Oh." I look at his loincloth. "Is there something... are you missing your...?"

"Of course not!" He shakes free of my hold.

"Then why are you attempting to flee?" I ask him directly. He scowls, and I grow frustrated and desperate. "If you leave, they will probably kill us both." I mean to sound cruel, like the elder, but I sound like me, and I sound scared.

"No. I will not let anyone hurt you." He says it as though he is a giant and the elder a lamb, and my heart flutters strangely in my chest.

"They will try if you do not fulfill your duty," I say, and I know this to be true. I slowly reach for his hand and take it, and I'm relieved when he squeezes my fingers. "Tell me what concerns you? I am a priestess. I can fix it."

He lifts my hand, studying my knuckles, and he walks toward me. My back meets the wall, and he is very close. He smells like oil and earth. Like a spirit of the land. "I do not think that what ails me is something I want to fix."

"If it stops you from completing the rite and saving our lives, then maybe you should reconsider," I say, and I slam my lips shut. Such talk is what gets me caned.

He doesn't cane me, though, of course. He laughs. He touches a piece of my hair. "I see how my mother looks at my father and how he, in turn, looks at her. I like it."

"That is the Union of Souls," I say slowly, as though he is stupid, which I don't think he is. But then... males. One can never be sure of them. "You will have that someday with the mother of your children."

He puts a hand on my belly. "But you are to be the mother of my child, are you not?"

I cover his hand with mine. "I mean your other children. I am to mother the earth spirit's daughter and raise her to follow the sacred acts."

"And what of our son?"

I cannot answer. His eyes are so dark. "Do you truly believe in the earth spirit?" he asks. "You did not choose this life. Did you choose the earth?"

"Such talk could get you stoned and slain."

One of his shoulders rises and falls. "If a man breaks his sacred vow to his United, then he, too, risks being stoned and slain. So does his wife. The only exception is if it is a priestess calling him away from their shared bed. But the priestesses do not summon, do they? You wait and you take what the elder and the order choose for you."

I'm terrified by his words and thrilled by them at the same time. I swallow thickly. "What do you want me to do? I cannot change the rites. I can only choose to enjoy them."

"I liked seeing you." He kisses the knuckle of my first finger. "On festival day."

"Here and now you can do more than see me."

His smile is sad, though I can see the spirit overtaking him beneath his loincloth. "I want you for more than only this night."

A half thought flies through my mind like a bird chasing a worm, and I watch his lips dance across the back of my hand. "I can do that," I mumble.

He stops kissing. It angers me. "How?" he asks before I can complain.

I can hear the elder's words as though I am studying at her knee. I remember drawing the symbols in the sand. "I am a priestess. If I become elder, I will bless the Union of Souls. It means binding one soul to another. I know the spell."

"But when I leave, we will not be bound in the eyes of

your elder or the villagers," he says, and I want to scrub the pout of his ignorant face.

"Of course not, but we will be bound through all time. That is what you desire, is it not?"

"Tell me more of what I desire."

I patiently explain. "When we go to the earth, we will know each other's true names. We will call to one another and walk hand in hand through the lands above the earth and beyond the sky. We will be one, but you will not be one with your wife, whom you will meet and love and be united to in the ceremony someday."

"I do not want some mystery wife of my uncertain future."

"Then what do you want?" I ask, because I long to hear him say what I think and hope he will say.

His expression is earnest. "I knew the day I saw you that I would want none but you."

I should tell him that he's a fool, that such feelings for a priestess are fantasy. I want to say such things in the elder's tone, to scold him so that maybe he will be happy whereas I will always be a priestess.

But the look in his eyes makes me wish his words could be true forever, and in that instant, I decide. "I will do the binding spell if you promise me that you will let the earth spirit take you so you and it can quicken in me."

His grin wakes up every part of my body and makes it thrum to the time of my heartbeat. "I promise, priestess. I will do all that you ask of me, now and in the lands beyond the sky, when we can be together."

It is a sweet dream.

The End

About Kelly Wyre

 A professional chaos manager and proud geek, Kelly Wyre enjoys reading and writing all manner of fiction, ranging from horror to romance, and believes she's here to tell stories and to connect people with them. Kelly relishes the soft and cuddly and the sharp and bloody with equal amounts of enthusiasm. She loves movies, stuffed animals, the smell of books, thunderstorms, naps, the ocean, gaming, psychology, studying the occult, kink, and all the colors of a bruise. In her free time, she strives to be the meditative star in the darkness. Or at least attempts to relax. Kelly resides in the southeastern United States. You can find her on Twitter at @Kelly_Wyre, on Instagram as @thefireswyre, or as part of the crew at demented-tours.com.

A Note From Kelly

Meet Me at the Gates was first published by Loose Id Publishing, and sadly they shuttered their doors some time ago. The rights to this novel returned to me. It's been revamped and reorganized, and I'm delighted it is back out in the world.

I couldn't have done this without major support. I would specifically like to thank all of my patrons on Patreon who helped me (and who had an unseemly amount of patience with me) in the process of creating this book:

AF Henley
Bengeance
Cheryl V.
Flu
Jamie H.
Jennifer C.
Kagamimi
Kourin
Liz T.
Lucy O.
Passiflora182
Phil H.
Rachel H.
Rebecca M.
Teresa R.
Wendo

As promised, all Patrons supporting me prior to April 2018 who completed at least one cycle received this Patron Perk. They are the official Start Up Team for Demented Ink and Tours.

MANY THANKS AND MANY, MANY BAKED GOODS.

<3Dee

Posting fiction, making videos, crafting jewelry and

art… If any of that sounds good, then come join Kelly Wyre at the **Demented Tours Patreon** – patreon.com/DementedTours

www.ingramcontent.com/pod-product-compliance
Lightning Source LLC
Chambersburg PA
CBHW071557150726
48000CB00004B/1500